I0699698

BRAVE HEART

ALSO BY EMMA HAMM

The Otherworld
Heart of the Fae
Veins of Magic
The Faceless Woman
The Raven's Ballad
Bride of the Sea
Curse of the Troll

Of Goblin Kings
Of Goblins and Gold
Of Shadows and Elves
Of Pixies and Spells
Of Werewolves and Curses
Of Fairytales and Magic

Once Upon a Monster
Bleeding Hearts
Binding Moon
Ragged Lungs

and many more...

BRAVE
HEART

For the women with dragon hearts…
And the men who serve them

Hall of H
L
Dracomaquia
Castle of the Lost
Umbral K
The Gloami
Solis Occasu

KINGDOM OF UMBRA
MALIS
STYGIAN PEAKS
FIELD OF SOMBER
CITY OF TENEBROUS

CHAPTER 1

Lore held onto the tree trunk with both hands, then leaned back to feel the wind in her hair. When she was little, she'd never have guessed that she would climb a tree taller than the castle without fear. She'd been terrified of heights as a child, and even the buildings in Tenebrous scared her sometimes as an adult.

But thanks to a dragon, she no longer feared steep drops. Or many other things.

Casting her gaze out over the land, she searched for a path across the Stygian Peaks. They'd been seeking a way to safely get down the mountain range for a couple of weeks now. Most of the trails were made by billy goats, and those beasts were far more suited to crumbling rock and sheer cliffs. Though they'd pondered if Abraxas could fly them all to safety, they'd agreed hiding the draconic form was the smartest choice of action.

That led to Lore climbing the trees every time they paused for breath. She hoped to find some trail that a wizard or warlock had made. So far, she hadn't been so lucky.

She really thought each time would be different, though. The path they'd been on today was wider than most of the other trails. It was easier for them all to travel side by side, rather than being stuck in a single file line.

Surprisingly, even this difficult journey hadn't ruined the spirits of her companions.

They had the eggs, although the box was heavy to carry with them. They had each other, even if they argued. No one had died. Thankfully.

So far, this entire mission had been quite the success, and they were all rather pleased with themselves. Lore was waiting for the other shoe to drop, but she supposed enjoying the moment would not make the world end.

She hoped.

Slithering back down the tree, she waited until her feet struck the ground before she turned to look at her companions. Wide-eyed stares watched as she shook her head in disappointment, and a round of groans all echoed down the mountain.

Goliath kicked a stone and grumbled, "Walking in the footsteps of a goat for another day it is, then. We should have sent Abraxas out to get ropes at this rate."

"We all agreed that sending him out at any time was only asking for attention. The longer we can hide from Zander and any of his spies, the better." Lore had tried to stop calling him the King. Even though, technically, he still was.

No one else had stepped up to take that role in the kingdom. No one was qualified other than the young man who stood at the back of their group, even if he hadn't been trained to be a royal.

Margaret, holed up in her castle with the rest of the rebellion, wouldn't want anyone to take the position, anyway. She'd rather the entire realm be free and let everyone figure out their differences. Even if that sent all of Umbra rolling into utter chaos.

Shaking her head at the thought, Lore looked over at Beauty, who still limped on her twisted ankle. "Is that getting any better?"

"Not walking around like this, it's not." Beauty looked down at the leg. "I don't know if it'll ever get to the point where we want it at, if I'm being honest. I need to rest and we know that's not going to happen any time soon."

Well, it could heal if they could get to their destination. The problem would be the journey there.

Lore pointed ahead. "There's a good stopping point up there, at least. Small clearing. Lots of trees around it. We could even have a fire, considering we're so tucked into the forest. That'll be nice, won't it?"

Everyone grumbled and walked away from her. Everyone except her dragon, who lingered behind the rest.

Abraxas stood far taller than anyone else in their group. While the others tired, he soldiered on like he didn't know what exhaustion felt like. Even though she'd seen him pass out before. But that was after flying as a dragon for days.

In human form? He seemed incapable of weariness.

Lore waited until the others were out of ear shot before she asked, "Are you sure they're even going to let us in?"

"The practitioners of Lux Brumalis may not be the most welcoming of sorts, but a band of magical creatures asking to walk into their city?" He lifted a brow. "They'll let us in."

She still winced at the thought of the place. Most magical creatures avoided that Lux Brumalis as though they would rather be set on fire than step foot on those cobblestone streets.

She still wasn't convinced they wouldn't.

Lux Brumalis was a city out of reach. Even beyond the King's eyes. It was a haven for the mortals and humans who thought they had a right to steal magic from the land. As such, it was also a city full of magicians, warlocks, witches, and their ilk. The King claimed to have allowed them to remain alive merely because they were entertaining. Lore and the other creatures knew better.

Magic wasn't as scary when it was wielded by humans. The King didn't care if a witch used magic, because that meant she was still a mortal. He could put a sword through her chest and all her spells would cease.

Magical creatures used magic with no price or any spell to cast. Sure, elves used rituals when they wanted something, but that power was freely given from the earth. Witches and warlocks sacrificed animals and people. Hags used blood magic almost entirely. All these humans eventually grew so twisted by their stolen power that they ended up looking very different from when they were born.

Lore didn't want to go to Lux Brumalis. She had no way of knowing what waited for them there.

"I know it's not your first choice," Abraxas said, stepping forward with his hands held out to her. "You fear what will happen when we step into that city. You fear it will swallow us whole."

She took his offered hands, holding them tight to her chest. "I know that they're going to ask for a price. I don't know what they'll ask for, and that terrifies me."

"Whatever they want, I will pay it. Someone in that city knows where the warlock who made this box was laid to rest. I can feel it." He tugged her against his chest, tucking her against the heartbeat that rapidly pounded beneath his ribs. "I will burn the city to the ground if they so much as touch a hair on your head."

The mere thought was foolish, but it made her feel better. Smiling, she tucked her face against him and inhaled deeply. "I don't think even the great dragon of Umbra could fight against an entire city weaved with curses and spells."

"You'd be surprised what I could do if you were in danger." He cupped the back of her neck and pulled her back so he could lean down and press a kiss to her lips. "I don't know why you'd question that, Lady of Starlight. You know a dragon's fire burns hotter for those he loves."

"Is that so?" Did she croon?

Lore hardly recognized herself these days. He made it so easy to be natural around him, even though they hadn't been around each other for that long. She easily said that she loved him, and that was new. Lore had difficulty remembering a time when she said those words to even her own mother, at least naturally.

"It is so," he replied with a grumble. "You know, they can set up camp on their own…"

She would love nothing more than a few stolen minutes with him. She'd wanted that for a while now. But finding that time together, alone, had been hard.

Whether it was their companions needing their help, or just the grime of travel standing in their way, Lore really hoped there was a chance for some privacy. Soon.

Otherwise, she was going to tackle him in front of all the others, and they could suffer the sight burned into their minds forever. If they didn't fancy watching, then they could leave.

"Sorry to interrupt. I know, I know." Goliath walked toward them, palms up in apology already. "I understand the two of you are quite over having to deal with any of us, and I'm the last person you want to see right now, but we do need help to set up the campsite. With Beauty's foot the way it is, and Zeph having never done this before, I could use some assistance."

She sighed and tilted her head back to look up at the sky. She shouldn't get angry with poor Goliath. He had been doing everything he could to respect their space. It wasn't his fault that their companions were much younger than the rest of them and needed more help because of that.

"I understand," Lore said, although her tone said she wasn't happy about this change. "I'll be right there. Did they at least find straight trees that are remotely suitable for the tent?"

Goliath scratched the back of his neck. "You know, I wish I could say they did, Lore. I really do."

"I'll do that too, then." She waited until he'd left before looking at Abraxas with a wry grin on her face. "We tried?"

If looks could kill, then the entire mountain would have fallen down at Abraxas's glare. "I'm tired of trying. Those three idiots wouldn't survive a day if we weren't here."

"Goliath would be just fine," she said, but she couldn't say that for the other two.

Beauty had been raised in a well-run house with a father who had given her everything he possibly could. That didn't lead to a young woman ready to take on the wilderness. Her time with the rebellion had taught her to fight, but not to survive. Beauty had spent most of her service making sure that Margaret's whims were enacted in Tenebrous. She was a brilliant fighter, and quick witted to boot. But a survivalist? Not so much.

And then there was Zephyr. The half brother of the King who should have been dead, and yet, miraculously, had survived all these years. He'd been locked up by his mother in the crypt, connected to one of the worst battlefields in history. It wasn't like the boy had a lot of time to get out of that hole in the ground just to practice being king. Anyone who saw him was more likely to kill him for being related to Zander than to help.

Sighing again, Lore pressed the heel of her palm to her forehead. Already a headache bloomed behind her eyes. "Let's get back to the others and hope we can find some privacy in Lux Brumalis, shall we?"

"We have a long way to go yet if we're waiting until we reach the city. I could fly us there, Lore. All of this struggle would be over and none of us would have to worry." His eyes had widened and his tone was a little too close to begging.

"You know we can't do that. There's a thousand reasons why you cannot turn back into the dragon right now, and you definitely cannot fly us to a city of witches." Lore tossed her hands up into the air. "They're already going to want to squeeze out every magical drop they can from the rest of us. What do you think a witch would do if she found out that dragon scales were within her reach?"

His expression turned dark and stormy. "I'll find the trees, then. Maybe breaking something will make me feel better."

He stomped off in the opposite direction and she tried hard to control her own feelings.

Lore was just as frustrated as he was. They were both tired of dealing with young mortals and scrambling across rocks. But he didn't have to take it out on her. She wasn't the problem here.

Walking back to the camp, she stepped into a scene of chaos. Beauty sat on a log and pointed imperiously at Goliath, who looked like he was ready to explode on her. Zeph stood in the middle of the tarps that would make up their tents, newly acquired from the elven stronghold they'd left two weeks ago. But the fabric billowed out around him and the lost expression on his face suggested he felt as though he'd gotten stuck underneath a wave and didn't know how to surface for air.

"No, Goliath!" Beauty shouted. "I don't want the tent to be there. If it's there, then the wind will catch it."

"And you know enough about building campsites to guess which direction the wind will blow?"

"Anyone can see that the wind is already blowing in that direction, and I refuse to wake up at midnight shivering because you did this wrong."

And even though she was angry at them for needing her, she... wasn't. Lore might want to be a little selfish with her man, but damn, she loved these fools that couldn't survive on their own.

She clapped her hands for attention and waited until silence fell in the clearing. That's when she started barking her own orders.

"Zeph, stepping off the tent would help if you're thinking of spreading that fabric out any time soon. Goliath, you're arguing because you don't want to carry things further into the corner. Bring the rocks over there if it means so much to Beauty. And Beauty," she paused, staring meaningfully at the other woman. "Stop being meddlesome when you can't help."

Beauty pouted. "I can help. I can point them in the right direction."

"You're making it harder on them with your opinions. Just let the boys set the camp up and enjoy resting for a moment. Would you?"

Still, the pout persisted. "I'm not good at doing nothing, Lore."

She supposed that argument could stand. Lore wandered over to Beauty's side and plopped down onto the log beside her. "Then we'll watch them together and you can tell me everything they're doing wrong. How does that sound?"

The relief that rocked through Beauty's body had her sagging against Lore's side. "I just don't want to be a burden," she whispered for only Lore to hear. "I know I've been slowing everyone down."

Lore ran a hand down her friend's back, then clasped her tight. "No one blames you for being injured, and no one is going to think you're a burden because of it. You've done enough, Beauty. Let us take care of you until you get to Lux Brumalis. Then I'll bargain with a witch to put you back together."

An answering shiver of disgust shook through Beauty. "I don't want a witch touching me. Magic like that isn't... natural."

"Fine, then. I'll get a warlock and he can tell you that you're being ridiculous." Lore rubbed her back and narrowed her eyes on the boys as they set up the camp. "But I'm still giving one of those witches a lock of your hair in case they need it for something later."

"That's not funny, Lore!"

CHAPTER 2

Abraxas knew he'd been a little too rough. He stomped through the woods, slapping branches out of his way without even looking to see if they were straight enough for the tents.

He was frustrated with himself, acting like an animal who needed to rut. He was a dragon, and they had a strict code of honor between the lot of them. Women were to be treated with respect. Everyone was, if he were closely following the tenets of what made a dragon "good". Yes, their companions were lesser in his mind than her, but he'd take care of them.

Not only because she would want him to, but because he enjoyed their company and the amusement they brought to his life.

So why was he so frustrated now? He had to peel away layers

of anger and rage until he finally got down to the bottom of it all. He wanted time with her to himself because he hadn't gotten that yet. And in the end, that's all that mattered.

No matter where they went, there wasn't any peace to be found. Other than the few moments in his hoard months ago, he'd never seen her without someone else being within earshot.

He desperately wanted that. Was it so wrong to wish for some time with the woman he loved? Moments when they didn't have to fear someone overhearing them, or worse, another person walking into the clearing and seeing what they were doing?

Peace. Quiet. Privacy.

Such were things that neither of them could wish for on this journey, but the few things that he needed.

A part of him knew that he should turn right around and apologize to her. She needed to know that he wasn't a complete idiot who had lost his mind. And that he didn't blame her for their circumstances. They were all in this together, and none of this was easy. Not for any of them.

Find the straight trees. That was the first matter of business. He couldn't return empty-handed and then expect her to accept an apology for him being an ass.

Abraxas took his time finding the right branches and limbs that would prop up the giant tent they'd brought with them. Then he made his way back to camp, following the scent of his companions and the ever present pull of the box that held the two other creatures who mattered as much as Lore.

He entered the clearing while trying to make sure the glower on his face didn't show. A quick glance to the right ensured his eggs were where they should be. They lay within the box. One of his friends had set them near the fire so they would stay warm.

A small knot inside him eased. They were still here. Even though the King must have tried to summon them by this point.

The charm Zeph had brought with him, well, that had done the job better than Abraxas could have hoped for.

Setting down the armful of heavy tree limbs, he searched for Lore. His heart thudded hard in his chest until he found her. She sat on a log beside Beauty, whispering to the other woman, who giggled.

The sight made his heart squeeze. Though the two of them had grown up in vastly different circumstances, they were the best of friends. The love they shared for each other was a bond even he couldn't break.

"Ladies," he said, approaching them with what he hoped was a remorseful expression. "What are you two giggling about?"

Beauty looked at him and dissolved into cackles again. "You!"

Oh, that wasn't good if they were laughing that hard. He cleared his throat and asked, "Hopefully, good things?"

The mischievous grin on Lore's face wasn't all that reassuring, but at least she replied, "Of course."

Why did he feel like she hadn't admitted the entire truth?

He turned away from the dangerous creatures who only wanted to cause trouble and resolved to apologize to her tomorrow. But first, he'd make sure they had a safe place to sleep tonight and that nothing fearsome would find them during the night.

Zeph stood with the fabric of the tent in his hands, clearly trying to figure out which way was up and which way was down. One might think after multiple nights learning how to put this together, that he might remember how. But anything made by an elf had to be difficult, and the tent had quite a few tricks that went with it.

"Give it to me," he muttered, holding out his hand for the material. "I'll set it up and you can watch again. But tomorrow night, if we have to put the tent back up, it's on you."

Zeph handed it over with a relieved expression on his face. "Thank you, Abraxas. I know you've been doing it a lot, but I just can't figure it out. Every time I try, it feels like the fabric twists in my hands."

"Magic isn't that hard to understand."

"It is, though. I'm supposed to just... ask it? What should I ask? And how often? What if I ask for the wrong thing and the tent kills us?" His face paled with every word until Abraxas feared the boy might pass out.

He understood Zeph's hesitation, of course. The tent was spelled so that anyone could ask it to be something on the inside, and that's what it would create. Magic had its limits, of course. No one could ask for an entire arena within the confines of the fabric walls, nor could someone create a castle within it.

But it wasn't that difficult to ask for a protected place with warm food and comfortable beds. Traveling like this was easier than what they'd been doing.

Abraxas shook out the tent, making sure there weren't any lingering pine needles on top of it before he started the lesson. Again. "You aren't going to create a dangerous space for us to be in, boy. All you have to do is ask for a safe, comfortable place to stay the night, and if it doesn't mind sharing a little hot food, then that would be very much appreciated. Ask the magic like you would your mother after you'd done something wrong. You might have to grovel to get what you want, but we're all used to that."

Goliath wandered past them and let out a snort as he dropped one of the branches Abraxas had brought. "That's the truth. Any man is used to that."

Groveling was what Abraxas should currently be doing at Lore's feet. Instead, he was putting together the tents so they could all be in the same damned space again. All night. Listening to a dwarf snoring and Zeph wriggling around in his sheets incessantly.

Sighing, he got his thoughts back under control. If he wasn't careful, then he would end up wishing the tent into a private room for Lore and him, and then no one else would have a place to sleep for the night. The last thing he needed was to anger the rest of his companions like that.

Or embarrass Lore. Then she might never give him the chance after all.

Mind cleared, he allowed the magic of the tent to prod at his mind. He could sense the power was curious about him and what he desired. It had no purpose other than to serve. And it did that job very well.

"Safety and secrecy for the night," he muttered, eyes drifting shut as he focused on the task. "Food to eat that will help us on our long journey tomorrow. Comfortable beds and perhaps a place to clean ourselves, as we haven't been able to do for some time now."

The magic coiled around his thoughts, moving through his mind as though searching for a sense of weakness in his resolve. This was the part that terrified Zeph. The sensation of the magic moving throughout his thoughts, digging deep into desires he likely didn't want anyone else to know about yet.

Abraxas didn't care. The magic wouldn't speak of what it found inside his mind. It couldn't. He let it play through his thoughts and brushed it aside when it offered him a more private room for the night where he and Lore could disappear from the others. It whispered that the walls would even be spelled so no one could hear their conversations, or lack thereof, inside.

"Another night," he murmured, letting go of his own desire to be with her. They could wait a little longer. "Tonight, I wish to keep my companions well fed and happy."

The magic retreated with no small amount of disappointment. Perhaps he and Lore were so obvious that even the spelled tent wanted them to get it over with.

Apparently, they were all getting to the point of frustration.

When he opened his eyes, Goliath had already stuck up the first pole. "Come on then, dragon. Let's get this up before the tent changes its mind."

It took a little work after that. The tent seemed to know what it wanted to be, and therefore, they could stake up the rest of it and then throw the fabric on top of the wooden posts. The magic wiggled itself into place with no more complaints and then the door fluttered in a breeze that wasn't there. Almost as though the magic was enticing them to take a step inside.

"Good enough," Beauty called out from behind them.

Abraxas watched her leverage herself up from the log and hobble toward the tent. The poor thing needed to stay off her feet more. But they didn't have the luxury of allowing her that time, and he feared she'd hurt herself even worse by the end of this journey.

He held out an arm for her to take, only to have Zeph beat him. The young man fairly lunged forward to offer his help, and Beauty gave him a smile that rivaled the sun.

Warmth pressed against his side, and he looked down to see Goliath had leaned against him with his hands against his heart. "Doesn't it give you butterflies?"

"Not really," he replied, taking a step away from the dwarf. "I think they're both awfully young and neither of them has any idea how to handle the other."

"Well, age isn't everything." Goliath levered a meaningful glance over at Lore, who had busied herself with picking up all of Beauty's things. "And on the matter of handling each other, I think you should be careful about calling the kettle black, eh?"

"What is that supposed to mean?"

"You know." Goliath's eyebrows disappeared into his shaggy hairline. He wiggled his hips, moved his hands side to side, and then elbowed Abraxas hard. "We've all seen the looks you two keep giving each other. The looks. You know what I mean."

"I haven't the faintest idea." Abraxas took another step away from him. "Stop talking to me."

"Just saying, dragon. You might want to get your own affairs in order before you point out holes in Beauty and Zeph's... friendship." Goliath popped the last word out of his lips, left it at that, and wandered into the tent.

The damned dwarf really had to meddle in everything.

Abraxas crossed his arms and uncrossed them while waiting for Lore to look up at him. "Do you want any help bringing things in?"

"I've got it." She barely even looked at him.

Had he stepped in it that badly? He searched around them as though he might find help from someone else, but they were alone. The others had all disappeared into the tent and there was no one out here to help him but himself.

"Fine," he muttered. "I'll see you in there, then."

Without looking back, Abraxas ducked underneath the flap and into the massive room beyond.

From the outside, the tent looked like a normal size that would hold three or four people. But from the inside, it was larger than most houses. He walked into what could be called a small kitchen, although no one would cook in it. The warm wooden cabinets had tiny daisies decorating their surface, and an ice box kept their dinner chilled. Pillows were piled at the back around a crackling fireplace with many colors that danced on every spark. Five doors, two on the right, three on the left, were painted with symbols for each of them.

Zeph brought Beauty over to the one with a pale pink rose on the outside, then released his hold on her. However reluctant that movement was. "Here you are," he mumbled, but his voice carried. "Will you be all right on your own?"

"Of course. I just want to get changed and cleaned up a bit." She looked over at Abraxas as though he'd done something wrong. "Someone apparently thinks the rest of us stink."

"That isn't why I did that," he called out.

Goliath wandered over to the door marked with a hammer and burst out laughing. "I'm sure he doesn't, Beauty. Can't you think of another reason he might want to be clean?"

The dwarf had better get control of himself. Abraxas bared his teeth in a snarl as Goliath pressed his front against his door, wrapped his arms around himself, and made kissing noises.

"You know, I've heard roasted dwarf tastes greasy, but I'm willing to try anything once," Abraxas snarled.

Zeph bolted toward his own door, the one painted with a blue sword. Clearly, he intended to hide rather than get involved with this argument. The young man was still uncomfortable when the rest of them argued like this.

They all froze as Lore ducked her head into the tent, arms full of

Beauty's bags and the crate of dragon eggs underneath her arm. "Would the lot of you grow up, please? I'm too tired to listen to you all arguing like children."

"I didn't do anything!" Zeph replied with an angry sound. He kicked the ground before walking into his own room, showing just how young he really was.

Goliath rolled his eyes and entered his room without another word. That left poor Beauty standing there, waiting for Lore to scold her.

Instead, all Lore did was hand her all her things, and then touch a hand to her forehead. With a soft shove, she pushed the human toward her room. "Get some rest. Get clean. We'll have dinner together without quarreling, like we used to, and then we'll make sure that we're ready for tomorrow."

He watched Lore as she headed to her own room, certain that she wouldn't say a word again. She'd already written him off again, just like she'd done before. But she stopped in the doorway, the eggs still safe in her grip.

Without even looking over her shoulder, she said, "There is another clearing nearby. It's not the best or most comfortable place on the mountain, but it's quiet and far enough away. If you're interested in meeting me at midnight."

His jaw might have unhinged, but he stammered, "That'll do."

"Then I'll see you later tonight."

He swore she flashed a small smile in his direction before disappearing behind the door painted with rays of silver moonlight. Abraxas controlled his reaction as he walked into his room with the painting of a dragon, and then carefully closed himself inside.

Then and only then did he pump his fist in the air and release a very controlled sound of elation.

CHAPTER 3

Lore waited until the very last moment to follow Abraxas out onto the mountain. Or at least, she hoped he had already headed out. She'd given hours of thought to his frustration and had concluded that she felt the same.

Sure, his anger had been unexpected, and he'd reacted like a child about the whole thing. But she also understood that he wasn't human, and she couldn't keep putting human ideals on him. The poor man wanted to be alone with her.

Though she knew what being alone meant. And she hadn't done that in a very long time.

Of course, she'd enjoyed the company of men in her life. Mortal and otherwise. She couldn't conceive, so who cared who she slept with? There were no consequences of sex for a woman like her.

Still, this wasn't the same as dragging some poor sap home from the bar and then being faintly disappointed with him. This was Abraxas. A dragon. The man who had consumed her thoughts and now she feared she might pass out the moment they finally acted on these feelings.

What if she messed it up? Lore thought she was good in bed, but how would she know? She'd never asked after one of her many one-night stands. And they hadn't wanted to talk afterwards, anyway. After that sort of meeting, everyone usually headed home and tried not to think about what they'd done.

That was probably a bad sign.

A really bad sign.

She looked down at her outfit one last time, in case it looked ugly. There weren't any mirrors in the tent, so she had to hope that the beautiful dress she'd chosen was enough. She'd summoned it from her old apartment in Tenebrous, and the magic had taken three nights to go through the tent. The white, spider silk nightgown clung to her body as though it were painted onto her, even though the cut was rather modest. It covered her chest and fell all the way down to her knees, but no one would ever call this nightgown anything other than sexy.

She hoped, at least. Lore didn't know if he was going to like this, or if he'd think she was trying too hard.

No, that was stupid to even consider. Lore shook herself as though someone had slapped her. Abraxas had made it very clear that he was interested in her, and that meant she could show up in a burlap sack and he would still want her. Clothing had nothing to do with his desire for her. She knew that.

Tip toeing through the tent, she tried her best not to wake anyone else. The last thing she needed right now was Goliath teasing her about sneaking off in the middle of the night. Everyone could sense the tension between Abraxas and her. And when they returned tomorrow, infinitely less tense, then the rest of them could tease all they wanted.

But first, she wanted to feel like herself again without the lingering pressure of getting this over with.

Ugh, that sounded terrible, too. She needed to stop thinking like that or the pit in her stomach would never go away and she'd be forced to return to the tent with her tail tucked between her legs.

She was ready for this.

She had been ready for this for a very long time.

The only reason she hesitated now was because it was happening. It didn't matter that they'd both been traveling for weeks on end and that the grime underneath her nails couldn't be scrubbed out in the tent's shower. They wanted this.

The cool air made her shiver the moment she stepped outside. She should have brought a jacket, or at least something to put over the thin material of her nightgown. That was foolish. She knew better than to risk a cold.

"You'll warm up soon enough," Lore told herself, even as she walked further away from the tent.

A dragon awaited her, after all. He could burn for the both of them and then she would feel the inferno of their desire.

That... also sounded horrible. She was rambling in her own mind like a two coin romance novel her mother used to read.

Lore picked her way through the underbrush and did her best to make sure it didn't rip at the nightgown. She didn't need to show up looking like she'd tumbled through one of the thorny bushes that stood in her way. The whole point of the nightgown was to be pretty, not ragged.

The moon filtered through the scraggly tree limbs that desperately tried to live on the edge of the mountain. The rays of silver light sank into her skin, and she absorbed the power without a second thought.

Life had changed in such a short amount of time. There were years of her life when she feared the moon, knowing that it was painfully obvious when she took magic from the world around her. Now, she could walk through the forest without fear as moon magic glittered on her skin like silver dust.

She looked up at the moon and felt all the anxiety ease out of her body. This was what she needed. Just a bit of extra courage, and thankfully, the goddess in the sky had never let her down before. Not even at a time like this.

The clearing she'd picked was little more than a rock face where nothing else could grow, but it would do for the two of them. If she came back with scratches down her spine from the rough granite stone, then so be it. She didn't mind.

A dark figure already stood in the clearing, and though she couldn't quite make out the tell tale height, Lore knew it had to be Abraxas. No one else would know they were meeting out here. And she didn't fear an unexpected visitor when the only other living creatures on these mountains were goats.

Sighing, she ran her hands down her sides to make sure that she still looked put together. She pulled her hair in front of her shoulders, making sure the pale strands had every hair in place. Lore pinched her cheeks just to be certain she didn't look frostbitten, but slightly flushed with anticipation.

She looked good. Lore knew this was the best it was going to get, regardless of how she wanted to be the sultry siren that called to him in the night. This would have to do.

Abraxas remained where he was, his back turned to her as he stared down the mountain. She desperately hoped there wasn't some enemy wandering up some hidden path to attack them. She'd only strapped one knife to her thigh, and that was explicitly for emergencies, not a battle.

Lore could do it, of course. She'd fought with less than a knife before, but she really didn't want any more distractions.

"You came," she whispered. Her voice floated on the breeze and carried what she hoped was the sound of her longing and desire.

They'd been waiting for this for such a long time.

The figure shifted, but when he turned around, it wasn't Abraxas.

Draven stood in the clearing, so far from his home. The moonlight changed his dark skin into something like an opal. Shimmering colors danced over the smooth peaks of his cheekbones and the planes of his revealed collarbone. He'd loosened the neck of his shirt, and the tight leather pants on his legs were torn from some battle he'd fought getting here.

How had she ever thought he was Abraxas? She could hear them now. The grimdags that were slid into their pouches on either side of his body. They called out for her, whispering that they'd missed how easily she plunged them into dark places that oozed and dripped. They wanted what she had given them. To kill. And to feast.

A shiver shook her shoulders. He shouldn't be here. He should be with his mother and the other Ashen Deep who had retreated into the earth, so they didn't have to fight anymore. A thousand other places were more appropriate for him to be in rather than the clearing where she was supposed to meet Abraxas.

As she watched, his eyes widened in shock, and then she recognized a look of strong appreciation. Followed by a swell of longing that he couldn't, shouldn't, have.

"Lore," he said, and there it was. The desire in his voice that turned it guttural and deep. "Of course I came."

This was wrong.

She took a step away from him, holding up a hand so he didn't get any closer to her. "I thought you were someone else. What are you doing here, Draven?"

Her words didn't deter him in the slightest. He matched her movements, following her even as she tried to retreat. "I followed you. I had to return to my mother to let her know I was leaving, but when I returned to the mountain, you were all gone. All of you."

"We had more work to do." Lore stumbled over a stone as she backed away. "You didn't give me any inclination that you were intending to follow us. Or to join our cause."

"I'm not interested in any cause." He lunged forward and she couldn't step out of his reach fast enough. Draven caught her around the waist, tugging her flush to his chest. "I came here for you, Lorelei of Silverfell."

This wasn't how it was supposed to go. This was so wrong and she couldn't reach for her dagger because he'd think she was reaching for something else. How had she confused this poor man so much?

"Draven, I'm sorry if I made you believe otherwise, but I'm not—"

Lore didn't get the chance to say anything else.

A clawed hand clamped down on Draven's shoulder and ripped him away from Lore. Though the deepmonger likely believed he was just as powerful as Abraxas, he was very wrong.

The dragon burned in Abraxas's eyes, which had turned from molten gold to a glowing ember with slitted pupils like a snake. He held onto

Draven's shoulder with one hand and had palmed Draven's head with the other. A single jerk brought Draven's ear nearly to his shoulder and forced him to freeze in place else he'd break his own neck.

All it would take was the slightest movement, and the light would fade from his eyes. Considering the impressive strength that already made Abraxas's biceps bulge, Lore didn't think Abraxas would require any effort to snap the elf's neck and move on with his day.

His face twisted in anger. Abraxas looked like some avenging god of the forge who would kill anyone for touching what was his.

Oh, Draven, she thought. You should know better than to try to steal from a dragon's hoard.

"Abraxas," Draven said, breathing hard. "I didn't know you'd be here, too."

"Clearly. Or you never would have touched her." His tone had darkened, turning toward the evil side that she'd only seen come out of him once.

He wanted to kill Draven, she realized. This wasn't a show of his strength or how much more powerful he was than the elf.

She stopped looking at Draven at all. He didn't matter, not right now. Instead, she forced Abraxas to meet her gaze and held that horrible fire with her own. He needed to know she was safe, and that she was still here. No one had stolen her or taken her away.

But worse, she had to stop him from killing the son of the Ashen Deep's Matriarch. The death of her son would cause an elven civil war when there were already so few of them to fight.

"Abraxas," she said. "He didn't touch me."

"He did," he snarled. "I saw him with his arms around you. I saw everything, Lore."

"I'm sure you saw something that looked bad to you, but that doesn't mean that anything had happened. There was a misunderstanding when I came into the clearing and I thought he was you. He touched me no more than Goliath."

Maybe a little more, but Abraxas didn't need to know that right now. He was on the edge of madness and wanted to kill the young man in his arms.

Draven's hands gripped at Abraxas's forearms, and the elf started to writhe in the dragon's grip. He sought to free himself, but that was only making the situation worse.

She flicked her gaze at the deepmonger and widened her eyes meaningfully. She was trying very hard to save his life, but that would all be ruined if he kept struggling like that. Thankfully, Draven seemed to get her message. He stopped moving and let her control the situation.

"Abraxas," she said again, forcing his attention back to her. "You need to release him."

"You seem to still be under the impression that I am either an elf or a mortal, Lore, but I am neither." His hands tightened their grip and Draven let out a little grunt of pain. "Dragons kill anyone who dares touch what is theirs. He should have known. He took the risk of touching you, trying to claim you as his own, and it is my right to take back what he tried to steal."

"He didn't," she whispered, taking another step forward. She couldn't look at Draven, not again. That was risking the poor man's life far more than he realized. "You seem to be under the impression that it would be so easy for someone to take me from you. Abraxas, I need you to think clearly now. I invited you here. I dressed like this for you. Not him."

She kept her words slow and quiet. A lullaby to soothe an angry beast who needed to listen to the man inside him. If Abraxas could focus on just her, hear what she was saying, then maybe he would realize that this was ridiculous.

Dangerous.

His massive hands clenched one more time on Draven's skull before he released the elf.

Draven fell to the ground, struggled to right himself, and then threw his body to standing. He reached for a grimdag at his waist, perhaps the only weapon that could kill a dragon.

She flung out an arm, stopping him where he stood. "No," she said, still not looking at him. "About a hundred paces up the mountain to the right is the tent we set up. Go join the others there."

"Lore," Abraxas snarled.

"Go." She repeated the word for Draven, but she never looked away from the angry dragon in front of her.

She waited until she heard twigs snapping under footsteps and the rushing of the elf as he ran through the undergrowth. That would keep him alive for a little longer, and she didn't want him dead. Sure, he had definitely gotten the wrong idea about what was going on between them. But that wasn't worth a death sentence.

"Abraxas," she whispered, stepping closer to him.

That was apparently not the correct thing to do. He flinched away from her while shaking his head. "I can't do this right now, Lore."

"I don't know what you want me to do."

"I'm too angry." He looked at her, at least. The sadness in his eyes hurt her heart. "I don't know how I would touch you. I need to..."

He didn't finish the sentence, but she already knew what he needed to say. "You need to be the dragon for a while."

Abraxas nodded, then gruffly added, "And I need to be a man so that

I can hold you. So I can make sure he doesn't..."

Apparently, all of this was more difficult for her dragon than she'd thought.

Lore knew they were walking a fine line. She knew that tonight had been ruined, although she wanted to grab at the edges of whatever time they might have had together and wrap it around herself like a warm blanket.

The chill wind blew around them, suddenly gusty as though a storm approached. She wrapped her arms around herself as she wished he would.

"It shouldn't be too dangerous if you stay away from any people," she whispered. "Stay safe, Abraxas."

"Lore..." He reached out a hand like he wanted to touch her, but those claws curled into his fists before he could even grasp a strand of her hair. "I'll return. I promise."

"I know." The power of his change dashed away her words.

She stood in the blustery wind of his wings as he beat them up into the air. She should have suggested that she'd go with him, but she had to pick up the pieces of what had happened. Goliath might try to kill Draven, too, for all she knew. There were things she had to do. And places he had to go to burn off that rage.

The dragon blotted out the moon and then he drifted away from her on the wind.

Lore swallowed hard. This was supposed to be their night. They were supposed to be happy together, at last.

Why did it always feel like the world was working against them?

Turning away from the moon, the sky, and the dragon beyond, she carefully picked her way back to the tent. Barefoot and defeated."

CHAPTER 4

Abraxas helped take the tent down three days after what he had come to think of as "the incident". Lore had been ridiculously understanding about the entire thing, and she shouldn't be quite so kind considering the circumstances.

He'd been foolish. He'd acted like an obsessive idiot who thought she was someone he could possess. It wasn't fair to her.

But when he'd seen that other elf with his hands on Lore? Abraxas hadn't been able to see straight. The only words in his head were remove and destroy.

Draven had stayed with them, much to Abraxas's anger. The deepmonger seemed to think it was acceptable to walk into their camp, offer his help, and that they would all accept him with open arms.

Some of them did, of course, but they were far more trusting than Abraxas.

He kept a close eye on the elf as he chatted with Zeph, tilting his very handsome face back to laugh at something the half brother of the King had said. Zeph didn't talk to Abraxas like that, not really. The boy only wanted to speak with the dragon when there was a dire situation that needed fixing. Otherwise, he went to the others.

Was he so unapproachable? Abraxas knew he was intimidating. He was a dragon. Someone would have to be a fool not to realize how dangerous it was to just walk up to Abraxas and ask a silly question like how to talk to a girl.

Huffing out a breath, he tried to tell himself that he didn't want anyone to ask him about relationships or girls. If someone were to approach him, then they needed to have questions about something far more important than whether or not Beauty wanted to talk to them. That was for certain.

The tent pole in his hands snapped.

The loud crack carried throughout the clearing and he froze as everyone looked over at him. He sheepishly held up the wooden pieces and said, "Too weak to take with us."

If anyone believed him after that poor performance, he'd be awfully surprised.

Sighing and ducking his head low, Abraxas tossed the shards into the bushes and finished taking the tent down.

"You know," Goliath's voice interrupted his thoughts. "If you asked that tent tomorrow night to make a prison for Draven, or to trap him in the fabric after we all left for breakfast, it might do it for you. I think the magic likes you."

"That would be a rather cruel death, even for the elf." Although, Abraxas couldn't prevent the smile from crossing his face at the thought.

He'd pay good money to see the deepmonger struggling with the tent as it tried to hold on to him while all the others had been allowed to leave without struggle. Such a sight might actually make Abraxas feel a little better, even though it was a petty dream.

Goliath picked up the other end of the fabric and helped Abraxas fold it. They were far enough away from the others to speak freely, and for that, Abraxas was thankful.

"I don't trust him," Goliath grumbled. "He shows up, out of the blue, and we're supposed to assume that's because of some change of heart? He's one of the Ashen Deep. None of them want to help without a price."

At least someone else had their senses about them. Abraxas felt some sort of relief that he wasn't the only person who thought it was suspicious that Draven had shown up out of nowhere, having tracked them across the mountain peaks.

He flicked his wrists and snapped the fabric hard. "Lore and I had intended to find some time with each other when he showed up. I hadn't reached the clearing yet, but I found him with his arms around her. She assured me nothing had happened, and that obviously she was still there for me, but…"

Goliath narrowed his eyes on him, and Abraxas knew he was about to get scolded. "Don't you second guess her for a second because of what that other elf did. You know how she feels about you. You two have been together far longer and gone through too much for you to question her now. Abraxas, do you hear me?"

He did. And he knew it was foolish to feel so… so…

Off.

No, that wasn't right. He didn't feel confident at all right now. Instead, he worried that he'd done something wrong, or he had somehow insulted her and driven her away. And they'd only just gotten past that.

Goliath cleared his throat, vying for attention from Abraxas's thoughts.

He looked back at the dwarf and carefully made the last pleat in the fabric. Abraxas refused to even look at his shaking hands as he tucked the tent into his arms.

"You are not yourself," Goliath said quietly as they stood staring at each other. "I just want you to know... Lore was interested in you simply because of who you are. Her entire being fell in love with you. We could all see that. If you think she wants someone like Draven, all I ask is that you don't try to become him. I understand your relationship and togetherness is already being tested and so early at that. But you have to remember she wants you, Abraxas. Not that gangly elf who couldn't give her anything other than opening old wounds."

And with that, like he hadn't stabbed Abraxas in the gut, Goliath wandered off to be with the others.

Abraxas stood alone, holding onto the tent and frowning down at the ground. He was right. Goliath was probably the only person in this crew that had a good head on his shoulders. He was the only one who understood what Abraxas was going through, as well.

Sighing, he joined his companions and handed the tent to Beauty, who stuffed it into her pack. "Who's carrying the eggs today?" he asked.

Everyone stayed quiet, and he knew why. The box was heavy. The eggs weighed exactly what they should, and that was likely about the same as a human child each. Everyone tired far more quickly when they had to carry that box.

To his shock, Draven cracked his neck and then shrugged his shoulders. "I'll do it. Looks easy enough."

Oh no.

No.

That wasn't going to happen.

Before the deepmonger could even move, Abraxas shook his head and stomped over to the box. "I'd rather carry them myself than let you do it."

He noticed that Lore rolled her eyes the moment he hefted the box into his arms. Even Beauty pinched the bridge of her nose and muttered, "If he wants to carry the blasted eggs, then let him."

He'd argue with anyone who wanted to change his mind, but Abraxas would not have Draven touching anything else that was his. The eggs were impressionable, and he didn't want them to get the wrong idea about the other elf. They clearly already liked one of his kind, and they were far too trusting at this age.

Everyone else knew how to read him. They stayed far away. However, Draven had yet to learn that poking an angry dragon was a bad idea.

"I can hold it for you," Draven said, his eyes sparkling with mischief.

"I think you've held enough of my things lately, don't you?"

Lore tossed her hands up in the air with an angry snarl. "All right, I think that's enough. We're all heading out. You two figure this out between the two of you."

All the others swung their packs and bags over their shoulders and started off on the goat trail they were following. Everyone except Draven. The elf remained where he was standing, lacking a pack or anything that would be helpful on their journey. And the smug smile on his face was one that Abraxas desperately wanted to punch.

"What?" he snarled. "The others are walking. Did that not give you the impression that you should move as well?"

"I think you and I could use a little chat. Considering we're going to be traveling together, I think it might be better if we settled things."

Oh, he wanted to settle things? The elf really thought he could talk about what happened between the two of them as though that would wipe away everything that he'd done? Abraxas had no problem at all doing that if the elf wanted to be pounded into the dirt.

He set the box back onto the ground and then cracked his knuckles. "I know you've been underground for a long time, so you probably haven't heard what they say about dragons. Even long ago, when there were more of my kind to create some sense of diversity, everyone always said you didn't want a dragon to punch you. Not unless you wanted to know what it felt like to swallow your own teeth."

"Oh, I don't wish to fight you. We both know that wouldn't end well for me." Draven held up his hands, but his posture said he was looking for anything but peace. "Now, I thought we could handle this like men. Not teenage boys looking for their first taste of blood."

Another insult, thinly veiled as a joke against the two of them. It was clear that Draven did not consider himself to be immature, as he was not the one who had desired a fight.

Abraxas still thought punching the other man in the mouth would end all this in a much more satisfying way than talking.

Still, he supposed the elf had a point. Lowering his hands, he sighed and gestured for the other man to speak. "All right. I suppose you have words you'd like to get off your chest, then?"

"I do."

"Then say them now, or get walking."

Draven tucked his hands behind his back, as though he were some royal father whom Abraxas had called upon. "I know you and Lorelei have a special relationship. You have been through much together while trying to save the kingdom, and for that, all of us must be grateful for what you have given up."

Where was this going?

"I'm glad to see you recognized our efforts," he replied dryly.

"And I know what I'm about to say will feel like an insult, however, I need you to actually think about it." Now that was an evil grin. "What do you have to offer her? You seem to think the two of you will stay together. That you will build some sort of emotional attachment and that, perhaps, you could build a life when all this is over. But do you really believe you can?"

He should have punched Draven in the mouth. That was better than this conversation.

Instead, he tried to do what Lore would have wanted him to do. Abraxas leaned back down, picked up the box, and started walking. He tried so hard to school his features into an expression of disinterest, even though he was seething.

"Hold on a second," Draven called out. "Are you not going to answer me?"

"That doesn't deserve a response. You don't know her, and you certainly don't know me."

"What can you offer her?" Draven asked again, his footsteps pounding to catch up with Abraxas. "I know what I can, and I'm certain it's better than what you could give her."

"Oh really?" That was hilarious. Abraxas shouldn't make the boy feel any more important, but he had to push. "And just what could a young man who's barely seen enough sunrises to know what a woman wants offer her?"

"Acceptance."

The word made Abraxas trip. He didn't like the sound of it and some warning bell in his chest told him to not give the boy any more time. He should keep walking. Find the others. Put himself in a place where Draven couldn't talk like this anymore, but...

"What do you mean by that?" he growled.

"I mean exactly what I said. Acceptance. Lore has been ignored by our kind for so long, simply because she's only half our blood. But if she was with one of the oldest clans of elves, then I could change that." Draven stepped in front of him, hands still tucked behind his back. "The elves would want to be around her more. They'd listen to her, that's for certain, and they wouldn't care so much about her half blooded status. Even my own mother would be more inclined to heed her words if she were with me."

Abraxas had no idea how to respond to any of these claims. The boy couldn't assume that the elves would listen to him. He was a child in their world, and though his mother was a very powerful woman, that didn't give him any more rights than other elves. He was just...

Damn it, he might be right.

The elves were notoriously difficult and rather focused on remaining pure blooded, so the magic didn't abandon their kind. Not to mention they didn't produce more children if they were only half blooded. But... They might accept Lore if she were with another elf.

Lore might want that. Her entire life had been spent waiting for someone to look at her, to give her the time of day. Her elven mother had been cast aside just for birthing Lore. So many of the elves had spat at her or told her she was little more than an animal for being who she was.

And Abraxas entering her life would only make things more difficult. Now she was a dangerous half blood who had the chance to change the very fabric of time if she kept going. Right now, she still walked the same path as an ancient prophecy and there were many who would stop at nothing to prevent it from coming true.

Her life would be easier if there wasn't a dragon in it.

But damned if he wasn't the villain in this story. He had laid waste to kingdoms before, and if it meant he had to tear this one down to keep her, then he would. He was a selfish and cruel man.

Lore was his and his alone.

"She's not something to be bought and traded," he said carefully, measuring his words. "You seem to think you can beg me to let you have her, as though I would ever hand her over like some prize to be won. She makes her own decisions, Draven. If you wish to take her from me, then you will have to try harder than to sneak behind her back and beg me to bow out of the race I've already won."

Draven's expression changed from one of triumph to anger. "You're trading her comfort and life for what? So that you can still have her around? She wouldn't want that. She wants, no, needs to be with her own people."

"Her people are already around her." He tilted his head to the side and eyed the boy as though he were nothing more than a beetle on the ground. "She has been rejected by the elves. Mortals cast her aside for her magical abilities. She's had to make her own family, her own people, for her entire life. You really think you can get her to throw that aside because you offer her something from her past?"

"Something she's dreamt about for her entire life," Draven replied.

"You might think you know her, but she told me things in that dungeon that she never would have said to you."

"And you want me to believe that you are more important to her than you actually are. She'd have talked about you at least once, Draven, if she shared the same interest that you do. And I've never heard her say your name if you aren't around." Abraxas placed the box on his shoulder and moved past the elf, who clearly only wanted to make trouble.

Though he worried that there might have been at least a little truth in the elf's words.

CHAPTER 5

Someone needed to save Lore from the stubbornness of men. Or the two idiots that were constantly fighting should just hit each other and get it over with. She had already decided that neither Draven nor Abraxas would get an ounce of her attention until they figured out whatever fight they had determined was more important than her sanity.

At least their presence and constant unease they brought to the group made everyone move faster. Even Beauty had tromped down the mountain with impressive speed to get away from the arguments being thrown out into the air.

"I don't think you know which way we're going," Draven would say.

"Well, I am a dragon and I've flown over this land countless times. We're going the right way."

"But how can you be so certain when you aren't even in the air? Perhaps we should pause again. Let's get our bearings and I'll climb up that tree to make sure we're actually going where you say we're going."

The grumbles, growls, and insults were grating on every nerve she had. They both questioned each other nonstop. And she understood why, of course. They were each trying to figure out who would come out on top, and as far as she could tell, that answer would always be Abraxas.

Who could compete with a dragon, after all?

She stepped through the last bit of weeds and realized, with wonder and shock, they were at the base of the mountain. They'd made it.

The sudden shock and relief that they'd actually gotten off the damned mountain had her staggering the last few steps. She caught herself on a birch tree, not some scraggly, sad trunk that desperately tried to survive on rough terrain. But a perfectly formed, straight as an arrow, lovely birch tree with golden leaves that fluttered in the wind.

The birch grove spread out at least twenty paces and then opened up into a brilliant wheat field that surrounded the walls of Lux Brumalis. Even so far away, the city was impressive. Stone turrets rose toward the sky and flew banners of every color. Each magical family had their own symbol, and each family had their own section of the city. The stone walls of individual manors marked where one family ended and another began.

Legends claimed the city had been built by a single family who then expanded through their children's marriages. As more bloodlines intertwined with theirs, they built more castles. Weaving them until the entire city was full of magical manors and prestigious buildings owned by rich and powerful people.

It was what every city desired to be, but no one had the funds to build. Other than this place, of course. Because even the poor would pay for a spell, or a trinket, or a charm. As long as the magic promised them to get them what they wanted.

A warm hand came down on her shoulder. Abraxas squeezed and murmured under his breath, "We did it."

They had. And she'd second guessed nearly everything on the way here. But they had made it. After all the struggles and long nights.

"Do you think someone remembers him?" she asked.

"Who could forget the warlock who indebted himself to a mad king?" His hand smoothed down, resting at the small of her back as he seemed to like best. "We can't give up hope now. Look at where it's gotten us?"

"I suppose so. Now we have to walk through the walls of Lux Brumalis and find a place to stay? Find someone to talk with us?" She pressed the heel of her palm to her forehead. "I hadn't given it much thought up until this point. Now that we're here, I feel like I haven't planned enough again."

Another voice interrupted them, and it was one that set her on edge. Draven merrily said, "Then it's a good thing you don't have to make all these decisions on your own."

Right. Because he didn't seem to understand that this entire trip was to figure out how to open the box of eggs that Abraxas had hardly set down for the week of their travels. This wasn't about making the right decision for herself, it was about making sure those eggs saw the light of day. And that would require them to open the damned box.

She ran her tongue over her teeth and started forward. "No time like the present to figure out if they're even going to let us inside."

Mostly, she just wanted to avoid the uncomfortable tension between the men on either side of her. She'd felt Abraxas's hand flex against her spine and how he'd let it drift just a bit lower.

She didn't want anyone to claim ownership over her. And while she knew that wasn't his intent, that was how it came across.

Meanwhile, Draven knew that he was baiting the dragon. The idiot wouldn't stop trying to see how far he could push Abraxas. He'd figure out eventually that that was a terrible idea.

Her legs didn't quite know how to walk on flat land anymore. Almost immediately, her thighs started to shake and everything felt a little wobbly. Maybe Lore hadn't realized how tired she was until there was an end so close to her sight. She could make it. Really, she could. All she had to do was put one foot in front of the other until they reached the walls.

Her companions apparently felt very much the same. Their sudden rush down the mountain and the pace that had become blistering slowed down to an almost crawl. They took the better part of the afternoon walking through that wheat field and staggering toward what she hoped might be a place to give them some sense of peace and quiet.

Finally, they made it to the city gates. The golden monoliths gleamed in the sunlight, perfectly polished as though not a single speck of dirt dared to mark the shining entrance to Lux Brumalis. Maybe there was a spell that made it impossible.

There were figures carved into the gold, she realized. Or perhaps they had used a giant mold to create such a monstrosity. She could admit it was beautiful, but the scantily clad women who seemed to float up the surface of the door were less impressive and more ridiculous.

The gates opened the moment they paused in front of them. No one stood on the other side. No guards. Just an empty space of pale white cobblestone that had clearly never seen a day of dirt in its life.

"Should it have opened so easily for us?" Goliath asked.

"I'm not really sure..." Lorelei had expected someone at least to talk with them. This was one of the most prestigious cities in all of Umbra, and they just let anyone walk in?

Abraxas heaved a sigh and rolled his eyes. "This city is full of the most powerful warlocks and witches in the realm. They don't need guards here. There are no laws. If you want to steal from someone with that much magic at the tips of their fingers, then you can try. They can also kill you for it with a flick of their wrist."

Right. Well, they all needed to be more careful than she realized while they were here.

Lore swallowed hard and tried to remind herself that one couldn't steal without actually knowing that stealing was occurring. But she'd make sure that people knew she had money to buy things with. Just in case.

She supposed they couldn't stand out here in front of the door forever. But they needed to get somewhere safe before someone noticed a band of people at their doorstep.

"We should split up," she said. "I think it would be easier for us to figure out the lay of the city without being a giant group. People might start asking questions."

Beauty heaved a long sigh, but then nodded. "You're right. Zeph and I will go to the right. It looks like there are more residential buildings over there and people will be more likely to talk if we're two mortals wandering around."

"Makes sense."

Goliath looked at her with a narrowed, suspicious gaze. His eyes then tracked Draven wandering closer to Lore's side before his brows snapped down in frustration. "The elf and I will go down the center. That looks like the most touristy spot and the two of us will attract less attention than you lot."

With an immediately negative reaction, Draven shook his head. "I'll go with Lore. Two elves walking down the center of the street are sure to be more interesting than a dwarf and an elf."

"Why? Do you think the two of us aren't interesting enough?" Goliath's tone was more than a little frustrated. "Lore's gotta hide those eggs Abraxas is carrying. They've got to at least figure out a way for the magical people here to not realize what's in that box. And that means being sneaky. Abraxas isn't exactly sneaky. The two of them therefore have to be together or we're going to lose the only reason we started this mad dash."

"All the better reason for Lore and I to hide those eggs while staying in the shadows—"

Goliath didn't give Draven the chance to argue any further. Instead, he grabbed the young man by the arm and forcibly moved him down the street.

Lore thought she heard Goliath add, "I want to talk with you about manners, boy."

Leave it to Goliath to take that task as his own. Maybe he would actually teach Draven something, but she had a feeling it was more likely that the two of them would start arguing as well.

Tension eased from her shoulders as soon as Draven was out of sight.

"I know he's going to be useful eventually," she muttered. "But he needs to grow up before I let him anywhere near me alone."

"The boy has a crush," Abraxas replied. He shifted the box in his arms, moving the heaviness to the opposite side. "I can't blame him. I had the worst crush on you when you first walked into the castle."

She glanced over at him and was horrified to find that her cheeks burned with a blush. "Did you now? That was difficult to tell."

"And here I was, thinking I'd been rather obvious."

"You were never too far from me, and I suppose that should have been warning enough." In truth, she'd always known. Abraxas wasn't good at hiding his feelings, and he hadn't even tried to hide them about her.

She tried very hard to focus her attention on the street they should go down. The left side of the street wasn't dark, per say. Nothing in Lux Brumalis would have the same dangerous energy as Tenebrous. Living in that city had certainly prepared her for the darker parts of Umbra. But this place seemed a little out of her reach.

At least she'd have Abraxas with her. He was much more used to the finer parts of life and of Umbra.

"I guess we're going left," she said, turning the way they were supposed to go. "We can ask around a bit, see what people are talking about and if there are any inns that might be safe for us. I assume a place like this has an inn, don't you think?"

He said nothing in response, and that was unnerving.

Lore glanced over at him at the same moment that he reached for her. Abraxas had set the box on the ground at their feet and now reeled her into his arms. She went willingly, because fighting against him would be like fighting a storm that barreled toward her. She could run from it, or she could turn her face up to the rain.

He growled into their kiss, his arms banding around her waist and holding her so close to his chest that she couldn't breathe. He nipped at her lips, forcing her to open her mouth for him to deepen the kiss even more.

She'd forgotten how easily he could consume her. And though she was embarrassed to admit it, she much preferred losing herself in him like this. He was... perfect. Everything she'd ever wanted and more.

Those giant hands flexed against her spine and oh, she wanted to climb up onto him and wrap her legs around his waist. It didn't matter that they were in a city where anyone could watch them. She didn't care that countless people could walk up to them at any moment.

They were alone.

For the first time in months.

"I missed you," she whispered against his lips. "I missed this."

"I know this isn't the time or place, but I cannot keep my hands off you." He took the choice away from her. Abraxas bent down, hooked his arms underneath the back of her thighs, and lifted her up.

He carried her like she weighed nothing more than a feather. Those long legs ate up the distance between them and the nearest wall. He flattened her spine against it, holding her with such ease even as he ground himself against her core. She'd wanted him for so long that she'd forgotten what it felt like to have a man touch her like this. To feel that clenching, wet heat that flooded through her entire body.

Abraxas dragged his lips away from her mouth and trailed them down her neck. "You have no idea how long I've been waiting to do this."

"About as long as me." She tangled her fingers in the long locks of his hair. Suddenly, she didn't care at all that they both needed a bath or that they hadn't gotten enough time to clean themselves. This was perfect.

Abraxas lifted his head and drew back. Staring down at her with a sudden seriousness that made her heart stutter in her chest. "No, love. I've been waiting for this since the first moment we met. I felt my entire soul pause when it saw you. Like some part of me realized how important you were. I knew the moment I laid eyes on you that my life would never be the same again."

Oh.

She'd forgotten how to breathe. How could he say something like that, knowing that her heart was already his? He'd torn her apart with those words, and she didn't know what to say. Lore wasn't a poet, but he deserved to know that she felt the same. Maybe she hadn't known immediately like him, but the mere thought of life without him was as if she'd asked an artist to paint a landscape in black and white. Without him, the world lacked color.

"Abraxas," she whispered. "I—"

A tiny bubble of magic popped over their head and suddenly glittering lights rained down upon them. Lore winced and looked up to see all those tiny sparkles of magic that she had not conjured. They landed on top of Abraxas's head and all over her arms. They were likely littered through her hair as well.

Lore glanced over his shoulder and saw a young woman standing there. Her brightly colored green skirts melted into a yellow bodice and matching head wrap. She sheepishly grinned and waved at Lore.

"Sorry," the young woman said. "I thought you might want something for the mood?"

Right, that had ruined the moment.

Lore untangled her legs from around Abraxas's waist and moved away from the wall. She nodded at the woman, who had already started off on her own way, before Lore snagged the box. "I can carry these. But we should get going."

"Agreed. My apologies. I shouldn't have gotten so out of control."

"Please don't apologize for that." He hadn't turned around to look at her again, so Lore had to say the words to his back. "I don't regret a single thing. Just that a young woman saw us, I suppose. But at least she wasn't completely scandalized."

He still didn't turn.

Lore shifted the box in her hands and then cleared her throat. "Are you ready to go?"

"Give me a moment," he grumbled. "It's not as easy for me to stop in the middle of things and then walk around without everyone else knowing what we were caught doing."

If she had a hand to press to her mouth, she might have hid the smirk. Instead, Lore grinned at him, then tilted her head back to the sun. "Take all the time you need. It is a compliment, after all."

"Lore," he growled. "You are not helping."

CHAPTER 6

One might think at this point that Abraxas had grown used to being denied time with Lore. But this was somehow worse. He had all the private time he wanted as they explored this city, but none of it was spent in the way he'd hoped.

He got control of himself fairly quickly, although he thought he should get some kind of medal for that. And then they were off, walking down the hidden streets of Lux Brumalis like the two of them had been here for their entire lives.

They turned the first corner down a real street, not just the entrance to the city, and Abraxas was nearly struck dumb by the sights that awaited them.

They were in the residential area. Laundry hung above their

heads from tiny apartments that were tinted a hundred different colors. Murals decorated the walls of every building. Some of them were painted with butterflies, others with birds, but the murals moved on their own. The paintings soared through the brick and mortar, flying across the buildings as though they were alive.

He could sense the magic in the very ground they walked on. As he watched a couple speed past them, colors glowed underneath their feet. Seemingly, the magic in the city guided people where they needed to go with swirling patterns that merrily danced below them. The couple turned another corner and brought his eyes to the first vendor he'd seen.

Obviously, the woman wasn't a peddler to tourists. Her hair had been pulled out of her face with a brightly colored scarf that twisted into a thick braid at the back of her neck. But she didn't even look at the customers who were lined up to buy her pastries. Instead, her eyes were above all of their heads as she moved her hands in an intricate dance.

Magic spread from her fingers. Sparks of colors turned into bright spots of glittering dust. As he watched, the pattern of sparkles changed into what looked like the image of a peacock. The shimmering spell floated down from the air and then landed on the thick cake in front of her.

Then, as if that wasn't a marvelous thing she'd just done, she bundled the cake up into a package, tied a bright pink bow on it, and handed it off to the customer who waited for it.

The man paid her with a vial. Abraxas could only assume that was payment for the cake, and then made room in the line for the woman behind him.

Laughter filled the air from above their heads. Abraxas flinched and looked up in time to see a young woman who leaned out over a balcony above them. She had a mountain of sheets, dresses, and shirts in her hands while waving a wand in the other. With a swift flick of her wrist, the laundry, which had been piled on top of her comically high, floated into the air and danced over to her wash line.

He felt another prickle of magic and leapt forward to grab Lore just before a floating line of vegetables hit her in the head. Shocked and awed by what he could see, he noticed that there was a brightly colored ribbon around the leading tomato with a name on it. As though someone were delivering food, and they wanted everyone to know who the vegetables belonged to.

"This is the strangest place I've ever been," he muttered, still holding Lore against his side. "I'm not sure this was a good idea."

"I think it's wonderful," Lore replied. Her eyes were wide as she let her gaze feast on everything around them. "There is so much magic here. It feels like I'm breathing it in."

She probably was. Dragons didn't use magic. Sure, the shape shifting was a kind of magic some might argue, but it wasn't like he cast a spell to do it. Magical practitioners in their world were elves, dwarves, and a couple other creatures who knew how to cast a spell.

None of them were quite so adept as a witch, however. Mortals had spent thousands of years perfecting their magic so that they were passably similar to magical creatures. But their spells were unlike anything creatures could do.

He'd always thought most mortals were upset that they weren't naturally talented like elves. But in fighting their way to the top, they had certainly become more powerful than the elves. Even magical creatures feared what a witch or warlock could do.

Maybe that was why the King had hired one of them. He'd never thought about it like that.

Lore slid her hand down his arm and linked their fingers together. "We have time to explore a little, don't you think?"

"What do you want to do?"

She pointed to an apothecary, although now that he peered closer at the sign, it looked more like a bar. "I was just thinking we might sit down and get a drink?"

"Are you trying to get me to court you?" he asked, amused that she'd been so sneaky about it.

"Well, a gentleman in Tenebrous certainly would have brought me out for a drink by now. Probably a few drinks." She spun in front of him, walking backward as she dragged him toward the apothecary. "We'd have gone to a few underground dances. The Umbral Knights always tried to shut them down, but they never managed. Not in the way they wanted to."

She painted a pretty picture, although that wasn't how dragons courted. He had half a mind to tell her that he would have kidnapped her back in the time when dragons still flew through the clouds above cities. Brought her to his hoard and showed her how a real dragon convinced charming women that they were worthwhile of their attention.

Later. He promised himself that someday, he would take her in the old ways. She might be afraid at first, but that fear had always made the experience a little more interesting for the elves.

Instead, he listened to her paint a picture of courtship and happiness. "So I would have teased you, then?"

"Oh, no." She shook her head fiercely. "I would have done the teasing. You'd have returned home multiple nights quite certain that I wasn't interested in you at all."

He followed her across the street, not caring that other people were watching them. "I did that."

"You should have spent many a dreamless night staring up at your ceiling while wondering what I was doing."

"I did that as well." He took the box from her arms and caught a lock of her hair with his free hand, giving it a soft tug. "You consumed my dreams and all my nights, Lady of Starlight. I have never been so exhausted as when we started this dance between us."

"Good." That mischievous look in her eye set his soul on fire. "I'm glad you suffered a little."

"And why is that?"

She turned and placed her hand on the door to the apothecary, but looked over her shoulder at him. "Because I was suffering too."

Abraxas had the stray thought that maybe she knew her laughter and teasing was a siren call. He wanted to follow her, no matter where she went. He trailed after her as though he didn't have another thought in his mind. Perhaps he should have been embarrassed by that, but if someone else had seen her, had seen the grin on her face and the way those ocean colored eyes sparkled, they might have done the same.

The inside of the apothecary had been set up to look like they walked into a room full of potions and spells. A faint fog filled the room, just enough to obscure most people from anyone's line of sight. He could tell there were people sitting all around them, but he couldn't make out any of their features. The only thing in the room that wasn't pale with smoke was the bar itself. Glass vials and jars lined the wall behind the figure who stood there, and every drink he could see in someone's hand was either bubbling, foaming, or had smoke pouring out of the glass.

It was a rather interesting idea, he supposed. Although he hadn't frequented bars much in his life. That was Zander's game and preferred choice of meeting place. Not Abraxas. He'd always ended up outside the establishment waiting to make sure no one tried to attack the King.

Lore stepped right up to the bar and braced her forearm against it. "What's the best drink you have?"

The woman who turned around was over six feet tall and had the deepest voice he'd ever heard coming out of a woman's mouth. "That depends on what you want, darling. There are a lot of drinks in this place."

Lore shrugged. "We don't want to get drunk, if that's what you're asking. We have some questions to ask around and hopefully speak with someone willing to take us and our friends in for the night."

The bartender looked Lore up and down, then peered at Abraxas. "I think you might find that a little difficult with a man like that looming over you."

"He doesn't loom." Lore looked over at him fondly. "He's just got an impressive stature."

"I'd say. Most people in this city don't want any trouble." But the woman started making them a drink. The one she eventually slid over to Lore was bright pink with swirling glitter that never stopped moving. "I call it the siren's call."

"Lovely name." Lore lifted it into the light, watching the sparkles move. "What's in it?"

"Magic," the woman replied with a snort. She looked over at Abraxas, apparently understanding that he wasn't going to drink. "And for you?"

"Someone who might know how to open this box." He gestured with it, although he knew it was a long shot.

The bartender clearly didn't want to deal with them anymore. She leaned to look around him and appeared disappointed that no one waited in line behind him. Sighing, she drummed her nails on the top of the bar. "People around here aren't interested in meddling in other people's magic."

"That's not going to work for me."

"You can try to convince a warlock to look at it, but it'll cost you a significant amount." Again, her eyes swooped over him from his feet to the top of his head. "I don't think you could afford a warlock. Maybe a witch if she's desperate."

He hated it when people judged him by what he looked like. Yes, he had been born to be a bodyguard with a face that was more suited to glaring than it was to smiling. That didn't mean he wasn't capable of payment.

"I think you've sorely underestimated me," he growled.

"I don't think so." The woman reached below the counter and picked up a dirty glass. She started cleaning it with minuscule, jerking movements. "I've gotten real good at reading people, and I think you're just like all the others that walk into our city looking for answers. You'll find nothing but disappointment if you want to open that box. Not without money or something else worth trading."

He was going to wring this woman's neck. If she wasn't careful, then she would find out why the mortals had been afraid of dragons. He even felt the fire burning in his chest before he noticed Lore's tiny movement.

It wasn't much.

Just the slightest flick of her wrist while she tucked a strand of hair behind her ears. But then the pointed tips were on complete display and the bartender froze. Her eyes caught on Lore's ears, and suddenly, her gaze flickered with hunger.

"Ah," the bartender said, picking her words carefully. "So that's how it is, then."

Lore lifted her drink and sipped it, her eyes watching the bar as though she hadn't just startled the other woman. "We're looking for a particular person, you see. I'd hoped to relax for a bit, but my companion has a one track mind."

Oops.

At Lore's slanted glare, he shrugged. They were in the perfect place to ask around. Why wouldn't he take that opportunity? If she were angry at him for that, then he'd accept the punishment.

There was nowhere better to get people talking than in a bar. Everyone's lips loosened with drink and they were far more likely to talk. At least Zander had taught him something, he supposed.

The bartender put her glass down and leaned closer to them. Her arms braced on the worn wood, and turned white as she pressed her forearms down hard. "There are people in this city who will pay a lot for certain items from the likes of you. All you've got to do is find the right one."

A bit of the fog drifted away from them, revealing certain patrons at tables that were already looking over at Lore and Abraxas. They had the same hungry gazes, and expressions he knew were born of desperation and greed. It was a bad idea to barter with their ilk.

He'd seen those same expressions in Tenebrous, although for very different reasons. The people in her hometown looked at him like that because they would kill to survive. These people would kill for power.

Lore didn't appear worried in the slightest. She took another sip of her drink and ignored the stares. "Certain items? I'd have to converse with these people who might give me that information. There are some things an elf is not willing to part with, you see."

"I think you'd be surprised at what they asked for." The bartender leaned even closer to Lore until her lips almost touched her cheek. "You'd be surprised what I would pay for, too."

All right, that was enough.

Abraxas slammed the box down right next to the woman's hands. Close enough to send a thrill of fear as the woman realized she'd almost lost her fingers.

"I think we'll ask someone else, if you don't mind." He smiled, though he knew the expression never made it to his eyes. "Now, do you know anyone else who might be helpful to us? Someone more agreeable."

The bartender's glare might have frightened him if he wasn't a dragon. "Give me a moment. I'll ask around to see if someone is interested in tampering with broken magic on a box that is centuries old."

With a flick of her hair, the bartender disappeared.

Lore kept her gaze on the vials behind the bar. "We might be in more trouble here than I thought."

"How so?"

"Witches and warlocks are always hungry for information, but I didn't think they would want to toy with us. I forget that magical creatures are now ingredients in rather powerful spells." She sipped at the drink again, then shook her head. "Even this is raw power. I can feel it. Two sips and already I could cast more spells than after three nights of soaking in the moon."

Abraxas frowned. "And that's a bad thing?"

"It is." She looked at him, then nodded behind the bar. "Especially when there are posters like that around."

He turned and faced a rather startling likeness of Lore herself. He hadn't noticed it when they first sat down because he'd thought it was a mirror. But now, he could see it was a magical rendering of her face. It looked around, smiled, and then graciously lifted a hand as though she were waving to someone. Beneath the portrait were the words, "The Savior of Tenebrous."

Shit.

"Well, that changes things," he muttered.

"Apparently, Margaret has moved forward with her plan to make us legendary around Umbra." She sipped her drink faster, perhaps trying not to look like she rushed to get the power into her system. "That means people will recognize us while we're walking around the place. I think we might want to keep our eyes peeled a little more."

"I think we should leave this place." He looked into the mist again, seeing that some of the foggy figures had stood up.

Perhaps those were people willing to look into the box. Or perhaps they were villains who wanted to take a bit of their magic. Witches and warlocks were unpredictable, and unfortunately, they were some of the few who didn't fear a dragon.

One figure in particular caught his eye. A woman stepped out of the mist. At least, he assumed it was a woman. The cloak that obscured her face did nothing to hide the lithe, thin body underneath. Rail thin, really. She stood with her hands loose at her sides as though waiting for him to look at her.

Or waiting for Lore's eyes to find her.

"Perhaps we go now?" she asked.

"I think you're right," he muttered, reaching for the box with one hand and Lore's arm with the other. "I think we can find someone else to help us."

She tugged him to a stop and placed three gold coins on the counter.

At his questioning gaze, she shrugged. "I don't want to owe anyone."

"Good enough."

Abraxas dragged her from the fog of that place while his gut twisted in fear. They weren't safe anymore, it seemed. Not that they ever were to begin with.

CHAPTER 7

Lore liked to think she had a sixth sense for danger. That sense had helped her survive for years underneath the noses of the Umbral Knights, and even in the King's palace while she tried her best to win him over and get close enough to kill him.

Now, that sense told her they were in a lot of trouble. And by a lot, she meant they were in an entire city full of people who wanted to kill them. Or maybe they wanted to squeeze out every drop of magic that she held in her body so they could figure out what made her different from them.

They stepped out of the apothecary while doing their best to act at least somewhat normal. Anyone looking at them would have thought they were a sweet couple who had come to Lux Brumalis to seek privacy. But anyone who knew them would wonder why they were clutching each other's hands so tightly. Or why they never once looked at each other.

Goliath and Draven walked around one of the corners near them, eyes wide and hands already ghosting around the areas where they hid their weapons. Good. At least they knew that they were all in danger. She wouldn't have to justify leaving.

"Lore," Goliath said as soon as they got closer. "We've got trouble."

"I'm aware of that."

"Your face is on posters all around this city," he continued, as though she hadn't spoken. "And there are people everywhere who keep whispering that you're inside the city limits. We've really got to get going."

"Then I suppose we need to find Zephyr and Beauty before we head out," she snarled. "Goliath, I already know all of this. We've seen the pictures too, and I understand the gravity of the situation."

She glanced over at Draven and noticed he had his hand on his side. The grimdags whispered that they hadn't tasted witch blood in a long time.

Damned things. They were going to convince him to do something foolish and then none of them would get out of this city alive.

"Normal daggers only," she ground out, watching the elf who rarely listened to her orders. "Don't let anyone know you have those things. We will only fight if necessary."

"You might find it more necessary than you think," Draven replied, narrowing his eyes on a crowd that had slowly formed. "You've been spotted, Lorelei. And I'm guessing they know what your friend is, too."

Lore strained her ears to listen to what the crowd was saying, but could only pick out a few strains of their whispers.

"Dragon?" one said. "No. There are no more dragons."

"The King said—"

"That man does look familiar."

"I think I saw him at Madame Blanchet's!"

Damn it, the deepmonger was right. They had been spotted in more ways than one, apparently. She'd been wary of what these vultures might do if they found out that Abraxas was a dragon, and she'd been so careful not to mention it since they got here. But one of their previous plans had gotten in their way.

"Where are those damned humans?" she muttered. Lore stood on her tiptoes to search through the crowd, but couldn't find Beauty or Zephyr. There was a single alleyway they should enter from, but there was no movement in the shadows.

Draven palmed a regular knife and drew it out of its holder. "We should start running."

"Not without Beauty."

Even Abraxas put his hand on her back, his muscles tense as he made eye contact with many of the witches and warlocks who were nearly licking their lips in anticipation. "I think it would be better if we ran. They're humans as well. I doubt any of these people will hurt them."

"You can't know that," she replied. "We're going to find them before we leave."

The two humans they were looking for careened out of the alleyway with bright red faces and horrified expressions. Beauty skidded to a halt first at the sight of the crowd. She grabbed onto Zeph's shirt and held him back even as he kept running. Thankfully, the girl was strong.

Lore shook her head. They needed to run too, as far as she was concerned. And they couldn't get to each other through the crowd.

Hopefully, Beauty had her wits about her. They'd find each other later, she supposed, even though it broke her heart to mouth, "Go."

Beauty clearly didn't want to do that. She always had a fight in her and clearly thought she could shove a way clear to get to her friend.

That wasn't possible. They would lose each other in the swell of people, and then what would they do? At least now, they had hope.

She glanced up at Abraxas and took his hand again. Hope. That was all she'd had for a while now, and she wasn't giving up on it yet.

A new voice hissed behind them. "Well, you all have a death wish."

Lore froze, knowing better than to look back at the person who'd spoken. "Not a death wish," she replied. "Only an incorrect opinion of a place like this. We'd thought it would be safe to seek shelter within the walls."

"Bullshit," the voice replied. "You want something, and you're willing to pay for it. Aren't ya?"

"Handsomely."

A chuckle echoed in her ear, deep and slithering down her spine. "I don't think you understand my question, elf. No one here needs gold. No one here wants what that dragon might have hidden in his trove."

Lore licked her lips and turned her head slightly. Not enough to see the woman behind her, but enough to make eye contact with her dragon. "You get us out of here alive, and I'll consider paying you what you want."

The look on Abraxas's face told her that was a stupid thing to agree to. But what other option did they have? An angry mob stood before them, ready to do whatever it took to eke out the slightest bit of magic from her and her companions. If Lore wasn't careful, she would lose everyone important to her in one fell swoop. She'd do anything to keep them all safe. Even risk herself.

He knew that.

The person behind them snorted. "I suppose that's good enough. You'll pay me something if you survive, I'll tell you that. Whether you want to or not."

She had to be okay with that. She had to know that risking this was worth it.

"Deal," Lore replied.

Her companions winced, but that was all right. She'd take the blame for this later when they were all alive and by each other's side once again.

A hand reached out of the darkness behind her, in the doorway of the apothecary, and tugged hard. That gruff voice muttered, "Then run."

She didn't have to be told twice. Lore spun around and raced after the dark figure. Though the woman wore a cloak that looked like it was dusted in emerald, the figure beneath the cloak showed no features whatsoever. She couldn't tell if this person had been in the apothecary with them or not.

They ran through the apothecary as the woman shouted out a word in the ancient language that sounded like stones scraping against stones. The mist disappeared. A crowd of people stood from their tables and they all threw their hands up to shield their faces as though they didn't want anyone to see who they were.

The woman hit a door with her shoulder and they busted into the back of the apothecary. The room beyond the mist was completely devoid of any decorations at all. Lore had only a few seconds to notice how barren it was before they ducked through another door and out onto another street.

To their right was a group of people who she could only assume were the tail end of the mob that had wanted a piece of them. They'd circled behind the crowd.

Smart. Very smart.

The woman took them down the alleyway and raced through the streets. They sprinted until Lore's lungs burned before they all stopped at the door of a handsome manor with exterior walls that looked eerily like raw emeralds.

"Is this your house?" she asked, her jaw dropping open in shock.

"We really don't have time for this conversation. Get inside."

She filed into the home with her companions in tow. And though she had been shocked by all of this, Lore really wasn't prepared for the pristine interior of the building. Everything looked too expensive to touch. From the hand painted green walls with writhing magical ivy, to the perfect green chairs that were plush and stuffed to perfection. A small fireplace at the back caught her attention, not because it was less glamorous than the rest, but because it was a normal fireplace.

Until it lit itself with bright green flames.

Right. Nothing was simple in this place.

She looked up at the ceiling as though that would give her answers, only to see that the ceiling had been painted as well. Pale green blooms opened and closed above her head. As if they were breathing.

The entire room was disorienting, but even more so was the flight from the middle of the street into what looked like a nobleman's living room.

Lore furrowed her brows and spun upon their unlikely savior. "And just who are you?"

The person threw back the hood of her cloak and revealed a very tall woman with statuesque features and a voice like thunder. "My name is Amalia, and you are in the wrong place if you seek help."

Lore retorted, "I think you've already helped us. So clearly you are the liar here."

Amalia paused long enough for Lore to get a good look at the woman. Her dark brown hair had been cut to her shoulders and framed her sharp features rather nicely. The solid chips of emerald in her eyes had been hardened by years of mistrust and fighting. Lore knew the look of another warrior when she saw one. The thin lines of her lips were already compressed into disappointment as she surveyed the people in her living room. Her broad shoulders could have held up the entire world if she wanted them to.

She was taller than any woman Lore had ever met, and that was the first reason why Lore thought Amalia might not be everything she claimed to be. The second was that the woman had saved them. And if the people in Lux Brumalis were that hungry for magic, then no one would have saved Lore and her companions.

Amalia gritted her teeth, a muscle in her jaw ticking before she ground out, "You should never have come here."

The woman ripped off her cloak and hung it on a small coat hanger near the door. The dress she wore underneath was similar to the rest of this house. Bright green, threaded with glimmering silver threads, and reeking of money.

This was not the person she'd expected to save them. Not in the slightest. She looked at her companions to get their opinion, realizing they were all still prepared for battle.

Abraxas stood by the door, apparently ready to run at any minute, though his eyes never left her for a second. Draven still had his hand on the knife. Goliath even flicked his eyes around them, clearly looking for something to fight with.

They didn't trust this woman either. Good. That would serve them well, she hoped.

"I'll agree that coming here might have been a mistake." She still thought that might be a lie, though. Lore held onto the hope that they would find someone or something that could help them. Perhaps even this woman. "I always heard Lux Brumalis was the gleaming pride of the King. The city where everyone wanted to go. Was I so wrong?"

The woman snorted as she walked past Lore toward the fire. "Certainly some might say that. Those of us who have lived here our whole lives know that's a lie."

"Then what would you call this place?"

"The city where magic goes to die." Amalia reached for a small cord next to the fireplace and gave it a pull. "Would you care for tea?"

This was by far the strangest interaction she'd ever had. Lore looked back to her companions, all of them still frozen where they stood. "I suppose water would be better. We're all out of breath from that run."

"Ah, right." Amalia pressed a hand against her stomach. "I suppose I should be as well. But I'll admit, it was rather invigorating."

Abraxas stirred from his corner. He moved to stand next to Lore, the box still clutched in his hands. "Perhaps for the person who wasn't about to be attacked. Why did you say magic dies in this city?"

She gestured all around them, as if the room itself was enough explanation. "People move here wanting to learn how to cast spells. All these green witches and wizards who think magic is good and power can only be wielded by the worthy. Give them two years here and they'll fall into the same trap as everyone else. They all want more. They compete for prestige and better materials and books, all locked away for the highest bidder. But the rich don't matter. It's who is in control. That's what counts. This city is eating itself alive for magic."

Amalia sat down hard on the nearest chair by the fire and lost herself in the flames. Lore watched that expression and recognized the posture of a woman who had found herself stuck.

"That's why you helped us?" she asked. "Because you're tired of this city and the people in it?"

"I'm tired of fighting with everyone for any kind of magical component. I'm tired of being the only one who doesn't have what she needs for spells." Those bright green eyes slanted over to look at her, and the fight in them was fierce. Powerful. "You're going to give me something that no one else has. Something that will make my spells stronger than anyone else's in this city."

Unease settled in Lore's stomach again. "And what is that?"

Amalia's gaze flicked over to Abraxas. "A dragon scale."

"Excuse me?" Abraxas snarled. "I don't think you'll be getting that."

"Then you can go back out on that street and deal with everyone else who wants the same thing. They all want a dragon scale. A lock of elf hair. The diamond tears of a dwarf." Amalia pointedly stared at each of them while she spoke. "Or you can give me a single scale and we'll all get what we want."

Lore's mind raced. This wasn't what she wanted. She hadn't expected to be trapped yet again by another person who thought they could take advantage of her and her companions. Unless...

Unless.

Lore meandered in front of Amalia's chair and crouched down. The woman clearly wasn't used to people being that close, because she sank back into the chair like she was afraid of elves. Maybe she was. She should be.

Lore chose her next words carefully. "A safe place to rest our heads for the night isn't worth a dragon scale. You and I both know that."

"Your lives aren't worthy of that?" Amalia shook her head. "You're bartering with nothing, elf."

"We need to find someone who knew the King's warlock." She nodded at the box in Abraxas's hand. "I think you know someone who can help us."

Amalia paled. Her hands clutched the arms of the chair so tightly they turned bone white. "Nothing is worth that information."

"Not even a dragon scale?" Lore leaned closer and whispered, "What about for two?"

She had her. Lore knew the moment greed and desperation merged together until the poor witch in front of them had no other option. The object of her desire was within reach, and that was enough.

Amalia narrowed her gaze and said, "That'll do. You can stay here for the night. Tomorrow morning, come down for breakfast and we'll talk about finding someone who knows that warlock."

"Good enough." Lore stood and added, "We still have two more companions who need to join us."

"I'll find them as well." A green tinged fog entered the room and coiled around Amalia's feet. Apparently, that was the thing she'd summoned. "Tea, please. And send for this elf's friends. We have guests tonight."

CHAPTER 8

Breakfast. With the person who could easily send them down a path that would kill them.

Abraxas had never seen such a thing in his life. And considering the woman had put them all in different wings of this massive emerald manor, he could only assume that they were walking into a trap. Which was exactly why he didn't let the eggs out of his sight for the entire night. He didn't sleep.

He hated every second of being in this place and intended to get them all to run.

But then he walked into the dining room, fully expecting there to be a wave of people who were immoral and dangerous waiting for them, only to find that his companions were already seated at the table. They all chuckled with each other, reaching for food and placing it on their plates with giant forks and spoons. Like they had been born into this genteel life.

Goliath sat beside Lore on one side of the table and it looked like the damned dwarf had bathed. He'd even brushed his beard out if the glistening curls were any indicator. Of course, Draven appeared quite at ease with these creature comforts. Though he'd placed his knife within reach, thankfully, it wasn't the grimdag. Abraxas didn't want to know what the witch would do, knowing such a powerful weapon was inside her home.

The mysterious emerald woman who had brought them here was absent, and that set him on edge. He hesitantly walked over to stand beside Lore.

"Morning," she said, looking over her shoulder while bringing a fork full of potato to her mouth. "Are you going to eat?"

He gave her a look that clearly said he thought she was mad for even trying any of it. Abraxas at least set the box at his feet, however. The movement cost him much, because if they had to run, then he would need to waste precious moments gathering it up while he also tried to get Lore to safety.

She looked him up and down, and he already knew what she saw. The bags under his eyes made his sight compromised, and the gritty feeling every time he blinked suggested that his eyes might be bright red as well.

"Did you not sleep at all?" she asked under her breath.

"Not a wink."

"Why's that?"

Did she really need to ask that question? He gestured around them and then let out a frustrated huff. "How could I sleep knowing that we'd willingly walked into the den of a lion?"

Lore reached for his hand and laced their fingers together. She dragged him closer to the table, her thumb rubbing his knuckles. "Because you are a dragon, and what is a lion when faced with a real predator?"

This was his fault. He'd led her to believe that a dragon was infallible. And in a way, he was. Compared to the other magical creatures of their realm, dragons were very difficult to kill. He'd spent centuries learning how to fight and how to make sure that both of his forms were formidable. But they were in one of the few places where he could die and that put him on edge.

She'd yet to admit how much danger they were in. And he needed to make that clear to her before she made some grave mistake that he couldn't fix.

The empty chair to her left screeched across the floor. Abraxas forced himself to remain still and not even flinch as he watched it round the table and land right beside Lore. It was then that he noted she'd hooked the leg with her foot and dragged it over.

He eyed the chair and then looked back at her. "What do you want me to do here?"

"Sit." She nodded while filling her mouth with some kind of mystery meat. "You're so tired you're seeing things."

"And you're talking with your mouth full in quite possibly the most beautiful place we've traveled to, so who's the crazy one here?" He didn't sit. Why would he? What if that witch walked through the door and attacked them?

"Sit down, Abraxas, before you fall over."

The mere suggestion was an insult. He remained exactly where he was, even if his legs flexed slightly to ensure he didn't keel over as she'd suggested he might.

The doors opened and in walked the emerald witch who had helped them. The woman looked a little worse for wear. She had matching eye bags of her own and her hair stuck up like a cloud of darkness around her head.

"Oh good," Amalia muttered. "Breakfast."

Without even looking at them, she slumped in the chair opposite Lore and snapped her fingers. The forks and spoons the others had served themselves with suddenly jumped up. With no one holding them, they served her with an accuracy that Abraxas wasn't sure he would have been able to mimic if he'd served her himself.

Not a single drop of food or sauce splattered on the table. And if it had, he was certain magic would have cleaned it up. Long before she noticed, at least.

Once the witch had served herself, she pressed her fingers to her eyes and shoved hard. "I was up all night trying to find anyone who would talk to you about the warlock who used to work for the King. Do you want to know how difficult that task turned out to be?"

Abraxas looked at his companions and found them completely dumbstruck. Even Lore's jaw had dropped open at the abrupt way Amalia had entered the room and then started talking as though no time had passed since the last time they'd seen her.

Clearly, they'd all been expecting more from this woman who lived in luxury, who had no interest in all the finery that surrounded her.

Like always, Abraxas had to be the one to respond to her. "I don't know that we all care that much about how difficult it was."

The witch dropped her hands from her face and glared at him. "Oh. So you think I should help you while you don't care at all about the repercussions for me?"

"We're paying you," he reminded her. "You're getting a magical component that no other witch or wizard has had in many lifetimes. I don't need to remind you how valuable a dragon scale is. Let alone two."

He was still quite angry that Lore would throw him to the wolves like that. His scales could create magic unlike anything this realm had seen in hundreds of years. The mortal witches and wizards alive today had likely only heard of dragon scales in spells as a myth.

Giving this woman, whom they did not know, an item that powerful was a risk they had to take. He understood that.

It didn't mean he had to like it.

Amalia glared at him, but the woman didn't have any argument whatsoever. He was right. Abraxas knew that with a finality that wouldn't give her any wiggle room here.

The witch sighed. "Fine, then. We don't have to be business partners in this. I can be merely a customer. This is a transaction, so to speak."

"Precisely." He placed his hand on the back of Lore's chair and tried not to look too prideful that he'd managed that conversation without a misstep.

Or, well, he supposed, close enough.

The witch pointed at his movement with a fork. "So you two are the leaders here, then? I suppose that makes sense. The two of you will want to interview the only people I could find willing to talk about that man. It's dangerous to even talk about him, you know."

He did. The King's father hadn't wanted anyone to know that he was working with a warlock. Zander's father had even more hatred for magical creatures than Zander, and that was nearly impossible. But he'd made concessions for the warlock because of what that horrible man could do for him. And in the end, it didn't matter.

Lore leaned forward and asked, "Why is it dangerous to talk about him if he's dead?"

The way Amalia squirmed in her chair made Abraxas's stomach turn. "Warlocks are never really dead, now are they? Anyway, that particular warlock was the strongest we've ever seen. He bound a dragon. He mastered the greatest magical creature to exist in this realm like it took nothing more than a flick of his fingers."

Abraxas had always hated that story. It was wildly inaccurate, but the witches and warlocks adored telling it like that. They wanted to think that the warlock had merely been powerful rather than ridiculously clever.

But he wondered... Perhaps this was his opportunity to save one of those scales.

Sinking down into the chair beside Lore, he steepled his fingers together and braced his elbows on the table. "What if I told you that wasn't how it happened?"

Amalia's eyes narrowed. "Are you trying to say the warlock who captured you wasn't the greatest man of our time?"

"He wasn't. I'm not afraid to say that, although many people would fear being struck down from the grave. I'll tell you the real story if you want to have it." He flared his fingers wide. "For a price."

She didn't seem like a fool. Amalia had to know that while power could be bought in items like dragon scales, it also came in the form of knowledge. Particularly knowledge that no one else had.

With a quick pursing of her lips, Amalia put down her knife and fork while narrowing her gaze on him. She stared at him, and for a moment, he felt as though she'd flayed open his mind. Searching through his thoughts to tell if he was lying.

"You want to tell me that truth?" she asked. "You have proof that the King's warlock is a regular man?"

"Oh, he wasn't a normal man. He was quick witted and his trickery knew no bounds." Abraxas arched an eyebrow. "I suppose you could go about thinking for the rest of your life that he'd trapped a dragon because he was powerful. You could worship him and his memory like the others."

"Or?" she asked.

"Or you could know the truth behind the story and perhaps that would help you later on." He shrugged. "I don't know how it might help, or why you'd want the information, but I do know it will eventually become useful."

Her narrowed eyes never moved from his. "What's your price?"

"One dragon scale."

She sucked at her teeth and shook her head. "That's a big price for such a story."

"Considering it ruins the name of the most revered warlock in the realm, yes. It comes with quite a price."

"And I still get one scale?"

"As promised."

He knew the moment he had her. Amalia's shoulders dropped lower and her eyes opened like normal. The witch had fallen for the bait, and it was information he would happily tell her. He'd grown tired after all these years of people claiming the man who'd trapped him was some anomaly in the warlock community.

He'd been a man. And men died.

She picked up her fork and nodded. "You have a deal then, dragon. Tell us the story of how you were enslaved to the King of Umbra."

Goliath snorted into his cup and then froze when everyone looked over at him. "What? Sorry, I've always wanted to know this story as well. It's not every day we get to hear about the great dragon of Umbra and how he was caught."

Abraxas gave him a censoring look, but knew what the dwarf meant. So many people had wanted to know how he'd been trapped, and so few knew the real tale. For a long time, it was only him and Zander.

He poured himself a glass of water before he started, knowing he'd need to drink something if he were going to tell it in its entirety.

"The King's father was a calculating general. He knew warfare better than any I'd ever met, and had studied it extensively for years. He caught me in my hoard, unaware that humans could get that high into the mountains. At least with so many armed men with him." Abraxas grinned with sharp teeth. "Even that amount of warriors wouldn't have stopped me. As far as I knew, I was the last dragon. I didn't care what they did to me, or how they went about doing it.

"Just as I planned on fighting them, a mist came out of the mouth of the cave. A mist so thick it was impossible to see through. I was trapped in the back corner. The King's men attacked, but then realized their blades could not cut my hide. They retreated, and that's when I heard him. Your warlock.

"He had found a book of dragon lore long ago and someone had painted one of my brethren. He conjured up an image of her that depicted how she'd laid eggs before her death. He told me where it was and I fell for that lie."

It was the worst part of the entire story. Abraxas had been so desperate to no longer be the last that he'd rushed from the cave. Right into a trap.

He shook his head. "I rushed to where they said the eggs were, and

I found them. Later, I learned it was just luck. The book had mentioned the mountain had once been a nesting place for dragons and the warlock took a risk. He was lucky that there were eggs there, and even luckier for what happened next.

"The box he spelled to keep the eggs was spell bound to his own energy. He had done it when he was still learning how to make magic, but the spell had never broken before. So why not use it now?

"He summoned the eggs long before I reached the cave. Timing was everything for your warlock. The eggs happened to be placed into that box before I could get to them, and then it closed. Forever. The warlock merely transferred that spell over to the King. And then if I no longer wished to be the last dragon, then I would do whatever that King wanted. Thus, he became known as the Mad King who made the dragons kneel."

Finished, Abraxas drained the glass of water he'd placed beside him. He let the room sit with it before he looked back at Amalia.

Her face had turned bright red. "Are you saying they captured a dragon by luck?"

"He was a talented warlock. One of the best. But he wasn't when he trapped me." Abraxas shook his head ruefully. "He became that man with countless years accessing the King's private library and all the confiscated books on dark magic. The King gave him unlimited access to unimaginable knowledge from the rest of your people. His magic and his talent came from studying, just like anyone else."

"Luck," Amalia muttered. "Who ever would have guessed that he'd lied to us all for so long?"

"He was an accomplished liar, and an even better cheat." Abraxas felt his shoulders curve in on him. "If a dragon could fall for his lies, then don't think you are above the man's charms. He had years to create the image he wanted people to think of. And years to make his vast power even more great. The King sacrificed many people and creatures to his warlock so the man could serve him better."

The witch slumped back in her chair, tapping her lip with a long-nailed finger. "That was worth the trade." She stood abruptly. "I'll let you know when the witch arrives who claims to have known him. You'll want to talk with her, I presume."

With that, Amalia left the room like he hadn't bared his soul and his greatest mistake.

CHAPTER 9

Lore could admit she'd never thought they would sit in a witch's living room waiting to entertain a guest. It felt... wrong? No, that wasn't the right explanation.

The witch had been kind enough to let them into her home. Amalia had made it very clear the danger and what she wanted for the risk, so Lore supposed that was to be admired. She was a woman who took control of situations and then decided to take care of herself first. And that wasn't a person Lore met every day. At least not in Tenebrous.

But this place also felt a little strange to be in. No one could look at the hand-painted flowers on the ceiling or the roaring fireplace, or the cushioned chairs, and not wonder where all this wealth had come from. Amalia claimed she wasn't the best witch of her age, but maybe she was and her lies were believable.

Either way, both she and Abraxas sat on an emerald velvet couch, waiting for Amalia to bring in whatever magical practitioner who claimed they could help.

She glanced over at Abraxas and wondered if he was nervous.

He'd placed the box of eggs on the floor between his feet, clearly not wanting to leave it out of his reach for too long. That was for the better. If this witch would put her life on the line for a single dragon scale, Lore had a feeling she'd do a lot more for baby dragons of her own.

Abraxas swallowed hard, then looked over at her. "Are we sure this is the way we want to do this?"

"I can't imagine there are many other options. Zeph couldn't open the box, and we both know Zander won't." She wrung her hands, twisting her fingers until she sighed. "But I'll admit, this is a risk we wouldn't usually take. Not together, at least."

"Witches," he muttered, and the word was filled with hatred. "No one can trust them."

"We're not trusting her. We're assuming that she's telling us the truth about what she wants. Power. Control. A dragon scale that will have her casting spells we eventually have to fix, I imagine." Lore tucked a strand of hair behind her ear. "And we haven't talked about the posters yet. I've been so wrapped up in all this that I didn't even consider Margaret would screw everything up from the Umbral Castle."

"She wanted to make a martyr out of you," he said. "I guess that still applies, even if you're alive."

She didn't want it to. Lore didn't want her face plastered over every city in this damned kingdom. The blessing of no one knowing her had been the one that she luxuriated in. Now? Everyone had seen her face, and if they hadn't, then they definitely would the next time they went to market.

Lore let her head drop onto his shoulder and bit her lip. "I just want things to go back to normal."

"Neither of us has that opportunity, Lore. Our lives have changed for good." But he still picked up her hand and tangled their fingers together. "I don't think I'd change a thing, though. Not now that I have you in my life."

Her dragon never failed to impress her, even in moments like this. Lore let her attention focus on the strength in his hands as he held onto her. Grounding her in the moment, in the now. He wouldn't let her fail. Not even in this.

The doors opened and Amalia stepped through with another hooded woman. This one was clothed in all black. Lore noted the dark skirts that were decorated with silver moons and stars. Classic witchcraft, it seemed, was the poison of this newcomer's choice.

"Another witch?" Lore asked, her eyes narrowing with suspicion. "Frankly I'm disappointed you didn't surprise me with someone more like the man we're looking for. A warlock."

Amalia threw her hands up into the air. "You asked me to find someone who knew about the warlock, that's what I did. Again, no one in this cursed city wants to talk about him. You get what you get."

"No," Lore growled. "We get what we pay for."

The new woman took down her hood and revealed a beautiful face underneath. Her pale face was shaped like the moon. Surrounded by pin straight dark hair and eyes equally dark, her features appeared more aggressive in all those shadows. The perfect bow of her lips had been painted blood red, and those lips curved into an evil grin.

"You'll get what you pay for," the dark witch said. "You wanted someone who knew the warlock, and I did. He was a great man then. I can tell you what you want to know. I am likely the only person who can tell you that in the entire city."

Such information seemed similar to what Abraxas had bartered with just this morning.

Lore pointed at the dark witch. "We paid her to find you. Now I'm assuming you want some form of payment as well?"

"She sees right through me." The dark witch looked at Amalia, that horrible grin still plastered on her face. "I'll admit, I thought you were lying when you claimed she was so courageous. She speaks to witches as though we are not dangerous at all."

Amalia quirked an eyebrow. "It's easy to be fierce when seated next to a dragon."

That was apparently the information the other witch had wanted. The dark witch's eyes found their linked fingers, and that was the only moment that horrible smile faded. Only a little, though, before she pulled up her shield once again.

Lore knew they would not get anything out of this woman, while she felt like Lore was protected. Witches were... difficult. Dark witches, in particular, were worse than the others. This one had a price that she wanted paid, and she would do nothing for Lore until the circumstances were exactly as she wanted them.

The witch's eyes flicked between her and Abraxas, and Lore knew nothing would be said if Abraxas remained in the room. The witch was here for Lore, not for a dragon. Strange. She'd never thought that magical practitioners like this would be interested in a lone elf, but here they were. The dragon had to go, or the witch wouldn't talk.

She squeezed his fingers. "I think you need to leave."

Abraxas jerked in her grip. "I'm not leaving you alone with two witches."

Lore opened her mouth to tell him they didn't have a choice, but Amalia beat her to the punch.

The green witch sighed and gestured with her hand for Abraxas to follow her. "She's only going to be alone with one witch. I'm not getting involved in any of this any more than I have to. If you'd come with me, terrifying dragon that you are, I'll bring you back to the others."

"I'm not leaving," he growled.

"You are," Lore replied. She looked up into his angry gaze and knew that he was worried about her. But they didn't have an option here. "It won't take long. And you know I can take care of myself."

He opened his mouth, closed it, then huffed out an angry breath. "I hope you know what you're doing."

"Most of the time, I know what I'm doing." Lore kissed the back of his hand and then let him go.

He'd tell the others what was happening. That was a good start. Draven would have more details because what elf didn't know about the magical women who liked to walk in the footsteps of those who had come before them? Goliath would agree with her dragon, but by that time, no one could do anything about the circumstances.

Lore would handle this on her own.

Her dragon slowly stood, gathered up his box of eggs, and glared at both witches the whole time he moved. "I'm going to be right outside the door," he snarled. "I'll hear if anything goes wrong."

"Keep telling yourself that," the dark witch replied. "You've never dealt with my kind before."

"I've dealt with more than you can imagine. I've killed creatures far more terrifying than you." Abraxas leaned close to the woman, his teeth bared in a snarl. "If you harm a hair on her head, witch, a pyre will feel cold compared to how I will kill you."

"Point taken." The dark witch never flinched, even with a dragon breathing death down her neck.

Amalia closed the door behind them without ever looking back. The finality of the lock clicking into place reminded Lore that she was at the disadvantage here.

"One of the local witches, I presume?" Lore asked, remaining seated as she was.

"My family has lived here for a very long time, yes. We are one of the oldest families in Lux Brumalis." Gathering her skirts, the dark witch sat down in front of Lore with all the grace of a noblewoman. "There is a lush history here, if you are inclined to hear it."

"I am not."

The smallest flicker of surprise lifted those perfectly painted eyebrows. "I see. You're a woman who prefers to get to business rather than idle chatter."

"I just want to know what your price is." Lore leaned forward then, bracing her forearms on her knees. "I fully understand that you are here because you want something from me. You wouldn't be offering information otherwise."

"You are correct."

"And I believe I am also correct in guessing that whatever you want from me will not be paid while we're in this house." Lore had dealt with witches before, as much as she hated admitting it.

"You're correct about that as well." The witch's grin grew wider until it seemed like it split her face in half. "You're much smarter than

I thought you would be. When I saw people putting posters up of your face, I felt certain that you were just another pawn being used for the rebellion's whims."

Lore shook her head and pressed her lips tightly together. "I wouldn't write those posters off as not using me. I don't condone any claims of a savior, but I don't control what they say either."

"Not controlling how they use you is not the first mistake you've made, I assume." The witch tilted her head to the side, obviously looking Lore over for any weaknesses. "I find it hard to believe anyone could take you by surprise."

"It wasn't intentional," she said. "I had no choice, and now I suffer the consequences."

"Ah." The sound was noncommittal, as though the witch had never been forced into making a choice she didn't want to make. "Well, this choice is yours. The other witches and I have a use for elves. Depending on your clan, of course."

There it was.

The indirect question that would weigh her merit.

Lore contemplated lying. She could tell the witch she was from any other clan of elf. Perhaps a Green Dale who had never left their meadow valleys and thus were plentiful when Tenebrous was built on their land. At least until that land changed from once plentiful greenery into a marsh and bog that grew no food again.

But lying would only make this witch more suspicious. Lying would prove that Lore was afraid.

She chose the truth while hoping it might get her more than secrecy. "I'm a Silverfell elf. My guess is you could make much use of me."

It was the first time the witch didn't hide her reaction. Her eyebrows lifted in surprise, then her gaze narrowed as though trying to scent a lie. "There aren't many of you left, if you're really a Silverfell."

"Not many at all." And there would be even fewer, no thanks to Lore. Her lineage would end with her.

"Prove it."

"How would you like me to prove it?" Lore asked, a flicker of anger making her tone a little too curt. "Do you want to see magic? Is that what you're asking for?"

The witch pressed a hand against her chest. "I'll answer honesty with honesty. Here's your truth, freely given, as I expect you to prove who you are. I'm not the one who has your information. My coven mistress sent me in case you were a liar."

"You mean she sent you in case the payment wasn't high enough for her liking." Lore curled her lip in disgust. "All you witches try to wring out the world for what you want. There is more to life than taking, you know."

"Spoken like someone who has taken nothing worthwhile in her life." The witch leaned forward ever so slightly. "Prove you're a Silverfell."

Lore hated doing this dog and pony trick. Humans were all the same. Whether they had access to magic or not, they desired nothing more than to see creatures perform magic without a spell. She expected Lore to jump when a human demanded that she show them something beautiful.

A fiber of her soul whispered that they shouldn't do this. She should leave because this witch wasn't even the one she had to talk with. But if she really were the link to the person they needed, then Lore would do anything to get one step closer to opening that box.

She let the magic pour out of her soul and linger on top of her skin. It was a simple parlor trick, really. Her skin sparkled like the moon, but that was the one thing that humans always gasped at when they saw the magic.

Apparently, witches were no different.

The woman's eyes widened, and she pressed a shaking hand against her mouth. "You really are a Silverfell."

"Why would I lie?" Lore asked.

"A thousand reasons. People lie to embellish the truth, or perhaps to hide it. But you? You took the truth right out of thin air and dangled it in front of me like meat before a starving dog." The witch nodded. "You will meet my mistress."

"And who is your mistress?" Lore let the magic fade from her skin.

"I'll inform Amalia when we're ready for you." The witch lifted her hood over her head and started toward the door.

"Stop," Lore ordered. She waited for the woman to hesitate before repeating, "Who is your mistress?"

The dark witch glanced over her shoulder and that grin morphed her face into that of a monster. "We are the chosen. The women who have survived after the gods turned their faces from us. The women whom men fear and desire. Come to us, child of the moon. Come to us and sacrifice, so that you might find what you seek."

A shiver traveled between her shoulder blades as the woman opened the locked door as though a key had never turned in it, and disappeared into the hall beyond.

CHAPTER 10

braxas didn't like that Lore was hiding something from him. After the witch left, his little elf had brooded. She'd stared off into the distance for far too long, her head in the clouds while she chewed on the nail of her thumb.

Something was off.

And he didn't like it when anything was off, let alone a detail she wouldn't confide in him.

He was aware this likely meant he had severe trust issues and that he should consider working on that. And he would. When they weren't trying to hide from a power hungry, undead King who couldn't be killed while they were also hiding dragon eggs in plain sight.

Which was why he called the others into his room later that

night. Abraxas knew he had little chance to get them to do what he wanted. Goliath liked to poke fun too much, and Draven disliked him for rather obvious reasons. But all three of them had one thing in common.

Lore.

The knock on his door sounded far too loud. He yanked it open with a snarl and pulled the other two men inside with a rough tug. "Would the two of you at least try to be less suspicious? We're in the household of a witch."

Goliath combed his fingers through the long length of his beard and picked out a tiny piece of bread that was likely there from breakfast hours ago. "She's been awfully nice so far, Abraxas. I think you should try talking to her. She seems sweet."

"I never trust a witch." He closed the door behind them with exaggerated gentleness. "You're a fool if you give her that much leeway."

The dwarf rolled his eyes. "I'll have you know, I met many lovely witches in my time in Tenebrous. They're no less trustworthy than the lot of us."

"They're still human."

"And humans do terrible things. I know, I know. However, so do we. Wouldn't you agree?" Goliath popped his fists onto his hips and glared up at Abraxas. "You have a hard time understanding that people are people, regardless of where they come from. You know that?"

Perhaps he did. Even though they were fighting for all magical creatures, it was still difficult to let go of old fears and hatreds.

Abraxas sighed and slid a hand down his face. "I didn't invite you to my room for a lecture, dwarf."

"People rarely do. That doesn't mean they don't need a lecture." Goliath turned around and surveyed the room with an unimpressed look. "She gave you the worst of our rooms, I think."

Yes, it was a little plain considering the house they were in. The floors had no rugs to hide the scratched wooden surface, and of course, he'd noticed that the bed was much smaller than normal. A single window and a wooden wardrobe were the only other furniture in the entire room. There was lovely wallpaper on the wall in a pale blue that mimicked the sky. Tiny enchanted birds flitted from one corner to the other. But he was fairly certain this room was meant to be for servants, not for guests.

Draven leaned against the wall, one leg lifted with a foot pressed against a painted bluebird that struggled to get free. "I guess it pays to be nice."

Abraxas already wanted to hit him. He would pay good money to pound his fist into that idiot's face. Just once. He didn't need to kill the man, that was overkill, but he would love to see blood spray from the pretty boy's mouth.

Still, he needed Draven for this plan, and that meant he had to at least pretend to be nice. Baring his teeth in what was likely a horrible smile, he ground out his next words. "Would you pretty please shut up for a moment?"

Draven lifted his hands in peace and then crossed his arms firmly over his chest. As though he would stay silent for more than a few sentences.

Not believing that posture for a minute, Abraxas looked back at Goliath. "Listen, both of you. I know you want to trust this witch who let us into her home. I would love to as well. But there's something going on here that none of us are privy to."

"Abraxas." Goliath sat down on the edge of the bed, hopping up to reach it. "I think you need to sleep, man."

"I think you need to be aware that she brought in a dark witch to talk with us and then kicked me out of the room to talk only with Lore. Why would they do that? They're my dragon eggs and I'm the only one here who has ever actually seen the warlock we're looking for." Abraxas crossed his arms over his chest. "I couldn't hear the conversation well, but I'm certain that the witch made a deal with Lore. She hasn't been acting right ever since."

He expected the two men to leap into action. Lore was in danger. A dark witch had named her price and that should be enough to set them both running into the streets seeking a solution. Instead, they both looked at him in confusion.

Maybe he wasn't only going to punch Draven. Maybe he'd turn the dwarf upside down and knock him unconscious with the floor.

Looking up at the ceiling, he muttered, "They called Lore a child of the moon. We are in a city full of magical practitioners who have not seen a Silverfell elf in centuries. What do you think they want from her?"

Really, did he have to spoon feed everything to these morons?

Draven was the first one to flinch, although it took him long enough. "I've heard stories that witches can siphon magic off of elves. If that's true…"

There it was. Maybe the boy had some sense in him after all. "They can, and they will. Dark witches would love to get vials of moon magic off a Silverfell elf, and who knows what they would do with it. But they could potentially control Lore and force her to work for them. Or they might use the magic to enslave others. We will have no control once they have Lore's power."

"That doesn't sound good," Draven muttered.

Finally, Goliath straightened his shoulders and seemed to understand this was more of a problem than he had realized. "What do you want us to do, then?"

"Sneak out of the house and see what information you can get out of people." Abraxas nodded at his window. "I'm on the ground floor. Easy enough to say we've all been talking for a few hours. That's not much of a lie. Even a witch couldn't taste that in the air."

Draven eyed him with a narrowed gaze. "You have another task for us, don't you?"

Astute as well. If they weren't in love with the same woman, he might actually like the elf. But as it were, he still wanted to wreck that pretty face. "If you have time, find Beauty and Zephyr. The two of them have probably gotten into more trouble and I don't want to let them continue to be fed to the wolves."

Goliath hopped off the bed and dusted his hands off on his thighs. "Easy enough. I'll see you two gentlemen later."

And with that, the dwarf hopped out the window as though he'd been doing that his entire life. Probably had.

That left only the elf in the room, and Draven eyed Abraxas with no small amount of disgust. "Look. I don't agree with you most of the time, dragon. But I see that you're trying to keep her safe, and that's all any of us could ask for. But if you use this time to leave or sneak her away from us... I'll find you again."

"I have no doubt about that. You wouldn't be so easy to shake off." He pointed to the window. "You two are the ones the witch won't notice missing the most. I'll cover for you as much as possible."

"Your will is my command." Draven bowed sarcastically, then slipped out the window after Goliath.

Abraxas hadn't spent much of his life waiting. He was a man of action and took great pride in that.

Sitting around waiting for them to return felt like death itself. The witch never came to his room, nor did she ask for his presence. He couldn't be all that surprised by that. She didn't like him, and she'd made it very clear that she didn't want to be around him.

Lore was the subject of her interest. And the dragon scale that helping them would get her. Of course, she'd have to deal with him when she wanted that. Abraxas assumed she would want to gather it up herself. Otherwise, she would have to trust that Lore would pay her.

He had half a mind to fly away with all his companions on his back and let the witch rot. Though he'd heard horrible things about owing a witch a debt. Perhaps it would be better if they paid up, after all.

The night passed with his companions wandering through the streets at night, and Abraxas did not sleep yet again. Perhaps he dozed off for a few hours. He wasn't all that certain. Night passed strangely in this place where so many people awoke whenever they wanted.

And the house made strange noises in the middle of the night. Not quite the creaks of stairs or the groans of a building settling into place. Instead, he could hear the house breathing. It inhaled the magic and power from all within its walls and exhaled dust.

A scratching came at the window at nearly four in the morning. Abraxas knew because he had stared at the clock for the better part of three hours. Watching it tick by and counting the seconds while matching his heart beat to the sound. Otherwise, he'd forgotten how to think. How to breathe.

He glanced over at the windowsill, half expecting to see some grinning witch's face while she held up the head of a friend. Instead, he was greeted by the mass of hair and glittering eyes of a dwarf.

"Help me in," Goliath hissed. "We don't have a lot of time. I think we're being followed."

That snapped him out of the stupor of exhaustion. Abraxas leapt up from the end of the bed, his muscles and bones creaking from the frozen position he'd maintained for hours. Reaching his arm out the window, he grabbed onto the back of Goliath's shirt and hauled him inside.

Then Abraxas stuck his head out and smiled down at the two familiar faces waiting on the other end. "Do you two need help as well? Or are you satisfied with climbing in on your own?"

Zeph rolled his eyes. "Get out of the way, dragon. We'll manage on our own just fine."

Easy enough, then. He slid back into the room and waited to say anything until his friends were all within reach. Zeph had somehow changed his clothing, and now wore a rather impressive dark blue suit of crushed velvet that matched his handsome eyes. And Beauty wore a flowing skirt and a matching pale blue shirt. Someone had cast a spell on her hair that made glitter sparkle on every strand.

They both looked lovely, and as though they'd been thoroughly enjoying themselves while the rest of them had gone through hardships.

"Where have the two of you been?" he asked.

Beauty tucked a glittering strand of hair behind her ear. "We were told to explore."

"And after we saw the four of you taken, we thought it better to hide for a while." Zeph added, as though that somehow made their appearance less suspicious.

Abraxas felt rather like a father scolding his children after they snuck out at night. "And hiding at what, some underground party, sounded like a good idea?"

Considering how red Beauty's face turned, she also felt like she was being lectured by a parent. "Well, we'd never gone to one of those before. And I've always heard it's best to hide in plain sight."

"Rather than seek out where we were and potentially try to save us?"

"Well..." She stopped, looking him in the eye and tried very hard to melt into the floor.

As expected, Zeph stepped in front of her as if he were thinking going toe to toe with Abraxas was a good idea. "Don't make her feel bad about this. We've been traveling for ages. She had a bad ankle. It wasn't like we could rush after you or take any unnecessary risks."

Abraxas leaned to look over Zeph's shoulder and asked Beauty, "Had?"

"Someone fixed it for me," she muttered.

"Good. Then both of you will be able to pick up the pace when we're finally ready to go. Until then, both of you should perhaps try to stay a little closer to the rest of us." Trying hard not to sigh dramatically, he turned his attention to Goliath. "Any news other than these two?"

He shook his head. "Took me long enough to find the young ones. I didn't have much time for anything else, considering I figured you'd want us all back before dawn."

"You were right." Damn, though. He'd expected Goliath to find something. The man was charming when he wanted to be.

Dark hands slapped down on the windowsill and Draven pulled himself out of the shadows. He eased onto the floor like someone had poured oil through the window, standing with a lithe grace that was both otherworldly and unnerving.

Abraxas always forgot how impressive elves were until he saw one move like that. "Well?" he asked.

"Not much. Few people know anything about the dark witches in these parts, only that they live on the opposite side of the city and stick to themselves. If they want something, they get it." Draven stretched out a shoulder, perhaps from running away from another witch. "I found some other elves, though. They've been living underneath the city, keeping away from the witches while using their potions and magic for other things. It won't be as comfortable a place to stay, but it's still better than a witch's house."

"Better than nothing." Abraxas walked toward the door of his room and then paused. He looked back over his shoulder and gruffly said, "Good job, Draven. I'm impressed."

He slipped out of the bedroom before the shocked expression on the elf's face could give him too much satisfaction.

He needed to find Lore. She'd want to know all this, even though she'd be angry at what he'd done. The woman had to realize that he would do whatever it took to keep her safe. Even if that made her furious with him.

Her scent was easy to follow through the halls. The witch hadn't tried very hard to hide where Lore's room was, although there was no answering sound when he knocked on the door.

"Lore?" he asked, slightly opening the door to the room. "Are you awake?"

"She's not," the witch replied.

Abraxas opened the door all the way with his stomach already in a knot. Amalia sat on Lore's bed. She'd crossed her legs and braced her wrists on her knees, the picture of poise and grace. Her emerald dress pooled around her hips and spilled down onto the floor.

"Where is she?" he growled.

"She's already gone to fulfill her bargain. Some people understand the importance of honor in witchcraft." Amalia didn't move, not even when smoke curled out of Abraxas's nose. "She's going to be fine, dragon."

"Where?" he asked again, barely sounding like a human.

"You can try tracking her down, but I promise you won't find her in time." Amalia lifted one delicate hand and held it up for his silence. "They aren't going to kill her. You'll get your little elf back in the same state she left in."

"Can you promise that?"

"No." Then she smiled, and it looked like just the dark witch's smile. "But a witch knows better than to make promises she can't keep."

CHAPTER 11

Lore knew the others would never have let her go after they heard what the dark witch had to say. And it was probably a bad idea to go on her own. But she couldn't stop now.

Lifting the hood Amalia had given her, she made sure it covered her face. No one could know she'd snuck out of the manor. She didn't want to risk another witch recognizing her from the posters. Lore had quite enough witches to pay at the moment.

The streets were surprisingly busy for midnight. So many people strolled beside her on the cobblestones. They ducked into businesses and walked out with bundles, their laughter ringing with bright gaiety. The city of Lux Brumalis never slept, it seemed.

She sidestepped a cart full of potions as the man wheeled it by her. She eyed the gleaming contents and wondered what magical component glowed in the dark. When he had nearly passed by her, she could see there were tiny glow worms in each potion bottle. Pretty, certainly, but they were living creatures who were likely being taken to their deaths. Everything here was like that. Pretty, but either a sacrifice or bringing about another's doom.

She shook herself out of the dark thoughts and kept going. All the way through the city as she passed by a hundred lovely sights. Fireworks that moved through the air like there was a real dragon above her head. Windows that projected light and sound and images to coax people within their walls. Even people with glitter in their hair and faces painted to look even more stunning than they already were.

If she were visiting, this city would hold some kind of magic for her.

The farther away from the green witch's home she went, the darker the streets became. Shadows slithered alongside her like snakes coiling through the windows and over the hedges. The buildings had crooked walls, not crumbling like in Tenebrous. These curves were intentional. They made every gothic structure in this section of the city intimidating.

Finally, she stopped in front of a building made of black wood, rare even in these parts. A wrought-iron fence surrounded the building with spear-like tips that would make sure no one climbed onto the grounds. Though, the gothic architecture should have been enough to warn people away.

Dark witches weren't accepted even among their own kind. At least, that's what Lore had heard a long time ago.

Steeling herself for whatever waited, she put her hands on the gate and pushed it open. The house seemed to lean closer to her. Or was she moving forward to the front door? Lore wasn't quite certain how to answer either of those questions in her head.

The front door opened and revealed the dark haired witch who had first spoken with her. The woman had removed her cloak, and the gown she wore was made entirely of black silk. Tiny silver patterns had been stitched through the entire dress, and as Lore stepped closer, she could see each stitch was a rune written in an ancient language.

Spells. The woman had sewn hundreds of spells into what she wore as though she expected to be attacked at any moment.

Lore supposed in a place like this, that was probably smart to do. The witches here were likely as cutthroat as Lore could imagine, and she had quite the imagination.

"You made it," the dark witch said. "I'm surprised. I honestly thought you would run."

"Running isn't in my nature." Lore lifted her chin and hoped she looked more brave than she felt. "You said there was someone here who knew the warlock, and that means I'm going to speak with them."

"If you're lucky." The dark witch didn't move aside for Lore to enter the house. Instead, she stepped outside with Lore and then turned to lock the house with a skeleton key.

Lore only caught the smallest glimpse of the interior of the home. While the outside was black, the inside looked warm and inviting. Mahogany wood accents, plush floor, thick carpets that led into another room she couldn't quite see before the door closed.

"Pretty home," she said as the witch turned around to face her. "I thought it would be filled with cobwebs and cauldrons."

"Those have their place." The witch's face split with that horrible grin again. "But our home is for living and there are better places for magic than indoors. Wouldn't you agree?"

She did, although Lore wasn't sure why the dark witches aligned with her own preference for magic. What she knew of their kind was very little. Dark magic had higher costs than most. She knew dark witches used sacrifices often, usually in some form of blood or murdered person.

So why was she here? What were they expecting her to give up?

"Follow me," the witch said. She hopped off the small porch and her movement revealed black boots that went up to her knees.

Curiouser and curiouser, Lore thought. She'd never met witches like this before, so that meant either this would be a highly amusing meeting, or a terrifying one.

She wasn't sure which she'd prefer at this point.

They rounded the house to yet another black gate that the witch opened with a wave of her hand. Lore realized they were going to a garden behind the house, and out of view of anyone who thought to pry upon what the witches were doing.

It was beautiful, really. They'd filled the entire backyard space with roses and hydrangeas that drenched the air with a cloying, sweet scent.

"I didn't think roses grew this time of year," she mumbled.

"They don't anywhere else." The witch paused in the garden and held out her arm for Lore to walk ahead of her. "We can make anything grow here. What is dead will live in the garden of the dark witches."

Lore paused beside her and met those black eyes head on. "And what happens to the living?"

"You'll find that out on your own, elf. You're smart enough to do that." The witch's smile never budged.

Lore stepped away from the dark witch and through a bubble of magic she hadn't even felt. She pushed through the magical barrier and the garden expanded before her eyes. Or not really a garden, but a field full of plush clover with a group of women waiting for her underneath a full moon.

They all wore matching black cloaks with the hoods drawn over their heads. More of that silver stitching was on all the hems of the gowns they wore.

All women, she presumed, although there could be a few warlocks among them. Either were equally dangerous, considering the magic they practiced.

Swallowing hard, Lore stopped in the middle of the field. She didn't know what to do next. No one had told her to walk forward or if she could speak. If the witches were casting a spell, she could suffer serious backlash with the wrong move.

The dark witch who had led her here should have come through the barrier as well, but she didn't. Lore was alone.

Lore took a deep breath and let power rise to the surface of her skin. The glittering moon magic filled her senses and dove into the spell the witches wove. They didn't care if she spoke, it seemed. They wouldn't care if she screamed, either. But the spell required that she go into the center of that circle they'd created with their bodies.

She put one foot in front of the other. This was what she'd expected out of the witches. They'd want some form of payment, and usually that was any material they could use in a spell. Lore should be thankful they didn't want her blood.

They had cleared away a small ring in the center of the circle. Only gravel remained in that spot. No earth or living thing that she could grab onto with her magic. They really didn't know how Silverfell magic worked, did they? All she needed was the moon, unlike many other elven clans. The earth didn't respond to her power.

The full moon overhead filled her with more power than she knew what to do with. Not that Lore had ever been all that talented with magic, but she could cast a shield none of them would get through if she wanted.

Considering the magical spell over her didn't seem to care if she spoke, Lore cleared her throat and spread her hands at her sides. "I am here, as requested. Now I need to know which one of you has information about the warlock."

None of them spoke.

"I'm not going through with this without knowing that you actually have information to give me. I'm familiar with the trickery of witches." She lifted a glowing hand as though about to cast her own spell. "I will put a shield over myself and walk out of here. Deals must be struck and payments must be paid."

"Just as we told you that sacrifices must be made."

The voice was ancient and came from the mouth of a witch who had seen many elves in her days. Lore knew better than to anger a woman with a voice like that. The witch would sooner cut her throat and drain her dry than argue with Lore's kind. That much was clear.

Lore licked her lips. "At the very least, I need confirmation that I'm not sacrificing for nothing."

"Then know I will provide information to you once we have our price."

She couldn't tell which one was speaking. None of the hoods let her see through the shadows underneath, and she was quite certain the voice had been amplified through all the hoods. It sounded like one woman, but many voices saying the same thing.

Lore looked up at the moon and wished not for the first time in her life that the moon could talk. What would it say to her now? Was she making a grave mistake that she'd regret for the rest of her life? Should she turn around now and save herself?

Or would the moon tell her that she had no choice in the matter either way? Lore could keep fighting against the tides of the world or she could ride them through the swells and the dips.

Perhaps this was a low part of the wave, but that only meant her trajectory was up from here.

"Agreed," she whispered. "Do whatever it is you had planned, and then I will have my information from you."

"You will," the circle of dark witches said.

She closed her eyes and hoped this wouldn't hurt too bad. Whatever they wanted to do, they could do. She would let them.

The first touch was a long-nailed finger on her right shoulder. She felt a horrible ice cold sensation trickle through her skin like water had been poured over her. But she knew it wasn't water. There was no sound or touch other than the fingernail.

Lore opened her eyes a crack and watched as a tendril of white magic peeled off of her skin. The witch pulled her hand back slowly and the little magical strand followed her like a moth to a flame. She swirled her finger in circles and the magic became a funnel.

The witch held out a small vial and Lore's magic trickled into the bottle that would capture it forever. Immediately, the witch corked it and held the bottle up to the light.

The silvery glow matched the rays of the moon.

"She's a true Silverfell," the witch whispered. Her voice differed from the others. The raspy sound of it came from a woman who had screamed many times in her life. "This is unlike anything we've ever captured before."

"True essence," another voice muttered.

"Magic from the moon. Not distilled or weakened by mortal hands." The third person who spoke had the voice of the leader. That voice wasn't easy to forget.

Lore hoped that magic was enough. Just the single strand that had been taken left her feeling woozy and slightly dizzy. She needed a moment to get her bearings. Even a few heartbeats were better than nothing.

Then that voice spoke again, this time even more powerful. "Drain her."

The witches descended upon her in a swarm of dark fabric and magic. Lore lost her breath. Even if she'd wanted to fight against them, she couldn't. The swarm of witches made it impossible for her to even think straight, let alone fight back.

Pricks of cold appeared all over her body and every single one started to hurt. Or maybe it wasn't pain. She couldn't feel her own fingers, hands, feet. Had she lost all sense of her limbs at all?

"What are you doing to me?" she slurred.

"Your sacrifice," the voices murmured in her ear. "Your sacrifice will not be in vain, little elf."

Why did it feel like she already regretted this decision? Lore swallowed hard and looked away from all the magic that poured out of her body. They were ripping at her now. The witches realized her magic didn't want to separate from this form and now they were pulling and tearing and tugging at the power underneath her skin.

They'd wring her dry.

She turned her head to the moon and looked up at the magical mother who had given her such gifts. It was like the celestial body told her to relax. Ease into the torment and the torture because it would all be over soon.

Silverfell elves had endured worse than this for centuries. She would survive, as they all did.

The moment they were done, all the witches stepped back as one. They moved away from her and no one moved to help her. Lore staggered to the left, barely catching herself before her weak knees sent her to the ground. The gravel bit into her skin. She slammed her palms down hard as her spine turned to liquid.

No, this wasn't how it was supposed to go. She'd given them a sacrifice and now she would be paid.

Forcing her neck to move, she peered up the dark column of fabric to look at the witch, who still stood beside her.

"What information do you have about the warlock?" She could barely understand the words that came out of her own mouth.

A swish of fabric and suddenly the witch had knelt in front of her and gripped a handful of Lore's hair. "If you can stay awake, I will tell you your information about the warlock. But listen well, elf. I'm going to say the words whether you stay conscious or not."

Her neck stretched back too far. Air couldn't make it into her lungs, and she saw pinpricks of black and white in her vision.

"A trick?" she croaked.

"Never trust a witch, darling."

And then all the light disappeared.

CHAPTER 12

The bubble of the magical shield parted around him. Abraxas didn't care if they knew he'd entered the clearing. He felt the witches hadn't conjured a spell to inform them who dared to break through their shield. Unfortunately for them, that meant they had let a dragon into their midst.

He crouched down, cursing his large form and how difficult it would be to remain in the shadows. The witch who had led Lore into this place stood nearby. She would see him if she looked over her shoulder.

Of course, the witch didn't. Her eyes were riveted to the horrible ceremony taking place in the center of this conjured field.

The witches all gathered around Lore, sipping at the magic that poured from her skin. The long tendrils of silver light were capped in tiny vials and bottles held in those wicked creatures' hands. Magic that would then be used for who knows what.

His body shook at the horrible sight. He wanted to rush into the field and grab onto the throat of the first witch who stood in his way. He imagined twisting her head around and watching as the skin of her throat ripped open around the bone white spine that would be revealed.

Abraxas knew Lore would murder him if he interfered with the witches' ceremony. His elf might be a terrifying woman of her own accord, and she had no problem with death, but she'd want to see this through to the end.

So he stayed to himself, lingering in the darkness while these horrible creatures did whatever they wanted to his Lore. All for information that was required to help him, because he already knew she'd do anything to make sure he and her friends were safe.

And now, she would do anything to hatch the eggs that she was so certain would bring about a new age.

His mind flickered back to the elven prophecy they'd seen not so long ago. The age of man was coming to an end, and even the elves had feared this new stage of the kingdom. Why? He would never know. There were few prophets left to ask.

The witches finished with their ceremony as Lore dropped onto the ground. He flinched forward, then forced himself to remain still.

A single hooded figure still held onto Lore, and the woman's raspy voice filled him with dread. "Never trust a witch, darling."

He couldn't interrupt, now. Not when there was a chance he could find out more information because Lore had been played for a fool. She should have known better than to ever trust a witch, and he would wring her damn neck the moment she woke up for risking her life.

Abraxas looked around for a way to hide from the witches. There were few options, other than a rather large topiary that had been trimmed into the shape of a bird with its winds held wide.

Fitting, he supposed, considering he was the only one who could fly.

Abraxas shifted in the darkness, moving slowly so no one would look at him while he slithered toward the safety of the topiary. And once behind it, he peered through the greenery to watch what the witches did next.

They left Lore alone in the field, apparently not caring at all that she was unconscious. They moved as one being, almost as though the magic they had stolen brought them all even closer together. Their dark cloaks billowed around them, undulating as though there was a wind that didn't exist.

He'd get to Lore soon enough. His elf could lay there for a while, considering she couldn't move at the moment and run off to do yet another stupid thing. The argument they would have after this would be quite the spectacle, but she'd be lucky if he didn't drag her off into the wilderness and leave her there, so she couldn't get into more trouble.

The leader of the witches finally stopped. She pulled back her hood and revealed silver hair that threaded like metal through the remaining dark strands on her head. A harsh scar across her throat explained the voice. Someone had tried to kill her once. He hated to imagine what she'd done to them afterwards.

With a wave of her hand, the air before them warped. Grass gave way to stone and a small bonfire lit as though it had always crackled there.

The display of power was impressive, he had to admit. They were not meager witches living on the edge of a village while hoping for scraps. These were dark witches with more power at their fingertips than he could ever hope to see elsewhere.

Abraxas needed to be more careful. If someone snuck up behind him, there was nowhere for him to go.

"That went better than I thought it would." One of the witches removed her hood, revealing emerald green underneath the black fabric.

Amalia.

The damned woman would pay for what she had done here tonight, although Abraxas would take his time ensuring that her punishment was creative and bloody.

"Did it?" the leader of the witches asked. Her raspy voice filled the clearing like a slap that cracked across the green witch's face. "You said bringing her here wouldn't interfere with our plan. She clearly knew more than she should."

"She only asked about the warlock, and I knew that wasn't information we'd give her." Amalia held up her vial of silver power. "We got what we wanted, didn't we? I don't think there's anything wrong with lying to get more power. She'll wake up. She's alive, isn't she?"

"Alive to continue asking about a man no one should remember," the other witch hissed. "The warlock needs to remain hidden. Or have you forgotten our bargain?"

Bargain? Now that sounded like something he wanted to hear more about. Abraxas leaned closer into the greenery, hoping no one would hear him as he tried his best to gain even a few more inches on the witches. At least they wouldn't know if he was trying to overhear them, not while they were arguing.

He hoped.

Amalia hissed out a long breath. "You know I haven't forgotten our promise to that fool. We're all required to follow his laws as long as he is alive."

Alive?

Abraxas felt his blood chill in his veins. Surely they were talking about a different warlock. One who hadn't ruined Abraxas's life and so many others with his magic that had given the King so much power. There were plenty of warlocks in the kingdom. Plenty of magical people who wanted more power and didn't care who they had to hurt to get it.

He couldn't possibly... No. It wasn't him.

The warlock was dead. He'd seen him die with his own eyes long ago when the King had gotten angry with a mistake. So many arrows had sunk into that warlock's back as he fled from the castle. There was no way he'd survived the attack.

The lead witch shook her head and stepped toward the fire. "We never should have helped him. Indebted to a warlock is no way to survive. Our coven should be so much stronger than it is, but that man tricked us. Now, we're forced to siphon power off an elf! Of all things."

"And what power it is," Amalia replied. She held the vial of moon magic up to the sky, letting the rays play against each other. "Can you imagine what we'll do with her magic? So much power in our hands. All we have to do is use this in a spell, together, and our reign will return. Rightfully, the dark witches will rule Lux Brumalis again."

He cared little that the witches were turning on each other. Let the magical practitioners fight against each other for who got to run the city. No one cared other than them.

What he cared about was the sudden realization that he'd been wrong, and the warlock who'd caused all this trouble was very much alive. The man could be wandering around this very city for all he knew. They had helped him fake his death, and he'd like more information on how that was possible, and how they'd hidden him all these years.

That warlock had so much death on his hands. He'd forced the remaining dragon eggs into a compromising position and thus caused the death of two other dragons. Four eggs now down to two.

Abraxas would have the man's head on a pike. He would track this warlock down to the very ends of the earth and then he would devour the man's heart while he watched. There were many ways to torture a man before he died, and he intended to use all of them.

The witches stirred, and one of them who had yet to remove her hood whispered, "I don't believe we're alone."

Damn it, had he made a noise? It wouldn't be the first time Abraxas had blown his cover due to anger, but he didn't want to take on an entire coven of witches while Lore lay sprawled out behind them. He might accidentally hurt her. Or a stray spell might land on his prone beloved.

If he had to fight, he would. Now he just had to figure out how to do that.

The witches all turned toward the topiary and the maze that was to his right. "A stranger?" one asked.

"Someone who thought they could get through our wards?"

He had. And if they wanted him to believe those wards were infallible, they had to look them over again. It hadn't even hurt for him to walk right through them. The spells were only there to hide the meadow they'd built with magic, not to prevent anyone from walking into the clearing.

The darkness of a shield poured from above his head. Unlike Lore's cool magic, that felt like a welcome power, this magic was dark. It slithered from the witch who cast it, covering him from the gaze of the witches beyond as they walked over to seek him out. They wouldn't be able to see through the shield, but that left him wondering who had thought to save him. It clearly wasn't Lore.

He glanced over his shoulder and realized the witch behind him was the same one who had led Lore into the clearing…

She pressed a finger to her lips, warning him to be quiet with a slight shake of her head. Then pointed at the witches who approached them both.

The women spent at least five minutes searching for them, although not as long as he'd assumed they would. They all gave up rather quickly, shrugging off the noise as some animal that had gotten into their meadow and then wandering off with giggles. Each one of them was so excited about the magic in their hands, they didn't even look back. Even the eldest witch walked through her shielding spell as though she wasn't concerned about who remained behind.

Finally, the witch who'd protected him let the shield drop. He felt the black magic leech the heat away from his skin as it disappeared.

He arched his brow. "Why?"

She shrugged. "They didn't invite me to the party."

"I'd imagine it was for more than that. What do you want, witch?"

"To see them upset when their new toy disappears." The woman crossed her arms over her chest, and a rueful grin spread across her face. "They think I'm too young and too uneducated to take part in gaining such power from an elf. I can't fight them on that. There are too many. But I can do this. Watching them scream in anger when they realize you've taken the elf back will be more than enough payment."

Who was he to look a gift horse in the mouth?

The witch might have motives other than this, but he'd believe her. If she wanted them to get out of the clearing without the other witches knowing, then that was as close as he'd get to an ally in this place.

"Good enough," he grumbled before walking past the still burning fire toward his elf, who was still passed out on the grass. "Do you know what they did to her?"

The witch shrugged. "Looks like they took all the magic she had saved up. Doing that can make some people very sleepy. She might stay like that for a few days."

"And how am I supposed to sneak past the other witches without them noticing that I'm carrying the woman they just drained?" He paused next to Lore, flexing his hands open and closed. He wanted to hit someone for doing this to her.

The dark witch rolled her eyes as though he were an idiot. "You aren't going to take her now. Dark witches perform all their magic at night, you dolt. If you walk out of here with her in your arms, they will definitely see you."

Don't hit the witch that's helping you, he reminded himself. "Then how would you propose getting out of here? I do believe that's what I just said."

"Leave during the daylight, of course. Dark witches hate the sun." She gestured to her ghostly white skin. "You'll be able to walk out with no one seeing you, that I promise."

He tilted his head to the side, still not trusting her. "I don't think I should thank you for all this information."

"I wouldn't. It means you owe me something." That grin turned into something dark and terrible. "Owing a witch anything is a bad idea."

"I'd agree." Still, he nodded at her. "We'll wait until morning, then."

The witch disappeared through the same shield that the others had gone through, and it felt like he could breathe again. The air rushed back into the clearing. Like the witches had sucked out any ability to feel comfortable until they were no longer around him.

Damned witches. They needed to leave Lux Brumalis before one of them got hurt.

Glancing down at Lore, so dangerously asleep at his feet, he supposed one of them had already gotten hurt. And he hadn't been able to stop it. Or at least, she wouldn't have wanted him to.

"Ah, Lore," he muttered as he sank down at her side. Abraxas leaned back on his hands and watched her with a careful eye.

Her lashes fanned out over her cheeks, and though he usually couldn't see the fine golden strands, in the moonlight he could see how long and thick they were. The shadow they left behind made her look tired, and he wondered if they'd been pushing each other a little too hard.

They didn't have to run themselves into the ground trying to hatch these eggs. Not while so many other factions in the kingdom were split in every other direction.

Abraxas traced his finger down her cheek, keeping his touch delicate so he didn't wake her from her rest. "Sleep well," he whispered. "You've earned the rest."

While she slept, he'd keep watch over her. As he always did.

And always would.

CHAPTER 13

Sunlight filtered through her closed eyelids. She could feel the heat dancing over her cheekbones while the sound of birds waking slowly brought her back to the land of the living. She hadn't thought she'd fallen asleep, nor did she remember returning to her bed.

Where was she?

Blinking her eyes open, she stared up at the clouds as they passed overhead. They were pretty; she mused. They had no right to be so lovely on a day like this. When she was struggling to figure out how to get what she wanted, while also being afraid of losing everything.

A witch didn't fear taking from another person. They devoured everything they could get their hands on. Otherwise, the world was likely to devour them. She supposed she couldn't blame them for stealing from her and giving her nothing in return.

After all, she had been the one incapable of staying awake when all she'd suffered from was a little exhaustion.

A shadow blotted out the bright rays of the sun as a figure leaned over her. She knew that silhouette anywhere. The long dark locks that fell in front of his face obscured his expression, but she already knew it was one of disappointment. He did that, her dragon. He found ways to be disappointed in her, even when she was trying to help him.

Reaching up between them, Lore pressed her palm to his cheek. "How did you find me?"

"You weren't all that hard to track," Abraxas replied. "Did you think this was a good idea?"

"Well, the witches were our only lead. And though I knew they might try to take advantage of me, I had hoped they were honorable enough to hold up their end of the bargain." Obviously, she'd been wrong. Lore hated admitting when she was wrong.

Though, it might be a little easier while in this meadow. She turned her head to the side and glanced around them.

This place had been terrifying in the darkness. She'd swear that there were beings waiting for her to make a single mistake, knowing that she was likely to fail at her task. They wanted to devour her flesh and drink her blood out of her skull.

But now, in the light of day, the meadow had taken on a new appearance. The green grass was so brightly colored it made her think of emeralds dripping from a woman's neck. There were few trees, but in the distance, she could see bright red apples hanging off their branches even though it wasn't the time of year for such fruit. The birds in those branches sang so prettily, it almost made tears prick her eyes.

This place wasn't one made by dark witches. They wouldn't come here during the day, so who shared this space?

"You're thinking the same thing I was," Abraxas murmured. "I'm not sure who or what originally created this haven in the middle of a city."

"But I think we both have an idea who might have done it."

Lore sat up even though that was the very last thing she wanted to do. Her bones creaked as she forced herself upright, groaning with discomfort. Her neck had cricked from laying in the same position for hours. And damn it, losing all that power made her muscles feel like liquid.

The witches hadn't been kind to her, that was for certain.

Abraxas watched her with an expression that said he had little pity for how she was feeling. "I suppose the warlock may have created this, but he wasn't known for acts of beauty."

"Neither am I." She braced her forearms on her knees and stared him down. "And yet, sometimes, I can put on a fancy dress and convince a king that I am worthy of standing by the side of a noble. We all wear many faces, dragon. Don't dismiss a man's abilities simply because he's never done something before."

She wished she knew what was running through her dragon's head. One moment, his expression was thoughtful, the next rather angry. And she didn't know why. Of all the emotions she'd expected, anger wasn't one of them.

Sighing, Lore rolled onto her hands and knees, then stood. "What are you angry at me for now? I already explained why I'm here without you or anyone else."

"It's the 'anyone else' statement that bothers me." Abraxas stood all too quickly, wiping his hands on his pants. Dirt smeared over the material. "You seem to think that people can change, is that it? Or maybe there's a good many people out there who are useful for their certain qualities, while others are lacking?"

What was he going on about now? She hadn't the faintest idea what he was trying to say. "The warlock might not have been known for pretty magic, but here he was, clearly a different person than he was before he started working for the King's family."

"That's not what you said. You said we all wear many faces." He tossed his hands up in the air. "I have to wonder if you see certain qualities in others that I don't have. Qualities that are more useful in certain situations, like this moment."

She took a deep, steadying breath. Yelling back at him would get them nowhere. Clearly, this was an argument about something she didn't know about, and she didn't have the upper hand here. If he wanted to yell at her, then he could do that for hours and she still wouldn't know why.

"Abraxas," she ground through her teeth. "Would you care to tell me what all this is about?"

His cheeks were even red with anger. She'd never seen him like this before, and Lore had seen him in many situations where he should be visibly angry.

Never like this. Whatever bothered him had festered.

His gaze flicked away from her, as though he couldn't stand to even look at her eyes while he said what he had to say. "There are others in our company who could give you what you're seeking. Others who could afford you the connections and the acceptance that I can never do. You know as well as I, loving a dragon is not a simple choice. That face you might wear in my presence will eventually become nothing more than a mask."

She tried to paw through his words in her head. She had said people wear many faces, yes, but she hadn't been speaking of herself. Was he angry at her because she'd threatened her own life by coming here?

"I don't want to risk my life, you know," she said, still very confused. "I don't know what you're trying to say, Abraxas. You know I don't want to rush into certain death at every opportunity. These witches were our first and what seems like the only chance to find the warlock."

"That's not what I'm talking about."

She tossed her hands in the air, losing her grip on the very thin thread of her patience. "If you could tell me plainly what you're talking about, that might be helpful. Because right now, I cannot imagine what conversation we're having other than the fact that I risked my neck."

"The conversation is that I'm standing here, in front of you, and I don't think I have any right to do so." He met her gaze then, and she realized he wasn't angry at all. He was sad. "Draven made it very clear what he could offer you, and I think he might be right. After all, if you were walking with another elf, you wouldn't have to sneak around like this. The witches would have allowed you both into this clearing. You would have had a protector long before they even tried to steal your magic. None of this would have happened."

What in all the realms was he saying?

Draven? She didn't care about Draven. The young elf had gotten underneath her dragon's skin, clearly, but that didn't mean the elf was right. There were plenty of fish in the sea for him, and plenty of young elven women who would love to entertain him in the cities once they made their way south.

And what was this ridiculous nonsense about Draven having

anything to offer her? Lore didn't care about the acceptance of elves. She never had. Those ranks of magical creatures had shunned her for years. Why would she pay their opinions any mind after this long?

"Abraxas," she started, not sure how to answer that rant. "I don't care about other elves. I renounced my people a long time ago. They have no use for half breeds like me."

"And what if he could offer you another path?" Abraxas pointed at the shield that hid them from prying eyes. "You haven't even considered a life on the other side of rejection, have you? Who am I to keep you from that acceptance when you might not even realize that you want it?"

"Where is all of this coming from?"

He ran his fingers through his hair, pulling at the long strands in frustration. "I don't know. I don't know. I sat here next to you, not knowing if you would ever wake up after they stole so much power from you, and all I could think was that what he had said to me might be right."

She needed to have a little chat with Draven about boundaries and how he needed to keep her name out of his mouth. That elf had been doing more damage than she had guessed.

Lore licked her lips and struggled to figure out the right words to say here. She didn't want Abraxas to assume she'd changed her mind, or that she was only saying this to placate him. Her reality was the only one that mattered to her, and the reality was that she loved him. More than anyone else. And that would not change no matter what other future was offered to her.

Making the man standing before her believe that was the truth, however, was the most difficult thing she'd ever done.

"I don't want anyone other than you," she said, hoping her words sounded truthful. "I've never cared about anyone the way I care about you. This world had always been one full of cruelty and hardship until I realized that you wanted to offer me something different."

"A life with me by your side will be no more easy than what you previously lived," he interrupted.

"What do you think I want after all this is over with?" She wanted to throw something at him. Did he assume she would hatch these eggs, win a war, and then what?

"Take the throne like Margaret wants you to." He stared at her like she'd grown a third head. "You see how everyone follows you, Lore. You've seen the posters and the way people whisper your name in the streets. You've become a legend to them. The woman who killed the King, tamed a dragon, and now you're going to have two more at your beck and call. You are soon to be a goddess, Lady of Starlight. Or have you not seen the writings on the wall?"

A flash in her mind's eye projected the mural on the floor of a lost city. A mural of a blonde elf standing before a city and a kingdom on its knees.

No.

That wasn't what she wanted at all.

She didn't want a kingdom or a throne or a crown. She wanted a quiet life with a dragon at her side and scaled beasts rolling in the sands at her feet. No one else. Just them and a quiet future growing plants in a garden and seeking out lost objects that needed homes.

"So you're under the impression that after all this is said and done, if we're even alive, that I will want to become a Queen? That I will take the throne and rule over all of Umbra?" Lore knew her face had twisted into some horrible expression of disgust.

Abraxas's expression twisted into something similar, although he clearly wasn't sharing the same line of thought. "I don't think you're going to have a choice in the matter, Lore. After we bring about the dragons, and we defeat Zander, do you really think they'll let you fade into the background?"

"You don't know that we'll do any of that."

"I do know." He swallowed hard. "I know that we'll complete our tasks and that this world is changing into something entirely different from what it was years ago. I know without a single doubt in my mind that we will succeed. Once we complete this. Once we move into the next stage of what Umbra is becoming, you will be at the forefront. Whether you want to be or not."

The words sent an icy chill down her spine. He spoke like he was uttering the words of a prophecy, even though she knew it wasn't the same one that he'd seen. That she'd seen. There was more here at play that neither of them knew.

"I don't want that life," she whispered. "And you have to know that I would choose you over all of that, Abraxas. No matter how difficult our path seems to have become right now, I will never choose a throne over you."

He met her gaze, and she saw that he didn't believe her. It was like another man stared back at her. "We all walk in the footsteps of heroes, Lore. And you are strong enough to stand with the greatest of them all."

"I am strong. But I'm exhausted." Not just from what the witches had done to her, but from all this. She took a step closer to him, holding out her hand for him to take. "I want a quiet life with you. I don't want to be anyone other than your Lady of Starlight. Their temptations hold no power in the face of your love."

The sadness never went away, even after she said all that.

Abraxas took a step away from her and tucked his hands behind his back. "The dark witches slumber during the day. It is safe for you to leave this place as long as the sun is in the sky. I'll meet you back at the house, Lore."

"I'm not going back to that woman's house." She shook her head. "We need to figure out where the warlock is, and I'm not leaving until the witches give me that information. But you can't go anywhere, dragon, we have words to say between us."

"I'll let the others know we are not staying in that house any longer, then." He turned away from her, only to toss over his shoulder, "Where are you going, so I can find you?"

She didn't know how to fix this. How to stop him from walking away from her.

"The forest," she replied. "Like always. There's one on the opposite side of Lux Brumalis. I've heard the trees are ancient."

"Be safe," he quietly replied before leaving her alone in the meadow. Again.

CHAPTER 14

Abraxas stomped through the streets of Lux Brumalis. He knew he looked as if he were going to burn the entire city to the ground, and he was feeling as though he might. How that woman always wriggled underneath his carefully laid control and unraveled all of his senses. He'd never understand.

He didn't know why he'd brought that entire conversation up. He didn't know why he felt so threatened by a young elf who was no competition in the eyes of the woman he loved.

The argument wouldn't change her opinion about Draven, that much he knew. If anything, it would only change her opinion about him. He'd known that the moment he brought it up.

But he'd been staring at her, completely unaware of anything around her while she lay on the ground, and he wondered if part of this was his fault. He could have burned all the witches to the ground with a single breath, and none of them would ever touch her again. All the things he could have done, or perhaps should have done, ran through his mind until he couldn't breathe.

And then she'd woken up, and all his rational sense bled out through his ears.

He hadn't been kind to her, and that was his fault. He should have listened or done anything other than berate her for not being interested in an elf that could give her a better life than he could. All because his own pride was smarting.

Abraxas stood before the green witch's house and realized he hadn't even told Lore what he'd overheard the witches saying. They knew where the warlock lived. They'd kept that information secret, and thought no one would punish them for it.

As he stared up at the emerald tinted windows of the house, footsteps approached from the opposite side of the building. Amalia rounded the corner, looking down at something in her hand which he could only imagine was the vial of Lore's magic. The grin on her face suggested it was that.

Here was his chance, he supposed. He could kill her now and take back the bit of magic she'd stolen. Or he could use this opportunity to his advantage.

He leaned against the fence surrounding the green witch's property and crossed his arms over his chest.

It took her a while to notice that he was in front of the house. Amalia's gaze flicked up to the gate that would lead to her front door, then realized rather quickly that said gate was blocked by a very large form. One she should fear.

"Oh," she stammered. "Abraxas. You're out of bed early, aren't you?"

"Am I?" Of all people, she should have guessed he might wake before the others. "I never went to bed, I'm afraid. I find wandering the city at night gives me far more information about Lux Brumalis than it did during the day."

All the color drained out of her face. She had to know. In that moment, she must have seen the truth in his eyes. Abraxas savored the moment. He wanted the witch to simmer in her fear so that when he put her out of her misery, she would know what it felt like to be in a dragon's trap.

Amalia's gaze flicked toward her front door. Was there something hidden inside that would help her? Would she capture his friends within those walls so that he never saw them again?

She wouldn't get the chance.

The witch lunged toward her gate at the same time he moved. Abraxas snapped out his hand like a snake, reaching so quickly she didn't stand a chance. She thought she could outrun him, but he only let her move the barest amount before he grabbed onto her wrist.

Shifting to the right, he yanked her hard. Reeling the witch back into his arms took little effort. She stilled, knowing when she was trapped. Witches were always waiting for the moment when they would become the fly in a bigger spider's web.

Abraxas locked his arms around her shoulders, forcing her to remain in place and listen to what he had to say.

"I saw everything," he snarled into her ear. "I know what you did to her, and I know that you are aware of where that ridiculous idiot lives. You're going to tell me everything."

"They'll hurt me worse than you." The witch didn't even tremble in his arms. If anything, she seemed to sag against his chest with relief. "They would pull out my nails one by one for even standing beside you, let alone telling you everything."

Did she believe a death at the hands of witches was worse than in the mouth of a dragon?

No one had any sense of self preservation these days. These foolish witches thought there were more terrifying things in this world than him, and that was because he'd been gone for too long. They hadn't seen a dragon in centuries, and they had forgotten the true terror lurked above them.

He tightened his grip, banding his arms over her shoulders until he felt her bones creak. "I know what witches do to their betrayers. Their torture is nothing like dragon fire. I know the truth has become legend, but let me remind you. Dragon flame can burn a person to ash in mere seconds if we wish, and destroy the soul as well. Or I can devour you slowly. Crunching your bones in a long, agonizing death that you'll experience for what feels like hours."

Flames burst to life in his palms. The fire sprites were hungry, but he wouldn't let them feast. Not yet. She needed to be afraid of them first. Then he would let them perhaps light the very ends of her hair on fire.

"You don't scare me, dragon." Though her words were brave, she shook in his arms. "My soul is already damned."

"These are the real things to fear. I can call upon fire sprites, and they are the ones who will burn you slowly. I'll tell them first to take your hair. All of it. Every part of your body will be scorched by their heat. Then I will tell them to take your flesh. I will tell them to take it in pieces, so you'll never know when they are going to scar more of your body. Piece by piece, until you finally succumb to death. For years on end, if I wish."

Perhaps he exaggerated a little. He wanted her to be afraid, however. He wanted her to know how horrible an end this would be for her if she didn't listen to him.

Witches couldn't do that. They would kill and maim very quickly, perhaps very painfully, but nothing compared to having parts of a person stolen for months until they couldn't live any longer.

"I will not give you the power that I stole," she hissed. "It is mine by right and I will keep it."

"I don't want what little moon magic you ripped out of her form, you idiot." Really, did he have to spell everything out for this witch? "Tell me where to search for the warlock. Your kind seemed to know where he is, or at least was, and that is enough reason to let you live."

"What do you want with that old fool?" Amalia seemed to be stalling, although he couldn't guess why. "His magic has been waning for years. He can do nothing for you."

"You don't even know what I want from him." Abraxas tightened his grip one more time. "I think you should be far more concerned about your own wellbeing."

She twisted in his grip, struggling now that she knew what he wanted from her. "I don't fear death. I never have."

"You should fear death from me." He jerked her hard in his arms, forcing her to pay attention to him once again. "I will not tell you again, witch. Give me the information, and I will let you survive."

She seemed to weigh her options. Knowing a witch, she'd want something in return.

Even as she opened her mouth, he could see the intent in her eyes.

"No," he snarled. "There will be no bargain. Your life is the only thing I will give you in return for this information."

"And if I don't know the information you seek?"

"Then I will rejoice in knowing you have spent months dying. I will visit you, in the end, so you can look upon the face of the man who killed you. There won't be much left by then. Just a mass of burned flesh and sunken eyes. But you will know me, even in your weakened state. And you will know that your arrogance was the reason for your death."

Though she still didn't seem as frightened as he wished for her to be, Amalia sighed. "The Hall of Heroes was the last place I heard he'd retreated to. That was years ago, mind you."

"He should be ancient by now, or dead." How had the warlock lived so long? Magicians and witches were mortals, no matter how much they attempted to prove otherwise.

"He is deathless," she hissed. "Wasting away but trading power for life. Considering his abilities, his life will be much longer than expected."

Abraxas had never heard of such a spell, but that would pose some issues. If the warlock had been giving up his stolen power to live longer, he may very well have little power left.

They'd cross that bridge when they came to it. "I'm a man of my word. Your life in exchange for the information. Now, you will release my friends as well."

"I will do no such thing. I will use their skulls to drink my wine!"

He let out a long, low hum. "That was the wrong answer."

Since the moment they'd harmed his beloved, he'd wanted to wring the neck of a witch. Now he had the opportunity.

With a quick twist of his hands, Abraxas snapped her neck. It took so very little. He forgot how fragile the humans were, and while he'd been careful to twist but not maim, he nearly took her head off with that movement.

She sagged in his arms, limp this time. Poor dead thing, she'd never stood a chance. At least he'd killed her quickly, however, when she could have suffered.

He twisted so no prying eyes would see what he'd done. He didn't need any neighbors seeing what he'd done. Not while he had plans to make, Lore to gather, and the rest of his companions to free from that cursed house.

With a quick movement, he gathered her up into his arms as though she'd fainted. She weighed so little. Abraxas almost felt sorry for what he'd had to do, and then another side of him felt sorry that he hadn't made her suffer. It was a troublesome sort of dichotomy which frustrated him to no end.

Then he strode up to the front door of the green witch's house and kicked it. It wasn't like he could knock. He didn't have a free arm. Hopefully, that would mean one of his companions would open the door and not someone he was unaware of who worked for the dead woman in his arms.

Thankfully, Draven opened the door.

The dark elf's jaw dropped open in shock and his eyes widened along with the exaggerated gesture. "Did you kill our host?" he asked.

"I did."

"Why?"

"Long story. Witches, covens, and dark magic were involved." He shouldered his way through the door and unceremoniously dumped the witch's body next to the coat rack. "She stole moon magic from Lore and left her in a magical field alone. And then they all joked about how they had fooled the elf while refusing to give her any information about the warlock. I took care of it."

Draven's eyes flicked from the body back to Abraxas. "I think this is the first time I've ever actually respected you."

"To that, I will only say that it's taken you long enough." He wouldn't spew out the angry words he wanted to say. Death made the young elf respect him? Killing someone was easy. It took very little effort and most of the time, it was done in anger. Keeping someone alive, or forgiving them, that was much harder.

Sighing, he scrubbed a hand over the back of his neck. Exhaustion suddenly struck him over the head like a mallet. "Where are Goliath and the others?"

Draven hooked a thumb behind him. "Parlor. They were talking about coming to get you two."

"Good. I'll go tell them what happened, then."

The elf hesitated, his eyes never leaving the body on the ground. "Do you want me to take care of this mess? Just in case someone comes looking."

"You know how to do that?"

"I do." A dark flash of some horrid emotion accompanied the words. Abraxas knew better than to ask questions.

He'd seen that look in other people's eyes before. That was always the beginning of a darkness Draven would battle for the rest of his life. He could pretend that it wasn't a second side of him. The other side of his coin that whispered terrible things in his ears tonight. But that battle would be hard pressed to win in a time like this. War called out to the souls who preferred bloodshed and violence. War lived on in those souls as well.

"Do with her what you will," he muttered. "I have no use for a witch."

Guilt twisted in his stomach again, a lasting knife from the woman whose spirit likely laughed in his ear. She would want him to feel bad for what he'd done, because she would feel no guilt at all for it. Witches killed. People died. Spirits lived on, or their magic returned to the earth where it belonged.

He could only hope she couldn't curse him from beyond.

The emerald parlor hadn't suddenly turned into something else with the death of the witch. He hoped that meant all her objects were actually bought and not willed into existence. His companions all sat in the bright green chairs, the three of them leaning forward as they tried their best to hide their plotting. The whispers filled the air. Perhaps so quiet it might have been difficult for magic to pick up on it.

Abraxas leaned his shoulder against the door frame and crossed his ankles. "We need to leave."

Goliath was the first to flinch. The dwarf put his hand at his waist, searching for a weapon he'd probably hidden, then relaxed when he looked to the door. "Abraxas! We thought the two of you were done for."

"Almost were. Lore made a foolish decision, and I made an even worse one to see what the witches would do." He gestured behind him. "Get your things."

They all stood, though Zeph hesitated. "Should we at least say goodbye to our host?"

He didn't think that would be necessary. "Can't. I want the rest of you out of the city before nightfall. I'll get Lore where she is and meet you all at the northern gate."

Beauty swallowed hard, her eyes a little too wide. She shifted by him while dragging Zeph behind her by the wrist.

The dwarf, however, paused in front of Abraxas with shadows in his eyes. "Why can't we say goodbye to the witch?"

"She's dead." No reason to sugarcoat the truth, he supposed.

"Why?"

"She hurt Lore." That red hot anger burned in his chest again, squeezing his throat like a hand wrapped around it. He wanted to fly back to that meadow and burn it all to the ground. He wanted those people to feel pain, more than just the one witch he'd killed.

"Hm," Goliath hummed under his breath. "How badly?"

"She stole magic. They all did. So much that Lore passed out, and I had to leave her there, alone, while I tried to at least glean some information from them. Unfortunately, even while I listened to them from the shadows, they let nothing slip." He twisted his neck to the side, cracking the tension there and then, only being reminded about the sound the witch's neck had made. "I got the information out of this witch, and then she swore she would take matters into her own hands. I did what I had to do."

Goliath reached up and patted his arm. "You did what you wanted to do, dragon. I sometimes forget how different you are from all of us. You don't find death to be quite so sad."

Of course he found death to be sad. He mourned the loss of the other dragons. He'd spent a century trying to find where the others were, and then dedicated the rest of his long lived life to protecting the remaining eggs.

Abraxas loathed death. He hated losing someone to a great beyond where he could not follow them, and he would never take death lightly. That wasn't... he wouldn't...

He watched the dwarf walk away from him and had the distinct impression that his life had shifted. Did he take death for granted? Abraxas had killed hundreds of people, if not thousands, at this point. He killed whomever he was pointed at, like a weapon that had no choice.

But now, he thought, maybe he did. Or at the very least, maybe he could have mourned those lives rather than simply take them and forget.

"Dwarf," he called out.

Goliath paused in the hallway that led back to their rooms. "Yes?"

"If I mourned all the lives I took, that sadness would weigh more than the world itself. I cannot shoulder such a burden." It was a poor excuse, and he knew it.

"Even a flicker of regret is better than being devoid of emotion." The dwarf attempted a smile, but the worry marring his expression wouldn't let such happiness through. "I'm not judging you, Abraxas. I fear for your soul."

And with that, Goliath turned away from him and went to gather his things with the others.

Abraxas wasn't quite sure how to take what he'd said. A dragon never feared for their soul. They killed when they had to, who they had to, and such a thing did not burden them. These mortals and short-lived creatures couldn't understand the guilt he'd carry for all those deaths.

They saw the world through a much smaller lens, he surmised. Though, sometimes, he wished he were more like them.

If only to value life more than he did.

CHAPTER 15

She hadn't been this angry in a very long time. That idiot dragon thought he could stomp off, lecture her, get angry, and that she wouldn't care? Lore had enough of his fiery antics and all his blustering.

He could go back to wherever his kingdom was, she decided. Or better yet, return to his hoard and leave her alone. She'd given him enough of her time and if he wanted to act like a child, then she would find someone else who didn't.

Of course, the thought of living without him made her stomach twist. She wanted to be with him. That was the worst part. Even this angry, she still wanted to make sure he wasn't running off and that she wouldn't see him again for weeks. The dragon was... part of her. At least, that's what her heart wanted her to think.

No, it wasn't that he was part of her. He had earned a spot in her soul and she loved the fool. He would always have a place with her.

This damn city twisted them into something they weren't. She couldn't think while Lux Brumalis sank its magical claws into her shoulders and puppeteered her thoughts.

She needed to get out of this false meadow and into the real moonlight. To a place where she wasn't gasping for clean air.

If she remembered the maps correctly, there was a forest to the north of Lux Brumalis. It might make her companions upset, but Lore needed time to think on her own. She had no idea what they would do about their witch problem within the house, so she supposed it would be all right for her to disappear for another day.

Abraxas would tell them all what happened. They knew she was safe enough. At least she wasn't in the clutches of a witch any longer.

The streets were surprisingly empty this early in the morning. As the sun changed from pink to bright yellow, a few people woke up, however. Those were the workers. They stood outside their shops, making sure everything was just right for customers.

Lore nodded at the few people who noticed her walking among them. Their eyebrows lifted in surprise, as though they recognized her, and maybe they did. She supposed that was all right, though. Let them know that the Savior of Tehebrous walked among them. She'd already given all she could to their esteemed dark witches.

The northern gate stood open, ready for whomever might dare to enter the city. Lore hesitated only briefly before ducking out of the golden doors and out into the wilds beyond. A small path led toward what wasn't really a forest, but more of an overgrown grove of trees.

Some magic called out to her. Or perhaps it wasn't magic at all, but the wilds that whispered a secret haven for an elf like her. An elf who had been missing from the northern reaches for so long.

The bright white birch trunks stood out from the yellow leaves that rained down over her head with every whisper of the wind. The ground was covered in golds and oranges, like the treasure trove of a dragon long forgotten.

Leaves crunched under her feet and Lore slowed the quick pace that had led her to this place. The tension in her shoulders eased as she finally took a deep breath, clear of magic and the cloying scent of power.

Wind toyed with the strands of her blonde hair, longer now that she'd been so far from Tenebrous for so long. The leather bindings of her corset stuck to her skin. Some sweat still lingered after that horrible magical experience. Lore reached for the clasps without thought and slid the leather straps free.

She carried the corset with her and whispered, "I could use a bath."

The forest seemed to shift in front of her. Of course it did. The magic from Lux Brumalis had leaked out from those esteemed walls and this place had become something more than just trees. It was alive in a way no other forest was.

Tree trunks bent out of her way and then she saw it. An emerald pool fed by a waterfall that lazily poured into the crystal clear depths. The rocks at the bottom were covered with emerald algae and tiny water lilies floated on top with bright pink blooms.

"Yes," she sighed. "This is exactly what I needed."

The trees seemed to bend toward her just slightly and then left her alone to her thoughts. Lore took her time stripping out of her clothing. She folded each article and left them in the sun to warm for when she left the water's embrace. But it would take a while for her to do so.

Lifting one delicately arched foot, she stepped into the pool and let the water glide over her skin. It was chilly, but not cold enough to take her breath away. A single plunge brought her underneath the water's surface. Her hair tangled around her face, then floated above her as she opened her eyes.

Silence. Deep, heavy silence made her think that she had forgotten how loud the world could be. Everything was so much above the surface, and here, she could finally have a moment of peace.

Eventually, her lungs screamed for air. Lore slicked her hair back as she kicked her feet up to the surface.

The pool had looked deeper than it was. She could stand in the center, though the water came up to her collarbone. Lifting her hands, she smoothed her palms over her head and turned her gaze to the golden leaves dancing overhead.

An echo of sound skated over the water. Not quite the crunch of leaves, but movement ever the same.

She turned toward the sound and froze. Abraxas stood at the stones where she'd left her clothing, his eyes wide as he looked upon her form.

Lore had the hesitant thought that she should turn away from him. Perhaps that she should hide herself. But then she realized she didn't want to. She was angry at him, yes, she wanted to hit him for what he'd said. But perhaps she wanted to claw her way down his back instead.

It had been too long.

For both of them.

When she didn't move, frozen as she was like a deer caught out in the wild, his expression changed. His gaze heated and his eyes changed to that deep, molten gold that she loved so much.

He said nothing. Only the sound of the wind filled the small clearing as he reached between his shoulder blades and slowly pulled his shirt over his head.

All the breath in her lungs whooshed out. She hadn't seen him like this since Tenebrous, and her mind had dulled the beauty of his body. Trim muscles rippled down his stomach. An arched "v" over his hips disappeared beneath the low slung waistband of his pants. All that bronzed skin, only marred by the faint mottling of scars from hundreds of years of battle.

His hands dipped to the buttons of his pants and she knew she should tear her gaze away. But it only felt fair that if he could see all of her, and the water was so clear that he certainly could, then she should see all of him.

The linen pants slid off him and she was surprised by his tree trunk thighs once again. She'd seen him in that skirt that parted over his legs, but this? Watching him in all his glory move like a panther through the forest... It was almost too much.

Abraxas strode through the water with all the power of a dragon, his attention never wavering from her.

She didn't move. Not even when he reached for her, water splashing around his thickly muscled arms as his hand scooped underneath her hair. He dragged her forward and sealed their lips together in a kiss that tore through her soul.

His other hand slid up her back, smoothing heat from his palm as the chilled water splashed against her skin. He rained kisses down her jaw, then nipped at her. The sudden spark of pain traveled down her spine.

"Fool woman," he snarled against her neck. "It took me a while to find you. You were supposed to return to the house."

She didn't care. "Shut up and kiss me again."

With a sudden wrenching of his arms, he tugged her flush against him. She could feel every inch of him, from the burning heat of his chest, to the heavy weight of his thigh pressed between her legs.

He kissed her, holding her so tightly she couldn't breathe. And then the kiss changed. He stopped trying to devour her. Stopped kissing her with a bruising force. It all eased into something not quite tentative, but lingering. As though he were savoring every moment so he would never forget the taste of her lips.

She drew back and the bitter taste of ash coated her tongue. "I won't apologize for doing what I had to do."

"I know." His lips were redder than before. Darker from the weight of their desire. "And I won't apologize for scolding you."

"Then I suppose we will have to accept that, together, we will argue." She was all right with that. But she had no way of knowing if he was.

Abraxas didn't let her have a moment of doubt. He tightened his arm around her waist and molded her body against his. She sighed as he gently traced his fingers over her forehead, down her nose, to her lips, where he lingered.

"You are beautiful," he whispered, drawing his fingers down her neck to her shoulder. "From the moment I first saw you, I hoped that I would touch you like this."

She tilted her head and watched his hand dip beneath the water. His fingers flirted against the side of her breast, not quite where she wanted him, but so close. Then his hand moved lower, smoothing down her waist to her bottom, then he grabbed onto the curves there. A gasp escaped her lips at the sudden roughness. He pulled her leg up to his own waist, holding her there as he strode out of the water with her in his grip.

The forest bent again, moving to accommodate his will as he walked them right underneath the waterfall and into a darkened cave beyond. The light of the sun filtered through the pouring water, and the spearing rays looked almost like the moon.

He settled her back against a bed of thick moss, never once appearing like her weight bothered him.

She arched her back as he settled between her thighs. Abraxas ground against her, and that sound she didn't recognize escaped her lips again. She'd never made that whimpering noise before.

Featherlight kisses rained down on her neck, over her collarbone, and then his hot breath fanned over the peak of her breast. "Have you nothing to say, elf?"

No. She couldn't think. Not when he closed his lips over her and drew upon her flesh with such force that she saw stars. Her hands flexed in the air, searching for something to grab onto. Her palms landed on the broad expanse of his back and thanked the ancient elves there was so much of him to hold on to.

He chuckled, and the sound echoed through her skin. "I don't think I've ever seen you speechless."

"If you can talk this much, there are better things for you to do with your mouth," she hissed.

He drew back so she could see his lifted brow, as if she'd surprised him. But then the heat entered his gaze again. His hand smoothed up her leg, drawing her knee up with the movement. Silver light danced over the veins of his hand and turned the depressions of her skin underneath his fingers into shadowy pools. "Yes ma'am."

Normally, now was the time she'd closed her eyes. She would tilt her head back and focus on sensations rather than looking at her partner. But she didn't want to miss a single movement of seeing herself reflected in those golden eyes.

He held her gaze as he shifted down her body. The muscles in his back flexed, lithe and so very strong. He lifted a hand and blew out a breath of fire, then sent the small sprite fluttering into the air. The new orange light made the entire cave flicker.

"I want to see you," he growled as he bent to work between her legs.

His eyes never moved from hers. Not when he draped her bent knee over his shoulder. Not when his tongue gently touched her folds. Nor when he found the small bead of nerves that made her lose all sense.

Lore's head slammed back against the moss. She lost control of her body. He gathered her up like an instrument only he knew how to play, and he certainly knew what he was doing.

He didn't just toy with her like so many men did. Nor was he concerned about tact or control. He wrapped an arm around her hips, tilted her to his liking, and then Abraxas feasted.

How was she supposed to remember to even breathe? His tongue was a masterpiece and all too quickly she felt that tense coil in her belly tighten and wrap around itself. Soon, but not quite. She couldn't quite...

A broad thumb pressed against her opening, swirling in a languid circle that mimicked the movement of his tongue. Around and around until suddenly, he sank his finger inside her and that was enough for the stars to align.

She gasped out his name, long and drawn out as her thighs tightened around his head.

He never stopped moving, following her up that peak with his tongue and then gently easing her down from that impossible height. Just as he had when they had flown through the clouds together.

Shaking, Lore touched her fingers to her lips, needing something to ground her even as her legs turned into liquid and her racing heart slowed to a deep relaxation.

She should move. She should take control and make sure he felt she was doing more than just lying here, but moving right now felt a little impossible. He'd somehow taken her mind in his capable hands and then crushed it into dust.

Abraxas grabbed her hip with his hand and lifted. "Roll over, love."

What? She would do what she was told because a man like this should surely not be questioned in bed. But the moment she rolled over and tried to push herself up, he instead pressed his body against hers. Abraxas traced the sides of her body with his hands, drawing her hands up over her head and then linking their fingers together.

"Breathe," he gruffly whispered in her ear. "I'll take care of you, little elf."

Oh, she was in so much trouble. Or perhaps so much pleasure awaited her that she would unravel at the seams.

The broad head of his manhood pressed against her seam and suddenly she realized why he'd said to breathe. She could see nothing, control nothing, and he was ever so large.

With a flex of his hips, Abraxas sank into the wet heat of her body. Too big, yet so right, the sudden stretching of her very core made stars spark in her vision again. The easy glide of his movement was too slow. He took his time, waiting long heartbeats to ease inch by agonizing inch until he finally settled at the base. Deep within her.

A low groan echoed in her ear. And he, too, seemed at a loss for words.

"Abraxas," she whispered. The sound of his name was enough.

One of his hands transferred her wrist to his other hand. He held both of hers in a punishing grip as his other hand reached down to palm her hip. With a sharp thrust, he drew back and slammed into her as though he could wait no longer.

He had valiantly fought to remain a man. He'd touched her with gentle fingers and an easy lash of tongue. Now, the dragon had come out and there was nothing she could do but endure the onslaught of power and pulsing need.

Her breathing turned ragged, and he bucked his hips even harder. His grip around her wrists started to hurt, but she was shocked to realize she liked even that. He had laid her body before him like a banquet. The dragon took what he wanted. And she would give him everything.

That tense, pulsing coil within her grew again. This time stronger than the first, and she knew this could unmake her. She wanted... she needed...

The fluttering ache deep in her body could only be satisfied by the long glide of his. She tried to catch her breath, but couldn't.

Her orgasm hit her hard and so suddenly it was almost shocking. The power of it made her entire body tense around him, and the guttural groan he made sent her over the edge. She held her breath even as she felt him throb inside her.

There it was. The moment she'd been waiting for, where they both hung over a precipice of need and desire, then flung themselves over the edge.

Abraxas slumped over her, careful not to let his weight crush her until he caught his breath. Then he rolled them onto their sides, wedging a thick thigh between hers. He smoothed her sweaty hair away from her face and let out a soft chuckle. "I've been wanting to do that for ages."

"Good," she said, still struggling to catch her own breath and uncertain she had the where-with-all to speak like a normal person. "Because as soon as we catch our breath, we're doing that again."

"Oh really?"

"Yes, really." She looked over her shoulder and licked her lips. "I've been waiting for you, I realized. Centuries of waiting. And I fear I won't ever be satisfied now that I have you."

He traced the outline of her lips. "Then I will endeavor to satisfy you, Lady of Starlight, Savior of Tenebrous, and Tamer of Dragons. Even if that is an impossible feat."

CHAPTER 16

Three glorious days with the woman he adored. That was the exact number required for him to find a little peace and happiness in this world.

The others were likely worried about them. He knew he'd told them to wait at the northern gate and that both he and Lore would return. But their companions had to be used to them disappearing by now. They waited. Lore and he adventured. Such was the life they led.

The explanation made him feel only a little less guilty for leaving them after the rather dramatic murder of a witch as they fled from Lux Brumalis. But these three days were worth whatever lashing he would return to.

He now knew the taste of her from memory. The feeling of her soft skin never left his palms, even when he flexed his fingers. Abraxas had spent centuries wondering what the perfect woman would look like for him, and he'd never guessed that the woman would be in the form of an elf who tore him down to flesh and bone with her gaze.

Still, it made him feel young again. All of it. Her scorching looks, her sharp tongue, even the moments when they fought. All of it made his heart beat harder in his chest and his breath wheeze from his lungs.

He watched Lore as she moved in front of him, standing at the very edge of the golden birch leaves. She looked over her shoulder and he saw his own thoughts reflected in her eyes.

They both knew this was the end of their bubble of safety. Once they stepped out of these birches, the real world would come back to them. Responsibilities. War. Finding a warlock who had single-handedly destroyed a kingdom. All of it would return and their small moments together would fade into the background once again.

"We'll keep moving forward," he said, quietly. "You and I haven't changed and we won't once we join the others."

"Are you so sure?" She'd braided her hair back from her face on either side of her head. The twisting coils looked almost like the scales of a dragon. "We had to run away to even get to this point."

"But now we're here." He gathered her up into his arms, tugging her back against his chest. Leaning down, he murmured in her ear, "We won't let it change. And if I feel you drifting away again, then I will whisk you off to the next hidden pool. I love you, Lorelei of Silverfell. We will make this work."

"In whatever way we have to," she replied, resting her arms on top of his. "I suppose we have to go tell them we're still alive."

"That would be for the best."

He thought she would straighten, pull out of his arms, and stride out of the forest as though nothing had happened. Instead, she linked their fingers together and dragged him from the trees with her.

Was this what acceptance felt like? She didn't care at all if someone looked at them, or if anyone had opinions about an elf and a dragon standing together. Lore never cared about those things, though. She stared into life's snarling face without hesitation or fear.

Sometimes, he wished he knew how to be like her.

Their four companions had set up camp just in front of the northern gate. Goliath, true to his normal tactic while he had to wait, had set up a fire. Food already roasted above it, rabbit again if Abraxas correctly guessed from the scent. Zeph and Beauty stood off to the side, whispering together with the box of dragon eggs at their feet. They were likely planning to go find Abraxas and Lore on their own, which would only infuriate the other two members. Draven leaned against the wall surrounding Lux Brumalis, arms crossed over his chest as he watched the others with eyes that saw far too much.

The dark elf was the first one to see them approaching. Though the two of them had struck up a strange sort of friendship, unlikely considering the circumstances, Abraxas still had a flare of pride and justice as Draven's eyes looked at their joined hands.

Anyone who saw them together would know something had changed. They might not guess immediately what that change was, but Draven had.

The disgust that crossed over his expression was enough to satisfy the jealousy that had burned deep in Abraxas's stomach for weeks. Ever since he'd seen the young elf, really.

Oh, that was a sweet taste on his tongue to know the dark elf had seen his prize lost.

Abraxas tugged Lore a little closer to him, tucking her underneath his arm. There was a time when she would have pushed away from him, or even insisted she could walk on her own. But now? She snuggled deep into the heat of his body and tentatively wrapped her arm around his waist.

Goliath glanced up at their approach and dropped the stick in his hand that he'd used to poke the rabbit. "Let the sun rise! Would you look at the two of you? Finally, if I do say so myself. I've been waiting for this for months."

Months?

Abraxas rolled his eyes at the dramatics and glanced down to see a bright bloom of pink spreading across Lore's cheeks.

He was rather stunned to see the color and how much it affected him. She was so pretty embarrassed like this. Prettier than he'd imagined. His stomach flipped over and his heart thundered in his chest again.

The feeling was entirely new to him. He didn't want to kiss her or press her up against a tree again. They'd already explored those options. Instead, this feeling was a nervousness that coiled around his heart and up into his throat. His hand flexed against her side, pulling her a little closer. The world disappeared around them. It was just him and her and this strange new consuming feeling.

Though Goliath seemed rather pleased with this recent addition to their relationship, Beauty looked disgusted.

He'd thought better of her than that. Was she siding with Draven after spending such a short amount of time with the dark elf?

Abraxas directed a glare over in her direction and asked, "What are you making that face for?"

"It's like finding your parents in the bedroom together," she muttered, then stuck her tongue out. "It's not something I ever wanted to imagine."

Her parents?

He glanced down to find Lore already looking up at him with her own disgruntled expression.

"Are we that old?" he muttered. "I don't think we're that old."

"She thinks of us like her parents," Lore growled. "And here I thought that we were all the same age."

"Translated to mortal years, the two of us. We're hardly old."

And he refused to believe anything other than that. If they translated their ages into that of a mortal timeline, then neither he nor Lore were any older than Beauty. The mortal was entirely wrong, and he was insulted that she would ever say anything differently.

Before he could argue with her that they weren't like her parents at all, and how dare she even think that, a booming echo rocked out of Lux Brumalis. The ground shook with the force of the angry magic.

He and all his companions turned toward the sound. The sound had echoed up the road that ran through the gates and down into the city. From deep within the very bowels of the buildings a dark mass erupted that at first looked like smoke, but then he realized it was fabric. Gauzy and thin, it coiled through the air like the veil of a dancer.

The dark mass tangled through the clouds before unfurling above the city. The smoke gray coloring then descended onto the house of a green witch who had once been alive. As he watched, all the fabric laid out over the house, the windows, even the grounds like a funeral shroud over Amalia's home.

"What is that?" Lore whispered.

"I killed the witch for betraying you," he muttered. "I'd guess they just found out she's dead."

It had taken longer than he'd expected. Witches were always checking in on one another. And he wouldn't be surprised if the only reason they'd found her body was because another witch had arrived to steal the magic from Lore's attack.

The concerning bit was the theatrics.

The witches would never make him believe they cared about each other. He knew they were cutthroat and there were no friends in a coven. So why were they covering the home of a lower witch who had no right for such a show?

A great wind gusted out of the city, traveling up through the road and blasting his hair away from his face. He tucked Lore tighter to his side and squinted his eyes to see through it. Along the wind came the scent of dark magic, though he didn't know why they'd cast the spell. The witches couldn't find him or his companions outside the city limits.

Could they?

The blast of power and anger rocked throughout the entire city one more time, almost like a child expressing frustration, and then the northern gates slammed shut with surprising force.

Silence fell after that. Then, as he watched, the golden gates turned red as blood.

"Well," Lore said, breaking through the sudden quiet. "That was rather dramatic."

Draven pushed himself away from the wall, where he'd stood just fine while the magic thundered through the city. The elf had a death wish if he wasn't at least a little afraid of what that power might do to him while he was standing about like that. "Apparently, that's what happens when you find a body of someone you liked."

With a slight tilt of his head, Abraxas surveyed the arrogant walk of the elf. "Ah, that's right. You said you would take care of the body."

"I did."

"And how did they find their fallen brethren?" Abraxas already knew they must have found Amalia in a state that angered them. Otherwise, they would have raided her house and been done with it.

Draven looked at his nails. "You said she hurt Lore. Or at the very least, she was the reason that Lore was harmed. I took care of it in the way of the elves."

He had no idea what that meant. Considering how likely the elves were to hide things, he assumed that meant the body remained in the shadows. Difficult to find. But then he looked down at Lore and saw her expression change to horror.

"You strung her up for them to find?" she asked, her voice trembling.

"As a traitor should be found." Draven nodded at her as though he'd done her a favor.

And maybe in the eyes of the elves he had. This woman had made a point to not only put Lore in danger, but manipulated them to take unnecessary risks.

Stringing up a body like that for someone to find? That was too far. Abraxas could imagine what the witches had found. The body must have hung awkwardly, considering the angle of her neck. And three days after her actual death, that body must not have been in the best condition.

The two elves glared at each other until he thought one of them would catch fire. And that was his job.

Finally, Abraxas angled his body between the two, focusing on Lore. "We have no intent to return to Lux Brumalis."

"And if we find that we need to return? What if we need a witch on our side? What if the warlock is actually dead and there is nowhere else for us to go?" Those ocean eyes met his, and he saw how terrified she was. "I am not a fool to assume this journey will remain easy."

He had no answers for that. If they had to return to this place, then they were in trouble. The witches were unlikely to forget any of them, and they wouldn't allow a dragon back on the premises once they used magic to see what he'd done.

"We'll be long gone before they get too much information out of her body," he finally replied.

"We don't even know where we're going."

"Actually, we do." Abraxas gave her a quick wink before he turned them toward their companions. "Before the witch died, she said the last known place where the warlock resided was the Hall of Heroes."

The two mortals in their company seemed confused. Perhaps they hadn't heard of the strange building where the magical creature's history was kept. Perhaps because most of the people who guarded that history were young men given up by their families to become monks.

Goliath scratched his beard and let out a low hum. "I've heard of the place before, but I'll admit, I don't know why the warlock would live with a bunch of monks. He didn't seem like a religious man, at least in the history books."

"He wasn't," Abraxas replied. "He loathed all those who walked the path of righteousness, and that is all the more confusing. If he's still there, and that's a large 'if', then we can end all of this once and for all."

He asked too much of them. They'd already dragged this entire crew from the very bottom of Umbra to the highest peak, and now they were here. They'd found nothing, yet again, and he was asking them to travel based on rumor alone.

It was too much.

He'd asked too much for far too long. They'd be insane to go with him on this journey.

Except Beauty rolled her eyes and shrugged her shoulders. "All right, fine. I suppose we have little choice if we want to see some baby dragons in our lifetime."

"There's more reason for it than that," Abraxas started, only to be interrupted by Zephyr.

"Sure, there might be more reasons than that, but we're all here for the baby dragons. Can you imagine what they'll look like?" He drew his hands together, locking his thumb and gracefully waving his fingers like a dragon in flight. "Soaring through the air like they do? What a sight."

"They don't actually fly when they're that young. It takes a while for them too—"

Lore squeezed his hand in hers, silencing him. "Don't ruin it for them. If they want to think of many dragons flying through the clouds alongside you, then let them dream."

It was his dream, too. He wanted to tell them all that he feared his heart would stop the first time he flew with another dragon beside him. It had been too many centuries since that last happened.

Looking around at their smiling, teasing faces, he was reminded that this journey was more than them saving the eggs. They traveled together, like some dysfunctional family.

A family he'd trade for nothing else.

"All right then," he said. "To the Hall of Heroes we go."

CHAPTER 17

They spent the next three days traveling north, further and further up to the Hall of Heroes. Lore had heard little about the place. She only knew that many magical creatures considered it holy.

Why either of these kings hadn't destroyed the building, she would never understand. Perhaps there were a few holy spots left in the world where no one would touch. No matter how much they wished to.

As they crested the last hill that would bring them to the Hall of Heroes, she adjusted the straps of her pack and let her questions fly. "If this place holds the history of all magical creatures, why wouldn't Zander burn it to the ground? Or his father, for that matter? The man seemed to enjoy harming all of our psyches rather than bodies."

Goliath reached the peak before everyone else, surprisingly. As the sunlight silhouetted his form, he turned toward her. "There's a spell on the Hall of Heroes that even Zander couldn't break free of. No one will harm the Hall, not even the mortals. And it's an ancient spell. No one has ever been successful in trying to break it, because no one can cast a spell to harm it either."

"A binding sort of protection," she muttered.

"The best kind." He spread his arms wide and gestured below them, as though he himself had built the structure below.

The Hall of Heroes was not quite a hall. The giant building spread out like a cathedral with spires that jutted up toward the clouds with circular stained glass windows that glimmered in the sunlight. It certainly looked like a holy place. Lore had seen many people seek out a building such as this so their whispered prayers might reach the ears of the gods.

The grounds were kept immaculately clean. Tiny meandering paths moved throughout what looked like gardens on one side, and the other side of the Hall was filled with a long, sprawling lawn.

"It looks a bit like someone's home and also like a church," she mused. "What a strange combination for a building like this."

"That's because it is a home," Goliath replied. "Many monks live here. All of them have pledged their lives to ensure the history of magical creatures is kept in pristine condition."

"Pristine condition?" she asked as the dwarf made his way past her.

Obviously, he wasn't interested in answering any more questions. He bounded down the hill toward the building with no fear at all that someone would attack them or that they might be in danger. He had no sense of self preservation.

But, as she watched him frolic through the fields, she thought maybe he was just happy. And happiness like that deserved to be felt.

Abraxas paused beside her and watched their other companions move down the hill. "What I don't understand is why a warlock would hide within the ranks of monks?"

"Are they really all that different?"

"Quite." He heaved a sigh, then held out his hand. "Monks appreciate, value, even worship, life. The history of those who lived is sacred to them. Warlocks don't value life. They only care about power and what others can give them."

"I suppose." But something in her chest whispered that people could change.

Perhaps the warlock they were looking for had changed into a different man. The past was filled with men and women who had become strange heroes, and this was the place for a man like him to transform into someone worthy of history.

She laced her fingers through Abraxas's and followed the others down onto the large lawn of the Hall of Heroes. Sunlight played across her shoulders and a bead of sweat trailed down her spine. She hoped that was from the heat, and not because she feared what would happen next.

No one came out to greet them. That was the first strange thing about the place. Were there no guards? Surely, the monks knew that anyone could walk up to the front door regardless of their intent.

Monks weren't fighters. This place would be so easy to attack.

The moment the thought crossed her mind, her feet stuck to the ground. She tried to pull them up, but it felt as though someone was holding her in place. She couldn't lift them, no matter how hard she tensed her thighs and pulled. The magic of this place immobilized them.

Lore sighed and looked toward the building. "I get it. You made your point. Please release my feet. You know I have no interest in attacking this place."

She could almost feel the magic grunt with unhappiness. It didn't like that the thought had even crossed her mind, and the trust was broken from that point on. However, none of her companions had stuck to the ground, so it would let her go with the others. For now.

Duly warned, Lore schooled her thoughts from that point on. No need to insult the magical building or the spell that gave it life.

They wandered across the grounds, all their eyes zipping from side to side. Lore had the distinct feeling that there was too much to see here. The gardens were impressive and already had a wealth of fruits and vegetables to pluck. It wasn't the right time of year for many of them, and yet, here they were. Ready as if magic gave the monks food year round. And then there was the building itself. No figures moved in the stained glass windows, but Lore's hair stood on end like someone watched them.

She meandered around the building until she reached what appeared to be a front door. The small wooden doorway appeared out of place in such a grand building, and yet, what else could it be?

She approached the worn wood, ready to open it and slip into the rooms beyond, only for it to open just as her hand touched the knob. She stumbled back down the steps and the young man who'd opened the door continued forward as if he didn't notice her.

He did, though, once he almost walked into her.

"Oh!" The young man's eyes opened wide with surprise. His head was entirely shaved, though it was covered by the hood of his pale yellow habit. A rope belt held the robe tight to his too thin waist, and as she looked down at his feet, Lore noticed he had on what appeared to be rather comfortable woolen slippers.

They stared at each other for a long moment. Lore wasn't sure what to say to a man who had dedicated himself to the preservation of the past. A monk's vow usually came with more than that, however, and what if he had taken a vow to not speak with women? She'd heard mortals did that. There were even a few churches in Tenebrous where the monks would actively look through her as though she didn't exist.

This young man was looking at her, though. He met her gaze with startling surety, then looked behind her at the rest of her companions. "Well," he started. "There sure are a lot of you."

What kind of statement was that?

Her tongue was well and truly tied, it seemed. Lore glanced over her shoulder, hoping that one of the other people in her group might be able to help her.

Of course, Beauty rushed forward and wrapped an arm around Lore's waist. "We're seeking shelter for the night, and also we've heard the Hall of Heroes is a sight to behold."

The monk blinked a few times. "You've come a long way north for shelter. And why are there so many of you?"

Again, the same question. Beauty's cheeks turned bright pink with a blush. "Maybe we were more here to see the Hall itself, I suppose, but we do need shelter. There aren't many places for a large group like us to stay in."

The monk pointed back to the way they'd just traveled. "There are inns in Lux Brumalis."

Well, he'd talked her into a corner, now hadn't he? This was why Lore didn't do conversations like this. What were they supposed to do now?

Clearly, the monk had no intention of allowing them to stay here. At least not overnight. And that would be a problem if they were planning to sneak around and find the warlock who had evaded them for years now.

Lore coughed and wiggled out from under Beauty's arm. "We're looking for information. Information that doesn't exist anywhere else, and I think you might have it."

That caught the monk's attention far more than needed helping. She hated the gleam in his eyes, but at least he was looking at her with more interest.

"Information?" he asked. "What are you looking for? The Hall of Heroes only keeps historical records. Of your kind, I presume you know."

Ah, there was the pointed stare directed toward her ears. Of course, he had to know that she was a magical creature. He had to see that she belonged here, whereas he did not, considering he was in a holy place for her people. Not his.

"There is a prophecy about a half elf that I'm interested in learning more about," she found herself saying. "I'm here for the truth, and I know this is the only place where I will find that."

His eyes flared bright with a light that wasn't mortal at all. Almost as though the building itself, or the power that gave the building life, was looking back at her. "Now that is a reason to enter the Hall of Heroes. And a reason to stay within its walls."

It wasn't that easy, though. She could feel Abraxas's glare burning a hole in her back. She wasn't supposed to mention anything about that prophecy, but honestly, the desire to know the truth had been inside her for a long time. Everywhere she went, there seemed to be a prophecy that followed her around. One he didn't want her to know.

She deserved to have that information, whether it ended in her doom or not. If it were about her, and she had to assume it was, then she'd rather know. If she'd already fulfilled that prophecy, then she could put this burning need to rest.

Any half elf would do what she'd done. Anyone with a good heart and a conscience would have tried to stop the King.

Or anyone who had nothing to lose. Like Lore.

The monk reached into the folds of his habit, muttering something that sounded like, "Lost them again, did I?"

Then he pulled out a handful of keys, loose rather than on a ring as they should have been. The sound he made echoed through the corridor, and even Lore flinched at the shout.

"Still have them!" the monk crowed. "I always put them somewhere they shouldn't be."

Lore's stomach sank. "Do you know which one opens the door?"

"Not in the slightest." His cheerful reply wasn't helpful.

She watched him put the first key into the lock, try to turn it, and then start muttering to himself. What kind of monk was this? Taking a few steps back toward her companions, she crossed her arms over her chest and let her head tilt to the side. She surveyed the monk with a critical gaze, but she still couldn't understand what was happening in front of her.

Did he really keep all the keys in his pocket loose, and then expect to find the one that opened the door?

"Who did you say lived here again?" she asked Abraxas. "The people who dedicated their lives to working here. You said families would send them?"

"As tribute," Abraxas replied.

"Or because they wanted to get rid of the young men," Lore mused. Considering the state of the man before them, she had to assume she was correct.

This monk couldn't survive on his own. He was here because no one else wanted to take care of him any longer, and the Hall of Heroes would take anyone who wanted to pledge to becoming a monk. It was a shame, really. If he'd been left to his own devices, he'd be dead by now.

"There we go!" the monk exclaimed, then shoved the door open. "If you'll follow me, I'll show you around so you don't get lost."

What? All that talk about how they couldn't stay here and now he was going to give them a tour? Lore looked over her shoulder at Abraxas, who shrugged. Maybe he'd been expecting this. Or at the very least, assumed it might happen.

Or maybe he was more used to strange people acting oddly than she was.

Lore took the lead and went first. No one else needed to walk into a trap, considering this was all her idea to come here. Or at least, it was something she'd gone along with. But surprisingly, nothing happened to her. There weren't even other monks waiting for them. They walked into the front entrance of the Hall of Heroes with no one but the monk ahead of them.

The front entrance was beautiful. The pale marble floor shone as though no booted feet ever crossed it. Three stories above them rose to the peaks of the main cathedral, and the beauty of it made tears prick her eyes. All that stained glass cast beautiful colors all around them as they walked. There was nothing in this section of the building, and how shocking it was to walk through what felt like a holy place with no pews or places to sit.

This room felt as though she should worship something or someone.

Lore's heart beat in her chest, as though it knew the correct god to worship. Or perhaps the question to ask.

"Welcome to the Hall of Heroes!" the monk exclaimed, his voice echoing up into the rafters. "This is a place of great knowledge, as I'm sure you already know. There are many people here who have dedicated their lives to preserving the history books that are found within these walls. Our jobs are of great importance to the remembrance of the kingdom's history."

She had a feeling there were plenty of people who disagreed with him on that matter. Lore hurried to catch up to him, knowing her companions were keeping a quick pace behind her. "And where are these books you speak of?"

"Everywhere," the monk replied. He turned around and pointed toward doors on every wall. "Each door will lead you to countless books about every magical creature alive or dead that you need to know about. We've sectioned them off by each hall that is focused on each species, but there might be books that cross reference subspecies, of course. That's where it gets tricky."

She struggled to follow his logic. Let alone guess where he was leading them.

"Now." The monk tapped his lips as though thinking deeply. "You first said you were looking for shelter for the night. And while the pursuit of wisdom is honorable, I'm certain you would rather find yourself a comfortable bed so that your mind is rested before you find yourself deep in the bowels of information, is that right?"

A headache bloomed between Lore's eyes. "Indeed."

"Good! There are rooms here for sleeping. Rooms for learning. Rooms for a great many things, I suppose. But visitors stay in the back quarters away from the monks. It's best not to interrupt us while we're working on our endeavors, you see."

The monk led them to the very back of the great hall, and past one of the side doors that had been left open. Lore glanced into the revealed area for a brief moment. The hairs on her arms rose in disgust at the dark magic beyond.

No practitioner of magic created a feeling like that. Only magical objects which shouldn't exist.

She felt the same oil slick magic of the grimdags in that room, only different. Twisted.

More intelligent.

The shadows shifted beyond. Oozing with a thickness that she'd never seen before. Lore wasn't so certain she wanted to find out what lurked in those shadows, or what had cursed the books down that hall.

The monk grabbed onto her arm and tugged her away from the sight. "Best not to look too closely at grimoires. One never knows what they might say."

Perhaps it was best that she rest before turning her attention to the books in this place, she mused. It sounded as though they would all need their wits about them.

CHAPTER 18

Abraxas knew this place was more than the monks were letting on. He could smell the dark magic from a mile away, and if this building was only supposed to contain history books, then why did it smell like that?

The monk who guided them also didn't act like a monk. At least, not the ones he'd expected.

While the young man wanted them to think him an idiot, and quite a few of the others did, this monk was smarter than he looked. The man's eyes flicked to the sides as they wandered and doors would close quietly at his glance. Doors that led down halls which Abraxas thought didn't contain as many books as they did magical items.

He'd always wondered why the kings had never come to this

place. History like this was ripe for destruction in their eyes. It would wreck the entire magical community to know flames consumed so many precious items.

Perhaps they'd all been lied to. The books here didn't contain just history, but spells and powers kept away from the people who could use them most.

Thus, the warlock had come here.

He joined the others as they settled in the small room the monk had given them. It was bare bones, as he'd expected from a holy place like this. But Abraxas paid attention to the little details which shouldn't have existed in a place like this.

The bed frames were made of much finer wood than most holy buildings would have. Sure, the monks could explain that away as a donation to their esteemed members who had given up their lives. But the sheets weren't even wool. They were made of finer stuff. Perhaps a cotton that had been spun so carefully it resembled silk.

The bare walls had once been painted with tiny blue flowers that crawled up the ceiling. Time had aged the delicate strokes and paled the flowers until they were almost gone. Narrowing his gaze, he stepped up close to the paintings and eyed them.

Draven paused beside him. "Something wrong?"

"I'm not sure." He didn't know, and that puzzled him. Abraxas should be able to tell if something was off. He'd always been able to smell magic a mile away. But this place? It was hard to tell what was real and what wasn't.

"Before we all get too settled, might I have a word?" The dark elf said it so quietly the others must not have heard him.

Abraxas waited for Lore to look at him before he lifted a brow and flicked his gaze toward Draven. She understood that they were going to step out of the room, and diverted the other three's attention to herself.

"Goliath," she said, her voice perhaps a little too loud. "There aren't nearly enough beds in here, so who are you bunking with?"

The dwarf argued without hesitation. And the theatrics of the dwarf's loud words gave Abraxas and Draven the opportunity to slip back out into the hall.

Abraxas had no interest in talking with the young man now that he'd won Lore in their secret battle. Obviously, he'd never tell Lore he felt like that. She wasn't a prize to be won, and allowing those thoughts to come to life would only insult her. But damn it, he had bested this young, handsome elf. He had a right to be a little prideful.

So when Draven grabbed his arm and tugged him closer to the opposite wall, Abraxas had a flare of anger that burned so hot in his chest he was certain the heat could be seen through his throat. Why did the elf seem to think he had any right to touch a dragon? Let alone a dragon who very much did not like him?

"Did you notice anything odd about this place?" Draven asked, as though he didn't notice the anger in Abraxas's eyes. "The monks are trying to hide something. I just haven't the faintest idea what that might be."

"Magic," he snarled. "Some of those rooms had more than books. Even the monk admitted there were grimoires here."

"But a grimoire doesn't sing like a grimdag." Draven's hand ghosted over the hidden sheath he kept the dagger in. "At least, not any of the grimoires I've seen in my life."

"You haven't been outside of the Gloaming before, boy. There are a great many magical objects that are as deadly as that little pig sticker you have."

Though the boy had a point. More than the elves had heard the singing voices. Abraxas had heard them as well, which meant the grimoires weren't elven made. He didn't know other creatures who were especially adept at creating magical objects. Even the dwarves weren't skilled in magic and forgery. It was either one or the other. The elves simply had many years to perfect both skills, and then learn how to intertwine them.

He winced as a thought passed through his mind. "If the warlock is here, then the man had to come with the intent to learn something. The grimoires likely contain spells, and the spell in this place requires that no one enter with malicious thoughts."

Draven nodded. "It's the perfect place to hide in plain sight. I had the same thought."

"Do you believe the monks here are practicing spells?"

"I think they're doing more than that." Draven pointed back to the room they'd been brought to. "My mother kept many alchemical books in her possession from before the wars. I've read a few of them, and there are written accounts of warlocks and witches using magic they carved into the walls of their rooms. I'm not saying those flowers are watching us, but I do think there is magic in this place that is always listening."

And that would make everything all the more tricky. If the very building could listen in on their conversations, then finding the warlock they were looking for could be near impossible. At least, if he wanted to hide.

Abraxas ground his teeth until he heard the bones of his jaw creaking. "Fine. I'll stand watch tonight to make sure no one tries anything. Tomorrow night will be your turn."

"And here I was thinking we'd finally have a good night's sleep once we got here." Draven ran his hands down his chest and then nodded firmly. "We'll take turns."

The boy surprised him. Abraxas was certain the elf would at least try to take a jab at him for the change in Lore and his relationship. Clearly they were closer than they'd ever been, and Draven was comfortable simply... backing off?

Suspicious, Abraxas decided the only way to get clarity was to ask. "Why are you still talking to me when you didn't get what you wanted?"

Draven flashed him a grin. "Women are fickle creatures, dragon. She wants you now, and I will admit, that was disappointing. But you'll make a mistake someday and I will be the person who picks up the pieces. Mark my words. "

As the dark elf walked back to the room, Abraxas had the distinct thought that he should have left well enough alone. That elf knew how to get into the heads of others, and now Abraxas wouldn't be able to sleep at night for fear that he'd say something stupid and Lore would go running into another man's arms.

Again. He had the same damn fear. Again.

Scrubbing a hand down his face, he resolved to keep these thoughts in the back of his mind. Otherwise, he wouldn't be able to watch over the others tonight.

Protecting his companions was what he'd been born to do. This was natural for him as he leaned against the door and crossed his ankles over each other. No one would interrupt his thoughts. Not tonight. No one would enter this room, for that matter, without attempting to go through a dragon, and he assumed everyone knew how foolish an idea that would be.

The hours ticked by as he stood outside their room, guarding all the people he held dear in his heart. And as he waited, Abraxas listed out all the reasons why Lore claimed to love him.

Every single moment solidified that he had nothing to fear. He'd done enough stupid things in their relationship and since they knew each other. And she was still here. She still loved him.

The elf would not convince him otherwise. The only thing that would send Lore running in another direction was if he let that damned elf get under his skin.

As light filtered into the hallway through the parse windows, the door behind him opened. Lore stepped outside and pushed her hair away from her face. "Why were you out here all night?"

He pressed a finger to his lips and pointed to the walls.

Lore's eyes widened, and he had a feeling she hadn't even thought that they would be listened to. She touched a hand to her ear, and he nodded in response. Of course they were listening. There were always people listening.

Dust motes floated around her head as she stepped into the hall with him and closed the door behind her. "There are many people here," she said, obviously choosing each word carefully. "The information we seek might be difficult to find."

"You shouldn't have asked for that information." He could scold her even with people listening to him. He hadn't wanted her to know about the prophecy for good reason. She would only find darkness and fear waiting for her.

"It's information I need to know." She crossed her arms over her chest and he knew the argument would only get worse from here. "I know you want to hide it from me, but the truth has to be here. If this is the place where they are hiding much information about many people, then the truth lies within one of these books."

Words hide between the others. She'd both told him that she would read the prophecy while also searching for the warlock.

"Some things are hiding in plain sight," he replied, although the words didn't seem quite right for the situation. He added, "Perhaps we should all split up. I wasn't impressed with the young man who showed us to our room, and there may be other monks here who could direct us toward what we seek."

That ought to tell her his thoughts. He wanted to explore on his own, out of sight from so many people who were watching their every move. If he had only a few moments alone, he might catch the scent of the warlock.

For good measure, Abraxas touched a finger to his nose.

Lore licked her lips, eyeing him before she replied, "It's dangerous to be alone. Even among books."

"It is." But he'd been in worse situations and still lived. He could return to his dragon form if he had to, and tear this building down from the top to the bottom.

"And it's been a long time since you've been in... danger."

Ah, that's what she meant. He hadn't seen the warlock in years. How would he even know what the man smelled like?

He'd shared the same concern when he'd first thought up this plan in the middle of the night. He had spent years working with the warlock, a little too close for comfort, but that had been a mortal lifetime ago. The warlock had disappeared and taken all of his things with him. Abraxas hadn't smelled the man in a very long time.

But he'd never forgotten the scent of black magic. The warlock had been unique in his power. All the magic he'd called upon had been stolen from magical creatures. Partly ones that the first king had captured and then fed to the warlock to keep him powerful. And then all that magic had been required to keep a dragon under their thumb.

Abraxas wasn't as amiable back then. He'd first been willing to give up the eggs for his own freedom, and the warlock had been called upon to convince a dangerous creature that being alone was worse than death.

"Dragons have a long memory," he finally replied. "With danger comes decay and malice. Those are hard to forget."

He hoped she understood that he meant the warlock smelled of those things and no one else he'd ever scented had. So much power corrupted a mortal's soul. And such a life could only turn a man into a monster.

Abraxas had hunted monsters his entire life. He'd seen dragons hunt them when he was a child and now he would follow in their footsteps, tracking down the man who thought he could control an entire species.

With a quick nod, Lore darted into his arms. She wrapped herself around his torso and he felt all the tension in his body leak out of him. Her touch eased the torment in his soul, and he wished he had the words to tell her that.

Instead, he curved his much larger body around hers and pressed his lips against the top of her head.

"Be careful," she whispered against his collarbone. "I don't like thinking about you being in danger without me by your side."

"I think if you look at our history, I'm the one saving you more often than the other way around." He kissed her head one more time before pulling back to look down into her eyes. "I do believe I should be the one worried about you."

Lore shook her head, brows furrowed in anger. "I'm not accustomed to worrying about someone else, Abraxas. I don't like this feeling at all, so I refuse to let go of you until you agree that you will not make any foolish decisions without me there to help you."

"I'm sure you would help me make the foolish decisions." He couldn't help but chuckle at the thought. She was far more likely to go rushing headlong into ridiculous circumstances. Not him.

But she knew how he felt about the warlock and all the rage that built in his chest from years of waiting to get his hands wrapped around that horrible creature's throat.

So he gave her a quick nod and made her a promise. "I won't do anything that you wouldn't do, Lore."

She rolled her eyes and stepped out of his arms. "That's not reassuring, Abraxas."

CHAPTER 19

They all split up and searched through the Hall of Heroes for days. Lore had thought it might be difficult for them to search for what they wanted, but the monks paid them no mind. And there were a lot more men in here than she'd thought.

Of course, there were no female monks. Only quite a few old men and some middle-aged men wandered through the halls with their arms full of books and their eyes on the floor.

Lore soon realized it was almost impossible to get them to speak with her. None of them even made eye contact with her, let alone talk.

They all had agreed to keep the monks' attention split between all of them. Goliath made up some story about having to search the kitchens, because he'd always heard that the Hall of Heroes had the best cooks. Beauty and Zeph made sure they both were available for talking and to ease the minds of anyone worried about so many magical creatures being in the building. Draven sort of disappeared, but she assumed that kept the monks busy seeking out the elusive elf. And of course, Abraxas was just too large to miss.

He charged through the hallways with obvious glee, enjoying making all the monks flinch as soon as they saw him walking toward them. He garnered far too much pleasure out of their fear.

Lore assumed the best she could do was to convince the monks to help her. She tried to speak to every single one who passed by her, even the ones that tried to rush. A few of them even broke out into a run when she tried to ask for their name.

Today was the fourth day here, though, and she was more determined than ever. All she had to do was pin one of these monks in place and force them to talk with her. There had to be a section on elves! They were one of the most well known and prolific magical creatures, or used to be. Their history was well recorded. All she needed was one damned monk to point her in the right direction.

She'd resolved to focus on the younger ones. There were only a few in the Hall that she'd seen so far, but they were easy to spot. Their eyes always strayed to her face rather than staying pinned to the ground.

What mortal man could ever stop himself from staring at pointed ears? That's what had gotten the elves in trouble all those years ago.

Finally, she found one of the young ones out in the gardens. He bent over a treasure trove of carrots that were ready to be plucked out of the ground. The poor boy didn't stand a chance.

Lore swept her hair over her shoulders, displaying the long length of her neck. She tucked the strands behind her ears. Hopefully he'd focus on those and not how thin she was after traversing across the entire kingdom. Or that she couldn't get the smell of travel off her skin no matter how hard she tried.

Still, she sauntered over to the young man like she was the most beautiful woman he'd ever dreamt up, and that she was here only for him.

"Hello," she murmured, hoping her voice didn't sound too hoarse from long weeks of travel. "I keep trying to find someone to help me in this place, but no one wants to be my guide."

His eyes widened as he stared at the ground. The young man turned as still as stone, clearly doing his best to not even look up at her. Had they all been told not to talk to the visitors? She wouldn't be surprised. Monks weren't known for their welcoming nature, especially to women.

But these were monks who guarded the most precious history of the magical creatures. These books were only maintained in the Hall of Heroes. Nowhere else. So why would they hesitate to speak with one of her kind? Shouldn't they be excited for an opportunity to talk with a real life magical creature?

Lore had finished with this game of tiptoeing around their ideals. She sank down onto her haunches, tilted her head to the side, and forcibly leaned into his line of vision. "I think you're the perfect person to help me."

The man's throat worked in a gulp. "I'm afraid that's not possible. I need to finish my work here."

"But you are the only one in this entire building that will show me where I need to go. I just need to find a book." She grasped the greenery of a carrot in one hand and pulled it out of the earth. The perfect size, shape, and color. Magic really was wondrous. "I'll even help you finish your work on time if you agree to bring me to the right section of this place. I think you know that I could spend a hundred years in here trying to find the information I seek and not find it."

He blushed, and the redness traveled down his neck, all the way into his habit, and then disappeared.

She had him.

He wouldn't look at her with those wide eyes and that bright red face if he wasn't considering it. "If you'll help me finish this later, then I suppose I could guide you. What are you looking for?"

Good enough. The men here might want to ignore that she existed, but none of them were so rude that they would deny her help when she forced them to look at her.

She didn't ponder how weak willed that made them. She straightened and nodded at the young man as though he were doing her quite the favor. "Lead the way to the section on the elves, then."

He gulped. "What book are you looking for specifically?"

The innocent tone didn't fool her. All the monks knew what she was looking for, and that was why none of them wanted to help her. No one seemed to be interested in her finding out the truth about that prophecy. Not Abraxas. Not these people.

Didn't she have a right to know if it was about her? Lore had buried her curiosities deep along this journey, but right now, she wanted to understand it. And if the dragon needed a distraction to find out what had happened to the warlock, then wasn't she owed her own distraction?

"I think you know what I'm looking for," she said, raising her eyebrows at him as though she were disappointed. "I'm looking for the history of elven prophecies. You know my people were more apt to write things down than let a prophecy go to waste. I want to know what those prophecies were. Particularly one about a half elf."

Again, the boy's throat worked in a heavy swallow. "Now, why would you want to know about a thing like that? Dark prophecies aren't worth anyone keeping an eye on, if you ask me. They always seem to end up in tragedy."

Dark prophecies?

Lore's stomach twisted. Even she knew that the darker prophecies were the ones more likely to come true. Something about telling the future lent people to seeing the bad things more than the good. Perhaps because that's what people feared the most.

Still, she had to know.

Lore nodded toward the building. "I don't have to explain my reasoning to you, do I? I'd like to see it."

He asked no more questions. The monk's eyes flicked up toward a window above them, and then he dipped his head. Tucking his hands into his bell sleeves, he started walking toward the Hall of Heroes at a pace that was almost difficult to keep up with. He would have sprinted if he wouldn't have appeared insane, she thought.

They walked in through a back door that led into a hallway full of books. It was one she hadn't explored yet, although she wasn't surprised. There were so many.

This hall was smaller than the others. The books didn't stack all the way up into the ceiling, but perched precariously on the edges of white oak shelves. The pale wood blended into the white marble floor while beams of sunlight filtered through the windows and lit the entire room with an ethereal glow.

Only the elves would have a room like this, she decided. No one else would require such an ostentatious section of a building that was already filled with beautiful rooms and objects.

She heard the sound of fabric swishing, though she could see the monk wasn't walking anywhere. Circling him, she noticed that his hands were shaking and the front of his habit had made the sound.

"That's all," he mumbled. "That's all I'm allowed to help you with."

"Why does no one want me to get my hands on that book?" She tossed her hands up in exasperation. "If it is about me, then don't I have a right to see it?"

She could have cut through the following silence with one of her blades.

The monk finally looked at her. He picked his head up and eyed her with a sadness that had brought tears to his eyes. "The prophecy is about you?"

Oh no. Why was he looking at her like that? "Some people think it is, at least."

She watched his attention focus on something behind her. He stared so powerfully that it was almost as though he'd pointed at a singular book. She turned to look and noticed there was a hardcover which had fallen over onto its side on the third bookcase down.

"I'm not allowed to give you any direction in this room," the monk said, though his gaze claimed otherwise. "The elves have made it very clear that no monk is to touch any of these books. If we even look at one, the magic here will burn out our eyes."

Somehow, she thought that was more myth than truth. The young man knew exactly what book contained the knowledge she sought, and he had no problems pointing her toward it. Thankfully.

Lore inclined her head and let out a long breath. "Thank you for the help you could give me, then. It will not be forgotten."

"Oh, I need no space in your memory, Lady." He bowed low, and the term he'd called her held more weight than it should.

Lady.

She wasn't a lady, or a noble, or anyone at all. She was Lorelei of Tenebrous. An elfweed smoking nobody who'd been dragged into all of this because her mother had a plan once. That was all.

Though, the reverence in the way he backed out of the room said otherwise.

Lore turned her attention back to the books on the shelves and tried very hard to not let herself be convinced that her life was about to change in a big way, yet again. Her hands shook as she reached for the book with pages that were gilded in silver. They were... lovely. So pure that it looked as though someone had dipped the pages in metal, and smooth enough that she could see her own reflection in them.

Her face had paled. She looked like a ghost whose hand was about to pass through the book.

The trembling of her fingers shook the pages as she flipped the silver bound novel open. The prophet's handwriting was lovely. Looping swirls leapt over the pages like a stag jumping through the forest. Someone had spent a lot of time to ensure that these prophecies weren't only remembered, but preserved with beauty.

Lore kept the book open, scanning through the ancient elven language while trying to find the symbol she knew meant half elf. She walked through the bookshelves, carefully making sure to not bump into a shelf that might be more important than the book she held. And then she finally stood beside the closest window and turned the book toward the sun.

She'd found the right place. It took about three hours, but she did it. Lore never moved from her position next to the window the entire time as she made certain that she was looking at the correct prophecy.

And there it was. Written in plain sight for her to see.

It was her. A depiction of a blonde half elf who stood above a kingdom. Just like the one in the castle they'd stayed at. The memory felt as though it were ages ago, and not just a few months.

The prophecy continued much the same as she'd already seen. The rumor of a half elf who destroys an entire kingdom, and that they should all be wary of what change she would bring. That the world would never be the same after this creature got her claws into the very realm they loved. She'd heard it before.

Lore trailed her eyes down through the list of horrible things the half elf would do, all of which she didn't care to read. If she were going to commit horrible sins, then she would have already. Lore had very little interest in making people's lives harder than they already were. Someone else would decide the fate of the kingdom and she would fade into the background like she'd always planned to.

But then her breath caught as she saw the very last line of the prophecy. The one that made her heart stutter in her chest and the weight of the world come crashing down around her.

Footsteps approached, and she looked up just as Draven recited the words from the prophecy. "But in the end, we need not fear the half elf. For she walks this path with a companion at her side. And that companion's name is Death."

She hated it. She hated this book and what she'd found out in this room.

Lore swallowed hard. "It doesn't mean what I think it means. I walk with a dragon, and it could mean him."

"Could it?" Damn it. His expression had twisted to sadness, and she knew that meant he believed the prophecy she now clutched too hard.

"My mother used to say that the half elf would still destroy our world, and then she would die. Leaving us all nothing but ash and ruin to fix in her passing. That was why the elves hated you. They fear the half elf who stands on her own because she could be the person that prophecy talks about."

"You knew," she accused. "You knew about this and you didn't tell me."

"Why would I tell you about an ancient prophecy you yourself claimed to not care about hearing?" He took another step toward her, lifting a hand as though he wanted to touch her cheek. He paused, hand midair, as she moved out of his reach. "You have to know that I wouldn't want to hurt you like this. Nothing I do is to cause you harm."

"This is something I should have known. You should have told me that the elves thought I would bring about the end of the world and then die." She slapped the book down onto the nearest bookshelf and ignored how the whole thing shook. "I refuse to stand about while everyone seems to think I'm walking toward my doom. I will not die on this quest."

"You very well could." Draven at least stayed where he was while she sought space to breathe. "All of us could die. We knew that when we started this whole foolish journey. We follow you to whatever end, and all of us will lay down our lives to make sure you live yours."

That wasn't what she wanted. Lore didn't want anyone to die for her!

She gripped the edge of a bookshelf and braced herself on it. The spines of the glittering books did nothing to ease the sudden tension in her chest, the weight that pushed against her heart and threatened to stop its beat. "I could never continue living if I thought I was the reason for one of your deaths. I would rather die myself."

"Then perhaps that is what the prophecy means." Draven hesitantly followed her and rested a hand against her shoulder. "You said it yourself.

A prophecy is not a path with no end. You could change it."

She knew he lied. Draven was the perfect elf, and he believed those prophecies to be true.

Lore released her grip on the wooden shelves and turned into him. They were but a breath apart, and normally she'd have noticed how close they were. But right now, she couldn't even see straight. "Have you ever heard of a prophecy not coming true?"

He hesitated.

And that was all she needed to know.

"Not even a single one?" She prayed he would respond then, but still, nothing.

She let the silence drop between them and walked away from his sad eyes. "I will be the first to break a prophecy, then. Mark my words, Draven of the Ashen Deep. Whoever wrote in that book will roll in their graves when I reach a ripe old age and decide for myself when I walk with Death."

She left the room while knowing deep in her very heart that she lied.

CHAPTER 20

Abraxas had all but given up trying to find this warlock turned monk who had learned to hide in plain sight. The ability to find such a man would require skills even a dragon didn't have.

But he enjoyed being here, even if it was a place full of mysteries.

He'd found a spot in the far corner of the Hall of Heroes, just outside the last door that led to a cliff's edge. Sea birds wheeled overhead, screeching out their plans to hunt for the day. If he listened hard, he could hear the faint chirps of their babies in the nests. This was a place for creatures who flew to languish and grow old. He liked that.

Abraxas sat on the very edge of the cliff, hands braced behind himself as he turned his face to the sky. He'd found it was much easier to concentrate on listening when he didn't have his eyes open. And he listened very intently these days.

He could hear the monks moving throughout the Hall of Heroes. In the days that he'd been wandering through their home, he'd pinpointed the sound of each of their steps. Each one walked differently, and that helped him rule out which ones of them were not the person he sought out.

The monks didn't want to help him. But they didn't want to help any of his companions, it seemed. Even Goliath, as charming as he was, couldn't get any answers out of these men. Not even what spices they used in their soup.

Maybe someday they would have a simple task. Wouldn't that be lovely?

He remembered the last thing the warlock had told him. The man had wandered into the cave where Abraxas had built his new hoard for the old king. He'd looked down at the crimson dragon and laughed.

"You are trapped here, aren't you? After all these years, you still haven't given up. Trapped by a mortal man and a little measly magic. All you magical creatures seem to think you are so much more powerful than you really are. But a taste of actual power can destroy you."

Abraxas had hated the man. He'd wanted to burn the warlock alive if he didn't know that would also mean the end of his own line. Of course, he would have done anything to keep those eggs alive. The baby dragons had become his sole reason for living in those days, and would continue to be so for many more years to come.

Until Lore. She had banished the dark magic from his mind with a single lift of her brow when he'd said something foolish.

She'd given him a second chance at living.

As the ghost of the warlock's memory glided through his mind,

Abraxas scented the bitter ash of magic on the air. First, he thought it was just the memory still lingering too long. But then the scent continued. Grew stronger, even, before it floated away.

His eyes snapped open. That was the warlock. He was certain of it. No one else could smell like the very end of days while still walking about like a normal man. And that scent hadn't come from the Hall of Heroes, but from the sandy beach just out of sight beyond the ridgeline. He could almost see the black magic in the distance. At the edge of Umbra, where the land met the sea.

The warlock really was alive. And he lived close to the Hall of Heroes. Just not within it.

Sneaky. The warlock told everyone that he was at the Hall of Heroes, and anyone with a little magic would have used it to find him once they got here. But, considering they didn't have a witch in their company, it had taken them this long for Abraxas to smell him. The warlock had lost his touch if it was this easy to smell him, though. A werewolf could have tracked him down ages ago.

He could not deny the hunger in his chest. Abraxas wanted to rip at flesh and rend bone from body. He couldn't deny himself the complete and utter satisfaction of seeing this devious man's face when he realized the dragon had tracked him across the entire kingdom.

Abraxas slipped off the edge of the cliff and plummeted through the air. He spread his arms open wide and felt the change take him with a speed that should have been painful. A dragon ripped its way out of his skin and great leathery wings unfurled through the air. He beat at the very sky with the anger that surged through him. Powerful and deadly, he soared over the cliff and then glided toward the sea.

The sun sparkled off the waves that rolled toward the sand. At the very ends of the earth was a small hut made out of driftwood. The pale, salt stained edges made it blend in very well with the sand. Though a tiny curl of smoke rose toward the sky from a brick chimney at the peak.

There were no other signs that someone lived there. Nothing but the smoke and the small house to draw people toward its walls.

The warlock he had known would have wanted adoring fans to find him. He'd have advertised long ago that there was still a way to seek out his magic. The man had always been more interested in money than in helping people.

Abraxas let the change fall away from him. The strangeness of the area made him consider that this form might not be the correct one to approach with. After all, the warlock likely didn't remember him as a man. He'd remember a dragon, however.

He fell onto the sand, striking it hard on hands and knees before he drew himself up to standing. His back hurt from that, and he was reminded how old he'd gotten in the years since he'd seen the warlock. Magic had not given Abraxas the gift of immortality or youth. He was not the young dragon who had been so easily tricked, however, and the warlock would know that soon enough.

Striding up to the front door, he half expected some projectile of magic to strike him in the face. But it didn't. Nothing attacked him, no screaming banshee blasted out of the hut. He could walk all the way up to the front step and knock on the door.

No one moved from within the home. Was this all some kind of trick? An illusion to bring a person into his carefully laid net where he could then capture them? Abraxas could only assume that was the plan.

The warlock knew how to fight his battles without ever having to land a punch. He'd loved to watch people struggle and then suffer. Surely this was no different from all those years ago.

He knocked again, waiting for the magic to hit him like a hammer. Abraxas braced himself, only to be rather startled to hear a voice come from behind him.

"I don't know who you're looking for, but I can promise you they aren't in that hut." The sound warbled with age, and that wasn't like the man he'd known. "I'm the only person who lives in these parts, young man. No one else would be mad enough to live by the angry sea. But if you'd like, you can come in for a cup of tea."

He turned toward the voice slowly. His hands shook with anger because this couldn't be the man he was looking for. And yet, the moment Abraxas faced the elderly gentleman behind him was the same moment he was struck in the face with that horrible scent.

The man who had spoken did not have a back bent with age. He still stood strong and proud as ever. But the homespun wool clothing was not the luxurious silks he'd always loved to wear. His dark hair had turned completely white, and he'd shorn it off at his temples. Wrinkles lined his face, some from frowning, quite a few from squinting, and age spots decorated his nose where he'd been sunburned one too many times.

This was undoubtedly the warlock he'd been searching for. The man who had caused so much pain and misfortune for countless years.

The anger bubbled up in his chest. It was too much to bear on his own and it needed an outlet. He lunged for the warlock and grabbed him around the throat. Abraxas used that momentum to swing the other man around and backed him into his own door. He slammed the warlock hard against the wood, satisfied only mildly by the heavy thud the back of the warlock's head made as he struck the building.

The warlock let out a little "oof" sound, then a wheeze as all the air in his lungs leaked out from the strike. It wasn't enough. It wasn't nearly enough when Abraxas had desired to see this man screaming in agony as fire consumed his flesh.

But the other man wasn't even struggling. He didn't attempt to hold on to Abraxas's wrists or do anything that a man in his position should have. He allowed Abraxas to take his anger out on him and never once winced nor cried out in pain.

Abraxas leaned forward until he snarled into this horrible man's face, "You took everything from me."

That was when the warlock moved. He reached up and very gently placed his hands on Abraxas's forearms. "I wish I could say that was surprising."

The words were croaked out of a throat dangerously close to being crushed, and yet, they weren't the words that Abraxas had hoped to hear. Surely that wasn't the only thing the warlock had to say? He should cackle with glee to know even a dragon remembered him. He should be pleased to hear he'd ruined the lives of so many, and now another one had admitted to the power he had.

Instead, the warlock almost looked sad and ready to accept whatever fate had come for him.

With another snarl, Abraxas released his grip on the warlock's throat. This wasn't how he'd thought it would go. He didn't want to kill a man who wanted to die. Abraxas had desired a fight and a struggle and a battle that would be told about in storybooks for years to come.

"I didn't track you down to kill an old man," he growled, spitting the words out with more venom than he'd thought possible.

The warlock touched a hand to his throat and massaged the bright purple skin there. "I don't blame you for that. There were many people who wanted to find me in the early years. None of them did."

"Where did you hide, then?"

"Here." The warlock gestured to the house behind him. "No one seemed to think that I would hide in plain sight. I'll admit, however, after all these years of hiding, I am pleased to know that someone has finally come to do the job."

No! Abraxas would not do the dirty work of a hundred people and exactly what this warlock wanted!

The man deserved a death that was painful and long. But he shouldn't want to die, or it wasn't satisfying at all. Then he was playing into the warlock's narrative.

The sand sucked at his feet, dragged him into a slow motion as he started pacing in front of the warlock. "You don't even remember who I am? Do you?"

With a long sigh, the warlock leaned against his door and slid down it until he sat on the front step. "I have harmed many people in my life. Killed thousands. I conjured black magic at the tips of my fingers and I sent souls to the afterlife who never should have been there. I wish I could say I was a good enough man to remember all their faces so that I could feel some measure of guilt. But I do not. So no, young man, I do not know who you are."

And if that didn't tear him up. He'd known this form would be difficult to remember, considering the warlock had rarely seen him as a man. But now he was disappointed to know there wasn't even the slightest bit of recognition.

The anger surged again, and Abraxas let the dragon's flame fill his throat until he was certain it glowed with the heat. "And here I was thinking I'd be rather hard to forget."

That must have done it. Even the warlock gulped, then nodded. "I had always thought it might be you to track me down. I've done terrible things to so many, but none of them had more of a reason to seek out my death than you."

"Stop it," Abraxas barked. "Stop trying to be a good man now that you're old. You cannot decide that your life's work was ill begotten this late."

"I'm not trying to save my soul, if that's what you're implying. I know I wasn't a good man in this life and I am not trying to hide that." The warlock spread his hands open, palms to the sky. "I cannot make amends for the path I walked. What I can do is accept the fate that I sewed into the very fabric of my life."

He hated this man.

Abraxas hated every ounce of what the warlock had stood for and now was trying to do. He didn't get to walk out of this without a scratch or mark on his body.

"I do not forgive you," he said. "I don't want to. The only desire in my chest is to kill you. I want to watch you burn and writhe in pain. Your screams will be a song I remember for the rest of my life."

The warlock nodded. "A well deserved song after all these years."

"I will do all this and worse," Abraxas said. "I will make you suffer just as I have suffered. You will perform one final spell for me and then I will tear you apart. I will rip your heart out of your chest and make you eat it before you die."

Again, the warlock nodded. The old man rolled onto his side and used the door to help him stand. But once standing, he returned to that straight backed, strong man he still was. Even though his magic had disappeared over the years.

The warlock eyed him, nodded one more time, and then opened his door. "Yes, I believe you are owed all of that, dragon. But first, would you like a cup of tea?"

As the other man walked away from him, Abraxas had the distinct realization that this man was not the same as the one he remembered. And so, before he let out the anger to shred this man into bloody pieces at his feet, he decided a cup of tea sounded all right.

CHAPTER 21

Abraxas followed the warlock into his home with only one thing on his mind. He would make sure that no one was ever harmed by this man again. Not a single hair on a man, woman, or child's head. If that meant they never left this shack, then so be it. There had to be other ways to release the baby dragons from their tomb of a box.

Except, he hesitated when he walked through the door and into the room beyond. This wasn't the interior of a shack by any means. Magic bubbled around him, creating a screen of power that made him think there was only a single room beyond.

But then he walked through the power and revealed the multiple rooms and levels of space where the warlock lived. The interior was almost completely white with the faintest sheen of blue. The floors, walls, all of it. A giant curving stairwell wrapped the inside wall, no railings for safety, and leading up to a second and third story. As he looked up, twin rainbow colored birds flew to the top level and perched on the floor, staring down at him with black eyes.

There were at least ten doorways, each covered by a different colored sheet of fabric that blew in a slight breeze. Which meant the windows must be open somewhere, or there was no glass at all.

The faint sound of bells filled the air every time a gust of wind passed by him. He remembered that sound, Abraxas realized. He'd heard it before when he was living in the castle at the same time as the warlock.

Those bells had always been in the man's quarters, but also attached to him at the hip. If that sound approached, then everyone knew the warlock was coming. It had become a warning sound in the castle during those times. A warning for people to run and hide and try their best to not let the dark magic man see them where they hid.

For Abraxas, the sound only reminded him of hours spent in pain. Hours knowing that someone would arrive soon to torture him, or worse, to show him the eggs and taunt him with what he couldn't have. No matter how much he tried to get them.

The warlock walked over to a small table in this center room and deposited a few items from his pockets. Two sea smoothed rocks, a feather, and something that looked like the scale of a fish.

"My name is Lindon," he remarked. "I don't think I ever told anyone in the castle what my real name was. Names have power, you see, and in a place like that, a man couldn't be too careful."

Abraxas knew that firsthand. And he'd learned it from the warlock in front of him who'd used his name to make him dance like a puppet.

He opened his mouth to say just that, but then closed it. One of the birds had launched off the third story and lazily floated down to them in wide circles. It didn't even flap its wings as it made its way to his master. Finally, the beast landed on Lindon's shoulder and clutched the cloth of his shirt with sharp talons. The bright tail laid over the warlock's back.

Lindon chuckled and gently stroked underneath the bird's chin. "It's called a sylph. A rare species in these parts. They've mostly been hunted for their feathers, you see. Air spirits like this create powerful spells." He rubbed the bird's chest with a gentle touch. "Every part of them my brethren use, but... I find them too beautiful to kill for magic."

Ah, finally. Abraxas knew this part of the warlock well, and that was because the man was a liar to his very core. He'd claimed to care for the magical creatures back then too, but every time his eyes would gleam with a knowledge of power.

The warlock, or Lindon as he was apparently called now, never passed up an opportunity to take power from whatever was weakest near him.

Abraxas crossed his arms over his chest and felt justified in knowing the man hadn't changed all that much. "So you have kept them here to make a point to the other powerful witches and warlocks, is that it? You're the only one who can use their power. If you choose to."

With a soft smile, Lindon let his hand drop away from the sylph that surveyed Abraxas with no small amount of distrust. "When I was young, yes. I would have. But these days I've found it's much easier to keep them as friends. Why don't you come into the kitchen, dragon? I'm afraid I wasn't expecting company, but I can explain a good many things over a cup of tea. Or perhaps something a little stiffer if we're going to be digging at old wounds."

Turning on his heel, Lindon made his way to a door with a bright blue sheet over it, and then disappeared onto the other side.

It could be a trap, Abraxas mused. The temptation of knowing more would always be his downfall. Abraxas hoarded information just as he did gold. Although these days, he hoarded friends, it seemed.

They'd all be wondering where he was. It had to be close to lunch time now, and they always gathered together to say what they'd found. His absence should tell them what had occurred, but he feared it wouldn't be enough to stop them from seeking him out.

It didn't matter, he supposed. No one would find him here.

Abraxas strode forward and pushed aside the blue cloth. The kitchen beyond, surprisingly, was quite small. Only a few countertops served their purpose, a single island in the center of the room with four seats on one side, and the rest was taken up by a very large white stove. Of course, the behemoth piece was enchanted because the claw feet moved the moment Abraxas entered the room. Almost as though the stove turned toward him, expecting something to be done about his presence.

Lindon stood before a wall of shelves, reaching for what looked like a glass canister of tea leaves. "Pay no mind to Mertyl. She's a lovely addition to the home, but the spell might have gone a bit awry. She can be overbearing. Best just to sit down and tell her what you want."

Well, he was out of his element talking to a sentient stove. Abraxas hesitantly took a seat at the center island and cleared his throat. "Tea would be lovely, Mertyl. Thank you."

A puff of smoke erupted from the top of the stove, which he could only take to mean she had understood. As he watched, a giant tea kettle floated down from another shelf over their heads and landed on top of the stove. Mertyl then rocked side to side. Settling in for work, he supposed. A flame burst to life inside the grates, and that was apparently that.

No, this wasn't the warlock he remembered at all. Any semblance of understanding disappeared out the window the moment Lindon patted the stove like a good pet, and then went about his business.

Lindon spooned multiple helpings of the tea leaves into small satchels and then handed Abraxas a cup. "I find earl grey in the morning to be particularly bracing."

"Is it poisoned?" Abraxas had to ask, holding the cup with both hands while he waited for the water to boil.

"I suppose I deserve that." The warlock reached up to his shoulder and helped the sylph step down onto his hand. He then set the bird on a small post that Abraxas hadn't noticed, before dragging a chair to the opposite side of the table. "It's not poisoned. I left that life behind me when I disappeared from the castle."

"You mean when you faked your own death?"

Abraxas would not let the man shy away from this story. A lot of bad blood had boiled between the two of them, and he intended to lance that wound today. They would both bleed, perhaps, but then it would be over and done with. Finally. After all this time.

Wincing, Lindon nodded. "I did fake my death. I'm sure that caused quite a commotion afterwards. For that, I do apologize. There are many things to apologize for though, and if we spent the entire time making amends for all the things I've done to you, I fear we would both be dead by the end of this conversation."

Probably. For more reasons than just time. "I suppose you are correct. Though, I'll admit, I'm not sure why you're wanting to talk to me after all this."

"It's a bit like purging my soul. I've never had the opportunity to speak with someone I wronged, and now I can actually explain myself." Lindon held up a hand before Abraxas could speak. "I know there's nothing I can do to convince you that I did what I had to. Because I didn't. There was a certain allure to that power when I was young, and I fell deep into that pool of darkness."

At least he owned up to it. Abraxas had little to say on that matter. It appeared Lindon knew quite well what he'd done.

The whistling shriek of the tea kettle interrupted both of them before it flew over their heads again. The floating kettle poured the perfect amount of bubbling water into both their cups, then the magic deposited it onto the shelf where it had started.

Abraxas stared down at the magic and sighed. "So, this is how you live now?"

"Hm." Lindon made the sound in the back of his throat as he stared down at his cup. "I'm not really deserving of it, now am I?"

"No."

"At least you don't try to lie and tell me that my soul can be saved with just enough magic to tip the scales. Not like those monks." He lifted the cup to his mouth, blew on the water, and then took a loud sip. "You're here to kill me, then?"

The question came so suddenly that Abraxas almost didn't know what to say in response. "Yes. I would love nothing more than to see your blood splattering the walls and the screams of my ancestors in my ears. You should die for all that you've done."

"I should." Lindon nodded. "I suppose I owe you some kind of explanation, though. To be honest, when I was young, I always revered the dragons. I memorized every myth about your kind. That was why I first got into magic. I wanted to be worthy enough to ride a dragon one day."

"You will never be worthy enough for that."

"I know. I really do know that now." Lindon placed his cup back on the table and laced his fingers together in front of him. "Like I said. I fell prey to the power and the wonder of having that much control over a very small number of people. I ran the entire kingdom and all with a simple wave of my hand. But I woke up one day and didn't recognize myself when I looked in the mirror. I'd become someone so vastly different from who I had ever wanted and it all became... too much."

That was it?

That was the story?

It had become too much, so the man had left. He'd buggered off, faked his own death, and left a kingdom in turmoil as everyone tried to fill the hole of power that he'd left behind?

"You left because you'd scared yourself?" Abraxas snarled. "You left because you couldn't imagine looking at yourself in the mirror any more after all you'd done? That's what you want me to believe?"

"It's the truth." Lindon shrugged. "I'll admit, it's not a good one. No one wants to find out that they had become a villain in the story when they'd always assumed they would become a hero. I left so I didn't hurt anyone else. Not even myself."

"But you hurt so many others when you ran."

Lindon winced again, and the expression seemed to sink into the wrinkles of his face. As though he made that expression so often it had marred his face permanently. "I am very aware of that."

He didn't feel pity for the man, if that's what the warlock was going for. He'd made his bed and yes, that would be a bed very difficult to lie in. But that was how life went. Sometimes, when a man became a villain like the warlock, that was the end of the path. Unless he wanted to dive deeper into the darkness.

The warlock watched him and paled. "I know what you're thinking.

You assume I want some kind of forgiveness or absolution from you, but that's not what this is. Not in the slightest. You and I know very well that the time for such things is long past. I know that my soul is tainted. I know what I did."

"Then why are you telling me all this?"

"So you'll understand." Lindon sighed. "And perhaps for my own peace of mind. I want someone to know the truth after all this is done. Someone should know that the great warlock who made even the King bend a knee ended his life as a sad, lonely man who regretted every choice that led him here."

And in that moment, Abraxas realized he would not kill this man. Death would only serve the warlock in the long run. Death would free him from this self imposed nightmare of a life. All that guilt he now felt would wash away with his death. And if there was an afterlife, then he supposed there may be more retribution waiting for Lindon. But Abraxas couldn't be certain of that. He might be playing right into what the warlock wanted.

Which, as he'd said himself, was peace.

Abraxas leaned forward, hands cupped around the hot tea in his hands. "You're going to do one more thing for me, warlock."

"I don't practice magic anymore."

Abraxas lifted an eyebrow and pointedly stared at the stove.

"Well," Lindon cleared his throat. "I don't practice the kind of magic anyone seeks me out for. Dark magic requires a lot more than people think. I refuse to sacrifice others or myself anymore. It's not magic that anyone should dabble in. Not even a dragon."

"I'm not asking you to kill anyone." Although, he could understand that most people seeking the warlock would ask just that. No one came to this man for good things. There were plenty of green witches for that, or perhaps a few light witches that remained in the world, although Abraxas didn't know if they were still around.

But this man could wallow in his own self hatred, if that was what he did these days. No matter. He would live out his life alone in this little shack with his ridiculous magical pets and a stove that knew more than most mortals.

Abraxas squeezed the cup so hard the ceramic edges cracked with a pop. "You cast a spell a long time ago on a box that holds the last remaining dragon eggs in this realm. No one can open the box other than the King."

Lindon lifted his hand in the air. "I'll stop you right there. I transferred the summoning powers of that box to the King. It was part of the spell I made a long time ago. Don't you think I would have summoned them to me long ago if I could undo that part of the spell?"

"I have the box."

Oh, it was satisfying to see the warlock's jaw drop open in shock. "How? The King can summon it again and rip it away from us."

"A friend of mine had a charm he found within a tomb in the Fields of Somber. It prevents more magic from being used, or at least freezing the magic. I don't know how it works."

All the blood drained from Lindon's face yet again. "You have a decaying charm as well? There hasn't been one of those created in years."

"Thus the use of a tomb to find one." Abraxas peeled his fingers off the cup before he shattered it and spilled boiling water all over his hands. "I'm not giving you a choice in the matter, warlock. You will return to the Hall of Heroes with me and you will take the curse off that box. Do you hear me?"

The warlock nodded, looking like he'd seen a ghost. "Aye, I hear you, dragon. I will not return to that place or they'll try to trap me in those walls again. But if you bring the box to me here... I'll try my best to take the curse off it."

His hands shook. His stomach turned in his chest and there were a few beats of his heart that simply didn't thud in his chest.

The warlock would help him?

"No tricks," he snarled. "I will not kill you, but I will make you suffer worse than you could ever imagine."

"Now is not the time for threats." Lindon stood and his age showed in the lines of his shoulders and the marks next to his mouth. "This day has been coming for many years. If anyone deserves my help, it is you. Of all people, I have harmed you the worst."

All Abraxas could do was hope the man wasn't lying. He wasn't sure what he'd do if the warlock changed his mind.

CHAPTER 22

He was late, and Lore didn't know when she should start to worry. Abraxas frequently forgot they were supposed to meet at lunch. Most of the time he was in the gardens watching the monks with a shrewd gaze. But she hadn't been able to find him there. Or in any of the halls they usually found him in.

She still shook with the realization that he had known she was going to die. That the prophecy claimed her life would be forfeited if she continued along this path.

And he hadn't told her.

He hadn't said a word at all, in fact, as though he didn't believe the prophecy, but he had to know that the elves were more reliable than most gave them credit for. And shouldn't she know if people assumed that she was going to die?

The longer he wasn't here to yell at, the angrier she got. If he didn't return to this place soon, then she would start weaving spells that would track him down. There were enough elven books here on the magic that Silverfell elves supposedly had. All she needed to do was pick up one of them and then she could hurl all the curses she wanted at his head.

The damned man had no right. That's all she could think about. Hour over hour, minute by minute.

By the time the sun had arched over her head to the opposite side of the sky, she was certain she would kill him when she saw him again. Thus, when she saw the outline of a dragon in the sky, she'd prepared herself with far too many daggers strapped along her thighs.

Goliath stood beside her, trying to hide his grin in his beard, but failing miserably. "Give the young man a chance, would you? Maybe he found something interesting flying off like that."

"We wouldn't even know he'd flown off if one of the monks hadn't seen him," she snarled. "And don't call him a young man. He's well over five hundred years old and he should have learned not to be an ass by now."

"Some of us never learn that." Goliath patted her arm. "Listen to him first, would you? You look like you're going to pin him down by every limb with a dagger and then threaten to skin him alive."

She hadn't told Goliath about the prophecy. She didn't want any of her friends to worry, not when she already knew how Draven felt about it. They'd all start watching her with far too much attention, and she couldn't stand that.

No one would kill her. That prophecy would not come true.

"I'll listen to him," she muttered. "But if he doesn't start talking the moment he lands, then we'll all get the spectacle of watching an elf try to kill a dragon. How's that sound?"

"Divine." Goliath didn't try to hide his laugh this time. "Although I don't know how much damage you'll do with those little letter openers. He's a lot bigger than you, Lore."

"He only needs one eye, though," she growled as she made her way out of the Hall of Heroes to the open plain that spread out beyond it.

Abraxas had already made his way over there. As though he knew she would come for him. And of course he did. She couldn't stop herself from rushing to those great wings, even though she didn't want to see him right now.

Or maybe she did.

This all was still confusing, even though they'd made things a little more serious between the two of them. She'd thought that by giving in to their baser instincts, the need to murder him on a regular basis would disappear. It hadn't.

She stomped toward him, crossing the field with surprising speed. He had to know she was angry. Just from the set of her shoulders and the way her hands kept flicking toward the daggers strapped to her thighs. He must know she wanted to throw him into the dirt and stick a blade through his chest. Or maybe kiss him because thank all the gods in the skies that he wasn't dead because she'd worried.

He landed so hard the ground shook at her feet. Lore had to side step a few times, so she didn't fall over herself.

"Abraxas!" she shouted, her voice carrying through the thunderous sound of his wings. "What are you doing?"

His booming voice was too loud this close, or maybe he thought he had to shout as well, considering it had been a while since he'd been in this form. "We have to go."

She lost her attention on his words as she stared at the size of him.

Lore forgot how large the dragon was, especially when he stood before her with his wings spread wide.

The crimson color of his scales stood out in the sunlight, sparkling like rubies. His neck arched up toward the sky, the spikes on either side of his head as large as she was. Had he gotten larger in their travels? No, surely he hadn't. He wasn't still growing... Was he?

The crimson scales around his wings glistened as though wet or coated in blood. She couldn't keep her eyes away from the sparkles, almost as though the very sight of him had enraptured her.

"Lore." He bent his head low so he could look her in the eyes. "I found him."

And those words rocked through her soul.

The ground seemed to tilt, and she had to reach out and place a hand against his snout to steady herself. Forget a prophecy that might not come true. Forget the elves entirely and damn them for their meddling.

"You found him?" she repeated. "You found the warlock?"

"I need you to get the box. Be quick about it and don't let anyone know what you are doing other than perhaps our companions. The monks might try to stop you, and I will burn this whole place to the ground if they try." He spoke quickly, and his eyes burned with happiness. "This is our one chance, and we're not letting it go to waste."

She had to go get the eggs, easy enough. Telling the others that they couldn't come with her, though... that would be difficult.

"They'll want to be there," she said. "We've all come so far to be here at this moment. They want to see the eggs hatch just as much as you."

"Of course they do. But we can't risk anyone else coming. They have to go somewhere safe. Somewhere we can meet them because I will not take any chances. Not now." A mad glint in his eye made her stomach turn.

He wasn't listening to her, not right now. He'd already decided what the next step would be, and Abraxas would stop at nothing now that this was within his grasp. She supposed she couldn't blame him for that.

These were his children. Perhaps not by blood, but they were his after all these years of looking after them. He wanted to see them after waiting for such a long time. Who was she to deny him that satisfaction?

So Lore decided that this moment wasn't about her. She didn't have to yell at him for lying to her, at least not right now. They needed to focus on what was right within their grasp.

"All right," she said, nodding. "I'll let them know and I'll get the eggs. Where should we meet?"

"Take no risks," he hissed. "If the monks try to stop you, then I expect you to cut your way through them to get to me. But we don't know who might be working with the King. If the monks let him know where we are, I don't know what will happen. And Zephyr's charm might not work much longer. We need…"

He paused, that mad look getting even wilder in his gaze. She knew better than to test him. Lore put both her hands on his nose and rested her torso against him. "It's all going to be fine, Abraxas. Trust me."

"I do." The words were filled with pain. "I trust you more than anyone else I've ever met, but I am afraid. We've never been this close before."

"And we will succeed this time." She didn't have any right to promise him that. Not when she knew just how difficult this would become, and very quickly.

But they had no other choice. This was their moment.

Pressing a soft kiss to the nearest scale, she turned and sprinted back the way she'd come.

Goliath still stood there, looking more amused than he had any right to look. "Back so soon? You're moving awfully fast."

"Room. Now," she barked as she raced past him. "Get the others!"

Lore didn't waste time to see if he was surprised by her order or if he'd taken off running like her. She knew Goliath. He would know how important it was that he listen to her.

Besides, how many times had she done the same thing to him when Umbral Knights chased them through the streets of Tenebrous? Those times seemed so far away now that she'd lived through this journey. Tenebrous seemed like nothing more than a dream.

She slowed her pace the moment she reached the Hall of Heroes. She didn't want anyone to think anything was wrong and thus risk all of this. Still, when she stepped into the building after smoothing her hair back, her ragged breath filled the rooms with sound. A few monks gave her a curious look as she tried to meander past them without drawing unneeded attention upon herself.

"Good day for a run," she said to one of them.

The man gave her a strange look, but it seemed as though maybe he believed her. That was good enough.

She made it to her room with no one trying to stop her, and she considered that to be lucky. Glancing around herself, she slipped into the room where they'd all been staying, then turned to peer down the hall. No one watched her, but her skin prickled as though eyes lingered upon her.

Everyone waited for her inside the room. Draven leaned against the wall as per usual, his finger pressed against his lips to tell her to be silent. Zeph and Beauty sat on the bed where the eggs were kept underneath, both of them watching her with curious expressions. And Goliath immediately made his way to stand beside her.

The dwarf gestured with his arms over his head, suggesting that she draw a bubble of silence around them.

Lore shook her head. Magic in a place like this would be noticed. That might be even worse than someone overhearing what she had to say.

Although, any words might be dangerous at a time like this.

Lore finally decided she'd have to mime the whole thing to them. She walked over to Zeph and Beauty, shoved them aside, and pulled out the box of eggs. She pointed to it, and then gestured with her hand like she had a wand. Hooking her thumbs together, she moved her fingers as though they were wings and then pointed out the window.

They all stared at her like she'd lost her mind until Goliath spoke. "Lore, I believe we've all had a trying day. I think Beauty and I are going to try out the gardens the monks keep raving about. There's a lot of vegetables there, and I'm sure they won't mind if we take some for the next leg of our journey." He winked at her. "Draven has mentioned there are a few books in the elven section that shouldn't be there. I think we should get those as well."

Zephyr jumped into the conversation, knowing that Goliath wanted to create more distractions. "If you don't mind, Goliath, Beauty mentioned there's a part of the Hall where the monks sleep. We haven't explored that yet, so I thought the two of us might try to find some monks to talk with us."

She watched them all leap to her rescue without question. Tears pricked her eyes, and she mouthed a quick, "Thank you," to them all.

Then she hefted the box of eggs into her arms. "That sounds like a lovely plan, all of you. I'll admit, I'm rather tired myself. I think I'd like to rest this afternoon, considering what I found in the elven section myself."

As she passed by Goliath, she muttered under her breath, "I have a feeling Abraxas and I will be missing for some time. He found him."

"Really?" Goliath projected his voice much louder. "Just make sure you don't go wandering off on your own. I've seen a few of those monks eyeing you. Who knows what holy men think of elves these days?"

"I'm sorry you can't come." She licked her lips and tried very hard not to cry at this goodbye. "Where can we find you all?"

The dwarf moved his arms as though he were conducting a symphony. The other three of their companions started talking over each other quite loudly.

She leaned down so her ear was right next to his lips.

"If you go past Lux Brumalis, heading back toward the Stygian Peaks, there is a standing stone on the cliff's edge. To the west. I know Abraxas will remember it. That's where we'll meet." He squeezed her arm, and it made her breath catch to see the tears in his eyes as well. "We did it, Lore? We really did it?"

Twin tears fell down each of her cheeks. "This is the closest we've ever been, my dear friend. He thinks this is the last chance we'll get. It's everything or nothing."

"Then you run with the rays of the sun." He touched a finger to the middle of his forehead and flicked his fingers at her. "Let the sun rise."

The last time she'd seen that reverent gesture was from the few rebellion people who stood in the crowd at her mother's death. They had flicked their fingers just like that, honoring her mother.

It made her feel like the saint some people were calling her. And Lore didn't know if that was a good thing.

The icy hand of Death landed on her back, as though he were guiding her to his side.

She nodded and sniffed. "Let the sun rise."

And with that, Lore sprinted through the Hall of Heroes like wolves were on her heels. Perhaps they were. Perhaps there was some monster racing along behind her with a cold breath puffing against the back of her neck.

CHAPTER 23

Abraxas was uncertain if he should feel like this. His stomach tightened, knowing that someone out there might be willing to help him in the way he'd been begging for everyone to do.

He felt Lore squeeze her thighs on his back as she held herself to him with only her legs. Both her arms were wrapped around the box of eggs, as though she were frightened the slightest wind would blow them out of her arms. Or perhaps she feared the charm would stop working and Zander would summon them back. His fierce little elf would go with them if that happened, and she would fight to the death to keep them at her side.

That was why he loved her. And, oh, his heart soared through the clouds with them.

He'd tried to tamp down on that feeling of hope. It was the most dangerous emotion he'd ever suffered as it clawed out of his chest and up into his throat. The hope that he wouldn't be the last. The hope that the eggs were still intact, and that they were ready to be freed from the confines of their prison.

The hope that Lore would still want to be around them once all of this became real. She had proven herself to be resilient and strong, but having the reality of three dragons with her at all times? That was a difficult task to accept.

Yet, he knew in his very soul that she would accept them as her own. She wouldn't abandon him or them.

The warlock's hut came into view and that hope twisted in his stomach until he felt like he might vomit. On the tail of that hope was the anxiety that the warlock had changed his mind. What if the man cursed them out of the sky? What if the warlock poisoned them all and made him watch the three people he loved die?

He cast his eyes down on the sands below, making sure that nothing flew up at them. But there was no one on the sands to cast a spell at them. Not a single person. The hut had its smoke curling up into the air, but other than that, all was silent.

Abraxas took his time landing, beating his wings many times to bring to life a sand devil that should have made it difficult for any prying eyes to see Lore slip off his back. She held her shirt up to her face so she could breathe through it and then waved up at him.

It was time.

He'd already decided that he would stay in this form for the entirety of what they had to do. Those eggs deserved to sense him in all his power, ready and waiting for them. They had not suffered through years of torment only to be greeted by another mortal reaching for them.

He let his feet touch the sand and tucked his wings into his sides. But his eyes never moved from the hut, nor did he stop sniffing the air to ensure that no one snuck up on them. And no one would. He'd burn any who tried to rush them.

Lore shifted the box in her arms and peered around them. "So where is he?"

"I don't know."

The front door to the hut opened, and out walked Lindon. One of the vibrantly colored sylphs sat on his shoulder, its own wings held against its side and its chin tilted high. He still wore those simple clothes and a soft smile as he walked toward them.

Lore dropped the box. She reached for her daggers and pulled one out before Abraxas could stop her.

He should have been angry at her for running at the warlock like that. This man was planning to help them, and she could ruin all that with her anger. But he only felt amused that she was willing to kill yet again for him.

At the last second, he spread his wings wide and held it out between them. Lore stopped before she struck the thin membrane, though she glared at the warlock through the thin skin that separated them.

"You," she spat. "You have ruined so many lives, you horrible monster."

"Indeed I have." Lindon didn't flinch from her anger in the slightest. He accepted it just as he had accepted Abraxas's anger.

She was shaking as she gripped her daggers a little too tightly. Abraxas knew if he lowered his wing that she would fly at the warlock without a single thought. She might not kill him, and shouldn't, but she would leave him with a scar for the rest of his life.

He moved his wing closer to her, forcing her to back up. "Feral elf," he said with a chuckle. "We need him to perform this magic and for that, I'm afraid he'll need his head attached to his shoulders."

"He has no right to even stand there alive. When this is all said and done..."

The words hung between them. She wanted his death to be their final success in his battle. He couldn't let her do that, though. He'd already decided there was not enough pain in the world to make the warlock suffer more than he already did.

Abraxas shook his head and put his wing down. "No, Lady of Starlight. We're leaving him as he is."

She looked up at him with an incredulous expression. Of course, she didn't understand, but the more she talked with Lindon, the more she would. They were not the villains of this story. The warlock was. And the man would suffer for a very long time yet.

Abraxas enjoyed knowing that Lindon would live out a very long life in sadness and disgrace.

"Elf?" Lindon repeated, his words floating over the sands. "Surely not a half elf?"

They both looked at him. Abraxas would let her deal with that if she wanted to, although he knew she hadn't read the prophecy. Except her face turned bright red with anger and her hands flexed at her sides again. That anger wasn't directed at Lindon.

It was directed at Abraxas.

Well, that complicated things if she knew what he had also read.

"I am," she replied, still glaring at Abraxas. "What of it?"

"Only that we're much farther along than I realized, and I am surprised to see it." Lindon bowed his head at her, the movement almost reverent. "You have a lot of people talking about you, My Lady."

"Please don't call me that."

"I'll call you what you deserve to be called, and nothing less than that." He reached up for the sylph and let it take off into the air. "I'm sure you realize the future is not so rigid a structure. There are many paths to take, many branches you can follow. But in all my years of scrying, your story is the one that always surprised me."

Abraxas watched Lore swallow hard. Her shoulders curved inward on herself, as though she were afraid to ask the question on her tongue.

It still slipped out. "Why's that?"

"You have so few branches on the tree of your future. Almost as though someone came along and clipped them all off, one by one." Lindon made a motion with his hands as though he were performing the action. "I don't want you to get discouraged though, my dear. You still have time to choose a different branch. Although, I believe there are only two left."

The bird circled them and the sun played through its wings. Rainbows of colors moved across the sand around Lore and he thought for a moment that this might be the last chance she had. It was a bone deep feeling. The kind of sensation that only happened once in a lifetime. She could choose one of two paths, and he hadn't put enough value on the prophecy itself.

Elves prophesied. They always did. But now this warlock confirmed the prophecy to be true.

She could die.

He wouldn't let that happen.

Abraxas bared his teeth in anger. "Prophecies are only there for the weak minded. They imply a story and people assume that story then applies to their life. It is the people who give the value to a prophecy which makes it come true. That is the way of the world."

"Is it?" Lindon lifted a single pale brow. "I'm afraid I don't agree with you, dragon. But if I remember correctly, you never put much value in magic at all."

He hadn't, and the warlock had pinned him with that statement. Not putting enough value into magic was what had gotten him caught in the first place.

"Enough," Abraxas snarled. "We're not here to argue the validity of prophecies or the logic of magic. You made a promise, warlock, and I intend for you to keep it."

Lindon rubbed his hands together as though they were cold. "Yes, indeed. And don't you worry, I will open that box. Like I told you before, this has been a long time coming. As long as you keep this location a secret and my existence far away from the knowledge of the King, then I am happy to break that curse."

Though he still thought it impossible, he refused to let doubt cloud his mind. Abraxas shifted forward, walking through the sands with Lore at his side. "Then we have brought you the cursed box you created all those years ago."

Lore had picked it up, but now she held her against her heart. So tightly he worried the curse might lash out at her. "Why are you willing to break it now? You created this with the intent of keeping Abraxas bound to the King. Can you even break it?"

"I can." Though, even saying the words made him appear more tired than before. "I have a little magic left in this old body. The last time I gathered any power was years ago, but I have enough to break that spell I created. I know you won't believe me, but this is penance. My last remaining power used to break my greatest spell."

It made some kind of perverse sense, he supposed. The warlock could get rid of everything that made him horrible. Though, Abraxas was certain he'd break down and rip power out of some poor soul again. What if his magical stove broke? The man didn't know how to live a normal life.

And that had nothing to do with Abraxas.

"Give him the box," he said. The words trembled on his tongue and he hated that he'd ever said it.

Giving that box to the warlock was the worst thing he'd ever done. More so than even sitting in that cave and threatening the King.

What if the warlock destroyed them? The man had the ability to do so.

Apparently, Lore shared the same thought. She walked the box over to the warlock, but she didn't release her grip.

Lindon pulled it from her with a small wince. "I am sorry that I've made you so distrustful of me. It is natural to not believe what I am about to do. I don't expect you or him to ever forgive me. Not even after I complete this spell. But I need you to back up because if anyone else is caught in this counter curse, then I cannot promise you will not be harmed."

"How far are you going?" she asked.

"Within eyesight. I just need some room." He glanced up at the sylph and a soft smile crossed his face. "I have all the help I need, half elf. Just as you do."

Abraxas swallowed hard and watched a man born of pure evil walk away with the most innocent creatures in existence. They had yet to be tarnished by the world or the people in it. Those eggs were pure. And such a temptation for a powerful spell.

Lore backed into him as they both watched the warlock.

Lindon took a long time finding the perfect spot on the beach. Every moment that he wasted made Abraxas's hide twitch with nervousness. The only time he could feel even a small amount of relaxation was when Lore put her hand on his side and breathed against him. They'd be all right. They had to be.

Finally, Lindon set the box down on the ground. He took a few steps back, then lifted his arms over his head.

Abraxas supposed he'd been expecting a bit of a show. Warlocks always liked to make their spells look far more than they were, but he didn't expect the sylph to let out a scream above the warlock's head and a sudden storm to descend upon them.

The sky turned black. Rolling thunderheads surrounded them with lightning crackling in their midst. The sylph's rainbow colors turned dark, and ash sprinkled down from its wings.

A pop of lightning struck down near the warlock's feet, but he never moved. He kept his arms raised above his head even as the sand turned to molten glass where the lightning had grounded itself.

Then he heard it. The deep, gruff tongues of a warlock's voice as it lowered impossibly deep. Like the crunching gravel of a mountain groaning as it was sliced in half by some immortal blade. His hands began to glow and thunder cracked over their head. So loud it made even Abraxas's ears ring.

The sylph screamed again, and the sound was that of a hundred women shrieking in the distance as their very life force was used to end a curse which should never have been.

Another bolt of lightning charged over their head. This time, it connected directly with Lindon's raised hands. The warlock let out a shout of rage and then directed all that power toward the box.

The metal strappings over each side burned red hot. A black mist grew around it and struck out a whip like darkness toward Lindon. The warlock let that magic wrap around his wrist. Then another lash manacled his free hand. Another scream of rage erupted from the warlock's chest as he battled with the curse he had created.

More lightning struck around the box and the warlock as they both fought for control. Ten spots of molten glass heated around them, bubbling and boiling into the ground. Soon, it would create a slick arena for them to fight.

But then Lindon snarled, "You were my creation and to dust I send you. So mote it be!"

The clapping of thunder echoed with his words and suddenly a white glow appeared in Lindon's chest. The ball of light traveled up his throat and then he let it slip out of his mouth. The light floated through the air, bouncing before Lindon before it landed on one of the dark whips around each of his wrists.

At its touch, the darkness disappeared. Again, the ball of light reached for the next and then followed the dark whips all the way to the box. The light enveloped the wooden frame and swallowed up the darkness within.

As quickly as it had arrived, the storm disappeared. Lindon fell to his knees in the sand, shoulders heaving with exertion and hands limp on his thighs.

The sylph floated down to his side. The tiny bird hopped a few steps before resting its head against Lindon's side.

"It is done," the warlock wheezed. "It is gone. And it took all my power."

Swallowing hard, Abraxas glanced down at Lore to see her eyes had widened and tears dripped down her cheeks. The greatest warlock of their age had given up all his magic to break his own curse.

Strangely, he mourned with the devil.

CHAPTER 24

Lore almost couldn't believe this had happened. The curse on the box was broken? She didn't know what to do now. Where did they go from here?

Of course, she'd dreamt they would get to this point. She hadn't lost all hope, and she'd hoped to free the baby dragons like this for months now.

But now that they were here, she didn't know how to keep going. She'd never allowed herself to consider what would happen after they succeeded.

The warlock sat on the sands with that tiny little bird next to him. He petted the creature on the top of the head, almost absentmindedly, as he watched the two of them. They were all staring at each other as if they were asking one of them to know what to do next.

Abraxas let out a low hum that echoed through his throat. "So it is done."

"It is." The warlock staggered to his feet and gestured to the box. "The King will still be able to summon the box, but there is no longer a curse to lash out at people if someone opens it other than the King."

"Was that the curse all along?" she asked. "The rumors were that no one other than the King's bloodline could open it."

The warlock shook his head. "It was the rumor the original king had spread. He liked people to think there was a chance to open the box and thus they would seek it out. But no. Only the King of Umbra could open that box. Not even the queen."

Which, so she'd heard at least, had happened at least once. But the original king had many wives, and a few of them liked to consider themselves worthy enough to open the box of dragon eggs. The first two queens had died that way, if the rumors were true at least.

Lindon cleared his throat. "I'll leave you two to it, then. I don't believe I am welcome for this part."

The low growl from Abraxas was enough of an answer, but Lore wasn't in the mood to be kind to the man who started all this. "Only those who are deserving have the right to see a dragon egg. Let alone the last two."

He inclined his head. "I understand."

He shuffled off toward his hut and she felt the smallest amount of pity for the man. The guilt he must feel considering he'd single handedly ruined an entire kingdom was a heavy burden to bear. Even for someone who deserved that burden. He'd made every choice that had led him here with a sound mind.

Still. She recognized the sadness in the rounded spine and the way he petted the bird who must go with him most places. The rainbow colors offered very little solace for a man who had a wounded soul.

"Sylph's often go to those who need the most healing," Abraxas murmured. "They find those who are suffering and they stay with them until the end."

"Is that so?"

"That's at least what the story is." He turned so he could look at her with one massive eye. "Do you feel sorrow for such a man?"

"Very little. Although I'd be lying if I said I felt nothing." She blew out a long breath. "I feel pity for those I shouldn't, and such is the life of a person with a bleeding heart."

"It's the mark of a good person, not a weakness." He flexed his wings, spreading them out on the sand so the sun could dance upon them. "I'm afraid to open the box. Or even have you try."

"Don't you want to open the box?" she asked, surprised he was still in his dragon form. "They're yours, after all."

He shook his head, and the great sweeping movement left divots in the sand from the spikes on his chin. "They deserve to feel the presence of another dragon not tempered by mortal form. Besides, Lady of Starlight, Lore of Silvefell, Savior of Tenebrous, you deserve to be the first person to see dragon eggs outside of the royal family. It's been over two hundred years since anyone other than myself or the King laid eyes on those eggs. I want you to be the very first."

She was honored. Her heart swelled in her chest and she straightened her shoulders. The dragons within those eggs might not be able to see, but they would sense that the curse was broken. They would know as well that she was the one who opened the box afterwards.

And someday, soon she hoped, they would see her once they had come out of their shells and they would know who she was. That she had fought countless months to release them from this horrible curse, all before ever having met them.

Her feet stepped through the wet sands. The waves crashed against the shore and the hushing sound was like that of a song carried by the sea itself. And there, just within her reach now, sat the box which could kill her if the warlock had lied.

What was life without taking risks?

Lore didn't hesitate. The locks flipped without a single spell cast in her direction. Then she put her hands on either side of the lid and opened it.

Red velvet cushioned the inside of the box and softly held onto twin dragon eggs nestled inside. Scaled like the hide of a dragon, each egg glowed in the sunlight.

The one on the left looked like a chunk of emerald that had been chipped off a cliff's edge. The sunlight danced upon it and in the reflection, she could see the leaves of trees as though the little one dreamt of flying through the forest.

Next to the emerald egg was one made of sapphire. This one she leaned closer to and placed her hand upon it. The images reflected within this one were of waves on a crystal clear ocean.

They were both so lovely.

Then her gaze flicked to the side, and she saw the spot where a third should have been. Where it no longer was.

Her heart ached for the sibling who would never see the light of day. For the dragon babe who should have been here in this moment, with the rest of them. That dragon should have had its time in the sun to fly with the others and give life to yet another type of dragon who would eventually take back the lands which were meant for them to take.

Her breath caught in her throat. For all the sadness that the missing piece brought, there was still this moment. They had the eggs.

She turned to Abraxas. His eyes were wide, and he'd stretched his neck up high so that he could peer over her.

"They're here," she said, although saying those words sounded a little foolish. Of course they were here. Of course, they were in the box, but they hadn't really known. They hadn't been certain those eggs would ever be in their grasp.

"I know," he said, his gaze filled with love. "They are as perfect as the day I found them."

They must be. Every inch of them was exactly how she'd expected a dragon egg to be, at least according to the stories.

She turned her attention back to them, her eyes wanting nothing more than to feast upon their beauty for a few moments longer. "You said that different colors had different meanings for dragons?"

"They do."

"Is it too obvious to guess that one is a forest dragon, and the other is a water dragon?" She didn't know if such a thing was rude to ask.

Abraxas laid his head down next to the eggs, nuzzling his nose into the sand. "In a way. There is a nature to us. Just as I am a crimson dragon and I lean toward protecting those that I love, or that which I consider to be part of my hoard."

"I've seen that before."

"I know you have." Even in his dragon form, she knew when he was grinning at her. "The two dragons you see before you have a proclivity for those things you mentioned. But they also will have very different thoughts and ideals. They'll become their own people regardless of their birthrights."

"And I imagine we'll be the ones who help them do so?" She grinned at the thought. "They'll be quite wild little things if the two of us are the ones guiding them through life. Can you imagine?"

"They'll face the world with a ferocity that no one has ever seen before."

"And a foolishness that will get them in quite a bit of trouble before they're finished." She'd never given thought to what her children might be like. She was barren, after all. Lore had always known she wouldn't have children on her own.

Except... these felt like they could be her children. If she wanted them to be.

Just talking about who or what they might be when they grew up made her heart flutter in her chest. She wanted to see them like that. She wanted nothing more than to watch these dragon babies grow up and spread their wings. Lore could already see every moment she'd share with them. As they stepped into the sea for the first time. As they took their first steps, their first flight.

All of those moments would be hers to keep. Hers to savor when she was old and gray and no one wanted to talk with her anymore because she'd gotten a little too cranky. She'd fallen in love with these babies already and she hadn't even seen them yet.

"Do you think they'll like me?" she asked, her voice quiet with worry.

Few people did these days. Everyone who knew her thought that she was rather pushy. Their companions followed her because she'd promised them these baby dragons and a new life. But did they really want to be her friend?

Goliath did, she knew that. But everyone else, she always wondered whether they were true in their feelings.

Her thoughts had run away from her. And as Abraxas always did, he let those thoughts go to the end and then quietly said, "They're going to love you, Lore. Just as I love you."

All her doubts faded away with those words. It was so simple for her to let them go when she had the proof in front of her. A dragon had fallen in love with her. A dragon, of all creatures, saw the value in her life.

That had to count for something.

With a quick nod, she braced herself on the edge of the box and stared down at them. "What now? I'll be honest, I didn't think much farther than this moment. How could I? We have always been so close to getting them and they've always slipped out of our reach. To be here, right now, with the eggs in our grasp..."

It was overwhelming. It was so much that she didn't even know where to start.

Abraxas let a long, low hum reverberate through his chest. "Do you know what I see when I look at the eggs?"

"No."

"I don't see the shell, but the life within it. Dragons have always been able to see through each other's physical forms and into what is inside of us. I see a strong young boy who wants nothing more than to cultivate greenery throughout Umbra. I see a steady, but willful young girl who dares anyone to stop her from taking what she wants."

Lore liked that. Each of these dragon babies already had such personalities, and her chest warmed at knowing a bit about them. "They're going to be a force to be reckoned with, aren't they?"

"They're going to take the world in their wings and teach it how to heal."

Yes. Oh, she prayed to all the elven ancestors out there for that. All she wanted was for Umbra to heal.

And with that thought, it almost felt as though the land sighed with her. It was the first time anyone had given Umbra's thoughts a voice and the entire kingdom, from sea to high peak of mountain, wanted that. Healing felt like a good idea.

"How do we help them do that?" she asked.

"Choose one." He said the two words as though they weren't earth shattering. "Pick one up and choose it as your own."

Lore shook her head. "My own? Surely you don't mean…"

"I want you to pick one, Lore. You've earned it after all this time looking after them. Children need a mother to nurture them, to help them grow and teach them how to be the best versions of themselves. I could not imagine anyone more deserving of that title than you." His gaze softened, and she saw herself reflected in his eyes. "Whichever one you pick will be your dragon, Lore. Just as much as I am your dragon."

She didn't deserve this honor. It wasn't right for her to pick one when there were countless other people in this realm who had done more than her. Better things. People who had dedicated their lives to making others better.

"I can't," she whispered.

"You can and you will. I won't take no for an answer on this Lore. Choose your dragon." He nudged the box closer to her with his nose. "They're waiting."

"What if I insult one?" she asked. "I don't want one of them to think that I don't like them."

"They won't. Dragons have been chosen by elves for centuries, although I suppose you wouldn't know that. In Dracomaquia, we allowed their riders to pick them when they were eggs. They would grow together, learning the best way to live with each other rather than either as a lower entity. You are choosing a friend for life, Lore. Someone who would warm your feet if you asked, but would expect the same in return from you."

She didn't deserve this. Lore opened her mouth to say just that, only for Abraxas to interrupt her again.

"Let your heart guide you, my love. If you give yourself permission to listen to that part of your soul, then I promise it will not lead you wrong."

She let those words wash over her and gave in to what she wanted. She closed her eyes and let the magic of the moon swell inside her. The power rose into her throat and filled her to the brim. Her hands moved toward the box as though the magic inside her wanted to choose. And she let it.

Her fingers danced over the sapphire dragon egg, then she gently lifted it out of the box. Opening her eyes, she looked down to see the massive egg in her hands and felt as though something inside touched her soul.

"This one," she whispered.

"Then so be it." Abraxas spread his wings out on the sand. "Now pick up both eggs, my love. I will wait no longer to meet them in person."

Blinking in shock, she stared up at him. "Excuse me?"

"It's time for them to hatch." He winked. "Let us bring about the age of dragons again."

CHAPTER 25

Abraxas gathered up the most important people in his life and decided that he would take no more risks. The time of the dragons had come again, and he was not going to waste a single second longer to see more of his own kind.

He waited while Lore clambered onto his back, practically shaking with the need to burst into the sky and leave this cursed place. His mind raced a hundred leagues a minute.

There were places for them to hide. Places where he could bring them, and Abraxas intended to do that right now.

While there was still time.

Lore settled herself onto his back, thighs flexing against his spine, and he beat his wings against the air. Against the pull of the earth that threatened to hold him down when all he wanted to do was fly out of this place and find them some kind of sanctuary. And he knew just the place.

Once in the sky, he let the winds carry him where he wanted to go, knowing that they had the time to get there now. Once he was among the clouds, with the wind along his back and the mist tickling his chin, all that urgency disappeared.

He was safe in the sky. His children were safe there too, as they had been created to be here above all other places.

This was where they were meant to be. And nothing would ever change that again.

Lore's voice traveled down his back, caught by the wind and thrown to his ears so he might hear her. "Did you know where these eggs were? You said you found them all those years ago."

The story was one of pain and torment. He could say it now that he had the eggs with him, however. It was a story that had to come out eventually and he supposed it was a good thing that she'd asked.

Abraxas tilted them slightly, weaving around a fluffy cloud tunnel that would have sent him tumbling at least a dragon's length out of the sky before he caught himself. "I knew their mothers, actually."

The silence that came after his admission was deafening. He hadn't the faintest idea what she must think right now. There were other dragons before those eggs had been laid. They weren't the children of the last female dragon, but even he didn't know where that dragon had laid her brood. Female dragons were incredible at hiding their nests, and even other dragons didn't know where to find them.

Somewhere, there could be more eggs laying dormant. Waiting for someone to find them.

But he thought he might have heard them crying out for help by now. At least, that's what he hoped.

Lore cleared her throat awkwardly. "Did you know them... well?"

Ah, that was why she'd hesitated. It must be difficult for her to think about him with his own kind. He knew he didn't enjoy thinking about her with Draven and how that elf might give her more than he'd ever could.

Those thoughts didn't matter. He couldn't put himself in her shoes because he would never be as intimidated by an elf as they would be by a dragon.

"No," he replied with a chuckle. "They were good females, from what I knew. I was still a very young dragon at the time of all this. I knew mortals were hunting our kind and shooting us down from the sky, so I stayed with my family. Our clutch was one of the last, as far as I know, that hatched."

"Ah."

He craned his neck around to see she had shifted the eggs to either side of her body. Lore held them against her side as though she'd held dragon eggs a million times in her life. And that made him so incredibly proud.

His heart swelled with the need to tell her more, and he couldn't stop the words from coming out of his mouth. "Their mothers were larger than most females. The biggest still alive and the strongest. They had traveled a great deal of distance together, knowing that they would lay their eggs in the same nest."

"Two dragons?" she asked. At least her curiosity hadn't dimmed in the wake of thinking that someone had once been in his life before her. "How many eggs do dragons lay?"

"A good deal between the two of them. Each dragon lays somewhere between three and six. I've seen clutches as large as nine." He tilted again, the wind whistling past his wings. "But that was a different time. They each laid two eggs."

When she said nothing else, he glanced over his shoulder to see she had moved them even closer to her body. "They're both the last of their siblings? Or are they from the same clutch?"

He shook his head. "I don't know."

Abraxas supposed that was hope burbling out of his mouth. He could only hope they were not blood related. They would be raised as close as brother and sister, but then, who knows what would happen? If they wanted to continue the line of dragons together, they would at least try. But if they didn't, then they would find other mates and the line of dragons would end again.

It didn't matter in the long run. The mere idea of repopulating an entire race of creatures starting from two eggs was a challenge most would never even attempt. They were children. Too small to even be considering such a thing yet. Perhaps someday he would have that conversation with them, but not any time soon.

Out of the corner of his eye, Abraxas saw the tiny island he'd wanted to find. When he was a child, he had found this hidden place as he explored the clouds. It shouldn't exist. It was just a small island in the middle of nowhere. Impossible to reach unless the traveler had wings as giant waves surrounded it and the undertows were brutal.

He could find it, however, and he would use this as the place to bring his children into the world.

Wings pounding against the air, he slowed them down until he was certain they wouldn't plummet to the ground. He knew how precarious a position they were all in. If he didn't land softly, Lore might drop the eggs. While they were sturdy, he wasn't certain they would survive a fall from this high.

Abraxas had never been so careful as he touched his back legs down onto the ground. He sank the tips of his wings into the sand and balanced upright like that. "Get down," he said. "I don't want to risk jostling you."

Lore didn't argue with him, although he could see she wanted to. She slithered between his spines, slid off his back hip, and then landed safely on the ground.

Only then did he fall forward and hit the ground with surprising force. At least the sand softened the resulting shake of such a large creature, maneuvering himself.

He turned to look at Lore and found her still staring down at the eggs in her arms. Her gaze had never been that soft. Or at least, he'd never seen her look at anything like that. It made him want to wrap her up in his arms along with the eggs, to tuck them into his chest and never let her go. There would be time for him to hold her, though. Right now, they needed to get on with his plan.

"Keep them safe while I work on the sands," he muttered. "They'll need to be fairly deep."

"You're burying them?" she asked, tromping along behind him even after he'd told her to keep them safe. "Why are you burying them?"

He didn't want to explain the entirety of what it took to hatch a dragon, but he supposed he had little choice in the matter while he was working. Sighing, he used the claws at the points of his wings to dig.

"Dragon eggs need to burn at a temperature you've probably never experienced before. Dragon fire is the only thing that will hatch an egg, and it is not easy to keep the temperature that warm. A mother dragon would burn the eggs beside her belly, but the sand will have to do."

Lore sat down far enough away from him, crossed her legs, and balanced the baby dragons on either crook of her thighs. "Why can't you hatch them the same way a female dragon would?"

He shifted to flash her his belly. "We don't have the same parts, Lore. A female dragon's stomach is like iron. Nothing can get through it, just in case someone tries to attack her eggs while they're still in her. The scales surrounding her stomach become even more impenetrable after she's laid her eggs. Dragon fire won't burn through it, and nothing could break the scales either." He shook his neck in a kind of shrug. "Male dragons are not so strong."

Abraxas wished they were, though. He'd have tucked those eggs tight to his heart and hoped they heard the thunderous beat while he waited for them to hatch. He wanted nothing more than to see those tiny snouts as they finally came out into the world.

Female dragons were larger and stronger than their male counterparts. They always had been. Perhaps that was why he saw Lore as capable enough to be his life partner. She scared him sometimes. Just like a female dragon.

Eventually, he couldn't dig any longer with his wings. He had to use his mouth to scoop up the granules of sand and spit them out into a pile beside the hole. It was disgusting work and took a long time. Eventually, his entire throat was coated with the horrible stuff and every time he tried to swallow, it felt as though he were swallowing broken glass.

The holes were dug, though, and that was the hardest part of hatching the eggs.

He spat out one last ghastly mouthful of sand and then shifted away from the nest he'd dug. "You can lay them within now."

"Are you sure they'll be okay?" The concern on her features had yet to move. "It feels wrong to bury them. What if they're scared of being deep inside the ground?"

"They were locked in a cursed box for years on end, Lore. They never saw the light of day unless it contained the face of the man who trapped them and had no interest in their well being. Being held within the arms of the earth is no less frightening than the life they've lived thus far."

And it was the sad truth, he supposed. They shouldn't have had to suffer the way they did, but this was their reality. They needed to learn how to live as dragons did. And this was the only way.

She took a deep, steadying breath, and then made her way to the hole. Elves were nimble creatures. She set the sapphire egg on the ground and held the emerald tight to her chest. She used her free arm to sink into the sand and created a mechanism to slow her fall into the depths. All said and done, it was likely about twelve feet deep, just shy of three Lore's. Her feet landed at the bottom, where Lore set the egg down.

Abraxas reached his head deep into the hole above her and muttered, "Grab on."

There were enough scales and horns for her to get some kind of purchase. But when she grabbed onto two of his teeth, he couldn't help but chuckle. The hot air from his mouth blasted her hair back from her face as he lifted her up.

"So trusting," he muttered.

"You're not going to eat me," she shot back as she picked up the sapphire egg. "Why would I fear your fangs when I know they have no bite?"

"Oh, they can bite." He flashed them in a grin. "I'll show you what they can do when we're in a more private setting."

Ah, how he loved to see her cheeks flare hot and pink. At least he could still make her blush, even in this monstrous form.

Lore set the sapphire egg down into the pit and then waited for him to lift her again. Once settled, she took a healthy amount of steps away from them all. "How hot is it going to get?"

"Extremely." He hadn't ever felt the heat from his mortal form, but he knew that it was likely going to be unimaginable for her. Dragon fire burned people into ash in a matter of seconds. This would be even more fire than it took to do that.

Pausing for a second, he looked over at her curious expression. "The sapphire one you chose. You know she will be considered a queen to my people. Correct?"

"I don't even know what that means."

"Then I will tell you once I am finished." He used his wing to scoop all the sand he'd displaced and shoved it back over the eggs.

He sensed their excitement almost immediately. They knew what was happening. Deep inside their dragon souls, they knew this was the moment to make themselves ready. They had to gather up all the strength in their little bodies for a difficult battle out of their eggs.

They would survive and shatter the gemstone shells that kept them hostage for such a long time. And then they would enter the world with the strength only a dragon had.

Abraxas took a deep breath, filling up his lungs until they almost hurt. His ribs opened, spreading wide to make room for all that air, and then the heat started. Dragon fire like this, the blue dragon fire that only rendered the world into ash and ruin, took more than just breath. It took intent with knowledge that only dragons had.

The light bloomed in his chest and cast a shadow over the sands as the sun started setting on the horizon. His flames licked out between his teeth as they traveled up his throat. The hot tendrils already knew what he wanted them to do. They knew the job they were created for.

Abraxas opened his mouth and let the fire spew forth. It rained down into the sand, heating it to impossible temperatures until every grain turned to liquid glass that would burn for hours on end. Still, more fire poured from between his teeth. It sank into the earth and even beyond, all the way into the bedrock and heated the stones to a hot glow that illuminated the sands.

Once there was no more fire in his lungs or even in his body, Abraxas let himself relax. He eased away from the glowing circle in the ground and then slumped beside Lore.

"A queen?" she asked, placing her hand on his heaving side.

"She will lead our people into the sunlight," he replied, resting his head on the ground beside her once he caught his breath. "All of dragon kind will know she was the first female since the great reckoning that nearly destroyed our people. She will have a significant amount of responsibility on her shoulders and we shall all look to her for guidance."

"That sounds like a lot of responsibility for one so young."

"You would know about that more than any other." He sighed as she settled against his side. Abraxas folded his wing around her like a blanket to ensure she wasn't too cold throughout the night. "I know you will help her through every step of the way."

"I can try." Lore covered her mouth as she yawned. "How long will it take until they hatch?"

"Every clutch is different. They've been dormant for many years." Not long, he thought. "Get some rest. I will wake you when the dragons are ready to meet you."

CHAPTER 26

L ore," a deep voice said in her ear. "You might want to get up for this."

But she'd been having such a lovely dream. Lore had been with Abraxas and the dragon eggs, and they had finally gotten the box open after all this time. Then they'd flown to an island where he'd said they were going to hatch the eggs.

Blinking her eyes open in the soft morning light, she realized that hadn't been a dream at all. They were on the island and the sands were shifting underneath her as Abraxas stood and shook himself.

Sand rained down on her. Standing quickly, she brushed herself off and tried to shake out her hair. "Abraxas!"

"Sorry, love, but we don't have a lot of time to stand around. You've got to get very close to that nest if you want to see what's going to happen." He lumbered closer to the dimly glowing sand. "The eggs are already rising."

"Rising?" She staggered over to his side, sleep sloughing off her mind as she realized what was happening. "Do you mean they're hatching? Right now?"

"At least one of them is."

The two eggs rose to the top of the molten sand. The gemstone egg shells glowed red hot, and Lore could no longer tell which one was which.

"Watch them," Abraxas muttered before he made his way down to the water.

She didn't take her eyes off them. But who could?

Abraxas returned as quickly as he left and opened his mouth above the eggs. Seawater spilled out and sizzled as it hit the heat of the sands. A great plume of steam hissed, billowing out in front of her until she couldn't see the eggs at all.

Lore lifted her arms in front of her face so the hot steam didn't burn her. But then, when she dropped her arms, she saw that Abraxas had laid his head down beside the now cooled eggs.

The green egg rocked left and right. The emerald scales that covered it already shivered with the tiny dragon's might. It struggled to free itself from the confines of the egg, and then a single crack split it from top to bottom. Like the tiny dragon inside had punched so hard that the shell didn't stand a chance.

Another crack appeared. Then a giant chunk of the emerald shell fell onto the ground as the egg rolled onto its side.

She couldn't see what happened after that. The egg obscured her view from what was happening, but Lore could hear the tiny shattering sounds. The cracks of the egg that never stopped until finally, it was silent.

Abraxas lifted his head and nudged the shell. It rolled away to reveal a tiny green dragon the size of a cat.

"A boy," he said, his voice glowing with pride. "A son."

Goo still covered the emerald dragon. The little boy waved his tail wildly, as though he didn't quite know how to control it yet. And his neck was much shorter than Abraxas's.

His giant head made Lore press her hand against her mouth to smother the laugh that bubbled there. His skull was comically large for such a small creature. Tiny wings on his back spread wide at the sound of her laugh, and he turned to hiss at her.

Those wings were no longer than her forearm right now. Too small to fly, and certainly too small to be intimidating.

"I didn't realize they'd be so small," she said, looking at Abraxas with wonder in her eyes. "Of course it makes sense, considering the size of their eggs. It's just that you are so much larger than they are."

"As it should be," he replied, keeping watch over the little dragon as it stood. "They will be wobbly for a while. Keep an eye on the other egg, will you? This one is already trying to move, and he'll be wandering off into the ocean if I don't stop him."

That was that? Already?

Lore was supposed to believe that he wasn't bursting at the seams knowing that a dragon had hatched right in front of him? She wanted to shout! She wanted to spin around in a circle and let fly spells that would raise up into the heavens because another dragon was in the world.

Of course, the longer she looked at him, the more she realized he was panicking. An actual baby stood in front of him, and the emerald dragon had already made quick work of learning how to use his back legs. Suddenly, it was very real that he had two infants to look after.

She turned to look at the sapphire egg, anticipation running like lightning through her veins. But the little egg wasn't moving. It didn't shift side to side like its brother had. In fact, there was no movement at all within the tiny egg that should have been struggling to free itself, just like its brother had.

Abraxas had said this one was female. That she would be the queen to lead them all.

Taking a deep breath, she stepped closer to the egg. Her feet touched the hardened clear glass it rested on, and she was pleased to find that it had cooled completely.

"Abraxas?" she asked. "This one isn't moving."

He turned so quickly the other baby fell over onto his back. Lore watched as the large crimson dragon leaned over the egg and nudged it with his nose. Nothing. Not even the faintest of knocking sounds could tell them if the dragon within the egg was aware of them.

"No," Abraxas muttered, and his voice cracked. "Not after all you've survived."

"Why isn't she moving?" Lore asked.

"I don't know. She should be trying to get out of the egg by now. He did." He looked over at the emerald dragon, who had stood up on his back legs, wings spread wide as he also stared at the sapphire egg. "This is how it is supposed to work. I breathe fire on them and they do the work to get themselves out of the egg."

"What if she doesn't?"

A choked sound echoed in his throat before he could catch it. "Then they don't survive."

No. Her heart broke for the little one who had endured so much only to suffer at this moment. The sapphire egg was their biggest hope.

She was supposed to come into this world and change it for the better. Now Abraxas wanted her to believe there was nothing they could do?

"There has to be some way to help her," she said.

"Dragons have to get out of their eggs. We could beg and plead for her to fight harder, but that doesn't mean she'll survive." He moved away from the egg, nudging the emerald dragon with his nose away from the nesting site. "I don't know what to do, Lore. This is the way of things."

"Well, it's a stupid way!" she shouted. "I don't care about your traditions or how dragons have always hatched their eggs! There has to be something we can do."

"I don't know anything that can crack a dragon egg."

Neither did she. But she wasn't willing to stand around and wait for the dragon inside that egg to die.

It was her dragon, damn it. And she was their elf.

Lore sank down on her knees beside the egg and reached out for it. Carefully, she pulled it to her chest and then wrapped her arms and legs around it.

"Listen," she whispered against the sapphire shell. "I know this world may seem big and scary. A lot of people have already done terrible things to you, and that's not fair. You have suffered more than you should have, and I know that's not what you chose. I wish I could take those memories away from you, but I can't. Right now, you have to choose to be brave again."

Nothing moved inside the egg. Not even the slightest of shifts.

"It might seem easier to stay inside that egg forever, but it isn't. You can try to hide from the world, only to realize that it always finds you." She smoothed her hand over the egg's surface. "I know that better than most. If I could take this fear from you, I would. All I can promise now is that I will be by your side every step of the way. I will never leave you. I will never disappoint you. My little dragon, you have to come out now."

Was that a slight sound inside the egg? Almost like a claw had tapped the inside, or a wing had pressed underneath her hand.

Lore tightened her grip around the egg. "No one can promise you that this will be easy. I won't lie to you, little one. But I will face whatever darkness comes for you. I know you're tired, but I can help. You just have to make one little crack. You have to fight for a little longer on your own and then we will be together. I promise."

There. She heard it for certain this time. A scrabbling of claws on the edge of the gemstone. Like the dragon babe within had heard her.

"You've got it," she said, letting excitement bleed into her tone. "Just like that. One more big push, little one. Then I will help you."

Suddenly, the smallest crack appeared in the egg. She heard the sound of a dragon's excited breath in her ear, but she couldn't focus on Abraxas right now. The babe in the egg had heard her, and she had promised she would help.

Lore heard the truth in Abraxas's voice when he said that no one could help a dragon out of their egg. She understood that there were cultural difficulties that came with that. But the dragon had already done the work. She could see the crack. Surely that was enough?

Releasing her grip on the egg, she reached up for the little shard of egg that she could already see was ready to fall off. It wouldn't make a big enough hole to pull the dragon baby out through, but it was a start.

She tugged at the shell and pulled it off to reveal the tiniest of holes. Laying her hand there felt as though she had finally connected with the dragon inside.

"Keep talking to her, Lore," Abraxas said. "She's listening."

"I know."

A tiny dragon claw reached out of the tiny hole and touched her finger. The blue scales shimmered in the sunlight, only to then withdraw.

There were no more sounds from within the egg. Lore could almost feel the baby's exhaustion. She'd been fighting for such a long time and now even this was too much. It was too scary. She didn't know how to pull herself out into the world when all of it seemed so terrifying.

"You have me," Lore whispered, curling her fingers around the edge of the shell. "You will never have to be afraid of the world again because I will tear the stars down from the sky if you need me to."

Impossibly, she felt something raining down on her body. The moon wasn't in the sky, but Lore looked up and could see it. The great mother gave her power that glowed through her arms and hands. That power was a message for her to take what she wanted.

And with that, Lore ripped the shell in two.

Abraxas let out a loud sound behind her, one of anger that she would ever do such a thing. It didn't matter. He could be angry at her for taking out the last female dragon, but they would at least have one. If she followed the way he wanted to do things, no one would ever see the dragons continue. They would only have two male dragons and she refused for that to be the way of things.

The shell shattered in her hands, breaking into two halves that would have fallen if she hadn't held onto the egg with her legs.

But now there was enough space for her to see the little sapphire dragon who had curled up into a tiny ball. Just like a cat. She shivered in her little cocoon, clearly terrified of the world that waited for her outside the safe walls of her egg.

"There you are," Lore said, softening her voice so it was a quiet lullaby. "I've been waiting my entire life to meet you."

The dragon baby lifted its head, and she stared into eyes black as night. There were galaxies in those eyes. No waves. Only a still ocean that met the sky and reflected the stars a thousand fold.

"You have nothing to fear," Lore whispered, but her words carried through the dim morning light. "You and I will be together for all our lives. I will watch you grow into the dragon you were always meant to be. And when I am old and tired, you will carry me into the night sky so the moon may fill my cold bones with something akin to heat. We will forge a path through this world together. We will not feel fear, for we will be the sword that carves a new age into this realm."

The sapphire dragon tumbled out of the egg into her arms. She stretched out her tiny wings, letting the sunlight play across the stained glass delicateness of her membranes. And then she scrabbled at Lore's arms, to wedge her tiny head into Lore's neck.

She couldn't hear the dragon's voice, nor had any way to know if the creature was speaking. But Lore could feel in her very soul that the sapphire dragon wanted to hear Lore's heartbeat up close.

Abraxas moved around them, his gaze wide and tone reverent. "I never thought to see the day that an elf and a dragon would unite like this."

Lore closed her arms around the tiny dragon and held her close to her heart. "And I never thought I would have the opportunity to become a mother."

It was a strange feeling. Like she'd ripped her chest open so this little one could crawl into the space she made for her. It almost hurt, yet was the most wonderful thing she'd ever experienced in her life. As though she welcomed the pain of knowing this baby dragon lived.

"I didn't know it would be like this," Lore said. "I thought…"

"You didn't know that a dragon soul bond is forever," he filled in. "You should have known, considering how much you love me."

"So arrogant."

He winked at her, and the emerald dragon spilled out between his feet as the little one tried to roll into view. "I'm yours, Lorelei of Silverfell. And you are mine."

She hugged her dragon tighter. She felt the same way for this child of hers now. And that terrified her as much as it sent her soul into flight.

CHAPTER 27

Abraxas knew they should hurry to get back to the others. He wanted to make sure there was time for them to figure out where to go and what to do next. However, this little island felt like a bubble of safety.

They'd only just hatched both the eggs a few hours ago and... Well, he wasn't ready to go anywhere other than here. The sands were warm. The sun was bright over their heads and danced across their skin. Lore laid out with his children, no longer caring about the sand in her hair.

And it was the most beautiful sight he'd ever seen.

His two children took to her like bees to a flower. Neither dragon baby could keep their eyes off her. The way she moved. How her hair sparkled like gold in the warm rays. He already knew they wanted to gather up every fallen strand of her hair and start their hoard.

Because he wanted to. Every time she moved, he found something new he wanted to remember and never let go. The mere idea of her existence made him want to start a new hoard consisting of items she'd touched or said she enjoyed.

Damn it, he was getting ahead of himself again. A hoard was not possible when they were moving around so often. He could only carry so much.

Abraxas folded himself into the heat of the sand and rested his head on the ground. The sapphire dragon had made quite the connection with Lore. He wasn't all that surprised, considering Lore was the reason she was alive.

He'd never forget the way his heart had stopped in his chest when he watched her fiercely bring the dragon babe into the world. His elf knew no rule or earthly barrier that would ever stop her from getting what she wanted. He admired her for that more than she could ever know.

The emerald dragon left her side, tumbling across the sands and staggering as he walked. It was difficult to get used to walking with only two back legs and dragon wings for arms. Abraxas knew it would take them a while to have the graceful gait that most of the dragons did.

He swore the little one had already gotten bigger. Soon they would be hungry, and then they would grow before his and Lore's eyes.

The emerald dragon skidded to a stop at his feet and looked up at him with bright yellow eyes. There was a moment when Abraxas wondered what he was doing, before he heard the little one's voice in his head.

"Is this our home?"

He suddenly remembered that dragonlings could talk early in their life, just not with their voice. They would learn how to speak in their dragon form, but not for a while yet. In the meantime, dragon babies could speak to other dragons like this.

He was horrified he'd forgotten. How long had it been since he'd seen a dragonling? Hundreds of years now? To forget this detail, to know that they would be able to converse so quickly, it made him ashamed.

With a slight huff of breath, Abraxas shifted so he could give the little one his entire attention. "No, this isn't our home. We're only here for a little while. Then our journey begins."

The tiny dragon scrunched his face up in confusion. "Then where is home? Where is your home?"

Oh, what a question. He didn't have an answer for that, and it killed him to admit such a thing. He'd never had a home since Dracomaquia fell. He'd come over to the kingdom of Umbra like so many other dragons in the hopes that he'd find a new home here. Instead, all he'd found was ruin and rot.

Of course, there were other places to make a home. The Stygian Peaks were largely uninhabited. Although there were plenty of giant spiders roaming the lands now. And even though they couldn't hurt him, of all people, Abraxas didn't want to be within at least ten leagues of them.

"I don't..." He started to answer, but then paused.

Lore had stood up with the sapphire dragon in her arms. She lifted the babe up into the rays of sunlight and spun around in a slow circle while the sapphire dragon flapped her wings. The little one must feel as though she were flying with the wind like that.

"My home?" He nodded at Lore. "She is my home. Someday, I hope you find a home just like her. Someone who makes you feel safe and welcome no matter where you are or how far you've traveled. For me, she will always be my home."

The emerald dragon followed his stare and looked over at Lore with an equal amount of wonder in his gaze. "I didn't know a person could be a home."

"Someday you'll learn that they can." Abraxas nudged him with his nose. "But right now, you are too young to understand it. So don't even try."

The dragon baby gave him an unimpressed look, clearly already thinking he was old enough for such things. Abraxas had a feeling the boy wouldn't understand it even if he explained the entire story to him.

He and his sister would learn what life would be like for them. They would choose a place to settle down and eventually decide how they wanted to go about their lives. The future they would bring about to this kingdom would be decided by them. He refused to allow any other to sway their thoughts.

Lore turned around, dropping the baby dragon into her arms so she could feel the world pull her back toward the sands. Her gaze found him and the way all her features softened made his heart race.

He wished he were in human form right now. He would run over to her, gather her up in his arms, and never let her go.

But they couldn't do that. Not right now. Not when the sun was already high over their heads and they had a long way to go. Their other companions were likely waiting for them, and he didn't need to make them wait much longer.

"Lore," he said, and his voice summoned her like the call of a siren. "I think it's time to go."

She tucked the sapphire dragon under her arm and made her way over to him. "I'm afraid to leave with them out of their shells like this. They're a lot more of a handful than I thought they would be."

They certainly were. Baby dragons wanted to explore the world. They weren't like most children who were born helpless and needing guidance. No. A dragon child was already halfway to being an adult when they were born. They had likely spent ages listening from inside the safety of their eggs. They had already learned so much before they ever saw the light of day.

"More hands will be helpful," he replied with a chuckle. "I think the others will want to see them. You told them our plan?"

"In not so many words." She set the sapphire dragon down on the ground so she could roll in the sands with the other. "Goliath knows, at least. He'll prepare the others."

"Did he tell you where to meet them?"

"He said you'd know the place." She tucked a strand of hair behind her ear, and his claws itched to trace the same path. "There are standing stones on the cliffs to the south of Lux Brumalis. He said it was safe there?"

Oh, he hated that place. Why did the dwarf have to pick the most difficult location?

"I know it," he grumbled. "The standing stones are historically a place where none can fight. Magical creatures have respected that rule for centuries, but it is not well known to mortals."

"Ah." Lore pursed her lips. "So you think it's too close to the witches and that they won't care about the honor of the standing stones site?"

"Precisely."

He needed to figure out another option, then. Risking the lives of these innocent dragonlings would not be something he'd do. Not even to get them back toward a home where they would be safe. It would take far too long to ensure the standing stones were safe.

Lore tapped a finger to her lips. "Didn't Goliath say they're on the cliff edge?"

"They are."

"Would it be possible for you to put me and the baby dragons on the beach and then go gather up the others from the standing stones? Then we'll be far enough away from the meeting site for the witches not to follow, even if they know where Goliath and the others went. And we'll be hidden from their view because we'll be on the other side of the cliff."

He pondered the thought and realized it wasn't a bad idea. "I can fly in low and hide us all against the side of the cliff to get there as well. They won't even realize that a dragon passed by them unless they're watching the sea."

"Which they have no reason to be doing." She lifted a hand as he opened his mouth. "I realize it's still a risk, Abraxas, but it's far less of a risk than other options we have. And you know, even if I'm alone with the dragons, I will fight tooth and nail to keep them alive. There are few people better to leave them with than me."

He knew that. In the very depths of his soul, he knew leaving Lore with the dragon babies was as safe as if they were with him. They were two sides of a coin. He could clear a battlefield with his breath, but she would pick off all the stragglers with her blades. One by one.

Sighing, he nodded. "It's as good a plan as we'll get. I don't see a reason to wait much longer, do you?"

"Not at all."

Lore clapped her hands and both the dragon babies looked at her as though they'd been trained to do so. Maybe she'd already taught them that while Abraxas wasn't looking.

"Come on, you two," she said as though she'd been born to herd dragons. "We're going on an adventure, and neither of us wish to leave you to your own devices. The last thing we need is the two of you eating up the entire island!"

He heard their voices in his head, twin cries of "I'm hungry!"

"You reminded them that they haven't eaten yet," he said, amused.

"You can hear them?" Lore's eyes widened as she turned to stare at him in disbelief.

He'd forgotten to tell her that, apparently. Abraxas cleared his throat and lowered his head with what he hoped was a sheepish expression. "Dragon children can speak to other dragons. They've yet to learn how to speak like I do. Soon, I suspect, they'll learn that. But for now, they can only converse with me."

"Ah." She appeared disappointed. "Well, I hope they know that we're going to get them food as soon as we can. Perhaps Goliath will have some of those honey rolls he likes to hide in his pack whenever he gets the excuse to make them."

He would not be giving the dragon children anything with sugar in it. The last thing he needed was two baby dragons zooming around the sands because they had too much energy.

"I will find them a deer to eat once the others have joined you," he replied. He then ignored the children as they tried to convince him that Goliath's sweet treats sounded much better than the bloody carcass of a deer.

The answer was no, but he wouldn't argue with the little ones when the decision was still his to make.

"Come along," he grumbled while trying hard not to chuckle.

He spread out his wing so Lore could climb on top of his back, although he knew she would have a more difficult time with two wiggling dragonlings in her arms.

And of course, he wasn't wrong about that matter. The two baby dragons wanted nothing more than to squirm their way out of her grasp. The emerald dragon kept shouting he could do it himself, while the sapphire one continued to climb so far into Lore's arms that she was practically on the poor elf's back.

They hadn't even gotten to Abraxas's wing yet. They were all still fighting on the sand.

Sighing, he looked up at the sky and prayed to the old gods for patience. If they could give him but a few moments, then he could handle the situation.

They didn't help, of course. But since when had the gods been able to control their creations?

"Enough," he grumbled, and the three struggling figures before him froze. The emerald dragon had paused on the ground next to Lore's right foot, and the sapphire dragon slithered out of Lore's grip to rest beside her sibling. "Lore, you will ride on my back. The two of you will be riding in my hands. I'll drop you off when we reach the sands and let you tumble to a stop. Perhaps that will teach you both a lesson."

"No!" the dragon babies shouted at the same time.

Even they understood that being held in his massive back claws would lead to a very uncomfortable ride while they were dragged over the water and then dumped unceremoniously onto the ground. It was a rather undignified way to arrive in meeting new people, and surely they understood how embarrassing that would be for them.

He had little pity. Abraxas eyed them with a severe look before the two of them sighed, hung their heads, and then approached Lore again with a much calmer demeanor.

"What did you say to them?" she asked, as though he had somehow had a conversation without her hearing.

"I talk to them out loud so you can hear what I'm saying," he replied. "They don't want to be dangled over the ocean for the entire trip."

"Well." She leaned down and gathered them up under each arm. "I can't say I blame them all that much. Will you two be good for the entire ride?"

He didn't have to translate their sullen "yes", considering they both looked up at her with wide, puppy dog eyes. She knew. How could anyone question if they were going to behave when they gave her a look like that?

Lore walked up his wing, then settled herself in her usual spot between two large spines. Once the two babies were settled, he felt her pat his back.

"I think we're ready to go," she said.

Ah, he wished he could say the same. He felt as though his heart would beat its way out of his chest for fear of what they were about to do. But there was a whole world out there, and he knew keeping anyone locked away for their own safety was a cruel fate.

"All right," he replied. "Then off we go."

CHAPTER 28

Lore stepped off Abraxas's wing with the two dragon babes in her arms. They wiggled already, so excited to be out of the sky that they couldn't contain themselves.

She adored them, but the idea of them running along the beach without a massive dragon at her side to help corral them... Well, it was intimidating.

"I won't take long," Abraxas said, his eyes still locked on the colorful bundles of scales in her arms. "Are you going to be all right alone with them?"

"Oh, probably not." She let them slip out of her grip and land in little plops on the sand. "They're likely going to run directly into the sea where neither of us will ever find them again. Of course I'm going to be fine, Abraxas. They're not that hard to watch."

"Are you so certain of that?" He leaned down to stare meaningfully into her eyes. "They are not normal children."

"No, they aren't." She looked down at their enormous eyes staring up at her and sighed. "We'll get along just fine. Be quick about it though, if you're taking requests."

He chuckled. "I'll have to make two trips, but I'll bring the most useful ones first."

Lore had a mind to ask him to bring Goliath. The dwarf had been around a lot more children than she had, and perhaps he would know how to entertain these two without losing them. But then curiosity got the better of her. She wanted to know who he thought would be more useful.

With a small nod, she ushered the baby dragons to get away from Abraxas so he could take off without spraying them all in the face with sand. And, as she shaded her eyes with a raised hand, she hoped that he would return quickly.

The massive dragon soared off into the clouds, heading to the standing stones.

"Well then," she muttered, looking down at the dragonlings at her feet. "What are we going to do until he comes back?"

The two children looked at each other and took off in separate directions. As fast as their little bouncing butts could carry them.

Lore glanced up at the clouds and let out a long, low breath. "Damn it."

She ran after the green dragon first. He was faster than his sister, and she didn't think he'd listen to her. The boy child had quite the hero worship for Abraxas, but the mortal elf didn't capture his interest as much.

He'd learn very quickly that elves were difficult to escape.

At least not when he was the size of a cat.

Her long legs ate up the distance between them and Lore leapt into the air. She captured the small dragon in her arms and rolled them both in the sands so that she was on her back and he had laid atop her.

"Don't you run from me," she scolded.

The audacity of the little man. He bared his fangs at her and chomped at the air, as if warning her that he could bite her any time he wanted. Lore bared her teeth as well, knowing full well that the flat edges in her mouth were nowhere near as intimidating as his. Still, she had no problem showing him just how feral she could also be.

"I might not have fangs like you, but I can summon magic whenever I wish, tiny dragon. I will chain you up with ropes made from moon magic and you won't be able to move until Abraxas returns. What do you say to that?"

The grumpy expression on his face was answer enough.

Lore stood, holding him tight to her chest even as he wiggled. "Now, where did your sister run off to?"

She scanned the sands but couldn't find the little one. The baby dragon should have stood out rather easily, considering the brightness of her scales. As she continued looking, however, Lore noticed a darkened edge of the cliff.

A small cave by the sea, it appeared. Not much of a cave, she suspected. There were very few tunnels in this area, considering the cliff edges were worn down every year by the waters that poured over them during the rainy season. But it was still a cave.

She looked at the emerald dragon in her arms. "A real dragon, your sister is. I bet she's found herself a cave. Will you behave yourself and follow me if I put you down?"

He nodded. Good enough, in Lore's opinion. He had to follow her. After all, his own curiosity would force him to investigate his sister's disappearance.

She set him down and he rushed toward the cave. Apparently, she'd been correct that the little sapphire dragon had wanted to get somewhere out of sight. Considering they were all trying to hide, Lore didn't mind the little one's plan. Even if it would make them more difficult for Abraxas to find them. They had some time to explore before the larger dragon returned.

The emerald dragon reached their destination first. He hesitated at the mouth of the cave, sniffing the air with one wing raised, as though he wasn't quite certain that he wanted to step foot into the darkness.

The damp air cooled the sweat at Lore's neck. She thought it felt rather nice. Though, perhaps it smelled a little too much of the sea for the green dragon. Seaweed was a particular scent, and if he was more inclined to frolic in forests, then he likely would not enjoy the air within.

She bent down and patted him on top of the head. "I promise, little man, nothing bad will happen to you."

Those giant eyes struck her straight through the heart. He trusted her, and not because he should, but because he'd never met anyone else. She was one of the first people he'd seen out of his egg. The innocence of his soul glowed so brightly, she found it distracting.

Someday, he would realize that there were bad people in this world. Or perhaps he already knew, considering how many of Zander's conversations he'd listened to. He must know that there was evil out there and such blind trust was unwise.

She wanted to gather him up to her heart and never let him go. He couldn't be allowed to wander ever again because if he did, then someone might… might…

A spike of fear burned in her chest. She didn't have time for this. She had to find the sapphire dragon.

With that fear came anger. It burned in her chest and suddenly she was so frustrated that the two of them hadn't listened to her. They knew she was the only one to look after them and still they took off into the wilds like there was nothing about to hurt them. They were just babies. A hundred things could injure them in the cave: people, animals, other magical creatures.

Lore scooped the emerald dragon up into her arms and stepped into the shadows.

The wet dripping sounds caught her ears first, but she couldn't hear any scrabbling of dragon claws on the stones. That was her first warning. The second was the strange glow in the back of the cave. She could see where a small outcropping of stone obscured her vision of the water. The light caught on the walls as waves gently moved, sending rippling patterns up onto the ceiling.

Only magical creatures could make light like that. Lore didn't know what that meant, or what creature she would have to fight now, but she reached down for her daggers nonetheless.

"If I tell you to run, then you run," she whispered into the emerald dragon's ear. "No arguing this time."

The spikes on top of his head pressed flat to his skull. She could almost hear his thoughts. He wanted to argue with her that he should protect the sapphire dragon. The need to serve already glowed in his chest. But he knew he was very small. Lore was the sapphire dragon's best hope.

She set the little man down on the ground and slithered over the slippery rocks. Algae clung to her fingers and clothing, but she ignored it as long as she still could grip the stones. Once close enough to the edge of the stones, Lore pulled herself over the edge and peered down into the grotto below.

The sapphire dragon had made her way to this cave for a purpose, it seemed. No magical creature threatened her well being, though Lore took her time peering through the glowing waters to be sure no merrow or siren made the light.

But there was only one small entrance to the grotto, and the water that came through it carried no magic.

If she had to guess, the pool of water was about knee deep. The sapphire dragon stood in the shallowest part of the waters, letting the tiniest of waves wash over her back and wings. The light wasn't coming from her, although Lore might have guessed it would. The dragon baby hummed as the water touched her, almost like she was encouraging the sea to come closer.

The light came from jagged crystals that jutted out of the stone all around the tiny dragon. Azure and glowing brightly from deep within, they seemed to simmer with magic.

Lore let some of her own power slip from her skin and touched a glowing finger to the surface of the water. She'd never felt power like that before. It didn't want to harm her, but it quite forcefully pushed her own magic aside. It didn't hurt, but the firm shove let her know that she wasn't welcome to take this magic.

It felt almost like ancestral power. She'd heard of such a thing before. Shared memories that the elves had left for those who came later. But all of those memories had been absorbed long before her birth. Besides, no one would let a half elf near such powerful and important memories.

As she watched, the sapphire dragon moved. The little one stretched out her neck on the water and let the salt help her float. Her tiny wings spread out around her as she allowed herself to trust that the sea would take care of her.

And it did. All the light in that pool glowed ever brighter until it suddenly beaded up into tiny balls of fairy lights that gathered around the dragon babe. They drew closer, ever closer, and then swirled around her in a tangle of lights and whispers.

Lore could almost hear the words, but they were in a language she did not understand. A small nudge against her armpit warned her the green dragon had joined them. Absent-mindedly, she tucked the other child underneath her arm as they both watched the sapphire dragon. She swam in a small circle and then lifted her head.

Her eyelids were lazily low on her eyes, but she still conveyed that Lore should touch the water again. Somehow.

Lore wondered if the dragon had spoken to her in her mind, as Abraxas claimed they could. But that wasn't quite right. She didn't hear a voice telling her to touch the power. She felt a compulsion to do so, as though someone had cast a spell and told her to move.

Lore dropped her hand back into the pool and suddenly, she could hear the little one speak.

"My name is Nyx." Her voice was quiet and burbled like bubbles deep underneath the water. "I am honored that you have chosen to stand with me throughout my life, and I find you quite pretty."

Lore thought the dragon had sounded quite proper and old until she'd said the last bit. Lore chuckled. "I find you quite pretty as well."

"I'm sorry I ran away. I had to come here to gather what remained of the memories." A few of the glowing lights bounced against her head and disappeared underneath her scales. "There are many for us to gather all over Umbra, but we don't know where they are."

That created a problem. Lore didn't want to think of another wild quest to add to their list when they still needed to return to the Umbral Castle and settle this whole affair with the King. And then she had no idea what their lives would look like. They could end up in another battle or a war. Zander was still out there. No matter how wonderful it felt to have the dragon babies, they were still not safe.

Oh, gods. This had gotten even more difficult.

"I think we can help you with that," she replied. "But there are some other things we must do first."

"I know." Nyx shook her head. "There are a lot of things to do, actually, but these will be the first to start. We gather the memories so that myself and Hyperion might follow the old ways as we seek to define the new ones."

"Hyperion?" Lore repeated the name, and then glanced down at the emerald dragon, who stretched up his neck. "Is that you?"

He nodded.

Somehow, all of this felt more real now that she knew their names. They weren't just described by color, but they were actual people with names and thoughts. Now, she had even spoken to one.

All that hope that she'd shoved down so far into her chest bubbled up. All of it. Since the time when she'd watched her mother shouting "Let the sun rise", to this moment. These two were more than just dragons. They were a future of light, and the two of them were so aware of that fact.

Swallowing hard, she swirled her fingers in the water and watched as the blue lights danced on the ripples. "I hope you know nothing will change what I said. It is my honor to stand beside you, and nothing will get between us. You and I are bound, little one."

She swore Nyx smiled.

"We're bound in more ways than you can imagine, honored elf of starlight." Nyx used her wings to glide on the water toward Lore and bumped her nose against Lore's fingers. "We should be going. Father returns soon, and I do not wish to worry him."

Father?

Oh, that was so strange to hear the little one call Abraxas that. She knew that, of course, they would look at him in such a way. He'd spent centuries planning to hatch them, and his voice had been the one that guided them through the darkness on many evenings.

But to hear him called father? The word sent strange shivers down her spine. She didn't know if they were bad or good.

"Right," she said, and then scooped the little one out of the water.

That power severed between them and suddenly Lore recognized the silence that surrounded them again. The painful silence of knowing it would be a while yet before she heard Nyx's voice again.

She wished the dragon babe could speak whenever she pleased. Soon, Lore reminded herself. Soon, they would be able to speak just like Abraxas.

They all started out of the cavern, the sapphire dragon in Lore's arms and the little emerald dragon tromping along beside them. Lore couldn't stop herself. She dropped a kiss on top of the baby dragon's head.

"I'm glad to know your name, Nyx," she whispered against the warm scales. "Now, let's go find your father."

CHAPTER 29

Abraxas had thought it would be smart to come back twice, but by the time he wheeled around the standing stones, his stomach had twisted into knots. What was happening with the dragon babes? They were too smart for their age and quick. What if Lore tried to run after one and another disappeared? What if Lux Brumalis had sent an army to his children, and they took the dragon babes by force? He could lose them all.

He landed hard on the ground, the thunderous sound sending up a cloud of dust and dirt that rained down upon his companions. The four stood near the stones but were knocked onto their hands and knees with the gusts of wind.

He didn't care. Abraxas almost didn't even have a question of whether they were all right. He didn't want to hurt them, obviously, but there were more important matters at hand.

The shout that echoed out of his throat was far too loud. "You're all riding. Now."

Beauty was the first to stand. His brave, wonderful young friend who had no qualms about hopping onto the back of a dragon and trusting that he would take care of her. Though her legs were wobbly, she raced across the ground with a determined expression on her face.

No questions. Only action.

That was why he adored the girl. Beauty didn't know hesitation.

Zephyr was on her heels. The young man's long legs ate up the distance between them and he flattened his back against Abraxas's side. Bending at the knee, he laced his hands together and caught Beauty's boot as she launched at him. He thrust her into the air with a small grunt, grabbed her hand that she'd shoved at him, and allowed her to haul him up onto the back of the dragon.

Two was good enough. He couldn't take much more on his spines without worrying if they would fall out of the sky.

He eyed the two magical creatures, who had hesitated too long. Goliath gave him a grin and a shrug, almost as though he had known he'd never keep up with the two younger companions. And that he knew what Abraxas would choose next.

That left only Draven. The dark elf who had no idea what was going on. He was also the only person who had never ridden a dragon, and the mere idea must have frightened him. He'd never seen an Ashen Deep look so pale.

Though Abraxas feared something had happened to his children and to Lore, this was the perfect opportunity to frighten the deepmonger one more time. And he very much enjoyed scaring this elf, who thought he could steal away his beloved.

"Hold on," he snarled.

The two mortals on his back clutched onto his spines, and then he took off again. Abraxas used all the strength he had in his wings to get into the air. Once there, it was easier for him to keep himself aloft. And that meant he had to glide to get the other two.

Like a giant hawk falling from the sky, he approached. Goliath stood with his arms raised above his head, clearly understanding what Abraxas was about to do. Draven, on the other hand, started running in the opposite direction.

Abraxas caught the dwarf with one of his great claws. He was careful to close his toes gently, making sure he didn't squish the man. Then he focused on the other who had lost all his senses. Didn't Draven know he couldn't run from a dragon?

Opening his claws like the bird of prey he must have looked like, Abraxas flew toward the elf. Though the sound of the wind in his wings might have given him away, considering Draven started weaving in his steps as though that might make it more difficult to find him.

It didn't make it any harder. Abraxas was so much larger than him, the elf didn't stand a chance.

He closed his free foot around the elf with a sharp snap. If he was a little rougher with him than he had been with Goliath, then oh well. The elf shouldn't have run. Maybe he would have been more gentle if he hadn't run.

Abraxas beat his wings in the air, striking harder than he usually had to. The weight of all his companions made it shockingly more difficult to fly. But he glided with them over to the edge of the cliff and then plummeted down into the air. The wind held him aloft, although the screams of his companions also gave him a jolt of happiness that made it easier to float through the air.

The currents of wind would take him back to the spot where he'd left Lore. They would find his loved ones safe and well. They had to.

Though his companions might have tried to speak to him on the journey, Abraxas wasn't paying attention. His sides already heaved with exertion and it took all his attention to keep them aloft. He needed to focus, so they didn't sink too low. He'd never get them this high up again if he lost his concentration.

Finally, they reached the place where he'd left Lore and the two dragonlings. They were farther than he remembered, or perhaps he had gotten too tired on the trip. Either way, when he paused to let down the two people in his feet, he realized that this would be a more arduous task than he'd thought.

Abraxas tilted his head back and used his wings to hover above the sands, the cords of his neck feeling like they might snap with the strain. He dropped Goliath first. The dwarf was surprisingly heavy. And then he let the elf slip from between his claws again, slightly easier than the first.

He let his wings slump onto the sands. His belly hit the warm grains hard. Wind wheezed from his lungs with the impact, but he had made it. With all of them.

A part of him was shocked they'd done it. Or he'd done it. His mind wasn't working quite right yet after that journey. He knew that it was a foolish decision to fly with so many people again. That much was certain. He'd need to work up to that many passengers on his back.

Beauty slid off him and walked around his front to pat her hand on his snout. "You did a good job. Perhaps you should rest for a while?"

"No time," he huffed. "Lore and the dragons are somewhere nearby. Need to make sure they're safe and alive."

Where were they? He needed to see them. A voice in his mind screamed that he was too late. That they were already gone, and then where would he find them? How would he find them?

"Oh," Beauty said, her voice carrying on the wind like the flutter of wings. "I didn't know they'd look like that. They're so small."

He lifted his head and saw the three of them walking across the sands. Lore held the sapphire dragon in her arms like a child. Upside down with her belly in the air, the sapphire babe snapped her jaws at the wind. While his emerald boy tromped along beside her, his spikes already raised as though he were expecting the humans to attack them.

Abraxas had no question that the emerald dragon would fight to the death to protect the two women behind him. But the boy needed to learn that when his women weren't worried or upset, that he also had no need to worry. Or rile himself up so much.

The relief that poured over him like a rush of cold water made his head spin. They were alive. They hadn't disappeared or died while he was gone. It was... exhilarating to know that they were where he had wanted them to be. He hadn't needed to worry at all.

Abraxas let the scales melt away from his body. Finally, after so many days of being in this form, he could let it go so that he could gather Lore up in his arms. He'd missed holding her against his heart and feeling the tiny sigh that she always let out against his neck. All of that and more.

For the first time in his life, Abraxas didn't mind becoming a man. He didn't mind letting go of the physical power that came with his draconic form. Because he knew that everyone was well.

He staggered to his feet, hands grasping at the sand as though it might help him propel forward. The others remained frozen in shock as he made his way toward the woman he loved and the first dragon babes in centuries.

Miracles. The lot of them.

But the moment he closed in on them, the emerald dragon reared up and spread his wings wide. The little man let out a long hiss that was almost intimidating and then spat out a small burp of a fireball that landed directly in the center of Abraxas's chest.

He patted out the flames with a small grin. "I didn't know you would already know how to summon fire. I'm impressed, little one."

The emerald dragon's voice snarled in his mind. "Human, I will roast your flesh and devour you whole if you touch my mother."

Mother.

Oh, his heart shattered into a million pieces and each one of them loved her more than before. They called her mother. His two children had never seen life outside of that box, but were already so connected with Lore that they felt comfortable enough to call her mother.

He'd never been so blessed. His life had never been better than this moment.

It took every ounce of his control to not kiss her. He wanted to wrap his arms around her so tightly he didn't know where she began and where he ended. However, the emerald dragon would continue to attack him if he touched Lore like that.

Sinking onto a knee, he held out his hand for the dragon's inspection. "Someday, you will learn that there are a few forms a dragon can take. One of them is the form you are in now. The form you are comfortable seeing me in. And then there will come a day when you realize it might be easier to walk in the skin of a man. That will be the day you remember this moment fondly, and how you threatened to burn a dragon."

"A dragon?" the emerald boy asked.

"Indeed." He pressed his offered hand against his chest. "You know me as Abraxas. The crimson dragon who brought you into this world."

The emerald boy looked confused, but at least he didn't spit fire at him again. Not when the sapphire girl was already scolding him as well.

She seemed... different.

Abraxas stared at the little one in Lore's arms, but he couldn't quite put his finger on why she had changed. She still looked the same, didn't she? This was the same child he'd left behind. But somehow...

Lore's voice interrupted his thoughts. "Nyx found what she says is called a memory nest. She wandered off before I could catch her and I found her in a pool of seawater with crystals and glowing lights all around her."

Memory nest? He'd forgotten all about them. Had his mother told him of their existence years ago? He couldn't quite recall. It had been such a long time since he'd spoken with other dragons that he'd never thought about a memory nest.

They had lost so much information about his own kind during years of war and pain. Already this little one had discovered more than he could teach.

"Nyx?" he repeated, the word filtering through his startled thoughts. "Did you call her Nyx?"

The grin that spread across Lore's face was one of sheer pride and joy. "I did. They've named themselves in your absence, or at least, Nyx has named them. The boy at your feet is called Hyperion."

"Hyperion." He sounded like a parrot, but he couldn't help himself. The boy had gotten a name and "emerald dragon" now seemed so silly to call him.

He might have named them himself, but Abraxas remembered the old ways enough to know that there were rules to this. Dragonlings with no mother were more apt to call themselves names from their family. Apparently, Nyx had found herself a memory pool that told her all she needed to know about their history.

With a slight grin on his face, he met Nyx's dark eyes. "And why did you choose those?"

The little one grinned, but she didn't answer.

Shuffling sands behind them warned there were a few visitors who wished to see what they had all been fighting so desperately for. Abraxas turned so they could see the baby dragons and saw the shock and awe on his friend's faces.

Beauty had tears streaming down her cheeks. She'd pressed her hands to her face, but that didn't hide the wonder reflected in her features. "Dragons," she whispered. "Real dragons."

"What was I?" Abraxas asked, the teasing tone hopefully softening his words. "They are only children."

"Yes, and those are so much easier to look at than your monstrous form." Beauty dismissed him and bent down to greet the emerald dragon. "Hello. I don't believe we've been properly introduced."

"They can't speak yet," he said. "They can understand you, though. His name is Hyperion."

"Hyperion." Beauty breathed out the word as though it were a prayer. "It is a brave name for a brave lad. Heroic, even. And I'm sure you will live up to such a name."

Hyperion bloated out his chest with far too much pride for a child so young, but Abraxas wouldn't ruin the moment. As with most people,

Beauty had already charmed the young dragon with a single smile.

Goliath approached next, his hands in his pockets and his beard moving with more emotion than he was letting on. "Your mother would be proud," he gruffly said to Lore. "This was what she wanted, you know. She didn't care about all the war or the death. She just wanted to see creatures like them given a second chance. I know she's looking down on all of us and knows that her work is finished."

Tears built in Lore's eyes. She appeared so emotional she couldn't even speak. She merely nodded and held onto the little one in her arms a little tighter.

Unsurprisingly, Draven remained behind the rest of them. His wide eyes looked at the spectacle in front of him, and Abraxas could almost sense how overwhelmed he'd become. This was a far cry from the young man's hole in the ground in a damp, dark forest.

"May I?" Zephyr had moved close to Lore and took a knee before her. "I know it was my blood that did this, and I think there are many apologies I need to say to these little ones."

To his surprise, Nyx wiggled in Lore's arms. Her tiny wings reached out for the face of the young man who should have been king.

Ever so gently, she brushed her wings along his forehead and cheeks. Then the dragon tilted up Zephyr's face and Abraxas heard her voice in his head.

"You have nothing to apologize for," Nyx said, and Abraxas repeated her words out loud. "Your family does not define you. Your heart is pure, forgotten son of the King. You will do great things, not despite the man who bore you or the brother who hates you. But because of who you are."

Ah, this young one would make a great queen yet. Her compassion did not fall on deaf ears as Zephyr lost all the blood in his face and all the tension in his shoulders at once.

Abraxas made sure he patted the boy's shoulder, while also checking to make sure he wouldn't fall over. "You're holding a lot of weight that isn't yours, Zeph. Even the young one can see that."

He eyed his companions and knew they all shared the same question now. The question that had haunted them since the beginning.

What next?

But when he looked at Lore, he already knew they'd both come to the same conclusion. He just had to be the one to give the plan breath.

"Get some rest tonight," he said. "Tomorrow we return to the last stronghold the magical creatures have. A place where these two will truly be safe."

Beauty wrinkled her brow. "Where is that?"

"The Umbral Castle," he replied with no small amount of disgust. "It's time to bring them home to Margaret, who I am certain will have some words to say."

CHAPTER 30

There were many ways to return to the castle, Lore supposed. One was to fly on Abraxas, which would take them the better part of a couple days. The other was to walk. And that route would take a couple of weeks.

Though they had to return, she knew this was when they had to split up as well. Abraxas couldn't take all of them. He'd made that very clear after carrying the others. Which meant some of them were going to journey back the long way.

It hurt to consider who she would take with her, and who she would have to leave behind.

These people had become more than just friends to her. They were her people. Her family. Without them, she didn't know where to go or what to do. They had gone so far with her and to know even for a few weeks that they would be apart... Well, it frightened her.

Lore didn't want to leave them. She wanted to walk back with the others. What would two weeks really do on foot? No harm would come to them.

"We are not going to walk across the entire kingdom with two baby dragons and expect no one to notice." Abraxas shook his head at her and crossed his arms over his chest. There was no arguing with the man. "They are going to get bigger, Lore. Every day they're going to be larger and especially once we start feeding them larger meals. By the time we make it to the castle, they'll be the size of a small pony."

"I don't care what size they're going to be. They are dragons, Abraxas. I didn't expect them to stay this size forever." Although she wouldn't mind if they did. They were quite adorable.

"Lore." He stepped closer to her so the others wouldn't hear what he had to say. "I know you're letting go of a safety net by leaving them. But we have to make the right decision, and you know that isn't wandering all over this kingdom again while trying to stay hidden. We're only going to run into more trouble."

Of course, she knew that, but it didn't make this choice any easier. While they were flying off into the distance with two dragon babes who were the future of their kingdom, her friends could be fighting for their lives. What if someone attacked Goliath while she was gone? What if they showed up at the castle missing one of her dear friends and she could have been there to save them?

Abraxas caught the back of her neck in his warm palm and drew her forehead to his. He inhaled, blowing out the air and then doing it again. Over and over until she breathed with him. All the anxiety in her chest disappeared until she felt as though she could think straight.

And he was right.

Damn it, he was right. They couldn't travel with two very sought after creatures because she didn't have the guts to leave her friends behind. They were all warriors in their own right. All four of them had fought on this journey. They would do so again and they would return to the castle alive.

Sometimes she had to make a choice that she didn't want to make. And that was all right. She could be sad and still do the right thing.

Swallowing hard, she nodded against him. "All right. We need to go back to the castle, and the others will join us when they can."

"I think it would be smart to bring Beauty with us as well."

They weren't as quiet as they thought they were. Beauty piped up, "Because I'm the only woman? Abraxas, that's low even for you."

"Because you're friends with Margaret," he snarled. "But by all means, I can say it was because I think you are weaker than the other three."

Beauty turned bright red. "Ah. Well."

"Not what you were expecting?"

"Sorry." She sat back down on the driftwood log where the others waited. "I should know better. I just wasn't expecting you to say that. We all know that we're the ones who get left behind."

And oh, if that didn't break Lore's heart. She didn't want them to think that was what her choice was. She didn't want to leave any of them in the dust. It wasn't fair.

"We wouldn't be here without you," she replied. Lore made sure to meet each one of their gazes before continuing. "I know that. I don't want any of you to think for a second that I forget you were the valiant few who stood by us while we fought for this crazy future no one else believed in. You have been here for months on end to help us, and I can never thank you enough for that."

They all seemed to wilt under her gaze. As though they felt a little disappointed in themselves for the way they felt. That wasn't right, though. They should never feel guilty for what their minds whispered at night when they knew damned well how much she loved them.

To her surprise, Abraxas spoke next. Though gruff and surly, his words rocked through her. "All dragon kind will remember your names. There is no forgetting in the ways of my people. We pass memories down through magic and no dragon will ever forget that you sacrificed so much so that we might live. Your bravery, your trust, changed the world. For that, all dragons owe you a great debt. And that will be repaid in full once you meet us all at the castle and I can do what a dragon must."

"We don't want money," Zeph said. "There's a lot of that going around the world, and I don't think anything in your hoard would tempt me."

"Then I will find another way, honored brother of dragons." Abraxas said the title as though he had spoken a new version of Zephyr into being. "You will be remembered, as I said. But I will do more than that. I promise."

Lore eyed all of her friends and wished she could bring them all. One more time. She wanted to look at them all until their faces were pressed into her memories, just in case. And she knew that she was only feeding into her anxiety about losing them.

"We need to go," she said, although her words stuck in her throat. "If we're going to get home before them, that is."

Goliath was the first to stand. He walked over to her side with a small smile on his face and pulled her into his arms. He squeezed her waist a little too hard, and then murmured for her ears only, "We'll all be fine, Lore. We'll meet you there and you'll see. Everything will work out."

Why did he always have to make her emotional? Lore bent down so she could give him a real hug in return. And then whispered in his ear, "Let the sun rise."

He released her with a bright grin and glimmering tears in his eyes.

She took her time hugging the other two they were leaving behind. Her boys. All the men who had helped her get this far and the ones she couldn't help but adore. Even Draven.

Lore stepped away from them all and grabbed Beauty's hand. "Do you think you can hold Hyperion?"

"If he'll let me."

Lore would have preferred to hold the wiggly boy herself. He was always trying to get out and fly on their rides. But Nyx needed her a little more.

The young dragonling had gotten quite clingy while the others were around them. Lore didn't know if the tiny dragon was still afraid of what humans could do to her, or if she knew something that Lore didn't. Either way, Lore was never far from the sapphire dragon's sight.

"I'll be nearer to the cliff," Abraxas said, nodding goodbye to the men in their company. "I'll meet you all there. Give me a moment to change so you don't get blasted with sand."

"Of course," Lore replied.

And then he was gone. She had been talking about what to do moments ago, and just like that, they were leaving.

It wasn't enough time with her friends. It wasn't enough time for her to say her goodbyes and yet, here she was. Lore took a shuddering breath and leaned into Beauty as the other woman wrapped an arm around her.

"It'll be all right," Beauty said. "They're all rather capable. I'm not worried about them at all."

But Lore saw the way her gaze lingered on Zephyr. The two of them had grown closer throughout the journey, and Lore wondered just how much more there was to it. Beauty was a lovely young woman with a heart of gold and a smile that could stop an army from attacking. Zephyr had clearly fallen under her spell.

Now she wondered how deep that spell had become.

She'd ask later, she supposed. There would be plenty of time to get the story out of the young woman while they flew toward the castle.

A boom echoed across the sands. Lore glanced over to see that Abraxas had already turned into the dragon. Their time was up.

She bit her lip hard, again casting her gaze to the three men she knew would follow them, but that still stung to think of them toiling to return. "Stay safe," she ordered. "I will not allow any of you to die, and I simply cannot imagine a world without you."

"We will not die," Goliath replied with a wry grin.

Draven pressed his fist to his heart. "I'll keep them alive for you, Lady of Starlight. As the dragon calls you. I think that name might stick, you know."

It sounded strange coming out of his mouth. Less like a nickname, and more like a prayer to a goddess.

Lore stuck out her tongue. "I have no interest in making that name stick, thank you very much. Just keep them alive, Draven. All of you look out for each other. The journey back won't be easy, I'm certain of that."

She squeezed Beauty's hands, and they both gathered up a dragon baby. The two children had eaten for the first time since hatching this morning. Abraxas had skimmed the water with his mouth open and brought back ten fish for each of them. Already Nyx was at least ten pounds heavier, though she was larger than her brother.

Walking away from her companions felt as though she'd given up on them. Yes, goodbyes were said. But she wouldn't be able to help them if they needed her. No one could call out to her for help and they would be limited with what magic they could use.

"They'll be fine," Beauty said with a small chuckle. "No one will even look at them if they do it right. No one remembers that the Savior of Tenebrous traveled with a dwarf. And if they remember that, they certainly haven't heard about the human man and the Ashen Deep yet."

Rumors traveled quickly in these parts, though. Lux Brumalis could have sent out a warning to all the cities nearby, and they knew who they were looking for.

"I just hope they don't make any foolish mistakes," she muttered.

"They probably will. But they will also get out of those situations without fail." Beauty hefted Hyperion higher in her arms. "We've got the most troublesome man with us, anyway."

She supposed they did. Hyperion had taken to trying to scare everyone when they were walking about. Especially in the dark. The only one he hadn't gotten a single shout of fear out of was Draven, but he'd been born in the shadows. Hyperion would need to work a little harder if he wanted to scare a deepmonger in the darkness.

Lore walked up to Abraxas with a heavy heart. She paused by his head and patted his nose. "I know this isn't easy for you, either. We might be walking into a trap in the castle."

"I don't think Margaret would have lost so easily." Although smoke came out of his nose with the words. "If she did, then I will have to lower my opinion of the elves."

"You should have done so a long time ago," she said with a slight chuckle. "I wasn't raised by the elves, and your good opinion of me should reflect only upon the mortals in my life."

"Ah, I believe you are more of an elf than you give yourself credit for." He shifted his wing so Beauty could walk up his side. "Although I don't think anyone in the kingdom has seen someone like you, Lore. Never before."

She rolled her eyes at his romantic words, but inside her chest, a warm fire burned at his approval.

"Just keep us in the sky, would you? The last thing any of us want is to tumble out of the clouds with these two in our arms." She tossed Nyx up into the air, keeping her hands underneath the baby dragon who had already learned how to spread her wings for the air.

The dragons couldn't fly just yet. But Lore thought it was helpful to show them that they could at least float. The more time they had with the wind under their wings, the less afraid of it they would be.

"You're not still afraid of flying, are you?" Abraxas asked.

"I will never be comfortable up in the clouds, dragon. My place is here on the earth with moss under my toes and dappled light from leaves on my shoulders." But she still clambered up his back.

She was getting far too used to this, in her opinion. Walking up his side was starting to become easy.

"I see," Abraxas replied. "You are a natural at it, so I find it quite disappointing that you've yet to learn how to love it."

And if she wasn't mistaken, the two dragon babes were quick to agree with him. Although, she could only assume that by the way he laughed. Deep from his belly, like he'd heard the funniest joke.

"What did they say?" she asked.

"You don't want to know." He snorted again, then another chuckle burst out of him. "They adore you, Lore. Even if they find your fear to be unfounded."

Right. And now the dragons were ganging up on her already. Why did she feel like the odd one out?

Arranging her grip more firmly around Nyx, she sat down and squeezed Abraxas hard with her thighs. "Let's get going, dragon. The sooner we get this over with, the better."

At her words, all three dragons made sounds like laughter as Abraxas spread his wings and they rose into the sky.

CHAPTER 31

Abraxas felt a tremble of apprehension shake through his wings the moment he saw the castle. He knew Zander was no longer within those walls. He didn't have to fear what bringing the dragonlings to that building would mean for their future. The rebellion might be questionable, but they all wanted the same thing.

Freedom for magical creatures and for no mortals to touch them again.

Still, as he glided toward the dark stone building, he couldn't stop the fear. Apparently, the two women astride him felt the same way. He looked over his shoulder to see that Lore had tucked Nyx even closer to her heart and Beauty had leaned toward Lore.

He didn't fear for the dragon babes' safety as much because

he knew Lore would murder anyone who laid a finger on them. But he feared for Lore. There was only so much a single elf could do against an army of men and women who wanted to steal what wasn't theirs. Lore didn't know when to stop and admit defeat. She would fight until the last breath from her lungs left her beautiful lips.

Damn it. He should just fly them to Dracomaquia. The Umbral Kingdom could fall and the mortals would tear each other apart to become the next most important person here. Give it a hundred years and the two of them would return if she wanted to.

Lore caught his gaze and shook her head. Almost as though she could read his mind.

Though he hated it, she was right. They couldn't abandon this place. Not when it was her home, and she had done so much to fight for everyone in this kingdom. And though he could easily leave it behind and never think of it again... She couldn't.

He sighed long and low through his nose, trying his best to keep the flames in his chest from burning too hot. He was having second thoughts and knew that meant little. But he refused to take any more risks than necessary.

It wasn't a risk; he reminded himself. The dragons and his mate were under his care and they would not be out of his sight.

Ever.

Wheeling through the clouds, he approached the castle and the courtyard where they had attempted to kill the King the first time. He could still see it now. How Lore had appeared on the ramparts like some avenging angel. She'd thrust her blade into the sky with a wicked cry of battle and then...

The King's magic. That damned warlock had affected more than any of them knew. A grimdag should have cut through that spell, and maybe it did. The last time he'd seen Zander, the man looked dead after all. But the magic wouldn't let him leave this realm, and that was enough to fear.

Many people milled about the castle, some of them carrying supplies, others in the training yard preparing for whatever Margaret had summoned them for. Abraxas didn't care to know.

All of these people paused and looked up when his shadow fell upon the castle. Abraxas knew how large that shadow was, and how many of them recognized it from countless years of terror that he'd inflicted upon many. Surely some of them still felt the shiver of fear, wondering who he had been sent to kill this time.

Except, the magical creatures who had flocked to the castle lifted their arms and cheered. He heard their cries of pleasure and jubilation even this far up in the clouds. They screamed out "Dragon", but not with terror.

He'd never been greeted with happiness before. Not in his life. No crowd of people had ever called out to him like the people within the castle now did. Almost as though he were a hero in their story.

It wasn't right.

Abraxas wheeled through the air, taking his descent easy so he wouldn't make the castle shudder on its foundations when he landed. And in the time it took for three great circles to lower them down into the castle grounds, a crowd of people had poured out of the doors.

He'd never seen this many people in the Umbral Castle. The building had always been halfway empty, leaving room for the King to wander the halls whenever he wished without seeing even a single servant. Even Zander's father had wished for privacy, although that man had wanted it because of the dark magic brewing in the secret corridors.

Now, there were hundreds of people everywhere he looked. They stood on the ramparts, jumped on the steps into the castle, and hung out of the windows to see the dragon who had flown to their home. He couldn't even count how many of these creatures were revealing themselves without glamour or cloaks.

Women with flowers growing in their hair. Men with all kinds of horns, antlers, and strange beaks that wandered without fear of someone seeing them. Dwarves. Elves. Even a centaur stood at the back with his arms crossed over his chest.

Abraxas's chest filled with that damned hope again. The feeling bubbled up in his chest, and he knew it wasn't right. He shouldn't let it free when there was still so much work to be done.

But he felt like a child again. He landed in the courtyard and gazed upon countless magical creatures, and it was like when he was a young dragon. He'd come here with his mother to visit with the dragons who still lived in Umbra. Abraxas had never seen creatures other than himself, and his eyes had been filled with the wonder of their forms.

Now was the same. He had forgotten how beautiful they all were. How honored he always felt to be in their presence.

They gathered around him with their hands clasped to their chests and their eyes wide with wonder. But he was the one who stared back at them with the same expression.

They were all here. So many magical creatures.

He hated admitting Margaret was right, but she had been. Just knowing that the castle was a haven for their kind had sent out a call. And no one could change that. Not anymore.

Lore patted his side, and he shifted to let her slide down his wing. But she stayed right where she was as a massive group of people approached them. He counted at least twenty of them, all moving at a slow pace to not scare them. The crowd didn't stop until they were almost within touchable distance, however.

And then they did something that shocked him to his core.

As one, the crowd of people sank to their knees. They lowered their torsos to the ground and laid their arms out straight. As though they were meeting a living saint who had given them a blessing.

He wrinkled his brows as more of the creatures did the same. Each of them falling to their knees with their arms outstretched, some touching the ground with their foreheads.

What was this nonsense?

He was the dragon who had killed so many of their family. They should have been throwing spears at him, or at least screaming in fear. And Lore? She was the person painted to save them, and who had then abandoned them in their hour of need.

A nymph lifted her head and met his gaze. "Great dragon. You have returned to us, just as they foretold."

Excuse her? What did that mean? He knew for a fact that he wasn't in any prophecies. He'd seen enough of them to know that crimson dragons, and dragons in general, were left out of such things.

A small sound came from behind him, like the choking of an elf on his back.

The nymph turned her gaze to Lore and something akin to love stretched across her face. "Savior. We have known you would come to us soon, but we did not think it would be with such blessings. The prophets were right indeed. You have returned to save us all."

What had Margaret done in their absence? Clearly, she had filled their heads with something that she shouldn't have. But if Margaret knew of the prophecy that the elves had spoken of, then she knew that Lore was going to die.

And he wouldn't let that happen. Abraxas would gladly look the prophecy down its gullet and breathe fire until that entire future fell apart. He would fight tooth and nail against it, and his beloved would return home with him.

He watched Lore swallow hard. She'd likely come to the same conclusion that he had. With Nyx in her arms, she stood and walked down his wing. It took her a long time to stand before the crowd of people, then she held up her hand for silence.

"I am no one," she said, a breeze catching her words and throwing them up to the ramparts. "My life started as yours did. In the pits of Tenebrous, where I knew not wealth or cleanliness. Your kindness to me now is greatly appreciated, but it is unnecessary. A woman born in the depths of poverty and hatred does not know what to do with a greeting like this."

She looked at the others and he knew what they must feel. They looked upon a woman who had been named goddess in their eyes and they thought she would save them. That she could. Her kindness would only reaffirm that they were right to honor her. That she was some woman who had walked out of a prophecy who had been promised to save them all.

His sweet elf had to work harder than that to get them back on their feet.

Another elf interrupted them all, and the sound of the woman's deep voice made his skin crawl.

"Welcome home," Margaret called out. "We've been waiting for your return, Savior of Tenebrous."

Lore's spine stiffened, and she watched as the Darkveil elf approached from the stairs. Margaret also took her time, letting everyone in the courtyard see her. Abraxas was horrified by the changes he saw.

She had been ill when they left, though her flesh was not riddled with any mortal sickness. Margaret's pale skin was now lashed with dark streaks of magic. The shadows at her beck and call were eating her alive.

The long tendrils snaked through her veins and left black patterns in their wake. He could see every vein and artery in her body, standing out in stark relief against her paper white flesh.

Her arms were the most decorated by that magic. Her fingertips had turned black with the magic that tried to consume her. He'd only seen such an affliction once in his life, and it was always because the person had used too much of their own power. Creatures might not need to sacrifice to gather power, but there were limits.

She must have sent her shadows out to watch everyone in the kingdom. Zander. Their company. Her own people who were spying. And the people she wished to know more about but couldn't afford to send an actual spy.

Her need for control would be her undoing.

Lore's mouth had fallen open at the sight of the other elf. She got ahold of herself, to his admiration, and tightened her grip on Nyx. "Margaret," she called out. "You're not looking well."

"I do what I have to for this kingdom," Margaret replied. Her feet touched the courtyard and an eerie silence surrounded them. He felt as though someone had put cotton in his ears. He couldn't even hear the other creatures breathe. "We've been waiting for you to come home."

"I did what I had to," Lore replied. "And as you can see, even though you tried to stop us, we succeeded."

"I never tried to stop you from hatching those eggs. All I needed was for you to follow orders and continue down the path that would change our world." Margaret lifted her hands and grinned. "You did exactly what you were supposed to do."

Lore shook her head. "I did nothing that you ordered. We followed our own path, and that is the only reason we have three dragons instead of one."

All the sounds rushed back in as the spell Margaret had cast lost its breath. She opened her arms wide as though they hadn't spoken until this moment. "The Savior of Tenebrous has returned to us! There is so much for me to tell you. Why don't you leave your dragons with Beauty and the two of us can talk privately? You will want to know everything that has happened in your absence."

Oh, that would not happen. Abraxas shook his back, forcing Beauty to get off of him.

The change took a little longer than he'd have wanted, but that was to be expected after a tiring journey. Finally, he stood before them all as a man. Flinging his dark hair out of his eyes, he strode up beside Lore and took Nyx from her arms.

His daughter snuggled her head into the crook of his neck, as though she couldn't stand to look at Margaret any longer. He felt the same way, but he couldn't put his face into Lore's shoulder and pretend they weren't here.

"She'll go nowhere alone," he growled. A few of the magical creatures beside him startled at the depth of his voice. "We started this journey together. We will end it together."

Margaret's lips pressed into a thin line. "If you must join us, dragon, then I suppose you can. Beauty will bring the little ones to the kitchens and get them fed."

He watched as Lore reached out a hand behind her for Beauty's. And though the young woman hesitated, she eventually laced her fingers with Lore's. None of them would go anywhere without the others. Margaret would need to understand that.

He hadn't thought it possible for Margaret's mouth to compress any further, but he'd been wrong. "As you wish," she grit out between her teeth. "The lot of you may come with me, then."

The clacking of her shoes echoed across the courtyard as all the magical creatures watched them. It didn't escape his notice that a few of the more daring creatures reached out for the hem of Lore's jacket as she passed. They let the fabric trail between their fingers with feather light touches and then held the digits against their heart.

Margaret had done a number on them if they believed just touching Lore would give them some kind of power.

They followed the Darkveil elf through the halls, which had been cleaned since the last time he'd been here. The castle almost looked like itself again, although there were more decorations and paintings on the wall. It was befitting a royal family, although he knew Margaret would be livid to hear him say such a thing.

She led them to the farthest part of the castle where the King's chambers had once been, then opened the door to reveal the massive room beyond. A giant table stood at the ready in the center of the room.

This was just as he remembered. And Abraxas had the strange feeling that they were back in time, somehow. Back to the moment when they had walked into this room and Margaret had claimed she didn't care about the dragon child in his arms.

That horrible creature who had not cared for his family at all walked around the table and then braced herself at the head. Her magic swelled again. Shadows stretched above them until they were cocooned in a ball of complete and utter silence.

She took a deep breath, let it out, and then let fly the words which erupted in his skull as though she had struck him over the head.

"The King has sent word that he will not rest until the throne is his once more. He doesn't want a battle this time. He is building an army to destroy everyone in this castle and will send out that army to murder every man, woman, and child with magic in their blood. If we do not relent the castle to him, then he will attack."

"When?" Abraxas asked.

"We don't know. Soon." Margaret shrugged. "There is only a short amount of time to plan before we lose everything."

CHAPTER 32

Lore had a hard time believing anything Margaret said, but she could see the exhaustion in the other woman's features. They'd fought for so long to get to this moment, and Margaret believed they could lose it if they weren't careful.

The King wasn't that wily. He knew that all he had to do was bide his time and he would find his opening. He could take back the throne if he wanted it.

"So he built an army when he disappeared?" she muttered. "And here we were, foolishly thinking he was trying to heal himself."

Margaret nodded. "We thought the grimdag would do enough damage to slow him and the curse which has given his family power for so many years. We were wrong. His curse is much stronger than we imagined."

She looked over at Abraxas, meeting his worried gaze with one of her own. "If we return to the warlock, do you think he could break that curse as well?"

Her dragon shook his head. "He used all his magic to break the curse on the box. He is but a man now, and I do not think he could gather enough power in such a short amount of time. It would take many lives to bring him back to what he once was."

Lore knew he was right, but that couldn't be their only option. They needed to take the King down once and for all. She couldn't think of any other choices. She was exhausted from travel and her lungs ached from panting as she battled her own fear of heights.

There were only so many options to beat a man who avoided death like the King.

Margaret sank down into her chair at the table and pressed her fingers to her lips. "You found the warlock?"

"We did."

"And you used what limited magic he had left to open that box?" She kept her fingers against her lips as though she were holding back the words she wanted to say. "Knowing that we might need his magic to fight against the King, you still selfishly opened that box rather than choosing the kingdom?"

"Selfishly?" Lore flung out her arm, knowing what would happen next.

Abraxas's chest pressed against her hand, just as she knew it would. He wanted to fling himself upon the elf and pull her head from her shoulders. He had every right to be angry. Their entire mission had always been to free the dragon children that were kept locked away by that evil man who had no right to their lives. For Margaret to imply that they had doomed the kingdom by making a selfish choice like the one they had made... that was cruel.

"I wouldn't change what we did," Lore said. "I know that it was the right choice to free the children from the box with the remaining power that the warlock still had to his name. He couldn't have hurt a fly when we met with him, Margaret. I don't think he had enough power to stop the King, even if he wanted to."

Her gut said that the warlock wouldn't have helped them if they asked him to kill Zander. She was quite certain he would have disappeared. Faster than they could have followed him. He wouldn't have said a word. Just disappeared and left them to their own devices without any explanation at all.

"We have to fight with what we have," Lore said. "And if you think he's going to attack soon, then we need to prepare the army we must have by now."

Margaret remained suspiciously silent.

Lore knew this could only mean there was more bad news, and she couldn't handle that without a little sleep. If they didn't have an army, then this would get very difficult, very fast. What had Margaret been doing while they were gone?

"We have an army to fight him with, don't we?" she asked.

Again, there was silence.

Lore screwed up her face in a long wince, then counted to ten. "Do you mean to tell me that after all this time, you have put all your effort into spying on people? You've brought countless magical creatures to the castle under the pretense that I would take care of them. You've built up an image of who I am and who my companions are with your own intent to control the population of Umbra. And in doing all that, you have failed to provide us with any warriors to fight?"

At least that forced Margaret to talk. "We have some fighters. But in case you hadn't noticed, the magical creatures of Umbra have been beaten down into nothing that looks like what we used to be."

"I have seen them." Anger made her words harsher than she intended. "I have walked through much of this kingdom. I have met the true denizens of countless capitals. So please, do not try to tell me that I don't know my own people."

"Then you should know already that they are not fighters. We do not have many people who are even willing to fight, let alone those who have ever picked up a sword." Margaret let her hands drop onto the table with a thud. "Zander might not have killed all of us off, but he did do one thing right. He took the spirit of our people and crushed it beneath his heel."

Lore couldn't believe the words that Margaret was saying. There were plenty of creatures who wanted to fight. That was how the rebellion had been born, after all. Her mother had regaled her with stories about generals who were just waiting for the right moment to strike. Creatures who wanted to battle and who knew how to bring about a new age.

Was all of that a lie? Had her mother been dreaming of a time that had already passed?

Lore didn't have to ask that question because of course her mother had been a dreamer. Of course those words were from a time that would never see the light of day again.

"How many?" Lore asked, swallowing her anxiety. "How many people can fight for us?"

"Two hundred." Margaret replied.

It wasn't a small number. That sounded good.

"And how many do you estimate the King will arrive with? I don't know the limitations of the Umbral Knights."

"Neither do we."

Abraxas cleared his throat, and they all turned their attention to him. "There is no limitation to how many Umbral Knights he can make. The smoke is a summoning spell, essentially. As long as there are shadows in this world, he can manipulate them to do his bidding."

Right, of course, there had to be another wrench in their plan. Lore pinched the bridge of her nose. "So, how many do you think he'll arrive with?"

He didn't reply immediately. Not until she dropped her hand and looked him in the eyes.

"Thousands," Abraxas said. "He will take no chances. There will be thousands."

She needed to sit down.

Lore groped for a chair and lowered herself into it. All of their options were disappearing out of her reach. She didn't know how to save everyone when they barely had anyone to fight for them. If the King could make the shadow monsters as long as there were shadows, then she couldn't stop him from making more and more soldiers until they were overwhelmed.

"They will keep us in the castle," she muttered. "That will be their goal. The longer we are stuck inside these walls, the better. They will wait until we starve."

"That is most likely his plan," Margaret replied. "He knows we're here and now he also has an infinite amount of time to wait. Death will not come for him. Therefore, he will exist until we no longer do. Or until some of us die without ever having to fight."

"He must know we will fight back before we allow ourselves to be trapped in such a way."

"I'm certain he does. That is part of his plan." Margaret flung a letter across the table. The handwriting was perfect, the marks of a man who'd been taught to write by the best in the realm.

The looping words swam before her eyes. Lore didn't have to read the words to know that they were filled with venom.

"So he warned you," she muttered.

"He wrote a letter that was delivered by one of my old spies. I killed the man for working with the King, of course. But he wouldn't have sent me a warning if he didn't want to fight. I know the King is egotistical, but even he wouldn't warn us of his plan without being assured he would win." She hissed out a feral sound. "And now we are to be ruined."

Lore tried her best to think of a plan. She ran through every option in her head, but none of them seemed to stick.

Until one of Margaret's shadowy tendrils touched her shoulder. And then Lore knew what to do.

Her eyes snapped up, meeting Abraxas's gaze with a fire burning in hers. "You said as long as there are shadows, the King will continue making the Umbral Knights."

"That was my understanding of the curse, yes. He uses the darkness to his advantage." Abraxas furrowed his brows. "What did you think up in that devious head of yours?"

"What if we don't let him have access to the shadows?" Frantically, Lore flipped the letter over and gestured for a quill. "Give me something to draw with. I need to show you all. I think this might work."

Margaret burst into movement and thrust a feathered quill into her hand, along with a pot of ink.

Lore bent over the page and sketched her battle plan. "We have enough magical creatures here that we should be able to cast a spell. Enough of us can call on the elements, and most of us know how to make at least a ball of light. The more we have, the brighter it is, the more likely we can kill the Knights before he can make more. Destroy them without ever having to deal with others."

It was a good plan. Better than any Margaret had come up with.

Abraxas set the baby dragon down onto the floor and leaned over Lore's shoulder to look down at her sketch. "And when the night comes? He'll make a thousand more and they'll advance, then. He won't give us a second chance."

"We won't need one. We'll fight like we have no idea how the Knights work. Retreat to the castle, and then that morning is when our actual job begins." She tapped the outline of the castle walls. "Archers here, with spells over their eyes so they can see through the light. Burn everyone and everything to the ground the moment the spells flare into life. Kill every last one of them and then it'll only be Zander left standing."

"We have archers," Beauty said. "I recognized a few from Tenebrous."

Margaret tapped her fingernails on the table. "And just how are we going to kill the King?"

She had no idea. It didn't appear that the King could die, and that would be the tricky part. "For now, we trap him. Capture him in whatever spell we can come up with. He's battled before and maybe he learned something from his nightmare of a father. But he's never fought magical creatures before. I think we can back him into a corner and keep him there until we figure out what to do with him."

And in the meantime, she intended to use the warlock's old library here to figure out how to do just that. Lore knew there were ways to break any spell or curse. If the warlock wasn't here to do it, then she damned well would.

Leaning back in the chair, she absentmindedly reached for Nyx. The tiny dragon coiled around her legs and pressed her sides against Lore. Somehow, the movement was more comforting than hugging the little one.

She wasn't alone anymore. It wasn't even just her and Abraxas. They had created a family here. One that would fight tooth and claw to take care of each other, no matter what. This was what Lore had always been missing in her life.

Hyperion struggled in Beauty's arms until the mortal had to let him go. He raced across the floor and hopped up into her lap, planting his clawed wings on the table and staring down at the paper as though he'd be fighting with them. At the same time, Abraxas put his hand on Lore's shoulder.

Her family. A proper family, perhaps not quite tied together by blood but no less close. These were the people she fought for and she would not fail. She couldn't.

Margaret eyed them all with no small amount of disgust. "I suppose it is the only plan we have, although I will say I think it's taking far too many risks. I will speak with the others and find those who are natural spellcasters. You can deal with them, if you wish."

"I'd prefer it. We must all use the same spell if we want this to work."

"Lore." Margaret looked her up and down as though there was something missing. "You have become something far beyond your knowledge while you were out traveling the kingdom. The people have an expectation of who and what you are. If you do not live up to that expectation, I'm afraid they will be sorely disappointed."

"I couldn't care less," Lore replied without even thinking about it.

She stood up from the table, her arms wrapped around Hyperion. "You have created an image of me for these people to cling to when they are afraid. I'll admit, it's a good plan. But meeting your hero sometimes proves that they aren't the fictional version of themselves. It's all right for them to meet the real me. They might like this version better."

She had nothing else to say to Margaret. They were all tired, and they all needed rest. More talk of battle and the end of the world would come, and likely for many days yet.

Abraxas eyed her, clearly having something he wanted to say but not knowing when was a good time. Even Beauty looked at her, startled that she'd cut Margaret off when they had only just gotten here.

Walking to the door with her arms full of dragon and another baby tromping along behind her, Lore turned around at the last second. "Margaret, I will join you tomorrow morning here to talk about our plan more. You'll have to have the spellcasters ready by then for us all to align on what spell will work best. There is more to talk about, I am sure."

"There is," Margaret snarled.

"Then we will talk about it tomorrow. For now, my family and I need to rest. It's been a long journey to get here, and none of us will brew up a good plan without sleep. I advise you to get some yourself." She pointedly looked at Margaret's arms. "Sometimes the cost is too great, Margaret. Even you should not give up your entire being for a kingdom. You will serve them better while you are healthy and well."

"I will serve them as I see fit."

Lore knew she wouldn't get anywhere like this. Arguing with Margaret was like beating her head against a brick wall.

Still, she couldn't help but land one last strike. "Then I'm sure you can understand that I also will serve them in the way I wish to. And perhaps that will not be the same way as you."

Lore turned on her heel and left Margaret fuming behind her.

CHAPTER 33

They stood outside in the hallway, his two children and the woman he loved, all staring at each other as though they didn't know what to do next. Eventually, their eyes turned to him. And he knew they were expecting him to do something about this.

He was the one with the ideas.

Abraxas opened his mouth to let something spew out, only to pause when the door opened behind them. Beauty walked out of the room where they had left Margaret and closed the door behind her, obviously trying her best to not make any noise.

She pressed a finger to her lips and gestured for them to move further down the hall. He didn't hesitate to do so. They all moved as one, as they were rather used to at this point, before stopping when

Beauty waved her hand.

"Sorry," she muttered, "I didn't know if Margaret would listen at the door or not."

Lorelei rolled her eyes. "Her shadows hear everything, anyway. I don't believe it's worth trying to hide from her without powerful magic of our own."

"Well, I don't care if she hears what I have to say. I just wish she would get some sleep." Beauty's words were almost a snarl impressive enough to live up to that of a dragon. "But she needs to understand that everyone could use some rest. We're all trying to do what's right."

He disagreed with her. Abraxas crossed his arms over his chest and leveled her with a look. He didn't need to speak to let her know that he didn't believe that nonsense.

Beauty flapped her hand at him. "I chased after you to ask if the two of you would like some time alone together. I know the thought of letting me take the dragons away from you is probably terrifying, but we'll just be in a room right next to you."

That was... kind of her. Abraxas wouldn't mind having an evening with Lore to himself. But would she be willing to let them go?

To his shock, Lore deposited Hyperion into Beauty's arms. "Good luck," she said. "They're an armful. Literally and figuratively."

"I can imagine." But Beauty looked down at them with no small amount of love in her eyes. Nyx even wandered over to the side of her leg and leaned against it hard, blinking up at Abraxas while looking more tired than he'd seen her in a while.

He forgot how young they were sometimes. They carried themselves like adult dragons, so it felt natural to treat them as such. But soon they would be grown and he would miss treating them like children.

He patted the top of Hyperion's head, smoothing his fingers underneath the tiny dragon's jaw. "You be good to her," he said. "She's our friend."

The dragon child wouldn't be good. Hyperion's eyes had already narrowed with the possibilities of mischief he could get into with an entire castle at his beck and call. Of course, the boy would have to get around Beauty first. And though she might look sweet as pie, Abraxas knew how fierce she could be.

If anyone could give the dragon children a difficult time, it was her.

He leaned down and patted Nyx as well. "I know you'll be good."

But she'd absorbed memories and was hardly the child she should be. Nyx had already taken on too much responsibility for her age, even though he'd known that would be their path. He mourned that they couldn't be children for long.

Lorelei shifted closer to him and wrapped her arm around his waist. "Come on," she whispered. "We could use a few hours of uninterrupted sleep."

To the normal person listening, they would assume she was innocently suggesting they get some rest. Even Beauty's face softened with pity as she looked at the two of them. But Abraxas's ears were keener.

A few hours.

They had more than a few hours of time if they were going to rest the entire night. And a few hours of sleep suggested she had other things in mind.

He told himself that she wasn't in any state to be looking for a few moments like they'd had in the stream. But it felt like forever ago since they'd been allowed to forget the world in each other's arms. He'd done the right thing. He'd followed her here and ignored his baser instincts.

A bed would be lovely, though. To be able to enjoy her knowing that she was comfortable and not fearing that he'd see a spider crawling in her hair. She deserved to lay in down feathers and not be thrown on her back in the wilds.

So he tucked her closer to his side, nodded at Beauty, and drew Lore down the hall toward what used to be her private quarters. He hoped they still were.

Beauty's voice trailed in the opposite direction. "Why don't we get the two of you something to eat? There's plenty of food in the kitchens, and I'm sure there will be quite a few people who would be happy to fill those empty bellies."

She had no idea what she was getting herself into. Those dragonlings would eat until they were gorged, and then they would do it again in the morning. Except they'd almost be twice their size in the morning if they continued feeding them at that rate.

He didn't mind. They would need all the weight they could get on their bones before Zander came here.

Lore let her weight sag against his side and he tucked her even closer against him. It felt right to hold her like this. Against his chest where she should always be.

They soon were staggering down the hall, so close to each other that they kept missing a step and then laughing as they stumbled to the side. Briefly, he wondered if she was trying to trip him. But then she hooked her leg under his, and he had no more questions about if that were her plan. Ridiculous woman, but oh, how he loved her for making him laugh.

He approached her room with a single thought in his mind. The time for talking had ended. Right now, he wanted to enjoy the woman he loved in every way possible.

Except, he couldn't just yet.

Lore came to a sudden standstill outside her room. There were posters all over her walls. Some were paintings, other screen printings that likely were all over the kingdom now.

Paintings of her.

Next to some of the posters were letters, hastily scribbled and messily written, but he could see what they were. Letters to Lore. Asking her to look over their children, brothers, friends. The closer he looked, the more of those letters he saw. Countless numbers of them, each one detailing why they needed help and if she would but cast her gaze upon the situation, perhaps it would change.

These were not letters written to a woman wandering the wilds. They were prayers to a goddess or a saint, hoping a divine energy would rain down from the sky.

"What madness is this?" Lore whispered. She gestured with her hand at all the papers that covered the wall and stretched down the hallways. "What did they think writing these would do? I'm not here to see them. And even if I were, I can't... I can't help everyone."

What did he say to that? Abraxas had never been in this position either. For all that she had been labeled as a saint, he was there with her on almost all the posters. A figure in silhouette behind her, or the beast she rode like a valiant steed into battle. He was never depicted far from her side. Like a weapon.

He swallowed hard. "I don't know what this is. I assume this eases their minds to think..."

"That I am some ancient goddess who came to life and was brought here only to save them?" Her hand scrabbled against the wall, searching for the door handle. "This is ridiculous. Margaret has told them so many lies that I can never live up to! What did she think would happen? Of course, the magical creatures are searching for someone to lean on. Someone they can say is more powerful than anyone they've met before."

"Are you not?" He knew it was the wrong thing to say, but it was the truth.

Lore froze where she was, hand still pressed against the wall.

He stepped closer and put his hand beside hers. The letter they both touched was written by a child. The little one asked Lore to look out for her father, who had come to the castle to fight with the rebellion. She wanted him to come home. She was afraid he wouldn't.

Lore's hand trembled. "I am not who they think I am."

"You are the only woman who not only tried to stop the King," he paused at the sound she made, "I know you were coerced into it, but you still did it. You were the only one to attempt to hatch dragon eggs after centuries. You have walked all over this kingdom to help me and I don't think there is another who would so willingly do so. Perhaps you are not a saint or a goddess, but you are special, Lore. At least to me."

"I was happy, you know," she whispered. "I might not have been pleased with my life. But I had elfweed and friends and quiet. I wouldn't mind going back to that and giving all of this up."

He leaned down and pressed a kiss to her shoulder. "And what about me?"

"You'd like elfweed, too," she replied with a small chuckle. "You'd have to get used to it, most people do, but then I think you'd be very pleased with how relaxed you'd feel."

Now, that was just ridiculous. He'd smoked elfweed before, but she didn't need to know that.

Abraxas found the door handle and turned it. So many posters and letters had been stuck to the wall with what he suspected was wallpaper paste. He had to wrench it open with a foolish amount of strength before the door would actually open. Only then did they get a glimpse of the inside of her bedroom.

It looked much the same. Bland. Vacant of any personality at all. Covered in a fine layer of dust.

Lore stepped inside and let out a soft snort. "Oh, of course. Margaret has no problem letting people put letters and posters of me all over the wall, but elves forbid that anyone come in to clean the place."

"We've slept in worse conditions." A little dust might make them sneeze, but he didn't mind.

Abraxas closed the door behind them, then stepped up behind her. He framed her hips with his large palms and tugged her back against his chest. Breathing in the wild-worn scent of her hair, he released her so he could trail his fingers down the backs of her arms.

"I've been fighting with the same thought since we came back," she said, her voice deep with emotion. "I thought they were all mad because they believed me to be someone I am not. But I think I have to come to terms with the realization that I might be her."

"Who?" he asked, his fingers curving around her wrists.

"The prophecy is about me, isn't it?" She shook in his grip, allowing him to lift one of her hands up into the air. "The elven prophecy you didn't want me to see. I found it in the Hall of Heroes, and Draven informed me that his mother thought I was the half elf it depicted. She who is destined to destroy the world and herself in the process, but brings about a new age."

His heart hurt for her. He should have been the one to tell her, not some callous young elf who thought it was an honor to die for their people.

Abraxas took his time, pressing her other hand to her hip with his fingers over hers. The other hand he held aloft as he swayed their bodies from side to side. "And if you are her?"

"I don't want to die. I don't think I'm ready to see what happens after." She clearly chose her words carefully, although some of the tension eased out of her as she said them. "That's what it says. That the woman who would do all that is going to die. So I don't want to be her."

"I won't let you die," he murmured against her shoulder. He pressed a kiss there, then another against her neck. "I told you long ago, Lorelei of Silverfell. If you die, then I will burn this entire kingdom to the ground. Umbra will become a graveyard and a shrine to the woman the last dragon loved."

"I wouldn't want that."

"I didn't ask what you'd want." He spun them in a sweeping step, as though they were dancing across the room. "You are my heart, Lore. I have no fear of what comes after life for me, but for you? I would follow you across the stars to find an ounce of your soul."

"And yet, now you have children." She turned in his arms in a graceful swirl, then stepped back into him. "They need you. If this prophecy is true and I am to die soon, then you have to promise me to keep them safe."

This was not the conversation he wanted to have. Anger burst to life in his chest at the mere thought that she would ask him to choose between following her into the afterlife and taking care of his children. The choice was too difficult. It hurt his heart to even think.

Abraxas released her hands and instead cupped her jaw. His hands were larger than her head, so he held her with a powerful strength. "You will live for me, Lady of Starlight. Brave Heart. You are the source of my madness, my torment. May all the gods have mercy on your enemies because I will unleash a fire upon them that will burn their souls for daring to touch you."

He felt her swallow against his wrists. Her wide eyes filled with tears and he hoped that was because she felt his honesty and not that he'd frightened her.

Lore lifted her hands and gripped his wrists. "My fierce dragon," she whispered. "The world would not be the same without you."

Abraxas pulled her forward so he could press their foreheads together. "Let us finish with this talk. Tomorrow we can worry and plan. But tonight, let me love you as a dragon should love his mate."

"I am yours," she said as he pushed her back toward the bed. "For now and all eternity."

"You are my light in the darkness," he replied. Abraxas resolved himself to kiss every inch of her. "My Lady of Starlight. You rival the moon."

For all she didn't want to be treated like a goddess, he intended to treat her as one tonight.

CHAPTER 34

Lore was unsurprised to find that Margaret had done nothing that Lore suggested. In fact, she couldn't find the rebellion leader for the next two days. Even though they needed to figure out what their next steps were. She had planned to talk with the spellcasters as a group, not to search for individuals throughout the entire castle.

Abraxas had decided to split up, so they could try to find out more information about individuals who knew how to cast a spell. There were a lot fewer than she'd expected. And every night, they curled up in each other's arms while they tried to forget what was coming for them.

She now stood in the Great Hall, where so many memories swirled around her like mist. Walking in here for the first time while the King himself sat on the throne. The countless beautiful women who surrounded her. The attack that had shattered the glass ceiling. Abraxas holding her while the Umbral Knights tried to take her from him. And even her last memory of standing in a cold throne room with wind whistling in her ears as she knew the kingdom had fallen.

Someone had put the glass ceiling back up. The throne was gone, instead there was only an empty podium where Margaret likely spoke with her generals when she needed to. Or perhaps they never used this room at all. They might have pieced it back together to leave it alone.

The doors opened behind her, and she had a thought that maybe Abraxas had found her. They'd planned to see the dragon babes before they had lunch. The children were well entertained by Beauty, who had insisted on keeping them with her so they could focus on the task at hand.

Maybe Margaret had asked her to do that.

"I'm not quite ready for lunch," Lore said. "But I'll join you in a moment."

"Oh." The light voice was not the gruff one she'd expected. "My apologies, Savior, I heard you were looking for spellcasters."

Lore whipped around in shock, to stare at a rather meek looking young woman. She had a tangle of ivy through her green hair and a dusted pattern of gold over her cheekbones, collarbone, and shoulders. Not an elf, at least not one that Lore knew about.

"I'm a lamia," the woman added, her eyes casting downward as though it were a disgrace to admit.

Not glitter, then. Scales.

Lore tucked her hands into the pockets of her pants. "You are right. I have been looking for people who are adept at spell casting. I didn't know any of the lamia were magically inclined."

"Some of us are." The young woman tucked a strand of hair behind her ear, and Lore noticed someone had woven the ivy through her dark braid. "My name is Thalia."

"It's nice to meet you." Lore almost introduced herself as well, but it was clear the other one already knew who she was. "I have a very specific spell I'm hoping to find people to help me with."

"Light casting. Correct?"

"Yes. I have a theory we might beat the Umbral Knights if we can cast out the darkness for long enough to wipe them out." She took another step toward the woman. "Do you think you could help with that?"

Thalia cleared her throat, eyes still downcast. "I think so. There are a few of my friends who could help as well. We aren't witches, though."

Ugh, she hated the thought. Another creature had said the same thing to her, as though witches were the only ones who knew how to use magic.

Lore put her finger underneath the other woman's chin and lifted her face. Slitted eyes met hers, like a snake. "Witches steal magic. We have power inside us that we don't steal. It comes from deep inside our souls because we are born to wield it. You are more powerful than any witch or warlock would lead you to believe."

Thalia's eyes widened with every word until she swallowed hard at the end. "Do you really believe that?"

"I know it to be true." Lore dropped her hand and stepped away. "If I could get more magical creatures to believe that, then I think this world would be a very different place. We are not weak, Thalia. We never have been. No matter how many mortals try to tell us that we are."

And now she sounded like some figure out of a prophecy. Lore wasn't a saint who had descended from the old gods, though. She was just a tired woman who had become overwhelmed by so much sorrow. She'd chosen to fight when so many others had chosen to become what the mortals said they were.

Thalia looked directly at her now. Perhaps Lore forcing her to reveal her eyes had shown the other woman that Lore wouldn't flinch away from her like she was a monster. Either way, Lore was pleased to see that she'd given up trying to hide who she was.

"Some of us came here to fight for you," Thalia said. "Not all. I'd argue most people only came for sanctuary. But when I heard about what you had done to the King, I knew in my soul that you would need help to continue your work."

That made it sound like Lore was fighting for the entire kingdom when she'd just been trying to save her own neck. Still, this was what she'd been hoping for, in a way. Lore couldn't afford to drive away this lamia when she had a connection to all the people who had joined the rebellion ready for a fight.

"Where are they?" she asked. "Or I suppose I should know who they are."

"They're in the training yards." Thalia suddenly glowed with energy, as though talking about this was what she'd hoped for. "We can find them there, if you'd like to see them all. I know it's not much, but we have been training for a while now."

Lore was no general, but she knew how important it was to have someone's approval. Battles were won with heart and determination, not just skill.

"Lead the way," she said, nodding at Thalia.

They walked through the castle with surprising speed. She didn't have time to stop for any of the others who tried to get her attention, and for that, Lore was grateful. She felt like she'd talked to the entire castle about their woes and trials, but she had probably only talked with a fraction of all the people packed into these walls.

"If you'll come this way." Thalia gestured toward a side door that had once led to the servants' quarters.

Lore nodded her head and trailed her through the kitchens, out the back, and into the open air. She filled her lungs with the scent of summer. The grass, the leaves, even the hay that they brought for the horses in the stable. The air was so clean here compared to Tenebrous.

"Savior?" Thalia asked, noticing that Lore had stopped.

"Do you ever notice how easy it is to breathe away from the city?" She could only guess Thalia had grown up in Tenebrous as well.

The lamia's eyes widened, but then she took a deep breath as well. "I suppose you're right."

Lore let her eyes drift shut and tilted her face to the sun. "You never get used to your lungs not having to fight for air. I remember waking up and losing my voice because of all the moisture and dampness. My neighbor lost her child to a cough. The little boy couldn't breathe in Tenebrous. When I came here, I took it for granted that these people got to breathe without having to fight for it. And then I realized most people didn't have to fight for air."

"We did," Thalia said.

"We did," Lore repeated as she opened her eyes. "I don't want any other children to die from a cough because the air is too wet."

The lamia reached out her hand for Lore to take. "Neither do I."

Together, they approached the training yards where so many people were already training. There were countless individuals there, each section with a unique weapon in their hands. Swordsmen. Archers. Even a few areas where people appeared to be fighting up close with knives. She also saw quite a few people with pikes in their hands, and she hadn't seen those weapons in a very long time.

"Huh," Lore said. "I didn't think there would be so many here. Margaret made it sound as if we were in dire straits."

"Well, we don't have thousands like the King will have. But we have a lot of fighters who are more than ready to battle on your behalf." Thalia bowed low and released her hold on Lore's hand. "I will find the other spellcasters. In the meantime, perhaps you would like to survey your army?"

"My army?" she repeated, but the other woman had already walked away.

This wasn't Lore's army. This was the rebellion's army, or perhaps one for magical creatures alone. She refused to take any ownership over all the lives here. Lore didn't know the first thing about planning a war.

If they insisted she lead them, then she would bring them to their doom.

Lore pulled at her shirt to ease the sudden heat that blossomed over her body. Then she meandered over to the area where people were fighting with swords. She assumed Beauty might be among them. The young woman had proven herself very good with a broadsword and could show some magical creatures how to do the same. They were of similar strength, she supposed.

Except all the breath wheezed out of her lungs when she found who was training the other magical creatures.

Abraxas stood in the center of the ring with a crowd of people around him. He'd taken off his shirt and all that broad expanse of muscle glistened with sweat. His hair was pulled back from his face with a tie, revealing his sharp and angular features. Every muscle in his body twitched as he walked in a circle around the other man in the ring.

This creature was almost as tall as Abraxas. His skin had a faint green tinge to it, suggesting some orcish blood in him. Then, once Lore could see his face, she had no question of his upbringing. The twin tusks that curved up from his bottom jaw were quite obvious.

Abraxas shouldn't try to fight an orc. Not alone, at least. Their kind were particularly outstanding fighters and were strong enough to snap a tree in half.

Though her lover was a dragon. This would be an interesting fight.

Lore leaned against the fencing that separated the fighting pit and watched with interest. The orc leapt for Abraxas, wildly swinging the sword in his hand. That wouldn't do, however. Abraxas knew how to dodge and he did exactly as she'd expected. He shifted two steps to the right, and the orc missed him. Then Abraxas brought the hilt of his sword down on the other man's back and sent him face down into the dirt.

The orc grew angry, as Abraxas must have assumed he would. Spitting earth out of his mouth, the enraged creature spun with a snarl. He lunged again, this time forgetting there was even a sword in his hand. Abraxas side stepped again, though this time he swatted the orc's behind with the flat part of his sword.

"You claimed to be the best fighter the rebellion has," Abraxas called out. "And yet you are easier to fight than a child. This is what we're throwing at the King's armies? We're going to lose."

The orc shook his head in anger, like some kind of angry bull. He would run at Abraxas again, and he would continue to be thrown face first or ass first onto the ground until he was littered with bruises.

This was not how to train people to fight. Frustrating his students would only make them less interested in learning.

Lore ducked underneath the railing and ignored the startled gasps from people around her. She kept her focus on the men who were ready to tear each other apart if she didn't stop them. The orc had lost his senses. Apparently so had Abraxas. The two of them would grapple with each other and end up in a tangled mess on the ground.

Like a breeze of wind, she slid in between the two of them and stood with her arms over her chest. The orc ran at her. He likely hadn't noticed the obstacle between himself and his prey. She felt Abraxas rushing forward as well. He wouldn't want the orc to touch her at all and if he did, they all would be in trouble.

But Lore wanted them all to learn that they needed to stop fighting like mortal men. She let the orc run so close that he nearly touched her when her shield went up. As it was, the orc struck her shield hard enough to startle himself. He stumbled back, shaking his head in confusion because he hadn't hit the dragon. Then he noticed her and his face turned a lighter shade of olive.

"Lady," he breathed, then fell to a knee in front of her. "My apologies."

The heat from Abraxas's chest burned her spine. She'd known he was there, so close that he'd almost connected himself to her as her shadow.

"You don't need to apologize," she replied. "You need to learn how to fight as you are. You could not get through my shield with your fists if you tried."

The orc looked up at her with wide eyes. "What?"

"Hit the shield, orc. Hit it with all your might and see if you can break it." She let her gaze roll over the crowd that had gathered more watchers in the moments that she'd moved. "We are not mortal men. We do not fight as they fight."

The silence in the training yards was deafening.

"I have disappointed you." The orc dropped his head again, pressing a fist into the dirt. "I accept your punishment as you see fit."

What had Margaret done to these people?

She let her shield down and placed her hand on the orc's shoulder. "You did not disappoint me. If you had picked up something heavier and used it to beat against the shield, you would have broken it. You think like a mortal man, and that's all right. We will teach you to fight like magical creatures, so that none may defeat you."

The orc nodded and left the circle. She wondered if he would treat his wounds or if her words hadn't quite gotten through that thick skull of his.

Though she had a bigger concern. The heat at her back had yet to move.

"That was a rather foolish bid for attention," Abraxas muttered against the back of her neck. "You seem to believe you are indestructible."

"I do not believe that at all, but I know my own abilities." She smiled. "Unless you want to fight me, dragon. We've never tried. Not really."

"Are you trying to goad me into making a show for these people?"

"Oh, it's already a show, darling." Lore spun and hit him hard on the chest with another spell similar to a shield.

The magic sent him sliding away from her, although somehow he kept his footing. Abraxas tilted his head to the side, unimpressed by her attempt at magic. Then he held his sword aloft.

She had no time to think. He came at her like a storm. The sword moved too fast for even her eyes to track, but that didn't matter. She threw up shield after shield with every step, her skin glowing with magic. The white light radiated from her body, reflecting the very sun itself in his eyes. And still he moved.

Lore shifted tactics. She took a knee on the ground and threw up a shield, then traced a line of runes into the ground. Abraxas lifted the sword over his head, and she stared up at a wall of muscle and strength. His arms quivering in the split second before he brought the sword down hard on her shield. His biceps flexed, his chest muscles stood out in stark relief, and her shield cracked.

His sword bounced away, but he controlled it in a moment and whipped it around until the tip pointed at her throat. "Yield," he said, breathing hard.

"No." She smiled and tapped her finger against the dirt. "You yield."

He looked down and smirked as he realized she hadn't quite finished the spell surrounding him. She could have. It would have caused all the water in his body to boil. Though it had taken her time, technically, she would have killed him before he killed her.

Abraxas lowered his blade with a smile. "You used your own magic. Eventually, that would run out."

"But someone else would come to assist before I ran out of power." She stood and brushed her hands off on her pants. "I believe we can say that I won."

"We'll call it a draw. I went easy on you."

The crowd clapped, and Lore took the moment to notice that there were very significant details in the way he fought. "You trained Zander, didn't you?" she asked.

"I did."

"I want you to teach me, then. Everything you know." She refused to let the shiver of fear wriggle underneath her bravado. "I intend to fight him again before all this is done. This time, I will beat him."

CHAPTER 35

If someone had asked Lore how she planned on beating the King, she wouldn't have answered... this.

She sat in front of a fireplace with two dragon babies running around her. Hyperion was dead set on catching Nyx's tail, something he apparently thought would be fun to chomp on. And Nyx was very much not interested in that option. She raced around Lore like the elf was a physical barrier between herself and the little dragon boy who had become the bane of poor Nyx's existence.

Abraxas sat on the other side of their rug, far enough away to not be involved in the chaos. He stared into the fire with a pensive expression on his face and a glass of wine in his hand.

She wondered if he could even feel the alcohol. Margaret hadn't gotten any of the good stuff from Tenebrous. Elves knew how to brew decent wine, but the dwarves were the only ones who had mastered getting magical creatures drunk.

She imagined it would take a lot of alcohol for a dragon to feel any of it. Still, he sipped at it while watching the flames dance.

"We spent the better part of the day fighting each other," she said with a soft chuckle. Hopefully, the newer memories would pull him out of the past. "And here I was thinking what you had taught him would be groundbreaking and new."

"He was adept at it," Abraxas replied. "I remember being surprised myself. But Zander never flinched away from cheating in a fight. Honor meant nothing to him. Therefore, he could beat most anyone in a fight. I know very few warriors who would throw dirt in someone's eyes to prove a point."

"Or to stick a dagger between their ribs," she muttered.

Lore remembered how Zander fought. He didn't care about kicking a person when they were down. Her ribs had broken at the first strike of his boots, and still, he hadn't stopped. He only wanted others to feel pain, and that was not the honorable way a man should fight.

Clearing her throat, she tried a different subject. "When you taught him how to fight, was his father still alive? I would have imagined that his father wanted to teach his son."

Abraxas shook his head. "The previous king had lived longer than he should have. Magic extended his life. Zander's life will be the same. The first king thought he was untouchable and thus his son would also become so. When Zander got his first bruise, his father beat him for hours to prove a point."

Lore winced. "And what was that point?"

"The true son of the king didn't bruise," Abraxas muttered. "So he would give Zander a hundred bruises until the boy learned how to stop the bruises from coming."

She refused to feel bad for him. That man might have had a horrible upbringing with a nasty father who only wanted him to feel pain, but that didn't justify what the King had done to her people.

Hyperion clambered over her legs, hissing with anger and his belly full of brightly colored fire. She needed to focus, and the children were not giving her the opportunity to do so.

Lore grabbed onto Nyx the second time she ran around and then used her foot to keep Hyperion away from them. "Stop it, you two. We're trying to figure out the best option for war here."

Hyperion sat down hard on his bottom and stared at her with an unimpressed expression. He wanted to keep chasing his sister around like a mad man.

She supposed she couldn't blame him. They wanted to play because they were children. And they should be able to. Unfortunately, that wasn't the life any of them lived.

Sighing, she kept her arms wrapped around Nyx and looked up to see Abraxas's eyes on them. He looked... softer. Like he'd been waiting for his entire life to see them cuddled up together in front of a fire.

Considering she was awkwardly sitting with one leg straight out, her hair likely sticking up in all directions, and two dragons in her arms who needed to get out energy before they even attempted to put them to bed. And here he was, looking at her like he'd never seen a more beautiful woman in his life.

"What?" she asked. "Why are you looking at me like that?"

"I just..." Abraxas shook his head and gave her a sheepish grin. "It's nothing. You said you wanted to know everything about Zander, wasn't that right?"

"No. First, I want to know what you're thinking. Why are you giving me that look?" She tilted her head to the side, eyeing him.

"I'm not going to tell you, Lore. Why don't we get back to the task at hand?"

"I want to know!"

"You don't need to know, so I don't understand—"

She shifted like she was going to throw Nyx at him. "Just tell me, Abraxas. What has you all soft and gooey like that?"

He sighed and leaned back on his hands. The firelight glimmered over his form, catching on the edges of his open shirt and creating deep shadows on his chest. "I've never loved you more than this moment."

Oh. Was that it? She couldn't imagine why. Lore looked down at the dragons in her arms and then raised a brow. "Right now? Not when we first met in the forest and I was wearing that beautiful gown with magical butterflies flying around my head?"

"Not even then," he replied. "Special moments like that will forever stay in my memory. But I love you for these quiet moments together, Lorelei. I love you most when you are happy, and I believe you are happy right now."

She supposed she was. Which was strange, considering they were talking about murdering a man. This was where she'd always wanted to be. Sitting by the fire with a loved one and their children. Warm with a full belly. It didn't matter where they were or who was with her when she had Abraxas and now these dragon babes.

"I suppose I am," she replied. "It feels wrong to say, knowing that we're going into the hardest battle we've ever fought through. But I am happy right now. Very much so."

"That is the best gift I could ask for." He leaned forward then, grabbing onto Hyperion and dragging the little one into his lap. "All I've ever wanted was to see you like this. Happy. At ease. I can count on one hand the number of times I've seen you so relaxed."

She imagined it wasn't often. They were struggling so much throughout months of torment and trials. And even though they were still in that state, she supposed she'd learned to take the little moments as the gifts they were.

Hugging Nyx closer to her chest, she sighed and looked into the fire with him. "All right. Tell me everything you think I need to know about Zander."

"You already know most of it. He'll fight dirtier than anyone you've ever fought before, even me. He'll try to catch you off guard or use other people to control your movements so that he can swoop in for the kill. He's not a good man."

"That's not what I'm asking." At least, she didn't think it was. Lore took some time to consider what she wanted to know. "He has a weakness. I know he must. If it's not a physical weakness because of the curse, then it has to be a mental one. What was it like for him growing up? Something has to give me an edge over him that no one else but you would know."

It was a hunch, not much of an idea really, but something that she could cling to. Lore needed a leg up over Zander, who had already beaten her in battle. Twice.

Abraxas narrowed his eyes at her. "Are you planning to fight him alone again?"

Yes. No. She wasn't all that sure. It might end up being that way, because she couldn't control how a battle shifted and moved.

If she had to fight him, and Lore had a gut feeling that they would face each other again, she could only assume that she would need every weapon in her arsenal. If she could get into his head, as so few people had done, that might be the one thing she needed to beat him this time.

"We are fairly even in our fighting styles," she breathed. "He has beaten me before, but those times, luck was on his side. As you said, he fights dirty. I have also unlocked all my power and I feel very comfortable fighting him with magic now. Perhaps he might have been a better fighter, but that doesn't mean he will know how to prevent someone with magic from cursing him."

Abraxas hummed out a long breath. "You don't think that will be enough though, do you? Otherwise, I'd be surprised at your confidence."

He'd read her mind. "No, I don't. I think he's well aware that I've learned more in my travels. He cannot assume that I am the same young woman who walked into his castle, no matter how much he would love for that to be true."

"He underestimates our kind," Abraxas replied. "You might fool him for a few moments."

"I tried that before. He seems to win, no matter how hard I try to trick him." And she couldn't afford to lose again.

"I could just eat him this time."

"And consume the curse that has been plaguing him?" The last thing she needed was to lose Abraxas. That simply would not and could not do. Magic was dangerous on its own, but she had no idea what would happen if someone devoured a curse.

He grumbled. "I suppose that won't happen then."

"Trapping him is the best option we have right now, and I agree it is not a good one." She snuggled Nyx closer to her, loving how the little one stuck her head in the crook of Lore's neck. "If we can get him to stay in one place for long enough, I think we can weave a spell that will keep him there."

"You're already using all your spellcasters to burn out the Umbral Knights." Abraxas always had to make the right point, even when she didn't want him to. "Which means there will be very few people who can help you with that spell. Do you think you would be strong enough to do it?"

"I have to be." Even if she didn't think she could.

Her magic had always been variable her entire life. The moon would give her the power she needed, but that didn't mean she was strong enough to trap Zander. They didn't even know what he had become.

His death and the subsequent curse which kept him alive had made him something else. He wasn't human, with a gaping wound filled with shadows. He wasn't dead because he was still walking around. But he wasn't alive as he was, either. In fact, she would swear the last time she'd looked him in the eyes, he had been missing the part of himself that made him human.

Life filled people's eyes with emotion and thought. He had lacked that.

Licking her lips, Lore tried to think of something else to say. How could she make Abraxas understand that this night was one to grasp at straws while they prayed one of Margaret's spies would provide them with information?

He cleared his throat. "When Zander was just a boy, I remember he used to attempt to make friends. First, it was with the servants, but his father killed them once he found out the prince was speaking with lower beings. Then it was with soldiers. But his father didn't like that either."

"One would think soldiers were good enough to talk to."

"Perhaps, but Zander's father thought it was better if he were alone. The less he knew about other people, the more his father could plant the seeds of his own hatred in the boy's mind." Abraxas seemed to ponder what he was going to say next, choosing his words carefully. "Zander became the man he is today because of his father. Because he was so limited in what he was allowed to understand or see."

She thought all of that made sense. Zander had wanted approval from the women he'd brought to his castle. Almost to a point where it had been strange. He wanted those women to give him an assurance that he seemed incapable of giving himself.

Now, if that was because his father had limited the boy to only interacting with family or that dastardly man who had ruined the kingdom in the first place, that would explain why Zander wanted others to exalt him. He still craved reassurance from his father, who would never give it.

"So you think I should convince him that even though we're not his father, that we might give him the approval he's been seeking?" She thought she could do that.

"No," Abraxas replied. "I want you to tear him down. If you end up fighting him alone and I don't get to sear the flesh off his bones, then I need you to look at him and tell him how small he is. How his father had been right all those years ago and that he would never turn into anything other than a little boy playing at king. Rip him apart, Lorelei. His opinion of himself is already so low, but you could use that during battle. It would distract him long enough that you might sink your blade between his ribs."

"I hate to use a man's fears against him," she said. "But I can do that. The spellcasters won't have much left after the light, but they all can amplify their voices across the battlefield."

"So you would take away his soldiers and then fill the fields with his worst nightmare. Countless people telling him that he is nothing and that he will die on that night." Abraxas nodded. "It is a cruel way to go, but it would be most effective."

It didn't settle well with Lore. Winning like that felt like cheating. She should fight him, hand to hand, beat him as the heroes of old used to.

But then she remembered all that he'd done. All that he'd tried to take away from her.

And it didn't feel so bad to let him burn like that.

"If we have any hope of beating him," she said, "then we will have to destroy not just his army, but his spirit."

CHAPTER 36

Abraxas stood on the ramparts, clasping his hands behind him as he surveyed the land beyond. Emerald hills spread out before him, reaching all the way to the edge of the Gloaming. His eyes could see farther than that, however. He saw the clouds that touched down to the sea so far from mortal sight. He knew that there was someone out there waiting. Someone who wanted to take everything from them all.

It was as though a piece of the King's soul was still linked to his own. Abraxas knew that wasn't possible. There were no lingering curses on him, or the warlock would have told him. Perhaps it was that he and Zander had been so close for such a long time.

Either way, he knew the man was out there. He could feel the dark magic calling out to him. Sense the power that bubbled under the surface of the King's skin. That evil man was planning a terrible attack, one that he thought the magical creatures could not stop even though they had amassed their own army.

But they had so few. Abraxas only had to turn slightly to see the people training in the courtyards. There were maybe two hundred good warriors and a handful of others who had signed up to fight without knowing what they were doing.

All of them were doomed. They would need so much more than what they had to defeat the King. Margaret had failed in her job and he would do his best to save as many of them as he could.

Abraxas was no hero, however. He was a selfish man, and he knew when to leave a situation like this. He owed it to them all to try. But the moment the tides turned where they would all fail, he would return to the castle, gather up his loved ones, and leave this place.

The dragon babes needed a chance to grow. Lore deserved to find peace in this world. And if she insisted on bringing their companions, then he would hide them on the coast until he could return for them again. Dracomaquia may be a dead kingdom, but there were still places for them to live. Gardens that needed only an adept hand to bring them back to life.

At least, he hoped.

The hairs on his arms raised as he noticed movement at the edge of the forest. Dark shadows that gathered up, clinging to the Gloaming before finally the darkness released its hold on the creatures within.

Three figures. One tall and lithe, another shorter and more bulky than he remembered. Of course, the third was the short, squat figure of the dwarf who had made more of an impact on Abraxas's life than he enjoyed admitting.

"Lore!" Abraxas called out, his voice slicing through the noise of the training grounds.

Everyone below him froze, all staring up at Abraxas as though he were about to announce they were being attacked. Even Lore had hesitated, her eyes seeking the gates to the castle.

He didn't mean to frighten them all, but such times were frightening, no matter how hard he tried to soften his voice. "We have guests," he shouted down to her. "Ones I think you would like to see."

The smile on her face could have brightened the very sky. If she had claimed to have sun magic, he would have believed her. The sight of her grin made him breathe easier. The time would come for the dark thoughts that always were on the edge of his mind. For now, he would enjoy seeing her happy that her friends had made it.

His elf took off for the side gate that led out into the fields beyond. Abraxas chose a more immediate path. He leapt off the edge of the ramparts, the dragon inside him growling in pleasure at the wind that rustled through the clothing at his arms. He landed hard on the ground, though his bones weren't affected like a mortal man. One fist struck the rock at the base of the castle, and he was surprised to feel the slightest twinge of pain.

Was he getting soft in his old age?

The door on the side wall of the castle burst open and Lore rushed out. Her blonde hair had gotten even longer now. It puffed around her head in a wild tangle like the nest of a bird as she sought him out.

"Where?" she gasped.

He pointed toward the Gloaming, where their companions walked toward them. Lore took off at a speed that surprised him, almost rivaling his own sprint as they both raced across the meadows. Her excitement fueled him. And suddenly, that glowing happiness that seemed to consume her filled him as well.

They had all been waiting for these three men to return. Safe and sound and without harm.

Abraxas wondered if he had been carrying the weight of fear for their safety without knowing it. His shoulders felt much lighter now that he saw three figures on the horizon.

"Goliath!" Lore shouted as they approached.

Abraxas slowed down, knowing that they would reach the men's side soon enough. Lore, on the other hand, did not. She launched herself at Goliath like a cat tackling its prey. The two of them soared through the air, then rolled in the dirt with a heavy thud.

He grinned at Goliath's swearing about foolish elves who did not know how much that hurt, while Lore grabbed onto him so hard the breath he'd struggled to find wheezed from his lungs again.

Shaking his head, Abraxas caught Zephyr's eye and arched a brow.

"I'm fine," the boy said with a grin of his own. "We're all fine."

"Thanks to me," Draven said with a sharp grumble. "These two were always getting into the most ridiculous situations. I will not travel with them again, Abraxas. I don't care who orders me to do so. It will not happen."

Lore staggered to her feet, grinning despite the fact that she'd nearly murdered her dwarf friend with that leap. "Oh, come on, Draven, you know you enjoy traveling with them. It's a challenge!"

"I don't." He pointed at the other two men. "They are like babies. Wandering around without a care in the world, certain everyone will do right by them and continue to be kind. They tromp through the woods so loudly I thought they'd bring about an entire army on our heads."

And with that, the mood changed. A gust of icy wind rushed over all of them, and he watched each of the expressions from those men fall.

"What happened?" he asked. Abraxas knew already what they would tell them, but he wanted to hear it from their lips first.

Zephyr cleared his throat. "We ran into a few of the King's supporters on the road there. Draven made quick work of them when they tried to attack us, so there were no concerns there. We didn't have to fear for our lives at all, even though they wanted to kill us for being..."

At his hesitation, Goliath added in, "Creatures. They called us animals and refused to let us speak."

Zander's influence had spread farther than he'd ever thought possible. The King must be so pleased with himself. All it took to ruin an entire kingdom was to whisper the differences between these people in the ears of those who had more numbers. A single ripple that spread into a wave to drown out all voices other than the majority.

He didn't want to know about those idiot mortals who thought they could attack any magical creature they saw. Abraxas would deal with them later, if he had the time. They would find out how dangerous it was to play in the world of magic without understanding who was more powerful.

Draven's hand fell to his waist, where he touched the hilt of a dagger. "I left the last one alive. Figured we could ask him questions, at the very least."

"What did he say?" Lore asked.

Abraxas knew. He'd been feeling connected to the King for nights now, almost as though his soul warned him of what was coming.

"The King and his troops are moving," Draven replied. "They've found safety in Solis Occasum. There was no one left there but spirits to ward them off. He's created his army there, in that cursed place. Apparently, he thinks he can not only travel through the Gloaming undeterred, but that he will raze the forest to the ground on his trip."

Oh.

Abraxas hadn't guessed that. He'd expected Zander to travel around the forest, as everyone did. Even the King shouldn't have been foolish enough to risk his entire army in the darkness of those woods.

Zander wasn't so bright that he would see the risk. Or he was so confident that he didn't think the risk was there at all. He would take the sacred forest and whoever protected it would die if they tried to stand in his way.

Even before he saw the expression on Draven's face, the way the young man was already preparing himself to beg, he wouldn't have allowed it. The Ashen Deep might not see eye to eye with their brethren on many things, but they were still the last of their people. The elves could not be expected to defend the forest on their own.

They would all die. No matter how many of those shadowy soldiers they killed, there would always be more. Even armed with grimdags, they couldn't take on the King's army by themselves.

Lore blew out a long breath, her wide eyes meeting his. This was the moment they've been fearing. The King had played his cards. Now, they had to do the same.

He refused to let any worry linger at the start of this. "We will not let the King get to the Gloaming. Your family will be safe, Draven. They have no part in this fight, and I'd rather burn the entire kingdom around it than let the King touch a single trunk."

An answering fire burned in Draven's eyes and he lifted a fist to press against his chest. The action of honor, one that so few people had ever given to Abraxas, meant more than Draven would ever know.

"Thank you," the deepmonger said. "My family will thank you as well. We have access to many weapons that many people want, but we are few."

"The King has struggled for long enough to put every magical creature on their knees when he has no right to do so." Abraxas looked at Lore then, knowing they both must share the same feelings. "We need to go back to the castle. We'll get these men settled and then decide what we are to do next. While I know Margaret would prefer to battle on these very fields..."

"I don't think that's the right choice anymore," Lore filled in for him. "I agree."

Goliath looked between the two of them with a rather startled expression. "You two are thinking of bringing the fight to the King, aren't you?"

"We are." Abraxas looked down at his friend with a soft smile. "As mad as it may sound, my friend, I believe that will be the easiest chance to catch him. Did the man you killed say anything about when the army will move?"

"By the week's end," Draven filled in. "He said they planned to allow the creatures a few more nights of rest before they would all be wiped from the earth."

"Right," Abraxas said. "They're so confident that they will win when the mortals aren't fighting against us at all."

Goliath lifted a hand and everyone's eyes fell on the dwarf. "That's an argument for a later time. We'll deal with the mortals. But for now, I believe food, drink, and rest were promised. We have a few days before the King plays his hand."

"We have less than a few hours to make the decision." Lore's voice sliced through their meager sense of hope. "If we want to beat him to whatever battlefield we choose, then we need to move now. Solis Occasum is too far from here for any of us to reach him without flying on Abraxas. And we have an entire army to prepare and move. We'll have to find somewhere flat, somewhere we can get the upper hand without letting the King know we've beat him there. Surprise will be our best and only opportunity in this circumstance."

She was right, even though Abraxas hated that she was right. "What are you thinking?"

Lore shook her head. "I don't know."

Goliath started walking toward the castle, forcing them all to follow him. "If he plans on traveling through the Gloaming, then he'd have to sail across the strait between Solis Occasum and our land. Which means he'll be going up through the sands that then lead to the Gloaming. There are old dwarven hills there."

Abraxas glanced over his shoulder at Lore, who shrugged as though she didn't know what he was talking about either. "Why are you bringing this up?"

"That's where my family is from, actually. Long time ago." Goliath bent and grabbed a handful of grass as he walked. And then, without acting like it was impressive at all, he lifted a small four-leafed clover to the sky. "There are a lot of weapons deep inside the earth. Should lighten the load considerably. If we can get to those holes, then I could supply an entire army with weapons."

"So we'd only have to take a few weapons each." Abraxas nodded. "It's a start."

"I can't promise there will still be dwarves there. But if there are, then I can say they'd likely join the fight." The dwarf's jaunty step felt infectious. "Not all is lost yet, you two. There are more people here than you can imagine who might help. Mark my words, we're getting closer to the end. And it'll be an end we're all satisfied with."

None of them said anything until they reached the door to the castle. Hope burned through all of their chests, he imagined. Hope that the dwarf was right, and this was all so close to being over with.

Abraxas held the door open for the others, waiting until Lore came through last. He muttered under his breath, "We'll have to get everyone ready before we bring this up to Margaret. She'll do her best to stop us."

"Oh, I know." She reached between them and placed her hand on his cheek. "We won't let her, though. You and I are legends to them now. To all of them. We've taught them to fight. We've told them not to be afraid of who they are or what they are. They will follow us."

He wasn't so certain they would follow him, but he knew that he would follow her to the ends of the earth. If she asked him to pluck the stars from the sky, he would battle the rest of his life to bring them down to her.

Abraxas pressed a kiss to her palm. "They will follow you, Lady of Starlight. And you will bring them to victory.".

CHAPTER 37

"Absolutely not," Margaret hissed. Her words carried the appropriate amount of venom for a woman who had realized she had lost control over her army. "I will not allow it. Running into battle without a single plan in place is the stupidest thing I've heard either of you say yet."

They stood in the middle of the Great Hall. Margaret had refused to see them in her private quarters, so Lore decided she would bring the information to her by force.

"Margaret," she started, trying her best not to lose her temper as well.

"Don't you Margaret me, little girl. I was the one who stayed with the rebellion after your mother died. I was the one who got us to this point. Don't think for a second you can use this opportunity to usurp me!"

Oh, that was it. Lore stepped forward and pointed her finger in Margaret's face. "That's what you think this is? You think I want to throw you back into the shadows and take over this meager army you have built? I am finishing what you started, Margaret. And I will do so with fewer deaths than your plan would."

Her companions looked on with shocked expressions, and Margaret's generals had already put their hands on their weapons. If she wasn't careful, Lore would start an all-out brawl in this room. Maybe that's what they all needed. This had been coming to a head for a very long time, after all. Margaret had pushed her too far.

The Darkveil elf chuckled, shaking her head as though she couldn't quite believe Lore's actions. "You think it is so easy to become an expert in war? You want to tell me what to do with my army, when you have only been here for a few days?"

"I find it adorable that you think it's still your army." Lore let her hand drop, then crossed her arms over her chest. "You're the one who told them I was a god. You are the one who made me into the Savior of Tenebrous when I am anything but. They will follow me to the ends of the earth, not because of anything I did, but because of you. If you think I'm trying to take over, well, didn't you want me to? This is all your doing, Margaret."

The silence that rang through the room was deafening. The two elven women glared at each other, and Lore refused to be the first one to break.

This was Margaret's fault. She had created this problem all on her own and Lorelei would be damned before she let this woman walk all over her again.

Margaret glared at her with too much venom. Too much hatred. But

Lore knew very well that Margaret could do nothing at all. Right now, she had seen all her fears come to life. Lorelei of Tenebrous, the Silverfell elf who she had painted as the only woman to save this kingdom, had come to take her throne.

"So what do you propose?" Margaret grit through her teeth. "That I give you the army I've been training for months? That I let you take all that I have fought so hard for, just like the humans would do?"

It was a low blow, even Margaret knew that. Comparing Lore to any of the humans wasn't fair. But she refused to let it stop her plan.

"I want you to tell them that you are working with the Savior of Tenebrous. Come with us. Fight by our side so you can see the battle for yourself. I know you are very skilled in your magic, and while yours leans toward shadows, we can still use that to our advantage." Lore had to force herself to hold out her hand, but she did. "I want you to say this was your plan, and I want you to be on the battlefield when we win. No one needs to know about this argument other than you and me."

"And everyone else in the room." Margaret took her hand, though, sneering the entire time. "You've backed me into a corner. Your mother would be proud."

"I know she would." Lore knew that her mother would be ridiculously proud to see how far her daughter had come. The problem now became how to live up to her mother's esteemed legacy.

She thought she'd done a good job of turning this situation around, though.

Lore looked into the eyes of the generals behind Margaret, knowing that her next words would mean more to them than the Darkveil elf. "It is now up to you. Her word has been given, and if Margaret does not show on the battlefield, then know all is lost. All of our people are watching now. They will either fight with us, or they will pray on the night that this battle takes place. Either way, you are the generals. You can give the orders. If she is lying to me now, then I will hold all of you responsible for bringing our army to the battlefields."

One by one, the generals thudded their fists against their chests. And though Margaret's eyes only widened ever more with shock and then anger, Lore knew this was for the best. Let them believe she was some avenging saint who came down to save them. She didn't care what they thought of her.

As long as they fought. As long as they won. They could think whatever they wanted of her in the aftermath.

Nodding her head, she left the Great Hall with her companions behind her. They were all silent, as she had asked them to be, until the door closed behind them.

Goliath was the first to throw his fist into the air with a silent whoop. "Now that was a damned show, Lorelei!"

"Thank you," she whispered, ushering them all further away from the door. "Don't let her hear you say that."

"I don't care if she hears it or not, bravo Silverfell! I didn't think we'd convince her of anything but look at you."

She didn't have time to feel the pride his words blossomed in her chest. They had to go. They needed to get a handful of warriors to start out with them so they could look over the field while they waited for the rest of the army to join them. A small few would start the battle, with waves of warriors coming to support them in the upcoming fight. Soon, they would be at the end of this story.

Her heart thundered in her chest. There was so much to do behind the scenes, but everyone already had their roles.

Beauty and Zephyr would stay behind. They still weren't interested in knowing what would happen if Zander saw his half brother, and Lore didn't want to take the chance of that exploding in all of their faces. The dragon babies would stay behind in the castle, where they were safe. If Beauty caught any hint of danger, the four of them would sneak out the back exit of the castle and disappear into the night.

Goliath would come to the battlefield. He was the only one who knew where those dwarven caverns were, and he would help both Lore and Abraxas find them before the army showed up. He also seemed to think there were a few traps they could lay out in the meantime, which Lore could only hope would be useful in the end.

Draven, while an impressive fighter, would return to the Gloaming to inform his mother of their plan. They needed to make sure the forest was impenetrable, should the King and his armies break through. The Ashen Deep would ensure any stragglers from the King's armies, or assassins sent to the castle behind their back, would die long before they reached these walls.

And after they'd confirmed the plan, Lore and Abraxas had prepared for their journey. They had everything packed. Weapons. Armor. Tents for the few nights they had before the King started his journey. It was a long shot, but this was their chance.

"Everyone ready?" she asked, breathless outside her and Abraxas's door.

"As ready as we'll ever be." Draven already had a pack over his shoulder. "Good luck to you all."

Lore nodded at him and then the dark elf disappeared. Wandered down the hall and blinked out of view as though he'd never been there at all. She hoped someday they would see each other again. But there was no way to know if they would both survive this, she supposed.

"I'm just going to…" Lore hooked a thumb over her shoulder. She refused to make eye contact with Abraxas, but knew he would follow her through the door.

She couldn't look at the others either, or she'd start crying and that wouldn't do. No one needed to see the woman leading them into battle with tears in her eyes.

But as she slipped into the waiting room, she let the tears fall. Two dragon babies waited on the bed. Their necks longer, wings larger, and eyes ever knowing. They must have felt that she was upset. Somehow. Or maybe they were more observant than she gave them credit for. They were so young. But for all their few weeks of life, they knew more than they should.

"It's time," Abraxas said behind her as he closed the door. "We are going to war, little ones. You will remain behind."

The raspy noises they made were clearly attempts to argue. And though she couldn't understand what they were saying, she could guess, as Abraxas's expression clouded. Even he struggled to say goodbye to them, and she'd expected him to fare better than she did.

"No," he scolded. "We don't have time to hear any of this. You are both far too young to be going into battle. You can hardly control your fire yet."

Hyperion snapped his jaws at the much larger dragon. His throat glowed bright red and a small burp of flame escaped from his mouth. It still wasn't enough to do any damage, or even burn the sheets. Though they were both the size of dogs now, quite large compared to what they had been only a few weeks ago, neither of them could fight.

Her heart ached as though someone had reached into her chest and ripped it out. She didn't want to leave them. No one did. But she couldn't risk their lives either.

"Please stop fighting," she whispered. The two dragonlings paused in their sounds and looked at her.

She was certain that it was because of her tears. They'd never seen her cry. They didn't even know what crying even was. They watched her with horrified gazes as tears leaked out of her eyes and dripped down her chin.

Lore walked forward and held out her arms. "Come here, please. I don't know if I'll ever see you again, and I want to hold you one more time."

"Lore," Abraxas scolded. "You'll come home to them."

She tucked their heads against her heart, stroking the sides of their flat cheeks. But she didn't look down at the two babies in her arms. Instead, she looked at Abraxas and knew the exact moment he remembered the prophecy.

Though neither of them wished to believe it was true, they would either be correct or proven wrong. She might never return. Never see these babies again.

Every part of her wanted to scream at the thought. These were her children now. They were part of her soul, and giving them up would be the hardest thing she'd ever done. Walking out of this room knowing that she might not see them as large as Abraxas. She might never get to see them fly or feast for the first time. She may never see them turn from child into adolescent. If she died on that battlefield, she would miss so many moments that would have been precious to her.

But they didn't have a choice, just as she'd never had a choice since the very start of all this. She had to go. She had to save her people, and not just because she was blackmailed into this from the start.

Lore had a duty to this realm, now. To all the people who looked at posters of the Savior of Tenebrous and whispered to their daughters that they could do anything. Magical creatures deserved someone who not only made them promises but upheld those promises. Someone who could and would change the timeline. She would rewrite the future and bring about a new age.

Just like the prophecy said. Now, all she could hope was that it wasn't right about everything.

She dropped a kiss onto each dragon's forehead, trying very hard not to cry on them.

"Now, the two of you be good for Beauty and Zephyr. They're going to watch after you while we're gone." She tickled the underside of Hyperion's chin. "You stop trying to bite Zeph. He thinks you don't like him. And you..." She cupped Nyx's head with both of her hands. "Don't grow up too fast, my darling girl. Just because the weight of the world feels like it's on your shoulders, doesn't mean you shouldn't stop to roll in the grass now and then."

Oh, her heart. She didn't know it would hurt like this. She'd thought heartbreak was something people said because they were sad. But it felt like her heart was breaking in two and that she needed someone to reach inside her chest and start it again.

One more kiss. One more for each of them so they would remember for the rest of their lives how much she loved them. How much they meant to her.

"I love you both," she whispered against their warm scales. "You were a dream come true, and I am so blessed to have met you before now. I hope I see you again."

Her hands didn't want to leave their sides. Her fingers stroked their scales, where their wings connected to their shoulders, to the soft membranes that soon would carry them through the skies. She would always remember how they felt. If her last moment came soon, this would be the memory she carried with her.

Lore had to step away. She cleared her throat and stood up, backing toward the door and holding her eyes as wide as possible so more tears didn't fall.

Abraxas had tears in his eyes as well, and if that didn't completely gut her. She didn't want him to cry, but how was he supposed to hold himself together when she had fallen apart?

"I can wait outside if you need me to," she whispered.

"No." He shook his head. "They have no need to fear that I will not return."

He walked over to the two baby dragons and stroked the tops of their heads. He smoothed their spines down as if that would ease their worry. "I'll bring her home, dear ones. I promise."

And then he walked over to Lore, tucked her under his arm, and brought her outside.

She couldn't breathe. Her babies were in that room and she hadn't ever thought she would have children. No one had prepared her for this feeling. This horrible nightmare of a feeling where she wanted to leap back into their room and never let them go. Even though that would be the end of their world as they knew it.

She hugged her arms around herself and heard Abraxas say something to Beauty.

"Keep them safe," it sounded like.

"You do the same with her," Beauty replied, her voice cutting through Lore's sadness. "We need her alive, Abraxas. All of us do."

A hand slipped into hers, and Goliath squeezed her fingers tight.

"You will be well," he said, staring up into her eyes. "We'll all be there with you."

He didn't know about the prophecy. None of them did.

Lore smoothed her finger down Goliath's jaw and into his beard, holding onto the side of his face. "Until the dawn comes," she whispered.

"Always," he replied.

But he had no idea what he promised.

CHAPTER 38

Abraxas soared through the clouds, with Lore and Goliath on his back. They'd all decided to scout ahead of the small army of warriors they brought with them. Namely, because Lore was so upset after saying goodbye to the dragonlings that it would have been a poor idea for the army to see her. They didn't need anyone losing hope because the figurehead of their war couldn't stop crying.

She'd gotten herself together about halfway through their flight. Perhaps Goliath had calmed her down with some words of wisdom, as he was apt to do. Abraxas couldn't quite hear their conversation. They flew through too many storms for him to hear much of anything other than the rumble of thunder and the loud crack of lightning that stretched toward the ground below them.

Such was the best kind of night for travel. He hoped that was natural luck and not one of the many spellcasters among them who had brought about a dark night.

Either way, it took him a while to fly over the Gloaming. They had to stay low, but not so low that they were in danger from the electricity crackling through the clouds. He relied entirely on small glimpses of the ground below them to let him know if he'd gone too far.

It made traveling difficult. He didn't want to overshoot where they were supposed to land and then soar over the King's men. But he also wanted to make sure they were close enough to their new battlegrounds when he landed. They would need to hide as quickly as possible.

More would arrive soon after. They had suspected it would take about a day for their troops to get straight through the Gloaming, aided by Draven and his family once the deepmonger had made it back to his own people.

Lore, Goliath, and Abraxas were to find the weapon storages and then do whatever they could to get all of those weapons out. Two days. They had two more days to get their plan into perfection before all hell would break loose.

His fire could only save so many. And unfortunately, that was getting harder by the minute.

He banked hard through the clouds and then plummeted from the sky. He tucked his wings close to his back, covering up Lore and Goliath from the pelting rain that must have felt like stones against their soft skin.

And then they broke through the clouds. He opened his wings wide, slowing them down quickly as they approached the ground.

He'd correctly guessed that they were just past the edge of the

Gloaming. Close enough to the battlefield so they could start their journey to find the dwarven hills at first light. And close enough to the forest that they would be safe in their tents tonight.

As long as Draven had done his job, that was. Abraxas hated having to trust the dark elf, but he assumed that the man would do everything he could.

Most of their plans these days required trust. The deeper into this battle that they went, the more Abraxas realized he struggled to trust anyone who wasn't Lore.

Landing at the edge of the forest, he spread out his wing for his two passengers to slide down his wing. Lore staggered as she landed, shaking herself but looking very lost.

Goliath walked up to his head and patted Abraxas's neck. Pitching his voice low, he muttered, "You need to get her head back on straight. She's going to get herself killed in battle if she keeps wandering around like this. I know those babies are important to the two of you, but we couldn't bring them. She needs to be the figurehead that Margaret made her, and she needs to be a lot more confident than she is right now."

He nodded and watched as Goliath started setting up their tents. Rather than change back too quickly, he stayed as the dragon. His heat would warm Lore more than he could as a man. And this way, he could bend his wing around her shoulders and pull her against him.

"Easy," he muttered, giving her as much reassurance as he could. "You'll be all right, love."

She nodded and he could hear her hard swallow. Maybe she didn't believe it. Maybe she thought that this was the end and that she'd said goodbye to her children for good. He couldn't guess what was going through her head in this moment.

All he knew was that he loved her, and his presence was the best he could offer.

Goliath waved from over at the tents a few moments later. Then the dwarf disappeared into his own tent, which he'd conveniently set up far away from theirs. This was the moment Abraxas needed to change back.

He let the dragon form melt away from him. Abraxas caught Lore against his chest as she sagged, and he held her against his heart.

"Come on," he breathed. "Let's get into the tent. Tomorrow will be easier, my love."

"Tomorrow," she repeated with a slight nod. "Tomorrow will be easier."

He didn't think she believed the words at all. Abraxas moved the tent flap aside and eased her through the opening. He crawled in after her while trying his best to figure out how to fix this.

She needed him, and he didn't know what was the right thing to do.

Lore flopped down on the hard pad that Goliath had laid out for them to sleep on. She didn't seem to even notice if there were rocks underneath her or if she was uncomfortable. Instead, Lore rolled over onto her back and stared up at the ceiling of the tent. Lost in her own thoughts.

He made a face at her dramatics. Abraxas settled beside her, laying down on his back as well and clasping his hands at his chest. "You seem troubled."

"There are a great many things to be troubled about," she replied.

"I know that. But we are going into a battle tomorrow, and you're already acting as though we have lost." He struggled to find the right words. He didn't want to make her even more angry than she already was, and he had never been good at finding the right words. "We have to fight as though we are certain we will win. Otherwise, he will win, Lore. And I cannot stand to suffer that fate."

"At what cost?" She rolled onto her side, cushioning her head on her arm. "All I want is for us to be happy, Abraxas. I want to run away with you and the dragon babes. To build a farm somewhere out of the way where we can all live together and watch those children grow. I'll grow elfweed in the back where the children can't find it, but you and I can smoke it on the front porch at night when they've gone to bed."

She painted a pretty picture with her words. He grinned, knowing that his teeth would flash in the darkness. "I'll teach them how to hunt, but it would take a while for them to figure out that they don't have to eat the entire deer. They'll get a lot larger than you're expecting. Much faster than you're expecting as well."

"I wouldn't mind. I want to see what they look like in their human forms as well." She reached out and rested her hand over his heart. "I want to see who they are in that form as well as watch them grow up into the dragons who I know will change the world."

As much as he enjoyed envisioning this future with her, he knew that this was a coping mechanism he couldn't entertain. "Why are you so certain that you won't see any of that?"

Lore shrugged. "I don't know. Just a feeling, I suppose."

He sighed and decided they were too far away from each other. Abraxas gathered her up in his arms and deposited his elf on top of his chest. "That's foolish. You know I wouldn't let anything kill you. I don't care about a prophecy or not. You are going to come home with me, Lore. No matter what that takes."

Her breath fluttered over his pulse, and he knew the exact moment that she'd fallen asleep. Exhaustion had turned into dark rings around her eyes, while worry lines marred her forehead even as she rested.

Not a single dream fluttered through her mind, and he knew because he stayed up all night watching her. Just as she was afraid of what would happen the further they went down this path, so was he.

Abraxas told her that everything would be all right. That he would protect her as no one other than a dragon could do. He would fight until the bitter end to see her chest lift with breath and a smile on her face one more time.

But even he now knew how difficult a fight this would be. She was without a doubt the elf in that prophecy. She was the one to bring about this new age, and as much as he wanted to transfer that fate onto Margaret, he didn't think that was possible.

They were going to fight this battle together. Side by side. Just as they should.

Abraxas just hoped that didn't mean he would have to watch her die so that the rest of the kingdom could enjoy their future. He wouldn't survive that.

He'd have to survive, however. For his children. For their future. So much rode on his shoulders, so many conflicting emotions.

The best thing he could do was stand guard over her in her sleep. As he'd done all those months ago when they had first arrived in her attic home filled with the wilted remains of elfweed and dust motes that floated like stars through the air.

The sun rose on the horizon all too quickly for his liking as the rain stopped. He listened to the sound of footsteps outside his tent. Many feet which had trudged through the rain and mud to get to this point on the battlefield. The army of their people had made good time in following them, but he didn't know if that was a positive.

Lore might need more time to get her head on straight. She likely would need at least a few moments to settle her stomach, perhaps even to paint on a new face that could smile when others asked how she was doing.

He wanted to make sure she was all right before he greeted the general that had arrived with the warriors who were to follow them. They were the ones who would set up specific camps around the area. The ones who would be the first to die.

"Lore," he whispered, squeezing her awake with a hug. "They've arrived."

"So early." She blinked her eyes open, still red and swollen from crying so much. "They were supposed to be here at midday."

"Apparently Draven and his family made their journey easier than we expected." He ran his thumbs underneath her eyes, pressing the redness into a pale white. "You look like you've been crying."

"I have been. I have every reason to be sad." She sighed though, and shook her head. "But I know they cannot see that."

A cool rush of magic surged from her feet to her face. The chill made all the hairs on his body stand on end, but it smoothed away all traces of her emotions. She was his Lore again. Fierce and proud and ready to take on the world for those she loved.

Still, he held her face in his hands and pressed a kiss to her forehead. "You are allowed to feel."

"Just not right now," she muttered, but forced herself to smile. "I know there is much we have to do today, and I understand that the army being here makes everything more difficult. You and I will be fine, Abraxas. I've slept on it. I mourned. Now, we will face the day with strength and courage."

He would give anything to allow her more than a single night to process what they had to do. Instead, all he could do was nod and open the tent flap for her so she could go out there and address all the people waiting for her.

Lore went first into the dim morning light, and he followed close behind. The rain had left a thousand dewdrops on the blades of grass that covered the battlefield. Sunlight caught in each droplet and made the entire field look as though it were sparkling with stars.

Fitting, he supposed, for the day that Lore was about to have.

The second thing he noticed was that there wasn't a general standing in front of them. It was Margaret herself. The Darkveil elf stood with pride at the head of all those people, waiting for Lore to walk over to her side.

"Great," Lore muttered. "Will I be forced to start the day off in a bad mood, then?"

"Hopefully not." He pressed his hand against the small of her back, hoping that it would warm her skin. "Let's go see what she wants."

Many eyes watched them as they crossed over to Margaret. The elf walked toward them, pausing far enough away from the others so that no one would overhear their conversation.

"Did you think I would let you take all the credit?" Margaret asked with a lifted brow. "You'll need me in the fight, anyway. It's been a long time since I've been in any active battle, but I am still a better warrior than most of these green young ones."

"And here I was thinking your overuse of magic had rendered you harmless," Lore replied.

"I haven't used so much magic that I cannot fight." Apparently, the Darkveil elf had no more use for such arguments. She cast her eyes upon Abraxas and that wicked, controlling look returned. "You are going to scout ahead, dragon. I want to send the King a message that we are ready for him to attack. Should he think he can beat us, he needs to be reminded that we have a dragon in our army and that is something he lacks."

"I don't think it's smart to let him know we're prepared for him," Abraxas replied.

"And I don't care what you think. I am still the leader of this rebellion. No matter how much that has changed in the past few weeks."

He opened his mouth, looked down at Lore, and then looked back at Margaret. "We have our orders already. The three of us were to seek the dwarven hills and supply the army with more weapons so that everyone could get here faster."

"I know." She waved a hand in the air. "I no longer believe that to be the smartest tactic, given the circumstances. The King cannot be allowed to feel so confident or he will have better chances at winning. I want to know exactly how big his army is, where he is, and how long we have. That is the best move in this situation. I will not rely on rumors alone to prepare us."

Damn it, he hated agreeing with Margaret. But her plan was a solid one. If they knew where the King was, then they could better prepare for the army that would attack them.

Lore needed him, though. She needed him to be here with her, and if his beloved still stood on shaky feet, then he had no other choice.

His elf grabbed his hand and squeezed hard. "It's not a bad idea, Abraxas."

He couldn't outright say that she needed him to stay. Not in front of Margaret, but he tried his best to say so with his eyes. He shouldn't leave her alone when she felt like this.

Lore smiled at him, though the expression didn't meet her eyes. "We knew we might have to split up. There is no battle yet, dragon of mine. Go. And return as swiftly as you can."

A shattering sound echoed in his mind, and perhaps that was his very heart splintering in his chest. He didn't want to leave her.

But he had to.

There was no other choice because they were at war.

So he wrapped an arm around her waist and pulled her against him. He kissed her as though the very sun was falling down around their ears and he would never get to see her again.

"Stay alive," he whispered against her lips. "Or I will make the world suffer for losing you."

She kissed him back. Softer. Less wild. "Come home to me, dragon. I have a future to plan with you."

Abraxas ripped himself away from her arms and took three steps back, watching her the entire time. Then, when he could no longer stand it, he whirled away from her and took off down the fields that would soon be coated in blood. A dragon pushed forth, raging against his skin for freedom.

For battle.

CHAPTER 39

Lore watched her dragon disappear into the clouds and felt as though a part of her soul had left with him. She knew he would return. He always did. And they needed the information he would provide.

But she missed him already.

"Good, now that he's gone we'll have at least some information about the King's whereabouts from someone more reliable than an idiot on the side of the road." Margaret flicked her fingers in the air as though she were dismissing a bug. "You will go with Goliath and find those weapons."

It took Lore a few moments to pull her gaze from the sky. "Yes. That was the plan."

"Then you should leave now. There will be plenty for the two of you to do when you get back." Margaret rolled her eyes. "This a war, after all. No one is going to sit around pretending that they are more important than anyone else. I refuse to sit and do nothing while the King prepares himself even further."

"Right," Lore whispered as the other elf walked away from her. "We'll get right on that."

She wasn't sure how to process Margaret's sudden involvement. She was too much on the best of days, and now she was firmly back in Lore's life. Margaret would take over, as she always did, but there was a sense of relief in that realization.

Lore didn't know the first thing about war. She'd never joined an army or fought beside others in battle. Stealing from shopkeepers in Tenebrous wasn't the same as... this. All of this was so overwhelming. A few hundred lives rested on her shoulders and required her to make the right decisions so that they went back to their families at night.

Her heart squeezed in her chest, thudding strangely as though it wanted to stop all together.

They would all have families to go back to, just like the family that waited for her. What if the two dragon babes weren't being good for Beauty and Zeph? They were a handful. The two beasts would run the entire castle by now, and they would have everyone under their thumb.

What if they'd gotten outside? What if they were lost, and no one knew how to find them because they had already disappeared into the Gloaming? What if the two of them had planned to come to the battle and save their parents?

She couldn't breathe. Maybe she should go back to the castle. Just to check on them. Then she could be assured that they were fine. She'd come back here. They didn't need her for all of this beginning part anyway, and then she would fight with everyone else.

A stubby hand slid around hers, squeezing her fingers tightly. "Lore," Goliath said. "We need to go."

Oh no. What if she should run and there wasn't time for that now?

She looked down at her dearest friend, and she hated the pity on his face. He looked at her as though he knew what was going on in her head, and he wished there was a way for him to stop the thoughts from thundering through her.

"I'm afraid," she said.

"If you weren't afraid, then I would call you a fool. There is so much that will happen in a very short amount of time." He squeezed her fingers again. "Take it in small parts. Tiny pieces that you can control. First, we have to see if we can find the dwarven hills. Then we will find the weapons. All of this will come more naturally like that. Don't you think?"

Not really. Lore had to do this, though, just like she'd always had to do everything they bid her to do since the start of this nightmare.

"Let's go, then," she muttered, casting a nasty glance toward Margaret. "I want to get away from here as quickly as possible. There's too many people expecting far too much."

Margaret wore a grin that was far too wide for her to have not seen Lore glaring at her. The two women didn't have to like each other to fight on the same side, Lore supposed.

The most frustrating piece of all this was that she respected Margaret. Probably more than anyone else. The Darkveil elf was confident in everything that she did. No one ever questioned her. Margaret didn't feel the anxiety or nerves that everyone else felt.

If Lore could have stepped into her shoes for a few days, she would have. Just for some relief from this emotion that weighed heavily on her shoulders.

She trudged along behind Goliath, who led her away from the crowd of people already setting up their own camps. He kept his eyes on her, perhaps a little too closely. Every now and then the dwarf would glance behind him as though he were waiting for her not to be there. Like she was at constant risk of running off on him.

"I'm still here," she grumbled. "And I'm not going anywhere."

"I'm just thinking that you look a lot like your mother when she first joined the rebellion," he replied. "She didn't want to do any of it, either."

Lore snorted. "My mother would have fought tooth and nail at every opportunity. She loved to fight. I can remember her coming home with a bloody nose more times than she came home with food for us to eat."

"But she didn't always want to be that way." Goliath grinned at her, his beard parting to reveal the cheerful expression on his face. "I remember my father saying that she was quite the fighter, but that she always wanted to run home to you. I guess you two are the same like that."

Lore didn't want to think about this. If she were that similar to her mother, then she would also die for this cause. She'd be buried deep under the ground or charred to a crisp by some errant spell while her children grew up on their own without a mother to hug them.

"I don't want to talk about her," she said. Lore picked up her pace to walk in front of Goliath, unable to look at his smile anymore. "She left her daughter alone and vulnerable. There is no reason for me to want to be like her."

"Or maybe you want to be like her because she loved you so much that it brought her to distraction." Goliath skipped ahead of her again. "I think any child would want a mother who loved them like that."

Of course they would. And every child deserved a mother like that. What they didn't deserve was a mother who was rarely there because she had some mad plan to save the world for her daughter.

Damn it, she was the spitting image of her mother. She'd become everything she had promised herself that she wouldn't.

"I don't know what else to say, Goliath," she said. "I don't want to become her, but I clearly am her. So here we all are. Wondering just how far I'll go."

The words of the prophecy pressed against her tongue. She wanted to tell him everything. The words wanted to spew out from her tongue so he could hear what would happen. She would die, or should die, if they were going to fulfill what her mother had wanted her to do. And that fate was not something she could escape.

Of course, both she and Abraxas would fight with every ounce of their bodies so that they could prevent that from happening. No one wanted her to die but...

Goliath raised a hand and froze in the middle of the field. "Quiet," he hissed. "Do you hear that?"

No, she heard nothing but the birds above them. Lore made a face and shrugged her shoulders. Goliath pressed himself into the grass, his ear against the ground as he lifted a hand to his lips.

She mimicked what he was doing. Lore also pressed her ear to the ground, although she wasn't expecting to hear anything until... There it was. The faintest sound of metal striking against metal in the distance.

No, not the distance. Through the ground.

Goliath's eyes had filled with hope and love. "There are still dwarves here," he whispered. "They're right underneath our feet, Lore."

She wanted to feel his happiness as well. His people were within reach, still living as they were meant to. They weren't wasting away on the streets of Tenebrous while begging for food. This moment must feel as though he'd struck gold himself.

But something didn't feel right. They were here, on the field that would become a battlefield, but she didn't see any openings like he'd said there would be. Goliath had made it sound like there were plenty of tunnels that would lead into those secret, underground hovels of his kind. Places where they could walk through halls made of gold that were filled with people who would guide them to where they still kept countless weapons.

"Where are all the places where we should be able to see them?" she asked. "You said there were many halls, but they sound so far away from us."

"Or so deep into the ground," he muttered. "They shouldn't be that deep into the earth. We only travel so close to the heart if..."

Goliath didn't finish that sentence, and that made her nervous. Lore waited for him to finish the sentence, then realized he would not continue. "Why would they go that deep, Goliath?"

He met her gaze with one of horror. "Only if they're preparing for war."

That was good though, wasn't it? If the dwarves already suspected that the King was coming to attack, that meant they had a secondary army which was ready to fight.

But that wasn't what Goliath's expression confirmed at all. The dwarf stood and took off down the fields, frantically searching for an opening that would let him into the realm below. She didn't know how to help other than to watch him dart around until finally, he fell to his knees in the earth.

"This has been recently overturned," he muttered, his hands scrabbling at the ground. "The earth here is softer. Someone buried them, Lore."

They couldn't be completely buried. They'd all have died down there without air, but... Who was she to argue?

Lore fell to her knees beside him and started digging.

It didn't take long for them to find the hole that careless hands had covered up. A blast of stale air struck her in the face, as though this tunnel hadn't been opened for a very long time. Coughing, Lore covered her mouth and backed away from it.

"Too dangerous," she wheezed. "Goliath, we can't go in there."

"They need us, Lore!" He whipped around to stare at her, begging on his knees. "They need us to help them."

What would she have done if these were elves trapped under the ground? She knew she wouldn't hesitate for a moment. They all would have plunged headlong into that darkness to find the people who were as much a part of her as her own soul.

She didn't want to go in there and risk not coming back out. Not when there was a war, but... Well, she'd do anything for her friend.

Lore weaved a minor spell around them, although it was only a meager enchantment for protection. It would do very little, but she wanted it all the same. "Let's go, then."

They walked into uncertainty together. Just as they would for years to come, she hoped.

Lore soon had to conjure a small ball of light to trail along behind them. She couldn't see without it, although Goliath moved as though he'd been here before. The dwarves had carved quite the home out of the earth. There were passages that split off from this one multiple times. Passages that Goliath ignored, but that sparked an interest in Lore.

She could almost feel the magic coming out of them. There were objects here that were incredibly powerful.

The tunnel was made out of stone. The smoothed surface had been textured just slightly so that it was still easy to walk down it, while the walls were polished into a grey and speckled slick surface. She'd thought she might even be able to see her own reflection in it if the stone were darker. It wasn't easy to make a mirror out of black and white granite.

All she could hear was the sound of metal hitting metal. The clinking noise grew louder the deeper into the earth they went, but she couldn't guess what it was. Just clinks that soon became more and more until she knew it was a hundred clanking sounds of something hitting another thing.

Goliath stopped in front of her so quickly she almost ran into his back.

"What is it?" she asked.

"Put out the light."

"What?"

He reached up for her little globe of magic and crushed it in his fist. The spell popped, sending them into a wave of darkness.

Except for the glow of red down the tunnel they stood in. The slightest glow that flickered like torchlight.

Or fire.

"This isn't right," Goliath muttered. "There should be dwarves in these halls. There should be more noise than just damned hammering."

"Well, there's no way to tell what is going on other than just to keep going forward. Isn't that what you would tell me?" She at least crouched to move quietly and pressed her hand against the wall. "Come on."

"Be careful, Lorelei." He swallowed so hard she could hear it. "I don't know what we're about to see."

Hopefully nothing. The wind might be hitting a metal piece against the wall for all they knew. These halls could still be abandoned, and they'd gotten all afraid of nothing.

Except, when she rounded the corner of the tunnel, Lore dropped onto her hands and knees, her breath stinging in her lungs. The blast of heat and moisture that hit her face was from a massive forge in the center of an enormous cave. It stretched up at least three stories, illuminated by the fire itself and the molten metal that poured from four massive cauldrons.

A hundred dwarves were all lined up against the walls, each one at his or her own blacksmith station, where they were hammering metal into flattened pieces. Other dwarves were at sharpening stones and sharpening blades into edges that were fine enough to behead a man.

"What are they doing?" she whispered. "That looks like a lot of weaponry for so few dwarves."

"They aren't for the dwarves." Goliath lifted a shaking hand and pointed to the blacksmith nearest to them. "They're all chained up."

Her eyes caught on the metal shackles around the dwarf's leg. Then she saw the next. And the next. All the dwarves were held to the wall against their will. The other end of the shackle had been hammered into the stone walls.

The dwarf nearest to them shifted and Lore could see the bloodied and raw edges of the wound the shackle had started. They hadn't been chained recently. They'd all been here for a while now, making swords and daggers.

None of this made any sense. The dwarves weren't making weapons because they wanted to do so. Who had chained them here?

More clanking, although this time it sounded far too familiar. Lore's eyes moved down the line of dwarves until she saw a metal suit of armor that moved without a man inside it.

An Umbral Knight. It walked up and down the rows, peering at the dwarves if they stopped working for even the briefest of moments.

"The King," Goliath whispered. "He's forcing them to build his army for him."

"But why is he doing it here?" she asked. "This is far from where his army should be based."

Unless he knew that this was where the actual battle would begin. Unless the King knew they were already here and he was making the last bits of armor that would erupt out of the ground to attack them.

Lore pressed her fingers to her lips. "He knows," she said. "He knows we're here."

Goliath's eyes met hers with horror and, silently, they both stood.

They needed to get back to their army and prepare for an attack. The King's eyes saw more than she gave him credit for. And this mistake might be her last.

CHAPTER 40

For a night full of thunderstorms only hours before, Abraxas questioned the clear skies of today. Not a single cloud obscured his vision as he crossed over the sea, and that was strange. Usually there were at least a few fluffy clouds that would hide him for a few moments, but no.

Today was only blue skies and a false sense of security that he didn't enjoy. There were too many ways for others to see him.

Although, he supposed that was the point of all this. Margaret had wanted him to be seen by the King. She wanted Zander to know that there was still a dragon for him to defeat.

Knowing Zander, Abraxas should fear that the King would shoot him down from the sky. After all, there were still two other eggs that Zander thought he controlled. Or at least, Abraxas had to assume that Zander didn't know the spell on the box had been lifted. Otherwise, this war would have started much earlier.

No boats were on the sea between the two outstretching edges of Umbra, and that was another detail which made him nervous. There should at least be a few fishermen who were out trying to bring in their catches of the day. Not a single boat floated on those calm waves, however, and he knew a warning sign when he saw one.

Even the locals knew there was something happening. The sea didn't suggest that there was evil here, but there was plenty enough to turn the waters red with blood in the coming days.

Solis Occasum appeared on the horizon. What had once been an impressive monolith of wealth was now a ruin.

When Abraxas had first come here with his family, he'd been shocked at how lovely the building was. The original family had built a castle at the very edge of the sea to worship the sun. The great metal piece atop reflected the rays wherever people wanted them to go. Usually, that was to three other towers that had long since crumbled. The square of light could always be seen overhead, like a spear of protection that kept the town near Solis Occasum safe.

Obviously, that safety hadn't lasted as long as they had expected. War came upon them far too quickly for any of them to run. The King's father had wiped them out in the matter of a few weeks.

The people who worshiped the sun disappeared, and with them the hope of the kingdom. They were the example the King's father had used to show the rest of Umbra what would happen to the areas that defied him. And as such, the entire kingdom had fallen. All of those people. All of those wonderful, glorious people who had shared so much love and light with the world had died.

And now, the son of the man who had destroyed it had invaded those sacred walls. Zander had taken what was not his, and he had forced them all to bend a knee to his will. That was the saddest part.

The souls in that building must scream every night. They must try to scratch at his eyes and force him to have nightmares of his own death. All of those actions would be in vain, however. Zander no longer cared about what others could do to him.

All he wanted was revenge.

Abraxas soared over those heartbreaking remains and saw the first Umbral Knights. As he suspected, they all turned bows and arrows on him the moment his shadow fell over the leftover city. They had been waiting for the right moment to kill the dragon who had betrayed their master. He stayed high in the sky so none of their bolts could reach him.

He wheeled overhead, trying to get a clear picture of what the King had planned beneath him. Except, this wasn't at all what Abraxas had assumed he would find.

There were many Umbral Knights, but not nearly enough to call an army. They were all standing within the ruins. Protecting what hid inside those walls, rather than preparing to march toward the Umbral Castle. And surely that was the plan. The man who Draven had interrogated had said as much. The King would move to the castle soon.

No army waited below him.

No. This was an entourage waiting to escort a king to a battlefield. What did Zander have up his sleeve now?

He took a long circle above, counting every Umbral Knight as he had been bid. But this wasn't right. A pit formed in his stomach because he knew there was something here he had missed. Too few Knights. Too many ways for Zander to have tricked them.

And then the King himself walked out of the ruins. Zander appeared rather healthy from what he could see, but a dead man could walk in this part of the world, so he shouldn't have been surprised.

Zander looked up at the dragon in the sky and pointed at him. Abraxas prepared himself for an onslaught of some new weapon the King had made, but nothing attacked him. No magic. No arrows. Nothing but Zander pointing at him as though the King wanted his dragon to look at him. To see what he was about to do.

And that was exactly what Zander wanted.

Abraxas winced as the King brought his hands together and the electric hum of magic filled the air. Even this far away from the castle, he could hear it. The whispering darkness that had always bound him to Zander's side no matter how much he wanted to free himself.

That magic had the same flavor as what the warlock had cast. It was the same spell that gave Zander life. He was certain of it.

Abraxas would know that power anywhere. And though he had prepared himself to wheel away from an attack, he had never guessed the King would bring his hands together in one solid clap that echoed throughout the very sky.

Then, impossibly so, dark shadows poured from Zander's chest. The King threw back his head and spread his arms wide, maniacally laughing as more and more darkness spilled off him until it was a stream of darkness. The shadows spread like some dark wave that had prepared itself to take over the world.

"Oh no," Abraxas snarled.

The shadows weren't some magical spell. They were the parts of the magic that made the Umbral Knights what they were. Every ounce of the dark magic that streamed out of the King already had a plan within it. An order from the King himself to destroy all who stood in their way.

The waves of shadow moved. Abraxas had assumed they would attempt to find whatever armor they could, but the shadows didn't. They rolled across the grass in the direction Abraxas had come from. Waves of darkness with a mind of their own.

The King had known, he realized. The King had known that they were coming and that meant there was someone in their ranks who had betrayed them. Someone who had told Zander to prepare differently. Otherwise, he would have moved his army through Umbra without traveling like this.

Abraxas didn't need to see any more. He changed directions and sped up as he went. The wind was on his side, but that also meant it would help blow the Umbral darkness toward whatever the King had set up to house them in. He had such little time to get back to the rebellion.

He had to warn Lore. All he could think about as he beat his wings through the air currents was that if he didn't get to her in time, that she might not make it. He had to be with her through the battle or he would never see her again.

It would be his fault that she died. His fault that the prophecy came true.

Abraxas flew over the shadows and fought against them until they both reached the water. Apparently, the salty sea gave that darkness enough hesitation that he could get ahead of it. Not by much, but enough that he had a chance to reach the rebellion in time. He could do this.

His sides heaved with breath as he reached the battlefields. In his frustration and exhaustion, Abraxas didn't even try to slow himself. He struck the ground with the full force of a dragon landing upon the earth and the ground shook and groaned with his weight. He didn't care. If it split wide open in a new canyon, then that would help them in the long run.

He let the change rip through him and stumbled toward the gathering of men and women who waited for him.

"Lore!" he screamed, his voice hoarse and ragged. "Where is Lore?"

A young woman struggled to the front of the crowd of warriors. Her dark hair was slicked back to her skull and a fine layer of gold scales dusted her neck and shoulders. "She's not back yet."

"What?" His mind struggled to catch up. "What do you mean, she's not back yet?"

"She went with Goliath to seek the hidden weapons left by the dwarves, and neither of them have returned." The young woman wrapped her arms around her waist, a worried expression marring her pretty face. "We thought to send someone after them, but we weren't sure if we should prepare the spells."

The sun was already high on the horizon. He glanced up and realized the King must know their plan about that as well. He'd been told everything. Down to every single detail of their plan.

Which one was the person who had betrayed them? Was it Margaret?

No, that woman was devious and deadly, but she wouldn't side with the King after everything he'd done to them. The only other people who knew about the plan in this much detail were her trusted generals.

Narrowing his eyes, he snarled, "By the time the soldiers get here, we won't be able to use the sun against them any longer. Your spells will have no use."

Another person moved through the crowd, pushing and shoving as she forced people out of her way. Margaret spilled forth, her eyes wild and her armor only half on. "Abraxas, what did you just say?"

"The King knows," he snarled, advancing on her with anger burning in his chest. "The King knows everything. He's set up some trap in this damned field because one of your generals told him everything."

"I trust my generals with my life," she spat back at him. "How dare you suggest one of them isn't true?"

"We're all going to die here." Abraxas pointed back to the fields. "The King has planted something out there. I don't know what. I watched him with only a handful of Umbral Knights begin their journey, but I saw him cast a spell that would create thousands of Umbral Knights. A dark cloud comes for us, Darkveil. A veritable wave of Umbral souls seeking whatever he's left out there, and there is nothing we can do to stop it."

Her eyes widened with every word, horror growing in her gaze. "This is a trap."

"We're all doomed if you don't make another plan in the next hour or so. The sea will slow the magic for a little while, but it will not stop his army from coming here. By the time the King reaches us, we'll all be dead." He gnashed his teeth, his body wanting to change back into the dragon without his control. "Get your people out of here before they all die."

"They came here to fight and damn it, we are all going to do so!" She spun away from him, hopefully to order people in different directions so they could all prepare for the wave that came for them.

"Margaret," he snarled. His voice pitched low and dangerously quiet. "Where is my mate?"

It was the first time he'd let the word loose from his soul, and now he couldn't pull it back.

Mate.

She was the other half of him and he refused to continue onward without her. She was everything that made him breathe and live and learn. The loss of her would tear him from his body until he was little more than what Zander had become.

The shadow of a great dragon who had loved and lost the most precious thing in his life.

"She's not returned," Margaret replied. He heard her voice shake with the words. "It is as Thalia said. They should have returned by now."

The edge of madness sparked in his vision. He could let all of who he was loose, release all control to the dragon inside him that wanted to burn this entire world to the ground until he found her. Part of him wished to do exactly that. He could. He was the only one in all of Umbra that could destroy the entire kingdom on his own, piece by piece. No one could stop him.

Except her. And she wouldn't want him to destroy all that she loved.

He held onto his sanity by a thread. Perhaps he would have lost all control if a scream hadn't risen through the ranks of warriors in front of him. They all parted like a wave as a young man with dark skin strode through them, holding up the head of one of Margaret's generals.

Draven took his time, letting everyone look at what he had done until he had stood before Margaret. Then he threw the man's head at her feet.

"You had a problem," he snarled. "I fixed it."

The head was familiar. Abraxas had known the man. He'd stood behind Margaret for a while and those his eyes had sometimes wandered from their conversation. Abraxas hadn't guessed that this was the one who caused all the problems.

Except, it would make sense. A man like that had every reason to stab them all in the back. All of this death and battle and fighting, that would bring any man to the conclusion that the easiest fix was to go back to the way things were. Unfortunately for this spy, Draven had gotten to him before he could run back to his king.

Abraxas narrowed his eyes on the deepmonger who had returned exactly when they needed him to. "Why are you here? Aren't you supposed to be with your family making sure that the Gloaming is the last place any stragglers end up?"

"Wouldn't you like to think that you can order me around?" Draven shook his head and then stood aside to point down the long row the crowd had made. "When I realized he'd betrayed us, I knew you would need more warriors until the rest of the army showed up."

A hundred Ashen Deep stepped out of the forest. Each one of them was dressed in leather armor that Abraxas hadn't seen in over two hundred years. Most held grimdags that whispered for souls to feed their never ending hunger. Some held mortal blades with serrated edges that would tear and rip at armor so the others could sink the grimdags into the space they created.

"This is far more Ashen Deep than you led us to believe were alive," Abraxas said.

Draven shrugged. "You don't need to know everything, dragon."

The ground below them rumbled, this time not from the heavy strike of a giant lizard hitting the ground from the sky. Dark magic crawled over Abraxas's shoulders and he knew they had run out of time.

He looked at Margaret and snarled, "Get your people together and ready them for a fight. They will need everything they have learned and more bravery than they thought possible. I'm going to find Lore."

"Abraxas!" she called out to his retreating back. "We need you here!"

Everyone needed him, he surmised. But he couldn't be a hero for all of Umbra. He only wanted to be a hero for her.

CHAPTER 41

L ore pressed her back to the wall of the cavern, squeezing her eyes shut for a moment so she could think without terror controlling her body. The question seemed to always be the same, no matter how many ways she tried to phrase it.

What do we do?

"Lore?" Goliath whispered. "I don't think we have a lot of time. There were enough Umbral Knights in there to be a serious problem."

"I'm aware of that," she hissed in response. "But there are also Umbral Knights outside of the tunnel."

And she had no idea where they came from. Goliath and she had both agreed leaving seemed the best course of action. Except, a group of Umbral Knights had already darkened the mouth of the tunnel.

She did not know how they had gotten there so fast. Lore knew for certain that she hadn't walked by any of the demonic soldiers while they were searching for the dwarven hills. So the fact that they were out front of this tunnel now stumped her. It felt like they were trapped.

They needed a plan to get out of here, but all she had were her daggers, a small sword at her back, and Goliath. He had his own daggers, but those throwing daggers wouldn't be enough for them to get through thirty soldiers on their own.

This situation was so much worse than anything they'd been in while they lived together in Tenebrous. She had complete faith they could handle five, maybe six, knights on their own.

But thirty?

Not a chance. The Umbral Knights would overwhelm them so quickly they wouldn't even be able to lift their blades. Which meant they needed another plan.

"Are there any other tunnels that would get us out of here?" she asked.

"I don't know, Lore. I'm not an expert on tunnels in this area. I grew up in Tenebrous, same as you." Goliath's tone was frustrated that she'd even ask such a thing. "I will not be the miracle that gets us out of here."

"Damn it." She looked behind them and noticed that the red lights of the forge had gotten even brighter. "And I don't suppose that light is because they're putting more effort into making more weapons?"

"I highly doubt we're that lucky."

She doubted it, too. Lore looked at their only escape and then back toward Goliath. "Do we make a run for it?"

He made a sound in the back of his throat and then gestured up and down his body. "Do I look like I'm the person who can make a run for it through Umbral Knights?"

Right, the short legs. That might make her plan a little more difficult than she'd expected.

"Well, what else are we going to do?" She supposed she could try putting him on her back. The extra weight would slow Lore down, but she might be able to sneak through the Knights and then take off running once they spotted her and Goliath.

It was a lousy plan, even she knew that.

The Knights in front of them shuffled, their armor clanking as they stood aside for something or someone. Was the King coming here? Had he found her that easily?

Lore let her hand drift down to the nearest dagger. If Zander wanted to fight her while she was stuck in this hole, then she supposed that was good enough for her. He wouldn't be the type of warrior to give her any chance to think, so she had to take this opportunity for what it was.

But Zander didn't walk toward the tunnel at all. Instead, they were both blasted with a wave of dark magic. She held her arm up over her face and tried not to cough as the shadows wiggled their way around her. There was something in that sudden wave of darkness that wanted to crawl inside her. It wanted to shove her own conscious mind out of the way and use her body.

Lore resisted. She pushed back with her own magic until the relentless onslaught moved past her. Then she could see the shadows for what they were.

It was the same darkness that spewed out of the Umbral Knights when she killed them. The shadows that would just find a new host unless she killed them with a grimdag.

But those shadows lacked form at this moment. They slithered across the tunnel floor as though they were ordered to come here. As though they knew exactly where to go.

"He's built an army underground," she whispered. "He used the dwarves to build an army right underneath our feet."

They had to go. They had to go now because once those shadows got themselves into an armored body, and there were plenty of them created by the dwarves, then they would be sitting ducks.

She groped for Goliath's hand, not taking her eyes off of the tunnel they'd just come out of. "Goliath, we have to go."

No one responded to her.

She looked down at her friend and saw that his eyes had gone black. He stood frozen in place, shaking as though someone had possessed him. Someone might very well be trying to, but her dear friend fought with every ounce of limited power he had.

Lore dropped to her knees in front of him, holding his hands in hers. "Goliath, you have to fight it. I don't think you can come back if you don't fight. And you have to come back to me."

His shaking intensified.

"I need you, dear friend. I need you to be by my side while all of this is happening. I can't do this without you." She squeezed his hands, as he had hers many times. "Fight, Goliath. That's what you would tell me to do. Fight it."

He took a deep breath, his entire body trembling with effort. And Lore prayed to whatever elven gods listened that he wouldn't disappear on her. She needed him. He was her rock. Her connection to a time when she hadn't been the savior. Just a scrawny street rat stealing to survive.

Lore remembered the first time he'd snuck her food in the apartment, telling her that someone had to look after a little elf girl if her mother wouldn't. He'd been here for everything. Her honest and kind friend who only wanted her to be happy.

"You told me to live once," she whispered so the Umbral Knights outside wouldn't hear her speaking. "Now I need you to live for me. You are my best friend, Goliath. Without you, I don't know how to continue."

He took a single deep breath in and held it. His face turned bright purple and the darkness in his eyes seemed to waver. There he was. Staring back at her with a ferocity that only a dwarf could muster.

With one great gust of air, he expelled all the shadows from his lungs. They fought against him. She could see the magic trying to crawl back to his nose and mouth. But he spewed it all out of himself in one great purge that she admired more than anything he'd done before.

And when his lungs were entirely out of air, the sluggish magic struck the floor with a wet plop and then continued toward the rest of its dark mass. Deep into the shadows of the tunnel.

"Well done," she said with a small chuckle. "And you always said dwarves weren't that good at magic."

"I almost didn't win," he muttered, his hands still shaking in hers. "But your voice pulled me out. Miss Lorelei, you know I couldn't leave you on your own. You'd make the worst decisions without me."

She tugged him into her arms and held him tight to her heart. "I would," she said, laughing. "I would."

She knew they had little time for this emotional outburst. They needed to get going, but she was so happy he had made it because she'd thought he wouldn't. Lore knew first hand just how strong the Umbral souls were, and he'd beaten death itself.

Goliath had never faced a creature like that before. Sure, he'd fought well his entire life. He knew how to battle most people and things. But curses like that were difficult for even the best of spellcasters.

He'd done her proud fighting it off like that. And also took a few years off her life from fear.

"Let go of me now," he said with a slight laugh. "We have to go, Lore. You know that mist is going to possess all the armor that the dwarves made and then come right back up this tunnel."

"I know," she muttered against his hair. "I just want a couple more seconds hugging you, if you don't mind."

He hesitated, but then wrapped his arms around her again. "For a second, Lore. But only that."

She tried to press all her love into him in that hug. She wanted him to know how much she loved him. How much she valued his friendship and how she couldn't wait until they could finally put all this behind them.

A voice whispered in her mind that he deserved to know about the prophecy. If anyone deserved to know she might have to say goodbye to them all, it was her dear friend.

"Goliath," she whispered, struggling to find the right words. "There's something I need to tell you."

Another shout echoed through the tunnel, although this one came from the fields beyond. The Umbral Knights all clanked together in formation, raising their swords at the fool who dared run at them.

Abraxas stood in the center of the field, clearly not at all threatened by the Umbral Knights who stood before him. "Lore! Goliath!"

Both she and Goliath stared at him through the armored plates before them. Lore would have been surprised if Goliath's jaw wasn't slightly open like her own.

"Your dragon is going to get himself killed," the dwarf said.

"Oh, I would guess that is his plan if I don't show myself." She stood up and grabbed onto his hand. "I think this is the best opportunity we're going to get. Are you ready to run?"

"As fast as these little legs can carry me." His brows drew down in concentration. "I'll be right behind you, Lore. Don't look back for me."

"I'm not letting go of you." She squeezed his hands. "We will get out of this together or not at all."

With one last look up at her, a bright grin on his face, Goliath turned toward the Umbral Knights and took a deep breath. Together, they sprinted through the group of the Umbral Knights before them. Lore hit the first few with her shoulder, throwing them off balance and into a few of the others. Then there was no chance for her to try fighting any of them.

They had to run.

Metal hands reached for them, but her legs carried them faster than an Umbral Knight could catch them. She wasn't sure where she was running to, only that straight should bring her to Abraxas and that's all that mattered.

Somehow, they made it through. By a miracle, she got both of them out of that tunnel, through the Umbral Knights, who were likely so surprised they didn't know how to act.

But they would have problems if they didn't keep going. Lore wanted to shout with laughter that they'd made it, but there would be time for celebration. Right now, she had to run toward Abraxas, who sprinted to them as well.

Her dragon caught her up in his arms with a quick swear. He pressed a kiss against her head and whispered, "You're alive."

"Still here," she said, breathless in his arms. "But I won't be for much longer if we don't get running. There are Umbral Knights everywhere."

"He knew we were coming." Abraxas released her so they could sprint in the opposite direction from the Knights. "I saw him in Solis Occasum. He had barely any soldiers with him. Draven killed the general he believes to have betrayed us."

Goliath struggled to keep up with them, but he still ground out through breaths, "At least the man's dead now."

"Not much good it'll do us," Abraxas replied. He leaned down and swept the dwarf up into his arms, running still as though the other man weighed next to nothing. "Fortunately for us, the Ashen Deep have decided to get involved with the fight."

Lore was so surprised she almost stopped running. "Excuse me?"

"Draven worked some magic." Although it seemed like he was reluctant to admit that Draven had done something right. "There's more people than we expected, and perhaps enough to survive the night."

"We'll survive longer than that. The spellcasters are here with us." She could lead them in a giant spell. Lore knew that was possible. She'd seen people do it before, although that wasn't quite what they were going for. The spell she'd seen was little more than a parlor trick to make people laugh at a party.

What they were endeavoring to do was larger than that. But it would work. She'd make sure it did.

"The sun's on the other side of the horizon, Lore." Abraxas guided them across the field of campsites. "Casting a spell now will only deplete the strength of your casters and the sun won't stay up long enough for us to kill enough Umbral Knights. And the King isn't here yet."

They all skidded to a stop in front of their makeshift tent. Lore whirled around to see the Knights had not followed them. Instead, she could see that they were focused on pulling out more and more of their brethren from the ground.

"He's trapped us," she whispered in horror. "We're stuck here waiting for him, because he knows nothing will stop until he is dead. They're immortal, and we die if we make only one mistake."

"And death for the Umbral Knights is but a mere period of waiting for the King to summon them again." Abraxas agreed. He let Goliath slip out of his arms and the dwarf landed on the ground with a hard thump.

"So, what's the plan?" Goliath asked. "If he's sent an army of undead soldiers ahead of him, how do we keep fighting them long enough for him to arrive?"

They didn't. That was the whole point of Zander's plan, at least from what she could see. By the time he arrived at the battlefield, safe and sound, without a care in the world, the opposing army would be dead. There would be no one left for him to fight and he would continue on toward the castle.

Defeating them, in his eyes, would be all too easy.

They needed a plan. A good one.

She opened her mouth, not sure what would come out. But before she could speak, another woman interrupted her.

Lore turned in shock to see that the Matriarch of the Ashen Deep had arrived with Draven. The woman's pale white hair glowed in the sunlight and the determination on her face was something to behold. Those white eyes saw right through Lore's fear, it seemed.

"We will fight," the Matriarch said. "The grimdags will kill the Umbral Knights permanently, while your weapons will only stop them for a little while. It is our duty to protect you and yours, now in your hour of need."

Lore bowed low, pressing both her hands to her heart as she honored the Matriarch. "I cannot ask your people to sacrifice their lives like that."

"You are not asking." The ancient woman smiled for the first time that Lore had ever seen. She'd filed her teeth into sharp points. "My people have waited a long time for a reason to slake their blood thirst. Let them fight, Lorelei of Silverfell. We know of you, and many of my people would be honored to fight at your side."

Lore walked up to the other woman and held out her hand. Clasped together, she pulled the Matriarch closer and whispered, "Until the dawn comes."

The Matriarch's eyes widened, but then she felt the woman's hand close around her forearm even more tightly. "Until the dawn comes."

CHAPTER 42

Abraxas had thought it would be easy to protect Lore. She didn't want to die, and therefore, shouldn't take any unnecessary risks. But the woman was damned well certain she would play a big part in this battle, and he refused to let her wander onto a battlefield with no one to look after her.

They all stood in one of the largest tents that Margaret had brought with her, packed shoulder to shoulder around a table with the remaining generals, the leaders of the Ashen Deep, a dragon, an elf, and a dwarf. As if that wasn't enough people in the room, all the egos that were building into a frenzy were enough to drive him mad.

Every person in this room had some opinion on how to plan their attack. They all agreed that a battle would have to be fought, even though the King wasn't here yet. The Umbral Knights would attack them. That much was for certain.

The Matriarch of the Ashen Deep leaned forward and pounded her hand on the map in the center of the table. "The Ashen Deep are not weak elves. We are more than capable of fighting throughout the night to give everyone a chance to rest until morning."

Lore shook her head. "I'm not taking that risk. You will lose too many of your own soldiers, and I don't trust anyone else to wield the grimdags if your people fall."

"So you believe enough of us will fall that there will not be another to take up the blade?" The Matriarch looked like she was about to launch herself over the table at Lore. "My people have trained their entire lives for this moment. What do you say to that, Silverfell?"

"That I have not trained a moment in my life for war, but even I can see how foolish a plan that is."

Margaret sighed and turned her eyes up toward the ceiling. "We all know that we have to fight against the damned Umbral Knights. They won't let all of us curl up in our tents and wait to attack in the morning. That simply isn't a reality that we can assume will happen."

He knew that Margaret was right, and that frustrated him to no end. There were only so many options for all of them right now, and none of them were good options.

He decided that the young people in the room had talked enough, and perhaps it was time for someone much older, who had been through a few wars, to speak. "Even if the Ashen Deep attack them, we know that whatever deaths they bring about won't help in the long run."

The Matriarch eyed him with no small amount of venom. "Death is death. The grimdag takes all its victims with it, and I don't think you can claim that fighting against them tonight would have no impact."

"It won't. The King can summon as many of those creatures as he wants. I think the best option would be to destroy as many vessels as possible." He lifted a brow, watching all the others as it dawned on them what he was saying. "There are a lot of suits of armor for them to possess out there, but little else."

Even Lore looked impressed with what he'd said. "Get rid of the vessels, therefore, make his army a lot smaller."

"Exactly."

She touched a finger to her chin. It was a very different plan than she'd offered up only moments ago. Lore was of the mindset that they all needed to throw themselves into the battle, even though he was very much against her doing so. There would be plenty of time for her to fight, but tonight was not one of those times that she needed to do so.

And maybe that was because he couldn't see her as well in the dark, and he wanted to keep track of her. But Abraxas wasn't about to admit that to anyone.

Even Margaret let out a little humph. "That's actually not a horrendous plan. But what do you propose we do? Keep the entire army up all night so that we're exhausted by the time the King gets here?"

If only they trusted that he wasn't a complete idiot and knew what he was talking about. Abraxas did his best not to let his eyes roll back into his head with the ridiculous question. "The Umbral army is only strong because of its numbers. There are limited soldiers out there, so we will have to minimize the danger. But if we keep the Knights away from us with a couple good shots, considering how many archers there are in your army, then I think we'll have the advantage."

Lore nodded, though still frowned. "We could keep everyone asleep in shifts. Archers for distance and then only a few people with daggers or swords to clean up the stragglers. We don't have to care about the grimdags, or risk any lives unnecessarily."

"Granted," he continued, "we won't be able to do that once the day hits. There are still quite a few Umbral Knights who haven't pulled themselves out of those dwarven tunnels."

And that was what he was afraid of. The mist was not exactly bright. The King had ordered them to kill, and that was what they would do. Their suits of armor made them a little more difficult to kill than the shambling zombies they'd seen in the Fields of Somber, but that didn't mean they were much more intelligent. An order was an order.

They were able to stalk through the streets of Tenebrous and keep the peace. Some could even talk, because Zander's father had given that order. And the order he'd given them was complicated. The task had to be incredibly detailed for the Umbral Knights to function like real people.

And as much as Zander liked to think he was as intelligent as his father, he wasn't. These Knights would shamble forward, continually trying to attack, while not having any other direction at all.

Abraxas knew the others would go for this plan, but he didn't know how to seal the deal. Unless, of course, he offered his own services.

He'd have to fight tomorrow on very little sleep. He wouldn't get one more night with Lore, as he'd hoped they would get. But this was war, and he had known this would turn into a nightmare.

Finally, when no one said anything else, he sighed and tossed up his hands. "I will also fight with whatever soldiers you choose. I will stay awake throughout the night and ensure that the sky is lit by my flame. When they need to aim, it will be a dragon who lights their way."

Margaret tsked. "You need to sleep for tomorrow."

Lore also seemed a little disturbed by what he'd offered. "So you don't want me to fight alongside the people who would die for me, but it's fine for you to go out there?"

"Yes." He met her gaze head on without a single hesitation. "And you know why."

He wouldn't lose her to some prophecy that an elf had spat out centuries ago. It wouldn't happen. And this was the first step he could take to ensure that he didn't lose her. No matter what.

Goliath moved closer to the table and pointed at a single spot in the center. "This is the best vantage point for the archers. It's high enough out of the way that the Knights would slow down having to climb that hill."

The Matriarch shifted closer as well. Her pale eyes peered down at the map, and again Abraxas had to wonder how she saw through the milky film. "And that would give our soldiers the best opportunity to strike at them. What do we do with the armor once it is vacant of the spirit?"

Well, he knew the answer to that, at least. "Destroy it," he rumbled. "Take a hammer or the blunt end of the sword and smash it to pieces."

The entire room stared at him in what looked like shock. Did they think he would be lenient with them? Why? He'd lived with the King for a long time, yes, and served with the creatures as well. But he knew better than anyone that there was no soul inside those horrible armored fools. They were conjured magic. Made to look and act as close to a person as magic could get.

That didn't make the Umbral Knights real, however. They were still just shadows inside a steel frame.

"We have no need to be afraid of them," he said. "Their numbers make them terrifying, but nothing else. If they are not ordered to speak, then they won't. They parrot what was given to them, and they only move because someone told them to. They are nothing more than the figment of what the King can think up. I, for one, am not afraid of that."

"Neither am I," Goliath said. He put his hand flat on the table and fiercely met every person's gaze. "We came here to fight. We knew this was our last stand and I am not willing to give up because of a change in plan. We fight until there is nothing left."

Lore laid her hand next to his, and her words filled the room with a brightness that rivaled the moon. "Let the sun rise."

Suddenly, the words took on a new meaning. They were said now in the hope that the sun would rise on a morning where everyone in this room was alive. In the hope that they would see each other again when the sun's rays touched upon their dirty and blood streaked faces again.

Abraxas put his hand on top of hers. "Let the sun rise."

Every person in the room followed. Their words lifted the phrase which had gotten them to this moment in time.

The Matriarch broke off first. Her expression softened as though she were pleased with the people before her. "I will gather my warriors. They will be ready to protect the archers throughout the night." She lifted a hand when Lore would have interrupted her. "Only half. They will change out through the night to ensure everyone is rested for the morning."

Margaret grinned. "I'll ready the archers. They will be prepared, although some of them will need to step aside and make more arrows. I'm not certain we brought enough for what the King had planned."

The two women left the tent with their people and a small amount of air filled the room. Abraxas felt as though he could breathe for the first time in a few hours.

Goliath looked between the two of them and then rolled his eyes. "Well, I suppose I'll wrangle up the soldiers who are good at smashing. I'm sure there are plenty of fighters out there who would love to take a hammer to those tin cans. You two just... hurry up."

He ducked out of the room and then they were alone. Again.

Abraxas didn't know what to say. He wanted to hold her. To kiss her. To tell her that everything would be fine because she'd be in her tent all night and then they would fight in the morning.

He couldn't tell her how frightened he was or how his gut twisted at the thought that this was their last evening. Instead, all he did was catch her by the back of the neck and draw her close to himself. He pressed a kiss to her forehead, lingering against the softness of her skin.

"I expect you to be careful," he said.

"I will be." She reached her arms around his waist and tugged him closer. "You are the one who will fight all night."

"Not much fighting. All I'm doing is providing the light." He pressed one more kiss to her head before stepping back. "Get some rest."

He watched as Lore wrapped her arms around herself. "I don't know how I'm going to sleep knowing that you're all out there and I'm tucked into our bed."

"Then just lie down and close your eyes." He gave her a wink, hoping that would make her feel at least a little better. "We'll need you and all the other spellcasters in the morning. Let us do the dirty work."

He didn't think for a second that she'd stay in her tent for very long. Lore didn't have it in her to not be involved, especially not now that they were so close to the battle. But he hoped she would at least listen to him. And if she ended up on the battlefield, he hoped she came to him first.

Ducking out of the tent, he strode through the many ranks of soldiers that were exiting their tents. Each and every one of these people looked to him as a symbol of their inevitable success. He'd do his best to help them, but... Well. A man could only do so much to save everyone.

He joined the others at the head of the army. It was easy to spot them with all the Ashen Deep standing on their own. They looked otherworldly in their strange armor and their whispering daggers that wanted to feast upon souls.

"Draven," he called out. "Are your people ready?"

"As much as we'll ever be."

"We need to cut through the Umbral Knights that are already headed this way." He pointed toward the large number of Knights that were gathering together. "Once we have a path to get to the mound, then the archers will follow along behind us."

"Easy enough." Draven pulled twin blades from his waist. "What are you going to do, dragon? Watch while we slaughter the masses?"

Oh, the elf really enjoyed baiting him.

"No," Abraxas replied. "I think I'll entertain myself by destroying what you leave behind."

He stepped out into the field by himself, waving at the others so they knew they should wait. And then he let the change ripple through him.

As the dragon, he could see so much better in the darkness. The Knights were gathering together as he'd thought, but they were in more of a formation than he'd expected. Abraxas should have guessed Zander would at least look at some kind of war book before he sent them off.

This might be a little more difficult than they had thought. Perhaps the Knights wouldn't be mindless, but they wouldn't know how to fight an army of the Ashen Deep. No one did these days. And he knew for certain that Zander would never guess the long dead elven clan would come out of the forest to fight alongside his enemies.

He looked behind him and saw the nerves in some of the soldiers' faces. He knew the archers had more fear in them than they should. The acrid scent made the air taste wrong. Their fear would get them killed.

So he stretched his long neck out and lifted his wings. Let that which terrified them give them strength.

Abraxas roared, long and loud in the darkness. He hoped the sound would reach all the way to the King's ears where he surely traveled to join them.

He hoped the King trembled in fear as the army behind him lifted their voices and screamed along with their dragon. And when it was finished, he glanced back and saw Margaret at the forefront of the archers. She held her own bow in her hands.

She met his gaze, then grinned. "Release the dragon," she called out. "Destroy them all!"

CHAPTER 43

Lore listened to everyone moving around her tent. So many people were marching into battle and getting into formation, ready to make sure that their home stayed safe and that they fulfilled their purpose.

And the person who had brought them all here was huddled in her tent, waiting for the day to break. It didn't feel right. She'd come here with a single purpose, and that was to ensure that she freed her people.

Remaining locked up and away from the battle was what a noble would do. She could only think that at this moment, she and Zander were the same person.

He was also avoiding the fight, even though she knew from firsthand experience that he was more than capable of battling alongside his Umbral Knights. But instead, he was taking the coward's way out. Letting others do the dirty work so he was in less danger.

Wasn't that what Abraxas had asked her to do? Stay here, away from any risk, and come in at the last moment. Refreshed. Well rested. How could she waltz onto the battlefield where everyone else had been fighting for their lives, and expect them to still respect her?

She stared up at the ceiling of her tent. A small seam revealed the full moon that rose above their heads. A good omen for a Silverfell elf, at least if she were heading into battle. The full moon always meant that they would win the battle to her people. They looked up to their mother as a sign that they were fighting for the right side and the right purpose.

Sighing, she tried her best to at least close her eyes. But the silver rays of the moon filtered down through the tent and touched her face, her hands, her shoulders. Almost as though the moon herself was keeping her awake. Keeping her aware of the sounds that surrounded her.

These people needed her. Not just to tell them what to do or to give them courage, but to show them how to fight like a real magical creature.

She couldn't stay in here while everyone else was out there. She just couldn't.

Lorelei of Silverfell was not some pretty noblewoman who made herself a false hero. She was the elf that kept moving. The elf that saw right through what the other nobles did and then moved in the opposite direction.

Rolling off her small mat on the ground, she reached for her armor. Each piece strapped onto her body like a second skin. Elven armor was enchanted to fit the wearer, and it had been made for a body like hers. The silver chest plate was etched with the symbol of her people. A star in the center with radiating waves of magic around it. The pauldrons on her shoulders had spikes coming off them, like the points of that star.

Black leather leggings kept her thighs protected, but also allowed her to move quickly. That was the only armor she would wear, even though Margaret had given her much more. The helmet was the only remaining piece that a Silverfell elf might have worn. But the plume of blue feathers wasn't Lore. She couldn't put that on.

Lore strapped two thin swords on either side of her hips and then strapped daggers up and down her thighs where she could reach them. The wicked blades were curved this time, perfect for hooking into an enemy and dragging them close enough to kill.

Her people had been warriors. They fought until their last breath and even then; they laughed up at the enemy who had finally killed them. She remembered the stories her mother told her about the ferocity of the Silverfell clan. Fallen too soon, but warriors each and every one.

She could not make the same mistakes as her ancestors. She would fight to win, not just to draw blood.

The flap of her tent fluttered in the breeze. But it wasn't a breeze who stood in the opening now.

Goliath crossed his arms over his chest and looked her up and down. "I thought you were supposed to be staying in your tent."

"Of all people, you know how impossible that was to ask of me." She tightened the last strap on her thigh and straightened. "I'm fighting with them, Goliath. They deserve that much."

"I figured." He gestured behind him. "Everyone is already heading out, so I thought I'd come and get you so you know where they're going."

"You didn't tell Abraxas?" Surprising. She'd thought Goliath would be on the dragon's side. But her friend didn't know about the prophecy, so maybe that was why he disagreed.

Goliath took a deep breath and then let it out. As though the weight of the world rested on his shoulders. "I worry about your safety, same as him. But I also know how long you and your family have fought for this moment, Lore. I will not take that away from you simply because I don't want to lose you."

Oh, how she adored him. Goliath had been her one constant in life since she was a child. Somehow, she wasn't surprised that he refused to fail her now.

Falling onto her knees, she drew him close to her chest in a quick hug. "Thank you, dear friend."

He hugged her back so tightly she heard her metal chest plate bend. "You look like the goddess she's painted you to be, you know. A Silverfell elf out on the battlefield will be a sight no one forgets. Not in times like these."

She supposed that might be right. Lore released him and pulled her hair back into a high ponytail, slick to her skull, then nodded at her friend. "To battle, then?"

"To battle."

They raced through the crowd of people in front of her tent and pushed through some of the warriors who hesitated. Lore could see the fear on their faces. She knew what they were going through.

They didn't know if they were going home tomorrow. Or if they would ever see their family or loved ones again. That fear had sunk into their skin and pulled at the bravery which had brought them here. It would continue to unravel them until they made a foolish mistake that would cost them their lives.

She refused to see that happen. These people were here because of her. They had traveled through the Gloaming, one of the most terrifying forests in all of Umbra. They had learned how to fight, even if it wasn't in their nature to do so. They had overcome all of that fear, and walked bravely to this pivotal moment.

"Where is Margaret?" she asked, searching through the crowd for that elf.

"She went with the first wave," Goliath replied. He kept up with her, and somewhere along the way he had picked up a giant hammer that he'd slung over his shoulder.

"Then who is leading everyone?"

"They have their orders." But she saw the grin on his face and how he was thoroughly enjoying himself. "Of course, there are a lot of ways this could go wrong considering there is no one to bring them into battle. Perhaps we should remedy that?"

She had no idea what he was about to do, but Lore had a feeling she wouldn't like it. She knew that expression on his face all too well.

Goliath's chest expanded and then he bellowed, "Look! Look, it's the Silverfell!"

Though his words had to have been difficult to hear over the sound of the crowd, she heard people repeat his words. The magical creatures surrounding her looked at the glowing figure who walked among them, and it was as though all their fears and anxieties had melted away.

Someone whispered her name as though in prayer.

"Lorelei."

"The Savior!"

"She fights with us?"

Lore didn't know when she had become a symbol of their courage, but she knew now that she couldn't forsake these people. She'd been right. Letting them fight on their own would only have led to more deaths, as they all questioned why they were here and what they were doing. They needed someone to walk with them.

If she could have ripped herself apart and thrown the pieces upon them like a blanket of stars, she would have.

Lore pulled out one of her swords. The glinting, elven-made blade shimmered in the moonlight. She reached up toward the moon, twisting her hand in the air as she beckoned her first mother to come down from the sky.

One of those stars was the soul of the woman who had given her life. The woman who had taught Lore to be brave and to have faith that she knew the right way to walk through this world without sacrificing pieces of herself. Her mother would guide her. Just as her soul always had.

A stream of moonlight broke away from the others. The ray danced through the air like a silken veil that a woman had let loose from her hand. It fluttered above Lore's head and then wrapped itself around her blade.

The light sank into the metal as though it had always been a part of the sword. And then her weapon glowed with all the light of the moon.

"The moon," someone whispered next to her. Their voice carried through the sudden silence of the battlefield. "The moon fights with her."

Of course it did. She was a Silverfell elf and though she hadn't been a particularly good one, nor was she full blooded, the moon knew a warrior when she saw one.

Lore lifted the sword over her head. "Tonight we fight," she shouted. "Tonight, we bring about the end of darkness in this kingdom. We have suffered in the shadows for long enough!"

An echoing shout rose as others lifted their blades. Every point glinted in the moonlight that suddenly seemed brighter. She could see better and knew where to bring this crew of warriors who had gathered together, even though they were likely supposed to be resting as well.

"We will not let our brothers and sisters die without us fighting beside them!" She looked up at the moon and felt her mother's spirit take her hand. "Let the sun rise!"

The shout echoed throughout the entire field. Warriors, archers, spellcasters — they all took up her chant. And though there were few, not even a fraction compared to the King's army, she felt the ground tremble with their words.

As one, they took off toward the battlefield. Together. As it should have been from the beginning.

Lore agreed that they would need to be rested tomorrow so that they could fight the King's soldiers better. She knew this would make their plan more complicated, but she also knew that these people deserved a chance to protect each other.

She refused to believe that the magical creatures of this kingdom were weak. They had survived through so much suffering. So much heartache and death and abuse. They would fight and no exhaustion or a single night of sleep would change that.

The wave of her warriors crested a hill, and then she saw them. All the Umbral Knights that the King had called out. She refused to falter, even knowing how many there were. It would be a long battle tonight, but that would not stop them.

She surveyed the situation that Abraxas, Margaret, and Draven had set up. The hill appeared to be working. Plenty of their archers were still standing and the Umbral Knights had created a rather impressive blockage for other Umbral Knights. The Ashen Deep swept in the moment an arrow pierced through the armor and Abraxas's flames lit the air for the archers to see.

However, the fields below them were swarming with Umbral Knights. There were so many. They moved like ants on an anthill, ambling toward the hill where the others would eventually be overwhelmed. Time was not on their side.

"Goliath!" she shouted.

Her dwarven friend raced up to her side. "What are you thinking?"

"Take them from behind," she said with a wild laugh. "We'll trap them between two waves of warriors."

"Risky," he said. "I like it!"

There weren't a lot of other options. Fighters from their side were already growing tired in the few hours it had taken for Lore and the others to decide they wouldn't stay in their beds.

They couldn't rush to the front lines without falling into the same problem that their friends now faced. Though they were still killing an impressive amount of Umbral Knights, there were just too many of them. But if Lore could split that army in half, they might make a bigger dent.

"To me!" she shouted.

Her sword flared brighter, as though it knew it had to become a beacon for the others to follow. And follow they did.

An army of creatures swarmed down the hills toward the back of the army of Umbral Knights. She had to make sure they didn't end up in the middle, just in case other Umbral Knights were still coming out of the ground. So she guided them all the way to the sands where they turned around and faced the Knights.

Lore stood at the front of her band of warriors and straightened her shoulders. "Have courage," she said, and magic made her voice swell over the crowd like the waves behind them. "Darkness cannot survive when there is light."

She lifted her sword, and the glow brightened. A shout rose from the depths of her belly, and she raced forward.

Goliath stayed at her side. Together, they struck the armored wall ahead of them with a ferocity that she knew made her ancestors proud. Lore bared her teeth and let her swords fly in whatever direction they wished. Her body knew how to fight. Her soul had done this a thousand times before.

A flash of metal caught her eye. She dipped low, dragging her sword along the seam that held the Umbral Knights chest plate together. The smoke billowed out of it like a dark cloud, though it turned around again. Seeking the same armor it had just fled from.

Goliath shouted and swung that hammer over his head. He brought it down on the helm of the Knight, crushing the entrance and the only eyes the creature would have. The smoke seemed to scream, but then left the field as it searched for a new host.

"That's it," she muttered. "That's how we're going to beat them."

Lore whirled and let a spell fly from her tongue. It amplified her voice, spreading through the battlefield. "Two warriors," she called out. "One to kill and the other to crush."

They heard her. The army shifted like chess pieces on a board. It seemed like it would work. Swords flashed in the moonlight. Hammers, blades, and maces swung immediately afterward, destroying what laid before them.

They fought like that for at least an hour. Though time escaped her. Lore's entire body felt as though it were covered in grime. Sweat, dirt, black magic... and blood.

She stepped over another magical creature who had fallen and looked around herself. It felt like she hadn't looked up in a while. Her side of the battlefield had dwindled on both sides.

It appeared Margaret's warriors had done the same. Though there were less Umbral Knights, there were less magical creatures as well.

She lifted a hand and swept a finger underneath her eye to get rid of the sweat that had pooled there. But when she drew her hand away, there was blood on her fingers. Was she bleeding? She didn't remember getting hit.

A wave of darkness approached her, but the person who stepped out was not an Umbral Knight. It was Draven. He raced toward her, catching onto her elbow. "What are you doing out here?" he asked, his voice fierce and angry. "Why aren't you in your tent?"

"I couldn't let them die alone," she rasped.

Lore lifted her sword and blocked an Umbral Knight from striking him across the back. She whirled with him, pressing their spines against each other as they both fought against two Knights. She plunged her dagger into the creature's eye and wrenched it out as Goliath wearily lifted his hammer over his head again.

They were so tired. When did her arms start shaking?

She spun around, breathless and tired. "You didn't come here to scold me."

"The sun will rise soon. We're gathering all the spellcasters, but then discovered you had left with half of them." He grabbed onto her elbow again as though he were going to drag her from the battlefield. "You need to come with me."

"They know what to do. I am needed more here." She spun again, catching a sword and tossing it aside. One more. She could kill one more.

Draven beat her to it. He whipped his sword so quickly she didn't see anything other than a flash of light. The Knight's head toppled from his shoulders and struck the ground with a dull thud.

"We don't have time, Lore. We need to go."

A roar shook through the air. The sound vibrated through her armor and made her heart squeeze in fear. She knew the sound of an enraged dragon, and when she looked up, Abraxas had spread his wings wide.

Fire poured from his mouth as he melted the armor of the Umbral Knights before him. That wasn't frustration. That wasn't exhaustion at having to fight all night. No, there was only one reason why her dragon would be that angry.

She turned and there he was.

Zander.

He rode on a black steed with eyes like fire. Magical creatures had swarmed him, but he cut through them with so much confidence it made her sick. Blood sprayed around him, painting his entourage of Umbral Knights with splashes of red.

"He's here," she growled.

Her heart said to go. Her heart said to fight him now because that was the moment she'd been waiting for. The moment the prophecy had said she'd been born for.

The whistle of a blade through the air made her flinch. She'd forgotten she stood in the middle of a battlefield.

Lore moved at the last second, seeing the weapon as though time had slowed. This Knight was larger than the others. He stood seven feet tall and carried a spike mace that he moved with too much ease.

It would have struck her in the chest. It would have pierced right through her armor if another person hadn't darted in front of her and wrapped his arms around the mace.

She watched in horror as Goliath carried the weapon to the ground with him. He hit hard, bounced twice, and then laid still.

He met her gaze and tried to smile, but then all the life faded from his eyes.

CHAPTER 44

Her ears were ringing. She couldn't hear anything other than a horrible sound that wouldn't stop, no matter how hard she pressed her hands against her ears.

He just... laid there. Staring at her with open eyes that had nothing in them. No soul. No Goliath.

Her worst imaginings were that he got injured in battle and make jokes with her about how he'd always wanted an elven nursemaid. They were supposed to get better together after fighting a war that would end all wars. He was supposed to laugh at how worried she was about him, because she was always worried. Maybe he'd find another dwarf when they saved the others. A lady who would take the place of his long-lost love, or at least prove to him that love was still... still...

Sounds rushed back in. The Umbral Knight who had killed Goliath walked over to the mace and put his hand on the handle.

He was going to pull it out. He'd rip Goliath's chest open doing that and then she would be standing here, staring at his heart that wasn't beating any longer.

A flash of rage burned through her until she couldn't recognize herself. She screamed, and the sound wrenched out of her body with a horrible strength.

Lore leapt upon the back of the giant Umbral Knight. She clambered up him, climbing his limbs as though he were nothing more than a tree shifting in the winds. She didn't care that she'd dropped her swords the moment Goliath hit the ground. An elf didn't need a weapon to kill.

Rage fueling her movements, Lore wrapped her thighs around the massive Knight's head. It spun, trying to take her off its back with grasping hands that she ducked away from. And then Lore screamed again. The ragged sound pulled itself out of her broken heart as she plunged her hands into the eye sockets of the Knight's armor.

"Fear me," she hissed. "For now you will know what it feels to die."

Her hands burst into a bright white light. Tendrils of magic crept down her arms and the Knight screamed in pain. For the first time, she heard one of their voices without magic parroting another's words.

"It burns!" The creature's voice was like nails scraping down stone. "It burns!"

She pushed harder into the helmet until the armored form went limp. Lore let the beast carry her to the ground, where she rolled from its back and landed on her knees before Goliath.

She didn't even have hands to touch him with anymore. The white light hadn't faded at all, and she could see there wasn't flesh there anymore. It was just... moonlight.

What should have been hands shook as she reached for him. A keening sound erupted from between her lips and she didn't recognize the voice. It wasn't her, it couldn't be her making that horrible sound.

Tears streamed down her cheeks, and she gulped for air that her lungs refused to take in.

He was gone.

He couldn't be gone because she'd... She'd promised him that she'd be there. She would stand by his side and nothing would touch him. They were supposed to fight together.

Until the dawn came.

Had she cursed him? Had her prophecy somehow leaked out of her body and made him yet another casualty of what she would become?

"Lore," the voice broke through her cries. "Lore, we have to go! Now!"

She looked up at Draven and rocked from side to side. "He's gone," she whispered repeatedly. "He's gone, and I did nothing. I didn't try to stop it. He's gone, Draven."

"I know." Even the elf's words were choked with emotion. "I know, Lore, but there's nothing we can do now."

He slid his arms underneath her, trying to drag her upright.

"Don't touch me!" she screamed.

A flare of magic burst out around her. Draven was pushed back from the force, his feet leaving marks on the ground as he slid. He braced himself with a fist and looked at her in terror.

He lifted a single hand, palm up, as though he were reaching out to a rabid animal. "We need to get you to Abraxas, Lore. Remember the plan. Remember the prophecy."

Her heart beat in her ears with a thud like the ancient drums of an elven army that descended upon her.

She lifted her head and watched the battlefield unfold before her eyes as though she were flying on the wings of a raven. A dryad screamed out, her cries cut short. A sword had sunk into her belly, while the next sliced her throat. The orc she'd trained hammered another Knight dead, but he turned around too late to see his partner felled. He screamed, and a blood rage came over him. Five Knights attacked at the same time and brought him onto his knees with five blades in his belly.

Abraxas's fire raged over the battlefield, but he was tired. He could not see who stood before his flames and the Knights were throwing magical creatures into the fire that burned a person down to their soul.

Then she saw them. The white, glimmering spirits of Silverfell elves kneeling all around her.

"This is what we feared," they said as one. "They will all die screaming, as we have never beaten the mortals before. This is why we sent you."

She took a long, steadying breath. Her fingers moved through the mud and the blood that coated the ground around Goliath. She picked up her twin swords, the ones that sang with moonlight.

"I'm staying," she said and her eyes turned toward Draven once more. "Tell Abraxas I love him."

His eyes widened, not in horror, but perhaps in fear. "Your eyes are white, Lore."

She stood. Her legs no longer shook. Her fingers held onto the daggers with renewed purpose. "Tell him the dragonlings need him. That this world needs him."

Draven shifted and sank onto his knees. He pressed his fingers to his forehead and flicked them toward her in the gesture of utmost honor among elves. "Goddess Eternal," he whispered, his eyes downcast as though he couldn't bear to look at her. "Your word is my will."

As she walked past him, Lore patted his shoulder twice. And though she shouldn't have been surprised, she saw that her touch left a handprint in silver burned through his shirt and embedded in his skin.

Lore should have feared herself. She should dread the magic that coursed through her veins and the horrifying feeling of power that was not hers. Yet another part of her knew this was the moon. She had become someone else so she could finish this.

Her ancestors walked with her. Side by side. A hundred Silverfell warriors with bows in hand and arrows that soared through the air. They felled any Knight who tried to attack her with spectral arrows that shattered the dark magic within it.

A hand slipped into hers. And as she turned her gaze to the side, she was met by her mother.

"We walk together, daughter." A crystal tear slid down her mother's cheek. "Together."

"Let the sun rise," Lore said.

"And so it does."

She looked at the horizon. The sun rose in a blood red sky, hovering at the same time as the full moon.

All it took was a lifted hand and a flick of her wrist to move all the Umbral Knights to the side. They struck each other and fell like children's toys. Leaving a path for her to walk to the undead King.

She could almost hear the magical creatures as they saw her. The Savior of Tenebrous, the last Silverfell, the woman who walked with Death.

"Lore!" Abraxas's scream echoed across the battlefield.

He would come for her. She knew he would. And then he would try to stop her from battling Zander on her own, and that simply would not do. She'd accepted this was her path. No one else could kill the King, but she had the power of the moon underneath her skin.

Zander's laugh reached her ears. "Yes, Lore!" He lifted his arms and beckoned her forward. "Come to die, little mongrel."

Oh, one of them would die. Or perhaps they both would. She didn't care anymore.

Goliath's face flashed in front of her eyes. This man was the one who was to blame for the death of a life so bright that Goliath had set himself apart from so many others. He was her best friend. A soulmate as no other had ever been before. A part of herself.

"Call your dragon to fight for you!" Zander screamed.

And while she knew Abraxas had already rushed to join them, she also knew that wasn't the way. This would not end with a dragon devouring this cursed being.

"No," she whispered, though magic amplified her voice through the entire field. "This stays between you and me."

She waved her hand again and all the Umbral Knights blasted away again. Even his bloodied Knights who stood beside him. His horse reared as more magic bloomed from her skin. Light peeled off of her and created a bubble of a shield around them. An arena, of a sort, to end this now and forever.

Zander's eyes widened, but then he laughed. "You've gotten more powerful."

"So have you."

"Ah, yes. But mine is stolen." He shrugged. "Doesn't matter. Power is power, and I think you'll be surprised at the new tricks I've learned."

He clapped his hands together and more shadows burst from his body than she could count. They were Umbral Knights, but... stronger.

They rushed toward her face like the one that had possessed Goliath. These weren't just shadow spirits. They had a purpose that was more dangerous than all the others.

White light rose through her hands and she lifted them as if they were the only shield she needed. The power that coursed through her flared, holding the shadows at bay. But the longer she held them up, the farther she saw her body starting to disappear.

Light consumed her to the elbows now. No longer Lore, but someone different. Someone new.

The King tired faster than she did. The stream of darkness broke, and he slumped over his horse, breathing hard.

"You have gotten a lot more powerful," he said with a small chuckle. "But you won't win with a few parlor tricks."

"Few?" she replied, walking toward him with slow, measured steps. "These are not a few. I am no longer the half elf you beat."

Zander swung his leg over the horse and jumped down onto the ground. He looked worse than she remembered. The rot had spread through his body in black veins that were puffy with magic and sluggish blood. The shadows in the wound at his neck undulated, like eels underneath his skin.

What had happened to him in the time since they'd been gone? She knew that keeping a body like his animated for longer than it was supposed to was difficult, but...

He gestured to himself. "Not what you expected? Apparently, it's not good to cheat death. The longer I'm alive, the uglier I get. I have you to thank for that."

"Ah, yes. You love to blame your failings on someone else, don't you?" She gestured at him with her sword. "I believe the last time we were like this, you won."

"The last two times," he corrected. "What makes you think it'll be any different this time?"

She didn't have time to answer. He lunged for her, too quick to be mortal and yet not quite impressive enough to be anything else. Lore shifted at the last second, letting his blow glance off her shoulder. His sword touched her pauldron and skidded off it.

He was right, though. The last two times she had fought him, she'd failed. Perhaps that was because she had fought alone.

Her mother's spirit slid behind her and lifted her arms. "Like this," her mother whispered in her ear.

Lore let the spirits guide her. Her blades were quicksilver in the moonlight, that gave her power. She glowed with power and that blinded the King as she whirled her blades. Lore spun in the air, her entire body moving in a great arc, and then landed in a crouch behind him.

The King stumbled back and pressed a hand to the wound on his cheek. "It's not just you in there anymore, is it?" he asked.

"I am prophecy," she said, standing with her shoulders squared and her back straight. "I am ruination and the end of the world as you know it."

"You are nothing but another half elf who will die by my hand." He bared his teeth in a horrifying snarl and then leapt for her again.

Lore blocked every one of his strikes. Their blades met and sparks showered down around them. A rain shower of gilded sunlight that burned and sizzled as it touched the ground.

"You have killed too many," she hissed, locking their blades and drawing him closer. "I want you to feel what they felt. I want you to experience a thousand deaths before I send you to the grave."

His arms shook as he pushed into her, trying desperately to get her to release his sword. "I cannot die, half elf. The curse protects me from magic and death itself."

All the people she'd lost before her vision. The hundred people who had fallen in this battle. The dead girls from his bridal parade. All the children in Tenebrous who had suffered for so many years.

Goliath.

So many people, so much blood on his hands. How did he even look at them? How could he eat with fingers that dripped with so much blood he must taste it on his tongue?

He was the man who had caused all this. Certainly his father had started it. She understood that. But he had continued the work of a madman and never once stopped to think about how dangerous that was. Or that he was becoming a monster himself.

Lore shifted her grip and let the moon magic crawl up to her shoulders. Her arms had disappeared, turning into white hot heat. The King's eyes flicked down to what was now her body and then his eyes looked up at her.

Finally, she saw fear in him.

"You are safe from many things, Your Highness." Lore dragged him closer with her curved blade and spat, "But you are not safe from me."

A hundred screaming souls of Silverfell elves plunged into her body. The light and power of the moon flooded into her body. She couldn't think or see or breathe. She was endless light itself.

And darkness. Deep inside herself, beyond the blinding starlight, there was a quiet, dark sea waiting for her at the end. Not terrifying. Not sad. Just peaceful and calm.

Without fear, she released her hold on one of her swords and lifted a burning hand. Like a spear, she shoved her fingers between Zander's ribs.

"You are no longer welcome in my home," she said, each word coming as a labored breath. "You will go back to whatever nightmare birthed you."

Zander's breath caught in his throat, but he croaked, "I am death. Eternal and inevitable. I will return."

"No," she replied, then twisted her hand until she could feel his black heart in her palm. "I walk with Death, and you are just talented at hiding. But there's nowhere to hide now. The grave sings for you, Zander."

A burst of light behind her was the first spell of her people. They drowned out the Umbral Knights, not allowing them even a second of shadow to hide in. She heard their screams even through the shield.

"What have you done?" he hissed.

"I finished it," she replied, then ripped out his heart. "And now I have finished you."

His mouth fell open and his eyes widened as he watched her lift his heart up to the full moon. Lore knew this was the moment the prophecy had depicted. A half elf holding her prophecy to the sky as her mortal form fell away, and she became magic incarnate.

Zander fell to his knees behind her, muttering some garbled sound of begging.

But she was not afraid. She wasn't.

All she wished was that she had a moment to tell Abraxas how much she loved him. Her eyes turned through the shield and caught upon the silhouette of a dragon that blocked out some of the light. He was her soul. He was all that remained of her to live on.

"I love you," she said, hoping her words flew through the magic and battle. "I will always love you."

Lore looked up at the full moon, tilted her head back, closed her eyes, and let the magic consume her.

CHAPTER 45

Abraxas turned his head away from the blinding light that filled the battlefield. It speared through everyone like a wave of power, rivaling the light of the sun itself. Through barely slitted eyes, he watched as countless Umbral Knights fell to their knees.

He'd seen the spellcasters gather as the first wave of their magic hit the field. Lore's idea had worked. And then the magic dimmed until a second wave hit. Not from the spellcasters. Even they seemed confused.

No spell could do what happened here.

The light had a mind of its own. Wriggling underneath the holes in the armor of the Umbral Knights and sliding into their hearts. It reached into the shadows hidden within the armor and pierced through the magic that created the Umbral Knights.

Over and over again, he heard the dark magic screaming. As though there were actual people inside that armor, but he was certain that wasn't true. The magic itself had met something stronger than it was, and that terrified the curse which had ruled this kingdom for so many years.

Finally, that bright light faded. It withdrew from the battlefield slowly. He wondered if that magic searched for anything that might still linger in the darkness, but there had been no darkness in that light.

Even his own shadow had burned away.

Swallowing hard, he turned his giant head toward the bubble of light preventing anyone from getting to Lore. He'd seen it bloom and knew she had denied him the right to protect her. Anger still burned in his chest for that.

She would learn that denying a dragon of anything had consequences.

As he looked around at the soldiers and magical creatures that stood, he realized they'd won. Not a single Umbral Knight stood. All that empty armor laid on the ground, either crushed by their hammers or shockingly dead after the magic that Lore had expelled.

That awe kept him going. He let the dragon form melt away and stumbled as he turned back into a man. His legs felt like jelly.

How long had he been fighting? All night. He was certain of that. Though it felt like he'd been going for days now, and he had no idea how much longer he could stand. Abraxas stumbled to the right, then the left, then managed to get his legs under him enough to walk.

A warrior walked by him with black eyes and a bloody grin. The deepmonger clapped a hand to Abraxas's shoulder. "We did it," he said, his tone surprised as they all should be. "We really did it."

Abraxas had a hard time believing it, too. They had somehow done the impossible, although most of that had been thanks to Lore.

His vision skewed, suddenly so blurry he couldn't quite see where he was going. How long had it been since he'd breathed fire like that all night? A very long while. He'd spent far too long in the castle, if that was what tired him out.

Lore.

He had to get to her.

He had to get through that shield so that he knew where she was and how she had fared. She'd survived, otherwise that light would have dimmed. She was still there. He knew.

He'd feel it if she were gone. It wouldn't feel like this. This strangely ill wave that crested over his head and spilled down into his stomach like he was going to throw up. That was exhaustion. His soul hadn't ripped out of his body yet, and he didn't feel any physical pain.

No. All that nausea and sudden anxiety was because he wasn't there with her. Not yet. But he would be soon and then everything would be set to rights.

Swallowing hard, he continued onward through the battlefield. His feet slid in the mud. He stumbled onto his hands and knees, then lifted his palms to see it wasn't mud. It was blood. His vision cleared, all the blurry edges of figures sharpening into people he recognized.

Draven. He walked toward Abraxas with a body in his arms and ash on his face. This was the first time Abraxas had ever seen the young man look... scared. Or sick. Or maybe that was sadness on his face. He didn't know. What would make one of the Ashen Deep sad?

And then his eyes trailed down to the body in the man's arms.

Goliath. The dwarf was limp in Draven's arms, even as blood trickled over the dark elf's hands.

"Abraxas," the raspy voice came from his right. Margaret limped up to his side. She held onto her left arm, the one she used to draw her bow, and he noted that someone had tried to cut her arm off at the shoulder. "Abraxas, it's over. Isn't it?"

He had the strange sensation that he wasn't in his body. Not really. Something pulled him away from them all. He could only note their injuries, but couldn't feel the worry or the anguish that should come after.

Even Goliath. His dear friend and the man who had helped them through so much. He could only feel the slightest ache in his heart, as though it were already full of some sadness he had yet to realize.

His stomach twisted and rolled in his belly. Abraxas turned away from Margaret and vomited on the ground, even though there was nothing in his belly to bring up.

Finishing, Abraxas wiped his mouth on the back of his hand and straightened to show Margaret, who walked toward them. But he didn't need to. Margaret's eyes had already welled up, and she took two large steps away from Draven.

"No," she whispered through her fingers pressed against his lips. "Not him."

"You knew there would be some casualties," Abraxas said through his teeth. "You knew we would lose some."

"I didn't think we would lose him." Margaret shook her head as though denying the sight before her. "I have known him since he was a child. I didn't want him to join the rebellion because he was too young and he convinced me. He was so..."

"Charming," Abraxas filled in.

His heart compelled him to move forward, and so he did. He walked across the bloodied field and put his hand on Draven's shoulder. Together, they looked down at the peaceful expression on Goliath's still face.

"Did he die well?" Abraxas asked. He knew that Draven would understand the question for what it was.

There were few deaths that were acceptable for people like them. The men and women who fought until their last breath and who knew their afterlife was filled with people the same as them. They had battled their entire lives, and Goliath had earned a death like that.

"He fought well," Draven said, his voice steely and his expression hard to read. "He saved her life."

The words were a knife to his gut. "And?"

Draven swallowed hard. And that was when Abraxas felt some emotion scrape inside him. Like someone had pressed a knife to his throat and no matter how many times he tried to swallow, he couldn't get past that pinprick of pain.

"Abraxas," Draven started, trying his best to speak. "She fought the King on her own."

He knew that. They all knew. They had seen the bubble of her shield go up and then the blinding wave of light.

He had seen it all. But what was Draven trying to say?

The eyes of the Ashen Deep turned dark and welled with tears. He moved toward Margaret and settled Goliath in her arms. Then, Draven backed away and fell onto his knees in the mud and the blood.

Abraxas watched the deepmonger intentionally put his shaking hands on his thighs. The pose was one of great remorse for the elves. He'd seen a hundred of them kneeling like this for days on end as they mourned a significant death.

"No," he muttered, backing away from Draven while shaking his head.

"My son." The Matriarch joined them with the remaining Ashen

Deep. Quite a few were still alive. "What has happened?"

Draven lifted his head and met his mother's gaze with one of deep and profound loss. "The prophecy has been fulfilled, Matriarch."

No.

He refused to believe it. He couldn't believe that he wouldn't know the instant she was gone, but then his stomach twisted again and that fucking nausea wouldn't leave him alone to think for a moment.

His heart thudded in his chest. Once. Twice.

"No," he muttered, refusing to acknowledge what his body had already known. His soul had felt her leave, and he had been sick with the anxiety of it since that damned light had flooded through the battlefield.

He wouldn't believe that. He couldn't.

Abraxas spun around and ran across the battlefield. He sprinted past men and women who helped others stand or who mourned the loss of loved ones. He leapt over the bodies of Umbral Knights, crushed beneath hammers and folded like a child had crumpled paper in their hands.

He'd never run so fast in his life. He reached the shielded bubble at the same time that the magic finally dissipated. The shield she had thrown up to keep him out fell down the moment he tried to touch it.

Abraxas stepped into the arena she'd made to destroy the King, searching for her, but his eyes only found the man who had fostered hate within an entire Kingdom.

Zander laid on the ground, gasping for breath. A giant hole in his chest glistened in the sunlight, blood dripping down his sides from where his heart should be. Sluggish black magic moved over the wound, but it was too weak to heal him. So it kept him alive for the few more moments that it could, even though that magic would die out soon enough.

He walked over to the side of the young man who had tormented him for years and stood over his body. Abraxas should have felt something. He should have been sad to see what had happened to Zander and yet... He could feel no pity for this man. Not even an inkling of it.

"Where is she?" he snarled.

Zander's roving eyes slowed down and then focused on the dragon who stood over him. He sucked in a deep breath that sounded like his lungs had already filled with blood. "Gone," he croaked.

"Where?"

The Once King coughed, the sound wet and rough. "A goddess. She became power and then... gone."

He refused to believe such a thing. Abraxas leaned down, ready to grab the shoulders of this rotting corpse and shake him until he told the truth. The ramblings of a madman would not point him in the right direction to find the woman he loved.

"Abraxas." Draven's voice cut through the anger and prevented him from grabbing onto Zander as he so desperately wished to.

Whirling around, he snapped, "What?"

The dark elf stood outside the area where the shield had been. Abraxas realized there was dust on the ground where the circle had started. Or not dust, but the lingering remains of Silverfell magic, coating the ground in lustrous detail.

He turned his gaze and realized that sparkling magic continued all around him. The entire circle, etched out onto the ground.

"I was standing outside the shield," Draven said, his voice shaking. "I saw it. We saw it all, Abraxas, all of us who were close enough to see through the shield. A light unlike anything I've ever seen. She became the rays of the moon and then she just... She disappeared. The magic ate her up. I watched her body become light itself. She didn't... She didn't fear it."

No.

He closed his eyes, squeezing them shut and taking a deep breath through his nose. He refused to believe that she was gone. That she was dead.

But then he felt the slightest touch on his shoulders. The kiss of a wind that shouldn't move like that. It tangled around his arms as though it were giving him a hug. On the next slow inhale, he could smell her. Sea salt and wild things growing in a field he could no longer reach.

That ache settled into his body. The nausea turned into an understanding that he had lost her and he was not there when it happened. He had promised her that he would be by her side and that nothing would ever take her from him.

She'd known this would happen, he thought. From the beginning. The moment she'd seen the prophecy, she had known what would happen to her, and she'd been trying to tell him.

Abraxas opened his eyes and saw that the silver dust on the ground had spread. Intricate patterns like that of a spell grew toward his feet. They were roots of an ancient tree, something whispered in his mind. Roots that would become a blessing made only by her sacrifice.

He stepped back and watched as they weaved together, spreading toward a single point within the circle. Like a man drunk, he followed them. His staggering footsteps led him all the way to the center, where the light tangled into itself in a bright circle of light.

A beacon of hope.

A place to remember.

Abraxas fell onto his knees as the pain hit him all at once. The loss of her. The future he'd promised her that no longer would come to life. The path he now had to walk alone, because he'd promised that he would be there for the dragon babes they had brought into his world.

He tilted his head back and let out a scream of anguish. All the rage he felt at this moment, the loss that made his hands numb and his heart shatter in his chest, came pouring out of him in a single roar of a dragon.

A dragon who had found his mate after centuries of searching and then lost her in less than a year of a mortal lifetime.

A gust of wind blew up, coiling around him in a great tempest of magic. It spun the sound of his heartbreak up towards the clouds, who consumed his sadness and turned it into rain. The storm appeared out of nowhere, but it did not match his rage. It was a quiet storm. Drops of water fell onto his face and hid the tears that streamed down his cheeks.

When he was finally spent, he let his head fall back and stared into the light before him. The light where she had last stood. The light where a goddess had come to this realm and blessed them with a sacrifice that no one would ever forget.

He lifted shaking hands and pressed them into the dirt where she had stood. As though he could touch her one last time.

He did not know how long he knelt there, shaking and in so much pain that he felt it throughout his entire body. Eventually, he heard the sound of humming around him.

Abraxas lifted his head and saw all the Ashen Deep in a circle around him. They knelt as Draven had first tried. On their knees with their hands pressed to their thighs. They tilted all their heads back toward the rain and let it drip down their cheeks to mingle with their own tears.

A hundred of them. And more people behind them as magical creatures from the army joined their mourning.

All of them. Here to honor her memory.

"Lore," he whispered. "I wish you were here to see this."

Because he could do nothing else, Abraxas sat back on his heels and placed his hands on his thighs. He turned his face to the sky. The rain poured over his face, as though someone touched loving fingers to his cheeks.

He had lived an impossible sort of love and having lost it made him realize that he had never felt so alone in his life.

EPILOGUE

braxas!" Beauty called after him.

He could hear her stomping through the halls and knew the anger in her steps. She had argued with him until she was quite literally purple in the face, but none of it would change his mind. He'd made his choice, and the others agreed with him.

Of course, she wasn't the only one arguing her point. There were plenty of people here who thought he should stay. No one wanted to lose a dragon to protect them, even though they had no reason to need his protection any longer.

He had fought for them. He had lost the greatest part of who he was, and paid the worst price any of them could ask of him.

Now he was ready to leave.

"Abraxas!" she shouted again. "You can't just give up on us like this!"

"I'm not giving up," he snarled. "I'm just leaving."

"We're already mourning so many friends." The sound of her footsteps paused in the middle of the hall. "Why are you making us mourn the loss of you as well?"

He paused in front of the room he and Lore had shared. A spike of pain drilled its way into the back of his head as though pain was the only way he could remember that she had once existed.

Abraxas took a deep breath. "I once told Lore that if she died, none of you would ever see me again. I wish I could tell you that was a lie, Beauty. But without her, I cannot stay here. I cannot suffer through her memories every hour of every day. Not like this. Her loss will drive me mad."

"And you think it doesn't do that to me? You think I don't walk through these halls waiting for her to order me around? Or for Goliath to make some snide jest because Zephyr and I are holding hands?" Beauty raced toward him. He felt her thud against his back as she wrapped her arms around him. "We can get through this together. If you stay."

He patted her hands around his waist, but he knew that wasn't true. He couldn't stay here when he knew that she'd once roamed these halls. The ghost of her would awaken something dark inside himself.

"I cannot do that," he replied. "You mourn in the ways of mortals. I have to walk my own path."

"Why?" She released her arms to stomp in front of him. "Why do you have to suffer on your own?"

"Dragons mate for life. If one of us loses a mate, then the other dies. I cannot choose that path because of the children Lore and I helped bring into this world. My mind will stretch thin soon, and I will not be able to tell reality from what I've conjured up in my mind. The farther I am from the memories of her, the better for all of us. The longer I will have."

Beauty's expression clouded. "So you're just going to pretend she never existed?"

"Oh, no." He could never do that. She was part of his very soul. "I'm running from her ghost, Beauty. But she'll always find me. Just like my thoughts will always find her."

He brushed past her and entered the room. There was only one thing he wanted from here, the rest he would leave behind.

Lore had left a single dagger behind. It was the one he'd seen her use most. Plain, simple, with a wicked edge.

Her mother's dagger. The one she had promised to never leave behind.

Lifting it with reverent hands, he slipped it into a pouch that he'd wear around his neck for the flight. Then he left the room without looking at anything else.

Beauty still trailed behind him, arguing the entire way. He'd heard it all by now, and she'd run out of arguments. Everything she said now was already what she'd said before.

They reached the courtyard together, where Zephyr and Draven already waited for him. They had rigged up the strange contraptions he'd asked for. Twin cages made of twisted metal and steel with large hooks on the top.

Hyperion and Nyx were in each one. The dragon babes hadn't taken the loss of their mother well. They both curled into small balls in the center of their cages, large eyes watching him as though they were afraid they might lose their father as well.

He walked up to Hyperion's cage and wrapped his hand around the bars. "It won't be for long, my son. Soon, we will be in the home of the dragons. We will discover our history together."

Dragons weren't meant to be in cages. However, these two still couldn't fly and he refused to stay here a moment longer. Which meant they had to stay in the cages so he could carry the two of them across the sea to Dracomaquia. He had no idea what waited for them there.

But it had to be better than here.

Draven stepped into his line of vision, arms crossed over his chest. "Are you sure this is what you want to do?"

"I have no other choice." Abraxas held out the rope and dagger in his hands. "Throw this over my head before I leave, will you?"

The elf caught the rope and dagger, then nodded. "You will be missed. I hope you know that."

Abraxas did. Of course he did. And he would miss them with every fiber of his being, but he wouldn't risk them being around when he lost his mind. A dragon was never meant to be without his mate. That loss would dog him until the end of his life. Hopefully, that would be well after the dragonlings were big enough to take care of themselves. But just in case, he had to bring them to Dracomaquia. Where he knew they would be safe from those who would hunt them.

He gave Draven a stiff nod, then turned to Zephyr.

The young man looked lost. He kept crossing his arms over his chest, and then uncrossing them. Finally, he reached those arms out for Abraxas.

He drew the young man into a hug. "You'll be fine without me," he said with a chuckle. "I'm not that important, young man."

"You are." Zeph squeezed him tighter before pulling back. "I hope to see you again."

Abraxas could lie. He could tell Zeph that they would. Instead, all he managed was a slight nod.

Then he turned back to Beauty. Tears streamed down her cheeks, and she kept shaking her head as he walked up to her. "You aren't leaving," she said through sniffs and tears. "You can't."

"I am," he replied, tugging her into his arms. Abraxas set his chin on top of her head and sighed as she grabbed onto him. "You are a strong woman, Beauty. You will overcome this and all of you, together, will continue the work that Lore set out for you. You will live up to your namesake in so many ways."

"I can't say goodbye to you," she said against his chest.

"Then don't." He peeled her off him, put his hands on her shoulders, and set her back. "We are friends, are we not?"

She nodded and ran a hand under her streaming nose.

"Then I will never leave you. My heart and yours will always be connected, no matter how far I go." He touched his chest and then tapped just below her collarbone. "You are part of me, just as I am part of you. Now, Beauty of Tenebrous, it is time for you to stand on your own."

She sniffed one more time before trying to smile through the tears. "All right. I just... I'm going to miss you."

"And I will miss all of you."

He had to change now or he never would. Abraxas would crumble under their sadness and he would stay. Thus, endangering everyone in the process.

Abraxas walked to the center of the courtyard, where he had changed into a dragon countless times. The change sluggishly came over him, as though even that form didn't want to leave. But then, a crimson dragon stood before them and the natural instinct of who he was came back. Those dragon babes were the one thing he had to protect now. He couldn't shirk his duty. He never would.

Lumbering closer to Draven, he lowered his head for the elf to loop the long cord around his neck. The dagger was comically small against his chest. But every time it clinked against his scales, he felt as though Lore were with him. She'd want this plan to happen. She would want her children to see where they had come from.

Taking a deep breath, he looked one more time at the companions who had become so much more to him.

"I will never forget you, my family." He lowered his head one last time, then he beat his wings so he could latch each of his claws onto the metal hoops at the top of each cage. Abraxas gave them one last look, then took off into the sky.

Neither baby dragon had anything to say. He couldn't speak through the knot in his throat.

As Abraxas flew toward the sea and away from the land he loved, he wondered what adventures would await them in the kingdom of the dragons. He did not cast his gaze toward the castle where his life had been ruined. He did not look down at the rolling fields that gave way to cliffs like the ones where Lore and he had hatched the dragonlings. The last crimson dragon kept his eyes forward toward the future.

But, if he had looked back one last time, he might have seen the light shift on a battlefield to his left. He might have seen the pulse of magic, like a soul struggled to return from the underworld.

The story continues in Torn Heart, preorder today!

ACKNOWLEDGEMENTS

All the books in this series wouldn't be what they are today without my beta readers and all the wonderful people who go into making this story come to life. Seriously. I cannot thank them enough, and this book is entirely for them.

I'll admit, writing this book was a journey in anxiety. I had so many ups and downs, so many mornings where I woke up quite certain I was dying (without any reason to fear that), and my own personal fairytale stood by me every step of the way. Tate, I love you for it. Thank you for being my rock.

And to finish these Acknowledgements off, I usually dedicate the book to someone who is really really special and in this case... It's you. My readers. My family. My friends. You are so much a part of my life and I couldn't do this without you.

ABOUT THE AUTHOR

Emma Hamm is a small town girl on a blueberry field in Maine. She writes stories that remind her of home, of fairytales, and of myths and legends that make her mind wander.

She can be found by the fireplace with a cup of tea and her two Maine Coon cats dipping their paws into the water without her knowing.

For more updates, join my newsletter!
www.emmahamm.com